CERCUEILS EN SPIRALE

BY
GN HETHERINGTON

First Published in 2022 by GNH Publishing.

The right of Gary Hetherington to be identified as the author of this work has been asserted by him in accordance with the Copyright, Designs and Patents Act 1988.

Copyright © Gary Hetherington

All rights reserved. No part of this book may be reproduced, stored in a retrieval system or transmitted in any form or by any means, electronic, mechanical, photocopying, recording or otherwise, without the prior permission of the publisher.

www.gnhbooks.co.uk

grâce à :

To all the lovely people who keep me going, especially my beaux parents, Bill & Chris Bailey, and my amazing friends & supporters Jackie Waite, June Russell, Sandra Scott, Pam Pletts, Suse Telford, Kathleen Pope, Margaret Cox, and Jennifer Trieb. And especially Julien Doré and Sheena Easton, for constantly inspiring me. Special shout out to Katy Anna Harris, Henry Douthwaite and Joseph Eisenreich for their amazing work on the audiobooks. They have been amazing, breathing life into Coco & Hugo in a way I never imagined, and I'm very grateful to them.

Huge thanks to Bastien Greve for all his hard work and patience and for making these books better. I'm sorry I make you blush *every* lesson!

As always, I couldn't do any of this if it wasn't for my amazing family - Dan, Hugo and Noah. They fill my every day with so much love and happiness. I can only hope I do the same for them.

Pour Charlie, Seth and Dawn. Jusqu'à ce que nous nous revoyions.

Notes:

The story and characters are a work of fiction.

For further information, exclusive content and to join the mailing list, head over to:

www.gnhbooks.co.uk

We are also on Facebook, Twitter and Instagram. Join us there!

The artwork on the cover, website and social media accounts were created in conjunction with the incredible talent of Maria Almeida and I'm indebted to her for bringing my characters to life.

For Charlie, Seth and Dawn. *Tu me manques.*

Also available:

Hugo Duchamp Investigates:

Un Homme Qui Attend (2015)
Les Fantômes du Chateau (2016)
Les Noms Sur Les Tombes (2016)
L'ombre de l'île (2017)
L'assassiner de Sebastian Dubois (2017)
L'impondérable (2018)
Le Cri du Cœur (2019)
La Famille Lacroix (2019)
Les Mauvais Garçons (2020)
Prisonnier Dix (2021)
Le Bateau au fond de l'océan (2022)
Chemin de Compostelle (2023)
Hotel Beaupain (2023)

The Coco Brunhild Mysteries:

Sept Jours (2021)
Métro Boulot Dodo (2022)
Cercueils en Spirale (2022)
Séance de Spiritisme (2023)
Quatre Semaines (2023)

Also available:

Hugo & Josef (2021)
Club Vidéo (2022)
Hugo & Madeline (2023)
Josef (2024)

DIMANCHE / SUNDAY

09H30

Captain Charlotte "Coco" Brunhild climbed out of the car, immediately dropping her feet into a puddle. She emitted a loud curse as the ice-cold water seeped through the holes in her boots, then passing through the tape which covered the holes in her socks. She was reminded, not for the first time that day, she ought to avoid taking TOO close a look at the state of her life.

She sat back in the car, twisting her feet, placing them on the heater in the middle of the dashboard. She reached into her trusty oversized antique Chanel bag and extracted a cigarette. Already her fourth of the day, although she had only been awake an hour and, more importantly, her finances were such that cigarettes were most certainly a luxury she could not afford. Regardless, she inhaled and threw back her head, frizzy dyed-blue hair cascading over her shoulders. It was Sunday, and she had planned on spending the day with her children, though as it transpired, the two elder offspring, Barbra and Julien had already made plans, and the two youngest, Cedric and Esther, despite being much younger, also had their own plans for the day. Even Helga, the surly German nanny who slept at the bottom of Coco's bed on a rollout, had a date with an elderly French bingo caller named Franc. *Everyone has plans but me,* Coco thought with an out of character petulance.

Coco blew smoke rings into the sky and closed her eyes. When her cell phone rang earlier, alerting her of a crime, she reasoned that if she was to spend another Sunday sans children, or a lover, or a life of any kind, then she might as well get paid overtime to keep herself occupied. She had been a police captain at the Commissariat de Police du 7e arrondissement for several years already, and whilst her clean up record was exemplary, her *perhaps* unorthodox methods had gained her a reputation. And there was the fact that her former commander, also her onetime lover and the father of her two youngest children, was currently spending a stretch in prison for crimes she could not bring herself to think about any longer. Whatever damage Coco had done to her own reputation it was nothing compared to what Mordecai Stanic had inflicted on her.

'Why are you sitting like that?' a gruff voice called out from behind her.

A smile moved onto Coco's lips. Although they spent most of the time bickering, she was fond of the young lieutenant who worked with her. Cedric Degarmo was a tall, athletic young man, with piercing blue eyes, a square jaw and rough, buzz-cut hair. He was also a half-decent cop, Coco reasoned. He had been assigned to her on his first day in the job, a day he also spent delivering Coco's third child on the filthy floor of a squat. She had called her child Cedric in honour of the man whose hand had guided him into the world, a fact she had since taken great pleasure in reminding the adult Cedric at every available opportunity, much to his chagrin. Whatever was between them, the two police officers had found a comfortable rhythm working together, despite the sparks of animosity which seemed to run through it.

Coco glanced down at her boots spread in front of her at uneven angles. 'I've got wet feet and I'm trying to dry them off. What's it to ya?'

Cedric opened his mouth to respond, but seemingly thought better of it.

'What are you doing here, anyway?' Coco demanded. 'It's the weekend. Don't you have gyms to frequent or poor women to stalk?'

'I'm always on call at the weekend,' he shot back. 'As I'm the only one without a family to spend time with…' he stopped.

Coco launched herself into an upright position. 'Well, ain't you a peach. Sometimes family life is overrated.' She turned her head. All the message had given her was an address. 'Where the hell are we, and why the hell all the secrecy?' She stomped her foot against the ground, water oozing from her boot. 'Not that I'm complaining, mind you. I'm all for overtime.'

'Maybe you can buy yourself a new pair of boots?' Cedric suggested.

Coco waved her boot in the air. 'There's plenty of life left in these old things yet,' she stated. 'All I need is some stronger tape. That's the trouble with you youngsters. It's all about chucking something away when it gets a little worn.'

'A *little*?' Cedric asked incredulously.

Coco blew a raspberry. 'Where the hell are we?' she demanded again. She looked around, as far as she could tell they were in the middle of a building site in the centre of Paris. Tall iron fences encased a tenement building in a sorry state of affairs. She surmised it was in the process of being demolished. The worksite was only a few steps away from another building. Coco strained her eyes to see it because it was surrounded by a tall brick wall with only a small gated entrance in the middle of it. As far as she could tell, whatever was behind the wall was in as much of a terrible state as the building which was about to be demolished. A sign hung above the wall. *Abbaye Le Bastien.*

'Why are we here?' Coco said, irritably stubbing out the cigarette. 'All the call said was that they'd discovered stolen goods.'

Cedric shrugged. 'Beats the hell out of me, that's all I was told too.'

'Are you the cops?'

Coco spun around. 'For our sins, oui,' she responded. 'And you are?'

The man stared at her. He was tall, with a long pale face and tired eyes. He pressed his hand against the hard hat he was wearing. 'My name is Aaron Cellier. I'm in charge of this site,' he snapped, fixing her with a bored look. 'You took your almighty time to get here.'

Coco tipped her head behind her. 'Well, it looks like there's a monastery over there. Perhaps I can ask for forgiveness.'

Aaron Cellier nodded towards the demolition site. 'You might need to when you see what I found in there.'

Coco flashed a look toward Cedric and they both knew what it meant. *This is going to be a long day.*

09H45

'You'll have to wear one of these before you can come onto the site,' Aaron Cellier barked.

Coco stared at the hard hat. It was round and orange with a protruding lip. 'It's not exactly my colour,' she replied tartly.

Cedric picked one up and placed it on his own head. 'Or your size,' he quipped.

Coco plonked the hat on her head, grimacing when she realised it did not quite fit over her skull and the abundance of wild blue hair. She tried her best to smooth it down. 'C'est bon?' she asked Cellier.

He fixed her with a withering look. 'It's the only size I have,' he tapped his own hat, 'usually there's not a problem.' He shrugged. 'If something falls on you, then it won't be my responsibility.'

Cedric snorted. 'If anything falls on her head, it would probably bounce off.'

Coco glared at him. 'Say, Monsieur Cellier, how's about you tell us why the Republic is paying for us to spend our Sunday afternoon in your,' she stepped into the work site, placing her boots carefully around a muddy puddle, 'rather fetching place of work.'

Cellier pointed ahead of them. 'I'm supposed to blow this damn place up this afternoon, but until you tell me what the hell is going on in there, my bosses tell me I can't.' He stopped. 'I have twenty-five men all sitting on their fat asses on double-time waiting to knock this down. If I can't do it today, who do you think everyone is going to blame? Me, that's who!'

Coco looked toward the derelict building. 'What the hell is the problem in there? Is there a body?'

Cellier shook his head. 'Not a body.' He shrugged and then

smiled. 'Well, not one, three at least, as far as I can tell.'

Coco spluttered. 'Whatcha talkin' bout, Willis?' she exhaled with a laugh.

Cellier gave her a dumbfounded look. He turned to Cedric. 'What does she mean?'

Cedric shrugged. 'I have no idea most of the time, so I wouldn't worry about it. She watches far too much ancient American TV late at night, because she has nothing better to do.' He exhaled. 'I think the point is, the report mentioned nothing about a murder, let alone three of them.'

Cellier sighed. 'I said nothing about murder, rather there are three coffins on the staircase in the building.'

'Three coffins?' Coco interrupted.

He nodded. 'Yeah. We figured we shouldn't really move them until you arrived.' He gestured. 'Follow me.'

It took Coco a few moments to understand what she was seeing in front of her. She stepped cautiously into the abandoned building, moving her head slowly from left to right. In many ways, it reminded her of her own tenement building, a few kilometres away, and she could not say that this one, which was about to be demolished, was much worse than her own. She moved gingerly through what remained of the foyer, dodging upturned boxes and wires hanging from the ceiling.

'I was doing my last checks,' Cellier said, appearing by her side. 'Ready for the demolition. And that's when I found them.'

Cedric pulled out his cell phone and turned on the light, illuminating the darkened vestibule.

'Them?' Coco interjected, her voice rising sharply. 'I only see one.'

Cellier pointed upwards. 'There are two more a few floors up.'

Coco and Cedric exchanged a concerned look. Coco lowered herself onto her haunches. A large, ornate coffin was situated at the foot of the winding staircase. 'And this wasn't there before today?' she asked.

Cellier laughed. 'I think I would have noticed three bloody great coffins in my building, don't you?' he demanded.

Coco shrugged nonchalantly. 'I dunno. I wouldn't be too surprised if one turned up in my apartment block and people just stepped over it.' She tapped her chin. 'When was the last time you were in the building?'

'Last night. About 17H00,' he responded. 'And it wasn't here then.'

Cedric looked at the doorway. 'And did you lock up?'

Cellier shook his head. 'The place is going to be demolished today. Half of the rooms don't even have floors. What am I going to lock it for?' He pointed towards the entrance gate they had just come through. 'The gates are locked, of course, and the fences are ten feet tall, so we've never had a lot of problems with squatters or troublemakers.'

Coco frowned. 'And there's no on-site security?'

He shook his head again. 'It's a pretty decent neighbourhood. There's not been a lot of need.'

Coco turned back to the coffin. She moved her hand across it without touching it. 'There's no name on it,' she stated. Her eyes fixed on a large engraving in the centre. It was lined with tiny stones and appeared to be some kind of relief, possibly a tree. 'This is interesting.'

'It doesn't really tell us anything, though,' Cedric moaned.

Coco stared at the engraving. She had seen nothing like it before. It certainly appeared old and was just unusual enough to make it appear unique. 'It might just tell us where the damn coffin came from,' she reasoned.

'The other two coffins have the same markings,' Cellier

added.

Coco pulled a glove from her pocket and tried to open the lid. It did not move.

'They also nailed the other two down,' Cellier confirmed.

Cedric faced Coco. 'What are we supposed to do?'

She shrugged. 'Beats the shit out of me.' She moved around the coffin. 'I don't suppose there's been any reports made about stolen coffins?'

'I don't think so. Want me to check?'

Coco considered. 'It's obviously some kids playing a prank, mais still…' she trailed off, glancing at her watch. 'As I'm on overtime, I think I'd like to satisfy myself there's nothing untoward going on.'

Cedric took a long, deep breath before emitting a sigh.

'What about my demolition?' Cellier interrupted, anxiety clear in his voice. 'I can't put it off. There would be penalties and the cost of delays would be astronomical, I…'

Coco waved her arms. 'Keep your panties on,' she laughed. 'I don't intend on crashing your big blow-up party, so how's about finding something to open these things so I can take a peek inside?'

Cellier whipped a long screwdriver out of a pocket on the side of his trousers. Coco raised an impressed eyebrow, her eyes flicking slowly over it. 'You've done that sort of thing before, haven't you, Monsieur?'

Cedric tutted irritably. He snatched the screwdriver and deftly began removing the screws holding the coffin lid in place.

Coco stepped back, winking slyly at Cellier, causing him to shuffle uncomfortably on his feet.

'Here we go,' Cedric said triumphantly. He yanked the lid away from the coffin, filling the foyer with a musty cloud of dust.

Coco took a tentative step towards him, peering over his shoulder. The coffin was filled with a withered corpse, covered in a long brown robe. 'Well, I think it's safe to say he's been there a while,' she stated. 'Say, Monsieur Cellier, show us the way to the others.' She smiled knowingly. 'I'll follow behind you so I can admire the view.'

Cellier flustered towards the staircase. Cedric shook his head at Coco. 'You have no shame, do you?'

'What?' Coco mouthed innocently.

They moved in silence up the stairs, following carefully in Cellier's steps. 'They're both on the third floor,' he called over his shoulder. 'Probably because the stairs are pretty much impassable after that.'

'If this is kids messing around,' Cedric posed, 'I don't get why they didn't just dump the coffins in the same place.'

'You think there's a reason they were arranged specifically like that?' Coco asked.

'I doubt it, but what plausible reason could there be?'

A reason had just occurred to Coco, and one she hoped was not true. 'Well,' she began. 'I guess it's public knowledge this entire building is coming down today. Someone might have figured it might just be a way to get rid of something without making too much of a fuss. They could have counted on no one actually checking.' She stopped at the top of the staircase to catch her breath. 'But you're right. It makes little sense they'd dump one coffin in the foyer and move the other two. If they were about hiding something, then it would be wiser to hide them all together away from prying eyes.'

Cellier continued quickly up the stairs. 'I told you. This is all just about damn kids messing around.' He stopped, pointing in front of him. 'Here we are, the other two.' He gestured to the missing floorboards around them. 'Careful where you're stepping, though. There's a reason this building has been condemned. It's practically falling down itself.'

Coco and Cedric stepped carefully across the landing. Two further coffins had been placed head to head, taking up most of the space. They were identical to the first one.

'Do your magic, Lieutenant,' Coco instructed.

Cedric nodded and began quickly removing the screws. He yanked off the first lid, revealing another withered skeleton in a robe. He passed on to the third coffin and began removing the lid. It took him only seconds before he removed it. He stepped back, his eyes widening suddenly. 'Merde,' he mumbled.

Coco peered over his shoulder to see what had caught his attention. She rolled her eyes. 'I'll call Sonny,' she exhaled slowly.

10H30

Dr. Shlomo "Sonny" Bernstein pushed his curls under the hard hat and clambered under the police tape which had been placed around the soon to be demolished building. He dropped his forensic bag and looked doubtfully towards the building. Coco appeared from the darkness of the doorway, Aaron Cellier a step behind her and it was clear they were involved in a heated debate. Coco stopped, grumpy face moving into a smile in Sonny's direction. She gestured for him to join them.

'Good to see you, Sonny,' she called.

Sonny stifled a yawn. 'You too. I mean, who needs sleep at the weekend? Or a life, for that matter.' He nodded at Cellier. 'Dr. Bernstein.'

Cellier returned the nod. 'Aaron Cellier. I'm in charge of this site. Say doc, can you talk sense into her?' he asked, angrily thumbing towards Coco.

Sonny smiled. 'I haven't been able to yet,' he chuckled. 'What's the problem?'

'The building is due to come down in,' Cellier began before checking his watch, 'three hours. It has to come down or else I'm screwed. But Madame here says that until you give the go-ahead, we can't do a damn thing.'

Sonny tipped his head to the building, his eyes widening in horror. 'Is it safe?'

'Bien sûr, that's why we're knocking it down,' Cellier retorted, his voice laced with irritation and sarcasm.

Sonny turned to Coco. 'And you want me to go in?' he asked.

She shrugged huffily. 'If I had them removed without your sign-off, you'd have the hump, non?'

Ebba Blom pushed her way past them, disappearing into the

building. 'Goddamn pussies,' she muttered in broken English. She was a slight Swedish woman with a shaved head and a fiery attitude, but was a formidable forensic expert.

Sonny shuddered. 'She's in a good mood today.'

Coco laughed. 'How would we tell the difference?' She grabbed Sonny's arm and began leading him toward the building. 'C'mon buttercup, I'll protect you.'

Sonny lifted the lid of the third coffin and peered inside. 'We have a dead body.'

Coco raised an eyebrow. 'I don't know where you get your sarcasm from, really I don't,' she complained. 'Now quit messing around and tell me what we're looking at, before the whole damn place falls down around us.'

Sonny nodded and quickly began examining the corpse in the coffin. He had briefly checked inside the other two coffins on the way up. 'Well, this is certainly different from the mummified bodies in the other coffins. We're looking at a Caucasian male, approximately 180 cm, 90-95 kilos. I'd estimate him to be somewhere between thirty and forty years old.'

Coco peered over his shoulder. 'How long has he been dead?'

Sonny appraised his surroundings. 'I'd normally check liver lividity, but under the circumstances, I'd prefer to do it back at the morgue. What I can tell you is that he's been dead no more than twenty-four hours, probably less because he's not in full-rigor.'

Coco moved slowly around the coffin. Unlike the other two aged corpses, the recently deceased was not dressed in a brown robe, rather jeans and a leather jacket. 'Is this cause of death?' she stated, pointing at the dead man's head. It was covered in blood, showing he had clearly taken a beating. 'Someone really went to town on him, didn't they?'

Sonny studied the face, his eyes moving slowly and decisively.

'You're right. He took quite a beating. I can't be sure if it contributed to, or was, in fact, the cause of death.' He lifted the head. 'I can't see any obvious trauma to the skull.' He stopped, his hands resting on the neck. 'Ah, I think we may have an answer here.'

Coco followed his gaze. He had exposed the neck, which was already displaying the early tell-tale signs of bruising. 'He was choked,' she stated.

Sonny shrugged. 'It's certainly possible. I'll know more when I get him out of here.' He unzipped the man's jacket and lifted the t-shirt. 'No obvious sign of trauma to the upper torso.' He took a deep breath. 'I can't rule it as a homicide yet, mais it is certainly a suspicious death.'

Coco snorted. 'You think?' she asked, her tone gently mocking. 'I see why they pay you the big bucks.' She glanced around the coffin. 'Do you think he was murdered in the coffin, or placed in it afterwards?'

Sonny flicked on his glasses, steering his attention around the wooden frame. 'I see some blood, probably from contact, but I wouldn't say he was attacked in the coffin. Not with the amount of injury to his face.'

Coco looked around. 'Ebba, where are you?' she called out.

Ebba appeared from the darkness. 'I'm here.'

'What did you find?' Coco asked.

Ebba glared at her. 'We're in the middle of a derelict building. You think I'm a miracle worker?'

Coco resisted the urge to respond. She moved toward the staircase. 'It would have taken at least two people, probably more, to drag the coffins up here. Hopefully, they left prints.'

'About two dozen in various states,' Ebba responded. 'I'll run them through the database when I get back to the commissariat.'

Coco tapped her chin. 'Sonny - you happy for the coffins to be removed?'

He nodded quickly. 'Very,' he said, hastening to the staircase and beginning his descent without looking back.

Coco moved back to the coffin and used her cell phone to take a picture of the dead man.

Cellier approached Coco cautiously. 'And what about my demolition?'

Coco ignored him and turned to Ebba. 'What do you think?'

Ebba glanced around. 'I don't think there's anything else here. The staircase pretty much ends after this floor. I've checked all the rooms on these floors. I think we've seen all there is to see.'

'What about my demolition?' Cellier pushed.

Coco moved to one of the broken windows. She pointed to a truck with a large arm and basket. 'Can that thing lift us up to see inside the other floors?'

'Yeah, but what's the point?' Cellier asked. 'You can see there is no way up.'

Coco shrugged and tapped her hard hat. 'If you want your little demolition, then I'm going to need to see inside the rooms on the other floors.' She gestured to Ebba. 'Come on, kid. We're going for a ride.'

Aaron Cellier rolled his eyes.

11H15

Coco stared up at the rickety cage attached to the van. She had seen pompiers climbing the side of buildings in such a way and it had always seemed exciting, but now, standing in the middle of a building site with the wind gusting around her head and up her skirt, she wondered whether her initial thought had been wise. She looked slyly to her side. Ebba Blom was standing, hands on hips, head trained upwards, and the excitement was clear on her face. *Well, I can't back out now,* Coco reasoned.

'Tell me you're not going up in that!' Cedric exclaimed, appearing behind them. 'For one thing, I don't know if it can take your weight.'

Coco's eyes flicked over the muscular lieutenant and she realised he was probably right. She looked to Cellier, and he offered a kind smile, gesturing for her and Ebba to get into the cage. 'Just hold on tight,' he said cheerfully. 'Give me a minute to get the engine running and then we'll be off.'

Coco and Ebba made their way to the cage and fastened themselves in. 'Did you find anything, Lieutenant?' Coco called out to Cedric.

He moved to the cage, placing his foot on the side and wobbling it. Coco stumbled, steadying herself on the bars and shooting him a hateful look. 'There have been no reports of missing coffins, if that's what you mean,' Cedric stated cheerfully, obviously enjoying the uncomfortable expression on Coco's face. 'And there are no CCTV cameras in this area, not working ones, at least.'

'What about the coffins?' Coco panted.

Cedric frowned. 'What about them?'

'They're unusual,' she snapped. 'Google the images or

something. See if you can find anything similar.' She gasped as the cage rocked and the truck roared into life. 'And there's another thing,' she yelled. 'Two of the coffins had old dead people in them and the third had a new body, which begs two questions. Who is the dead guy, and what happened to the old skeleton that was in the coffin in the first place?'

Cedric shrugged. 'As you're fond of saying, beats the shit out of me.'

The cage jerked upwards, throwing Coco and Ebba forward, closer to the building. It moved slowly, allowing them to see inside the various floors. Ebba extracted her cell phone and began recording their movement upwards, all the time staring intently in front of her, keen alert eyes focusing.

'Each floor looks pretty much empty, apart from rubble,' Coco noted.

'I'd agree,' Ebba stated. 'All the same, before you sign off on the demolition, I'd like to go through my recording just to make sure I'm not missing anything.'

'Knock yourself out, kid,' Coco replied. 'What do you think happened here?' she asked, desperately trying to take her mind off the jerking cage, slowly climbing higher and higher.

Ebba spun her head. 'Are you talking to me?'

'Non, I'm talking to my four imaginary friends sharing this rickety cage with us,' Coco retorted. 'Bien sûr, I'm talking to you.'

Ebba considered her response, seemingly unable to hide the fact she was pleased to be asked. 'I thought it was kids messing around,' she began, 'but the dead body changes that.'

Coco nodded. 'It does, doesn't it?' she responded. 'I don't know why, exactly, but I'm sure it does.' She fixed her gaze on the different floors of the condemned building. 'There's nothing else in there, is there?'

'There doesn't seem to be,' Ebba agreed with evident reluctance. 'I'd like to get in to make sure, but I don't think the people who did this could have got up here.'

'You're probably right, especially since there doesn't appear to be complete floors or stairs,' Coco agreed. She squinted. 'I think whoever dumped those coffins wouldn't have been stupid enough to go any further. At least we've checked.'

'Then you'll let the demolition go ahead?' Ebba asked.

Coco shrugged. 'I don't see how I can stop it,' she answered. 'Besides, I think it's clear that this was just meant to be a dumping ground, somewhere to dispose of something where the perp knew it was about to be blown to smithereens.' She shook her head, blue frizzy hair bouncing around the hard hat. 'It still makes little sense, though. Why go to such elaborate lengths, and why steal three coffins?'

'People are whack, you know that,' Ebba suggested. 'Just because we think there should be a reason doesn't necessarily mean there's going to be one.'

Coco turned her back to the building, her attention fixing on the property next to the demolition site. She imagined it was as large, but could not be certain because the entire property was encased in a high brick wall. 'Ah, I remember now. It's a church, or something,' she said aloud.

'What is?' Ebba asked.

Coco reached across and pointed, causing the cage to wobble. She steadied herself and exhaled. 'Next door,' she answered breathlessly. 'There's some kind of church over there.'

'So?'

'So,' Coco snapped, 'if you were gonna steal three coffins without worrying about how far you had to drag them, seems a pretty good place to start, doesn't it? Especially since it appeared the two skeletons were wearing what looked like robes.' She shrugged. 'It's a place to start, at least,' she added, before turning back to face the building. 'In any event, I think we're done here,' she suggested. 'This building has told us what it needs to for now.'

Ebba scratched her head. 'It has?'

'Oui. It's told us that whoever dumped the coffins in it did so for a very specific reason.'

'Then surely that means you have to stop the demolition?' Ebba interrupted.

'Not really,' Coco said as she continued staring ahead of her. 'The building is dead,' she stated. 'However, it's given us a great big clue. Somebody sent a message here, we just need to figure out what the hell it means…'

The cage lurched forward, throwing Coco into the arms of Ebba, who immediately pushed her away.

'C'mon, Aaron!' Coco screamed down to Cellier. 'Give your future girlfriend a break up here! I bruise like a peach!'

11H45

Coco pulled back the large ornate brass knocker and dropped it against its cradle, a loud piercing crack permeating the air. She looked at Cedric. 'They're never going to hear that. Why don't they have a bell?'

'Can I help you?'

'Jesus, Mary & Joseph!' Coco screamed, jumping backwards. 'Where the hell did you come from?'

A tall, thin man with wispy red hair and a tired, kind face smiled at her. Coco glanced downwards and noticed he was wearing a brown robe. 'Désole, Father,' she said immediately, making the sign of the cross across her chest. Her brow crinkled as she realised she had probably done it back to front and she was again reminded of the abundance of times she had spoken inappropriately in front of a man of the cloth. Her father, an Orthodox Rabbi, had once told her that he was sure the Devil himself had commandeered her tongue. She had responded before thinking - *that's what all the boys say*. It had cost her a slap and a month-long grounding.

The kindly man continued to smile. 'I'm a monk, not a priest, child,' he said in soft tones, which, unlike her father's, seemed to contain no malice. 'My name is Frère Gerard Leroy.' He extended his hands. 'Welcome to *Abbaye Le Bastien.*'

'Are you in charge?' Coco asked in the politest tone she could muster, trying to hide how uncomfortable she was around any sort of religious person. A hang-up originating from her father, who had very firm and definite opinions concerning his wayward and unwed daughter.

He gave her a warm look. 'We are a brotherhood. There is no hierarchy,' he replied before smiling again, 'though I am the oldest brother, so in that respect, I suppose you could say I am the senior.'

'Bon.' Coco nodded, extracting her ID and holding it up to the gate. 'I am Captain Charlotte Brunhild of the Commissariat de Police du 7e arrondissement,' she gestured to Cedric next to her, who she noted was staring at his feet as if he was about to be told off, 'and the lapsed altar boy next to me is Lieutenant Cedric Degarmo.'

Frère Leroy continued smiling. 'What can I do for you, Captain Brunhild?' he enquired.

Coco strained to see around him. As far as she could tell, there was no graveyard. 'I don't suppose you're missing three coffins, are you?'

Leroy chuckled. 'Well, I don't know what I was expecting you to say, but it most certainly wasn't that.' His eyes narrowed with concern. 'Coffins, you say?'

She nodded, extracting her cell phone and scrolling to find the picture of the coffins. She held it up in front of the monk.

'Do you recognise this?' she asked.

He pulled a pair of glasses from his pocket and narrowed his eyes. 'Oui, I do.' He stated with a puzzled frown.

'The engraving is yours?' Coco pushed.

Frère Leroy shook his head. 'It's not actually an engraving, rather a relief,' he explained. 'We carve it out of the coffin lid ourselves. It is the emblem of our monastery, you might say.' He stared at the image again. 'You say there are three of them?'

Coco nodded again. 'Oui. If they belong to your monastery, wouldn't you notice them missing?'

Leroy considered his answer, tired eyes flicking between the two detectives. He twisted his lips. 'Our coffins are kept in the crypt which is beneath the monastery.'

Coco considered. 'And how do you access this crypt?'

'Via a long, winding staircase,' the monk answered.

'And how often do you go down?'

He lowered his head, as if ashamed. 'Not as often as I would like, I'm afraid,' he tapped his legs. 'I have very painful arthritis in my knees. It makes stairs practically impossible. Most of my brothers, however, make the pilgrimage several times a year. Memorial days, religious days, that sort of occasion.'

'And when was the last time anyone was in your crypt?' Cedric asked.

Leroy shrugged. 'I couldn't say for certain. I'd need to check,' he replied. 'Though it is not an everyday occurrence.'

Cedric nodded. 'And how many coffins are down there?'

'Forty-two,' Leroy responded. 'Mainly brothers who have passed, but also specific donors and supporters of our monastery who requested to be laid to rest in the crypt and that request was granted by the Church.'

Coco glanced over his shoulder. 'And you're saying the only access to the crypt is via a staircase?'

Leroy shook his head. He pointed to a corner of the monastery. Coco narrowed her eyes, focusing on a long, narrow window at ground level. 'That is an access window to the crypt, it's where the coffins are brought in.'

'Or brought out,' Coco mused. She looked at Cedric. 'Get Ebba over here. I want her dusting for prints.'

Frère Leroy frowned. 'You surely can't be suggesting someone removed coffins from the crypt?'

'That's exactly what I'm suggesting,' Coco retorted. 'Now we just need to figure out why the hell…' she bit her lip again, 'désolé, but you get my point. All I know is that on the building site next door, we found three coffins you have confirmed came from here.'

Leroy's eyes flashed red. 'I didn't say they came from here,' he stated matter-of-factly, 'rather that they appeared to be the same design as the reliefs we use.'

'Potato, potahto…' Coco murmured. She moved closer to

the gate. 'How about you run your little inventory and show us around this crypt?'

Leroy's lips moved, but he said nothing.

'Unless your next words are going to be "where's the search mandate?" then I don't see what the problem is.' She stared at him. 'Is there a problem, Frère Leroy?'

He shook his head quickly. 'Bien sûr, there isn't.' He looked towards the demolition site. 'You say they were found in there?'

'Oui,' Coco replied. She noticed his expression again when mentioning the demolition site and the way his eyes flashed with something she could not quite ascertain. Was it fear? Whatever it was, she reasoned, at the very least she was sure it expressed confusion and concern.

Leroy stepped back and unlocked the gates. He gestured for Coco and Cedric to follow him towards the monastery. 'Follow me and I'll have someone take you to the crypt.'

Coco smiled. 'That's more like it, Frère, lead the way.'

The first thing Coco noticed about Frère Mathieu Moreau was his hair. It was thick and jet black, nestling on the top of his skull in a clump and falling over his forehead, brushing against his right eye. It almost called out to her: *Run your fingers through me and push me away.* She could see how soft it was, and even from the distance between them, she could smell the sweetness of whatever shampoo he used. It was musky and sensual. She shook her head, brushing the thoughts away. He was a kid, she reasoned, and a monk at that, but when she forced her gaze away from his head to his face, she found it even less helpful. His pupils were large and round, as dark as his hair, and they stared at her in such a way she felt sure her underwear was slipping away from her. She hoped it was because the elastic had long since gone, and not the carnal thoughts which were stabbing at her brain like laser beams.

Frère Mathieu smiled at her, revealing full, thick lips and white, even teeth, and he moved towards her, the swishing of the robes revealing a small portion of his calf. It was dark and slender, with a slight covering of hair. *It's been a long time between men*, she thought, turning her head away and closing her eyes, trying to imagine something, *someone*, who would distract her from the emotions coursing through her lonely body. It bothered her in a way she could not describe to herself that she should be caught in the trap of a man again. *I'm better than this.*

'Merci, for your patience in waiting,' Mathieu said, grabbing her hand and shaking it. His brow furrowed. 'Frère Leroy asked me to show you the crypt,' he said. 'Rather an odd way to spend your weekend, mais, I am here to serve,' he stated with a mock bow.

His hand was warm and soft, and his voice was light but masculine. Coco fought the urge to say something funny, or flippant because she feared it would betray something she did not want to reveal. *I'm lonely.*

Mathieu cocked his head, assessing Coco carefully. It was almost as if he was studying something he had never seen before.

'Yeah, I got bugger all else to do,' Coco snapped, immediately biting her lip. She had not meant to be... she had not meant to be herself in that moment. Not knowing what else to do, she pulled back her shoulders. 'I am Captain Charlotte Brunhild from the Commissariat de Police du 7e arrondissement and I am here because I am investigating something that happened in the building next door,' she blurted as she searched for something to say.

'The demolition site?' Mathieu interrupted. The tone of his voice had lost its initial warmth, replaced with what Coco could only imagine was concern. Why would he be concerned, she reasoned? Whatever it was, it was the same concern she had detected in the eyes of Frère Leroy.

'Non, the ice-cream stand at the end of the road,' she snapped, biting her lip again and wondering why on earth she was being rude to the nice monk whose sackcloth could not hide the killer body she imagined he was hiding beneath it.

A smile appeared on his face. He took a step closer to her, which only made Coco retreat further backwards.

'What do you want from me?' Mathieu asked.

Coco stuffed her hand into her pocket and extracted her cell phone. She stabbed at the screen, attempting to retrieve the pictures of the coffins. Finally, she found them and thrust the phone under Mathieu's nose. She did not want to show him a picture of the dead man, not yet, at least. Not until she had more to go on. Mathieu touched her hand, and he raised it closer to his face. 'What do you make of this?' she asked.

'It's a coffin,' he said.

'No shit, Sherlock,' she immediately retorted. She grimaced, making the sign of the cross across her chest. 'Désolé,' she offered. 'I'm Jewish, so I don't know if I did that right.'

He smiled. 'You did it perfectly,' he stated, 'other than it was upside down.' His smile extended. 'To answer your question, it's a coffin, not unlike the ones we have in the crypt.'

She tried to study him with fresh eyes, rather than ones which were likely to cloud her judgment. Whatever had caused his voice to falter a second earlier had disappeared. Now, he just appeared like any other young man. Admittedly, an excessively handsome young man in a weird fancy dress outfit. She still wanted to lick his face like it was a lollipop.

Behind her, Cedric coughed, fixing Coco with an irritated look. 'Even guys in frocks aren't safe from you, are they?' He mumbled under his breath. 'Want to show us the way, Frère?'

Frère Mathieu nodded. 'Oui. Follow me.'

Coco watched him walk ahead of her, her eyes lowering to his robe as it swished against his body.

12H00

Coco fought the urge to panic as they began the descent down the narrow winding staircase to the crypt. Frère Mathieu Moreau slowed his pace, placing his body to her left. The staircase was open on that side. Therefore, his manoeuvring protected her from the risk of falling into the darkness below. He said nothing, but she knew he had done it deliberately, no doubt hearing the panic in her fast breath. It took her a few moments, but she soon relaxed, although she could feel Cedric's hot, impatient breath on the back of her neck.

'Is there far to go?' Coco called out, trying desperately not to sound desperate. Mathieu had turned on a light switch at the top of the staircase, but it had done little to illuminate the crypt below.

Mathieu reached around and placed long fingers on her arm. Coco was sure it was meant for reassurance, but the charge Coco felt signified something altogether different to her. *Stop acting like you're in heat.* She could almost hear Cedric's voice. He did not need to say it, because Coco knew it was true.

'Not far now,' Frère Mathieu said.

They continued the descent in silence. Coco could hear the trickle of water running down the uneven wall her fingers brushed against. She felt claustrophobic and had to fight the urge to turn around and run back towards the light of the floor above.

'We're here,' Mathieu said finally. He pulled a torch from his robe and illuminated the space in front of them.

Coco took in a sharp breath and stepped cautiously from behind Mathieu. She was not sure what she had been expecting. It was a crypt after all, but the entire basement was lined with upright coffins, all standing sentry.

'Why are they all standing up?' Cedric asked.

'It is our belief the deceased should remain upright as if they are in constant conversation and eye-line with Dieu,' Mathieu answered as if he was reading from a brochure.

Coco moved slowly between the coffins. 'Well, they're the same as the ones on the building site.' She frowned, straining her eyes. 'I don't see any missing ones, though.'

Mathieu gestured. 'Follow me, the room takes a twist to the right, there are more there.'

They moved quickly. 'Is there a particular way you arrange them?' Coco asked. 'I don't see any names on the lids.'

'There is no pattern,' Mathieu answered. His lips twisted into a smile. 'Rather it's a case of first come, first served, you might say.'

'Then how do you know who is who?' Cedric interjected.

'We keep records, of course,' Mathieu replied. 'Mais if I'm honest, this place isn't really about visiting those who have passed, rather a place to lay them to rest. Often it is enough. Though to answer your question, Frère Leroy is assembling the records for you now.' He trailed off. 'However, I don't see any missing…' he halted. As they turned the corner, they faced a gap in the line.

Coco counted the square spaces where it was clear something had been removed. 'Three empty spots,' she said before clapping her hands together. 'We have a winner.'

Mathieu's hand moved to his mouth, his eyes locked firmly on the empty space. He shook his head slowly. 'There's something very wrong here,' he murmured. His voice was distant, as if he was trying to process something that he did not understand could be possible.

'That may be the understatement of the year,' Cedric grumbled. He turned his head. 'We've just come through the monastery and as far as I can tell, it was locked.' He frowned. 'Is it <u>always</u> locked?'

Mathieu nodded. 'Oui. All the time,' he replied.

Coco pulled in her chest. He had just lied. She was sure of it.

'Apparently they used to keep it unlocked,' Mathieu continued, 'and the gate as well, but over the years there have been those who sought to take advantage of it.'

'Advantage?' Coco asked.

He nodded again. 'The homeless, kids looking for fun, or trouble, and others…'

Coco watched him. Even in the half-light, she could see the colour spreading across his cheekbones, making him appear even younger than he already did. She fought the urge to watch him squirm, instead stepping away from the ante-room and back into the main section of the crypt. She hurried towards the access window. It was darkened, covered with some kind of protective sheet, she imagined, but there were a few holes, throwing pinpointed light into the crypt. She stopped, eyes moving slowly across it. 'How does it open?'

Mathieu appeared by her side, pointing at two handles. 'You press in the button, lift the handle and push it open.'

Coco stood on her tip-toes and pushed open the access window. 'It's coffin sized,' she stated.

Mathieu stared at her with the sort of inquiring look she was sure had led her to becoming pregnant before. 'That's rather the point,' he laughed. There was no maliciousness to his tone, rather it was playful in a way which Coco considered he had no way of being.

Cedric tutted again.

'It wasn't locked,' Coco stated.

Mathieu shrugged. 'Why would it be?' he asked with a frown. 'You can only open it from inside.'

Coco and Cedric exchanged a knowing look, realising what it meant. Coco moved her hand across the ledge. 'It doesn't seem broken,' she considered. 'Which suggests they did not force it open from the outside.'

'Is that important?' Mathieu asked.

'Probably,' Coco responded quietly. She turned back to Mathieu. 'Were you here yesterday?'

He smiled sadly at her. 'I'm always here,' he answered. 'And I have to confirm, I saw no coffins being removed.'

Coco turned away again. 'And yet they were, which begs the question - why and where did our corpse come from?' She moved back into the crypt. 'Can we look around a little more?'

'Oui,' Mathieu replied. 'Mais, I don't know what you think you might find.'

Coco smiled. 'A dead guy who was apparently thrown out of his eternal resting place.'

Mathieu gave her a quizzical look. 'You really are unusual, aren't you?'

Cedric pushed past him. 'You have no idea,' he groaned. He moved away, casting his gaze between the remaining coffins and using the light from his cell phone to illuminate his way. 'There's no obvious sign of anything untoward,' he stated finally.

Coco nodded, her fingers tracing across the coffin next to her. 'Then that only leaves us one option…'

'What's that?' Mathieu asked.

'We're going to have to open each of these,' she responded.

He gave her a horrified look. 'You can't be serious!' he cried. 'It wouldn't be allowed, I'm sure.'

She moved her head around the crypt. 'I don't see we have any other choice.' She tapped the coffin lid. 'One of these bad boys could have been sharing their bed with an unexpected guest and we need to figure out why.' She fixed Mathieu with a quizzical look. 'It seems to me one of your brothers is missing, possibly replaced by someone else. Don't you want to find him?'

Mathieu nodded quickly. 'Oui. Bien sûr. Mais, I don't know what you imagine happened here, or what we can do about it.'

Coco turned her head, staring at the young monk. She took a step towards him. 'I think someone in this monastery knows exactly what happened. That's what I think. And what do YOU think about that?'

He fixed her with an intense gaze. His eyes clouded. 'I think you're the first person in a very long time...' He stopped abruptly, biting his lip before continuing, 'the first person EVER who has actually asked me a question and has bothered to wait for a response, or to care about what I might say.'

Coco felt her cheeks reddening. She shrugged as nonchalantly as she could. 'Alors, that's me, Coco. I'm all about the bass.'

'The bass?' Mathieu spelled out.

Coco shrugged again. 'Yeah, y'know? It's a song.' She looked helplessly at Cedric. He shrugged. *You're on your own.* She stuck her tongue out at him before turning back to Mathieu. 'What I mean, *Frère*, is that I'm all about the... the...'

He smiled at her. 'The bass?'

Coco's mouth twisted, embarrassed that he was mocking her. 'I'm a cop. I'm here to bust your chops, or help you. Whatever you want, I'm easy either way. I can be your best pal, or your worst enemy.'

He smiled again. 'I'd prefer the first.'

Cedric cleared his throat, clearly expressing his irritation.

Coco turned to her lieutenant. 'Call Ebba and tell her to get over here, pronto. And in the meantime, you wait for her and help her check the coffins in here.'

'What are we looking for, exactly?' he demanded.

Coco's eyes flicked over the crypt. It was dark, and it creeped her out, but all of her instincts told her there was likely a lot to be learned from it. 'We're looking for answers,' she replied after a moment.

'And where will you be?'

She shrugged. 'We have a dead body, mais we also have a coffin whose space he filled. I'd like to figure out who is missing and where the hell he is right now.' She gestured to Mathieu. 'Peut être, you'd like to take me back to Frère Leroy?'

'Bien sûr,' Mathieu replied. 'Follow me.'

Coco watched his robe tightening as he strode towards the staircase. 'I can't think of anything better, so long as you walk very, *very* slowly,' she whispered.

Cedric rolled his eyes and turned away.

12H30

'Do you know this man?' Coco presented the photograph of the deceased man they had discovered in the third coffin. In the time they had been waiting for the monks to speak to them, Ebba had sent her a message informing her the dead man's prints were not in the police database. Coco had concluded they needed help, and they needed it quickly.

Frère Gerard Leroy leaned forward and stared at the image. He slouched his shoulders, his hands covering his mouth. He had suddenly gone very pale after staring at the bloody face. He made the sign of the cross across his chest, muttering a prayer which sounded Latin to Coco's untrained ears. 'The poor man,' Leroy said, shaking his head slowly. 'He must have suffered greatly.'

'We can't be sure yet,' Coco responded. 'Mais, let's hope not. Do you recognise him? I know it's not a great picture, but it's all we have to go on right now, so I would appreciate any help.'

Leroy glanced briefly at the screen. 'Je suis désolé, mais, I don't believe I know this man,' he answered swiftly, before turning to his left and presenting the cell phone to the man seated next to him. Coco followed them, her eyes locked on both of their faces, searching for a reaction which would tell her whether or not it was genuine. The second man shook his head, but said nothing. Both their faces remained impassive and told her little. Whatever their thoughts, they did not seem inclined to share them with her.

'This is Frère Henri Aries,' Leroy announced, gesturing to the other man.

The monk next to Leroy identified as Henri Aries leaned forward, pushing a piece of paper toward Coco. He was smaller than Leroy, with a round face covered with a thick beard. 'Here is a list of the missing souls,' he said.

Coco smiled, taking the paper from him. Her eyes scanned the paper. 'There are only two names here,' she said after a moment.

Frère Aries nodded. 'It appears,' he replied in a deep, baritone voice, 'the third missing coffin belonged to one of our more mysterious inhabitants of the crypt.'

'Mysterious?' Cedric asked keenly.

'Oui,' Frère Leroy replied. 'The press actually labelled him, *le fantôme à un million d'euros.*'

Coco frowned. 'What do you mean?'

Henri Aries shrugged. 'It was nothing, of no significance, really. You know how the press like to create headlines. The details aren't really important, in my opinion. He was a man who wanted to share his wealth with us. His instructions to his avocat were explicit. He wanted his eternal resting place to be here in our crypt and he did not wish there to be any fuss or bother. You might be surprised, but these kinds of bequeaths are fairly common, especially amongst those who have the sort of money they would rather not share with family they consider ungrateful.'

'You knew who he was?' Coco questioned.

Leroy nodded. 'He was a friend of the monastery, and the youth centre. However, the instructions from his client were clear, and we were asked to accept his remains and in return sign a confidentiality agreement not to reveal his true identity.'

'And that was allowed?' Coco asked with clear incredulity. She vaguely remembered hearing the story on the news, but had paid little attention to it.

Frère Aries smiled at her. 'You heard my brother. There were a million reasons why it was allowed.'

Coco and Cedric exchanged a look. 'And you didn't think there was anything suspect about it?' Cedric asked.

He nodded. 'Bien sûr. We're monks, but we are still intelligent men,' he responded. 'Mais, the Church's own avocats examined the death certificate and spoke at length with the deceased's avocat. We also had our own pathologist examine the body and, in the end,' he shrugged, 'it was agreed there was no real harm in granting someone's last request to be buried here in our crypt and for his name to be kept a secret.'

Coco snorted. 'Yeah, like you said, you had a million reasons to agree.'

Leroy moved his shoulders. 'They ruled the death to be entirely natural, and the money allowed us to continue our work in the community.'

'And he was in one of the missing coffins?' Coco pushed.

'Oui,' Leroy replied.

'And you won't tell me his name?' she continued.

He shook his head. 'Not without permission, non. It was a legal requirement, after all. I'm sure you, of all people, can understand that. In any event, I see no relevance to what happened. His death was of natural causes and bore no suspicion. Whatever happened yesterday, it is unrelated.'

I'll be the judge of that, was the first thought which flashed through Coco's mind. She also hoped of the three corpses, this was not the missing one, but she had a sinking realisation it was likely to be. 'What can you tell me about the other two coffins?' She looked again at the paper and read the names aloud. 'Paul Bardot and Anna Nols?' she asked.

'Paul was a much beloved brother here in our monastery,' Leroy stated, shaking his head sadly. 'He died nine years ago. He was a dear friend and I can't believe they have desecrated him in this way.'

Coco jotted down the names. 'And what about Madame Nols?'

Frère Henri Aries cleared his throat. '*Mademoiselle* Nols was a patron of the monastery. A single woman with no family whose dying wish was to be interned here.' His eyes narrowed coldly. 'Tell me, Captain Brunhild. When can we have them back?'

Coco moved her shoulders backwards. 'Now, that's a question, isn't it?'

Aries gave her a quizzical look. 'That's why I asked it, obviously,' he snapped.

She held his gaze. There was something about the holy man she did not like. 'There's a lot we have to figure out. Like for starters - how were the coffins removed?'

The two monks exchanged glances Coco could only describe as shifty, and it confused her immensely. Was she just being overly suspicious? It was far more likely than the alternative that two elderly monks were in cahoots. And yet… And yet…

Frère Leroy cleared his throat. 'As I'm sure you have realised by now, this monastery is a place of peace. We keep the door and the gates locked, mais I would imagine a person with criminal intent would likely make short shrift of them.'

Cedric interrupted. 'When we examined the crypt, it was apparent the only way to easily steal the coffins is through the access window, which was locked from the inside.'

Aries stared at him, the expression clear on his face. *And your point is what, exactly?*

Cedric leaned forward. 'Whoever removed the coffins had help from someone in this monastery.'

Frère Leroy slammed the palms of his hand onto his desk. 'That's an outrageous thing to say!' he cried.

Coco raised her hands in an attempt to pacify him. 'The Lieutenant has a point,' she said in as gentle a tone as she could muster, 'and it's a point we need to explore. Stealing coffins is one thing, the fact remains, whatever else occurred, we are most certainly looking at a murder that happened very recently.' She paused, allowing a moment to pass, hoping her words reached them. 'And while I'm sure you are all above reproach, the one thing in which there can be no dispute is that three coffins went missing and we need to understand when, how and, more importantly, who is responsible.' She stared directly at Leroy. 'And therefore you are going to have to help us with that, because once the press gets wind of this they're going to be all over your as…' She bit her lip. 'They're going to be all up in your business, and none of us want that, trust me.'

He shrugged. 'I don't know what you want me to say,' he sighed. 'I have no explanation as to how the coffins were removed and I certainly don't understand why it happened, nor do I know the poor soul who was murdered.'

Frère Henri Aries pointed to the wall clock. 'Frère Leroy, it's time for prayers. Our brothers will be waiting.'

Cedric sighed. 'Well, they're going to have to keep waiting. We're investigating a murder.'

Frère Leroy fixed him with a consolatory look. 'And believe me, Lieutenant Degarmo, during my prayers, I will ask Dieu to do whatever he can to assist, mais…' he spread his hands in front of him on the table, 'if I don't ask, then he's not likely to answer, is he?'

Coco noticed Cedric pressing his fingers angrily into his thighs and she reached over and touched the back of his hand. She turned to Leroy. 'Very well. As long as our forensic technician can have full access to the monastery while you say your prayers, I see no problem in delaying further conversations. After all, I hope she will be able to tell us more after she has been here.'

Leroy and Aries looked at each other. Leroy nodded quickly. 'Very well. While the brothers are in prayers, I will ask Sister Grainger to remain with your technician and offer her all the help she needs.'

Coco raised an eyebrow. 'You have nuns in the monastery as well?' she enquired.

Frère Aries snorted. 'Estelle Grainger is not a nun,' he retorted in a tone which suggested something different altogether.

Leroy pushed Aries's hand. 'For want of a better description, Estelle is our housekeeper,' he blurted. 'She manages the day-to-day running of the monastery, so that the brothers and I can spend our time doing what Dieu asks of us.'

'To pray and shit,' Coco nodded, muttering the words under her breath. 'Tell me, what exactly do you do here at *Abbaye Le Bastien?*'

Frère Leroy smiled softly. 'We pray. We help.'

Coco raised an eyebrow. 'I pretty much do the same thing, so what's the difference between you and me?'

'Dieu,' Aries snapped.

She shrugged. 'You're probably right,' she conceded. 'I only pray to Dieu went I want to get…' she lowered her voice, 'when I want something.'

'There's nothing wrong with that, enfant,' Frère Leroy interjected. 'At the end of the day, that's really all any of us do. We just do it for different reasons. Dieu is good.'

Coco locked eyes with him. 'My experiences may differ from yours,' she countered.

Leroy nodded. 'I don't disagree, mais, that's not really the point.'

'You said you helped?' Cedric interrupted. 'What do you mean?'

Leroy cleared his throat. 'For many years we ran a centre for local youths in the adjacent site. It only recently closed because it was badly in need of repairs. We also run a kitchen to feed the homeless each day.'

'A soup kitchen?' Coco asked, her interest piqued.

Aries laughed. His laugh was cold and hard. 'Well, obviously, we serve more than soup.'

'And what else do you serve up?' Coco asked. 'Do you also provide shelter?'

Leroy shook his head. 'Non, I'm afraid not. We don't have

the space, nor the resources, and such things are very difficult to arrange, and what with the permits and money we would require to bring the Abbaye up to code, it is just not workable.'

Coco nodded. 'And how do you get your money?'

'We have several donors, of course, mais we also have a shop where we sell our own handmade products,' Leroy replied with pride. 'We have a vegetable garden and a small vineyard. We make jams, marmalades and our wine, all at very reasonable prices which directly fund our work here.'

Coco looked impressed. 'Cool. I'll have to check it out. I'm always on the lookout for an excellent wine, the cheaper the better.'

Frère Aries cleared his throat and pointed at the clock. 'Frère Leroy. Prayers,' he said forcefully.

Leroy rose to his feet. 'I'm sorry we can't be more help,' he said to Coco and Cedric.

Coco nodded. 'Okay, but I think we'll need to talk more later when we have a better idea of what we're dealing with. And,' she paused, looking out of the window to the courtyard in the centre of the monastery, 'we really need to figure out why three coffins were taken from here and placed on a demolition site.'

'I'm not sure what answers you think we can give you,' Aries snapped.

Coco locked eyes with him. 'I'm not sure either, but I need to understand how three coffins made their way out of here, with apparently not a single one of you noticing.'

Leroy and Aries stared at each other but said nothing.

'This will not go away,' Coco warned. 'And once the press gets wind of it...' She whistled loudly. 'Well, you know how they like to kick up a fuss and I'm sure the last thing you want is anyone looking too closely at you. You know how people like to put two and two together, particularly when it comes to the Catholic Church.'

'What do you want me to do?' Leroy demanded.

Coco and Cedric moved towards the doorway. Coco stopped. 'It's in everyone's best interest to put this to bed as quickly as we can and to do that we need to understand how three coffins were taken from your crypt and how one of them now contains a dead body who we can't even identify because someone beat him so severely he's unrecognisable.' She stopped, waiting for her words to sink in. 'That is what I want you to do.'

The monks exchanged a worried look. Leroy nodded. 'I'll be in touch.'

Coco nodded. 'Sooner rather than later, if you don't mind.'

13H45

Commander Imane Demissy smoothed her purple hijab and pursed lips painted the same colour and stared in Coco's direction.

Coco tried her best to hold her gaze, knowing full well exactly what the commander was thinking. *What have you done to me this time?* They had been working together for barely a year and their conversations usually began and ended with Demissy chastising Coco for one thing or another, accusing Coco of single-handedly trying to sabotage both of their careers. Coco's eyes flicked lazily over the commander. She was dressed as if she had just been dragged away from some highbrow soiree, which Coco expected was exactly what had happened. Demissy was married to a world-famous violin player and her lifestyle, outfits and jewellery were as far removed from Coco's own as possible. Coco stole a look at her boots, hoping the tape which held together the broken soles was not visible. It was.

'I received a telephone call whilst at a fund-raiser for the Prime Ministers's children's charity,' Demissy began, pacing in front of Coco's desk. 'Which informed me there have been not one, not two, but three coffins stolen from a monastery. That in itself is bad enough, but to be further informed that one of the coffins is missing its former inhabitant to make room for a more recently deceased person, who,' she paused, fixing Coco with a withering look, 'as yet remains unidentified.'

Demissy flopped onto one of the chairs opposite Coco's desk, her face immediately crinkling in shock. She reached beneath her, quickly snapping back her fingers, staring at them, aghast.

Coco looked at her red fingers. 'It's not blood,' she stated reassuringly, handing Demissy a tissue before adding, 'most likely ketchup.'

Demissy wiped her fingers hurriedly, while mouthing, *most likely*. She balled up the tissue and placed it in the overflowing bin. 'Did I miss anything out in my assessment?' she continued, seemingly speaking to no one in particular. 'Ah, yes, I did. I fielded a call from the most senior Bishop in the Catholic Church on my way over here. He was demanding to know what I intended to do about it and assure him I had my best men on it.' She pursed her lips. 'I never knew I could be such a good liar.'

Coco rolled her eyes, before glaring at the smirk which had appeared on Cedric's face.

'The Bishop has insisted the Church's own press office deal with this,' Demissy continued. 'He is rather keen that we keep it away from the press, especially after it appears you scared the life out of two of the most senior and well-respected monks in the country.'

Coco shrugged her shoulders. 'I merely pointed out the fact that unless they helped us figure out what the hell happened, the vultures in the press will not be patient and they'll start making up their own stories to put on the news.'

'The press may be vultures, but they're pussycats compared to the damn Catholic Church,' Cedric grumbled. 'They close ranks and erase stories before they have a chance to hit the headlines. They've had plenty of practice, just ask choir boys up and down the country…'

'Lieutenant…' Demissy interjected. Her tone was even and brisk, but it was determined.

'You've got a point,' Coco conceded. 'Mais, I don't really care what the Church does so long as they don't get in our way, and if they keep the press off our asses, I won't complain.'

Demissy tapped long nails on Coco's desk. 'Well, regardless of all of that, we're the ones everyone is going to demand answers from. So, where are we exactly?'

Nowhere. Coco coughed. 'We're just waiting for Sonny to let us know when he's ready for the autopsy, but the dead man's prints didn't show up in any of the usual databases. The monks didn't recognise the photograph of him.'

'And you believe them?' Demissy asked.

Coco considered her answer. 'I'm not sure, but he was pretty messed up. Peut être when Sonny gets him cleaned up, we might have a better chance of identifying him. What bothers me the most about the monastery is three coffins were removed without any of them noticing.'

'And you think they're lying?'

Coco shrugged. 'Just because they're monks doesn't mean they can't also be liars. However, unless we lean on them, I don't know what else we can do to get them to talk.'

'They may just have nothing to say, because they saw or heard nothing,' Demissy retorted. She turned to Cedric. 'What is your evaluation, Lieutenant Degarmo?'

Coco's jaw dropped, but she said nothing, shrugging huffily at Cedric. It was not lost on her Demissy most likely would prefer to have Cedric as her Captain, rather than Coco. He cleared his throat. 'The fact is, we can't really rule out some stupid prank.'

'A prank?' Demissy asked doubtfully.

He shrugged. 'Why not?'

'Other than the fact one old stiff was replaced by a newer model,' Coco quipped. 'That doesn't seem to be much of a prank to me.'

'Hmm,' Demissy tapped her lips. 'That does rather change the dynamics of the situation, doesn't it? I'm not sure how exactly, but it does.'

'I think we can rule it out as just being a prank,' Coco interrupted. 'The three coffins is interesting, but what about the fresh corpse? All I can think is whoever dumped him assumed his body was going to be lost in the demolition and we would be none the wiser. It doesn't seem much of a prank to me when you look at it that way.'

She reached into her bag and extracted a cigarette, quickly lighting it and ignoring the withering look from Demissy. 'The only problem with that theory is - why the hell put the coffins on different floors? I mean, the chances are if the man in charge of the demolition hadn't seen the first coffin on the ground floor, he may not have checked all the floors above. Drag all the coffins upstairs and hope no one spots them. That makes more sense.' She blew smoke rings. 'We have three coffins, carefully arranged. I can't help but thinking that means something.'

Demissy moved her head slowly. 'I can't imagine what. Can you?'

Coco considered. 'I don't really know. A ritual, perhaps? A message to someone? If we find a suspect, I'll be sure to ask them.' She stood and moved across the cramped office floor. 'The idea of a prank is an interesting one, but it doesn't really hold up under scrutiny if the plan was to get rid of a dead body, because that would go back to hiding the coffins away from prying eyes. Because the way it went down kind of backfired, non?'

'Then could it have been a prank AND something else?' Cedric suggested.

Demissy frowned. 'What do you mean?'

'Oh, I don't know really,' he responded reluctantly. 'Peut être someone took advantage of a prank to hide a crime?'

Demissy moved her head slowly between Coco and Cedric, shaking it slowly. 'None of this makes any sense.' She sighed. 'Which brings us to the demolition. Are you happy for the demolition to take place?' she asked Coco in a way which made it clearly sound like a test.

Coco shrugged. 'I don't see we have a choice,' she replied. 'The buildings going to come down in one way or another and Ebba has done what she can. She has taken photographic and video evidence and checked for forensics as much as she can. It's barely standing as it is, and it would most likely be dangerous to keep sending officers in. And truthfully, I don't think there's anything else the building can tell us, not standing at least.'

'I don't understand what you mean,' Demissy interrupted.

Coco smiled. 'I'm not sure I do either,' she admitted. 'Only that if the building is significant to how the coffins were arranged, or why there was a dead body placed there, we don't necessarily need it to be standing for it to tell us. We need to look into what it used to be, what it was used for and why it was being demolished, and,' she paused, 'what it has to do with the monastery.'

She stared at Demissy. 'If you want us to stop the demolition, then it's going to have to come from you, or someone higher than you, because Aaron Cellier and whoever he works for is going to be mighty pissed off if they don't get to light the dynamite, or whatever the hell they do to blow it up. And their first argument is going to be that this was nothing more than a criminal seizing an opportunity to destroy evidence of a crime, and honestly, I don't necessarily disagree with that assumption at this stage.'

Demissy turned away as if she was contemplating her options. 'And Ebba is sure there is no more to be discovered in the building?'

'I went up in the cherry picker with her,' Coco answered. 'And I don't think there's anything else in the building.'

Cedric's cell phone began ringing. 'It's Ebba,' he said, reading the display. 'Hey, Ebba. What's up?' he answered. 'Okay. And you're sure? We'll see you back at the site. It looks like we're going to allow the demolition to take place.' He listened intently to her talking for a few minutes before finally disconnecting the call and dropping the cell phone on the desk. 'She says there is no sign of a break-in at the monastery. She's taken prints and will run them through the databases when she gets back. She also did a prelim examination of the grounds and she found nothing out of the ordinary.'

'And no missing corpse?' Coco asked.

He shook his head. 'Nope. And she looked inside the other coffins, just in case any of them were doubling up. They weren't. She also said she went with the officers through all the rooms and couldn't find anything suspicious. In fact, she said the place was pretty much empty.' He shrugged. 'I suppose that's how monks live, eh? No TV's or shit like that.'

Coco stubbed out the cigarette. 'Then where the hell is our missing corpse? You know, the fact there is no evidence of a break-in means there is only one possible answer. Someone in the monastery has to be involved in one way or another.'

Demissy visibly shuddered. 'Don't say that,' she snapped. 'Just don't say that.' She rose to her feet, glancing at her watch. 'I have to get back to my lunch. Mais, oui, the demolition can take place. You're probably right, there's nothing we can do to stop it and probably not a lot of point in trying. Get yourselves over there and monitor it. Pay particular attention to anyone in attendance. Whoever did this may just decide to come back to witness the demolition. We can't be certain they've heard we discovered their plan.'

Coco widened her eyes and pointed at them. 'You can be sure I'll keep these peeled.'

Demissy sighed wearily. 'Keep me informed. My phone may be off, but message me if anything happens.' She stopped by the doorway, peering at Coco. 'Oh, and Captain Brunhild?'

'Oui?'

Demissy's jaw tightened. 'Just be careful and don't… don't upset anyone, d'accord?'

Coco looked offended. 'Who, moi? As if I would.'

Demissy shook her head and disappeared into the hallway.

14H45

Coco nodded towards Aaron Cellier, the demolition site supervisor. He smiled, giving her a thumbs-up, the gratitude and relief clear on his face.

Coco was still unsure whether she was doing the right thing in allowing the demolition to proceed. She knew she could not really stop it, but more importantly, whether or not she stopped it, whatever happened next with the investigation, she was sure she was going to receive heat for whichever way she went. She was satisfied there was nothing left to discover in the physical shell of the building, and that was going to have to be enough, but she was convinced there was still much to discover about the building's history and why it had been chosen for such a macabre and bizarre ritual.

She turned her head. The monastery cast a dark shadow over the demolition site. She looked again at the building that was about to be demolished. Frère Leroy had mentioned it had been some kind of youth centre and Coco could not dodge the thought that came to her, particularly while taking into consideration her own previous interactions with the Catholic Church. She shook the thought from her head.

Whatever she had experienced in her own past, Coco knew she could not allow it to distract her from the investigation at hand. The building that was about to come down in front of her was very likely the key to the complete mystery, but she was sure there were likely many people who would object to her poking around. Her mouth twisted, and she realised it was not the first time, nor would it be the last, when her job forced her to butt heads with bureaucrats and those whose only interest was self-preservation.

'Is it okay if I stay for the demolition?' Ebba asked, appearing by Coco and Cedric's side.

Coco looked around, wondering who the Swedish forensic expert was talking to. 'Sure,' she shrugged. 'Everyone loves a big bang,' she added with a wink. 'Cedric told me you found nothing at the monastery that might help. Are you sure?' There was no bite to Coco's tone, just desperation. She was conscious the day was wearing on and she was yet to catch a break.

Ebba snorted. 'Well, I did the best I could, although they sent some trout to supervise me with the intent of making sure I didn't get to poke my nose around places she didn't want me to see. So, of course, I looked twice as hard in every corner she tried to shoo me away from.'

Coco flashed the forensic technician with an impressed smile. 'And?'

'And I found nothing,' Ebba conceded. 'Primarily because there's fuck all in there. Wardrobes filled with nothing but spare cassocks and bedside tables with bibles and crosses. If there are places to hide anything, I certainly didn't see them, despite the old woman following me everywhere.'

Coco nodded, recalling Frère Leroy mentioning the monastery had a female housekeeper, a woman by the name of Estelle Grainger. 'What's she like?'

'A bitch,' Ebba retorted. 'That's what she's like,' she added bluntly.

Coco chuckled. 'Don't hold back, Ebba, whatever you do!'

Ebba shrugged nonchalantly. 'I tell it like it is. I thought you, of all people, would appreciate that.'

Cedric nodded. 'She's got a point, there, Captain,' he added, before turning to Ebba. 'The question is - was she just an ordinary pain, or was she being a pain because she was hiding something? That is the question, and the answer makes a lot of difference.'

Ebba turned her head back towards the monastery, narrowing her eyes as if trying to recall what had happened in minute detail. 'There was something about her that was off.'

'Off?' Coco interjected, her voice rising with interest.

'Yeah,' Ebba agreed. 'I mean, she looks all prim and proper, like a nun or whatever the hell she is, but she just seemed wrong.'

'Wrong?' Cedric interrupted with a sarcastic laugh. 'Great deduction skills, Ebba!'

She glared at him. 'I'm a forensic technician. You're supposed to be the cop. You do the detecting, okay?' she said, stomping away from them towards the crowd who had gathered for the demolition.

Coco tutted in Cedric's direction. 'Speaking of someone being bitchy… Ebba seems to be trying to open up to us, don't you think? But she's sensitive, I think, and she doesn't take criticism well, perceived or otherwise.'

Cedric's eyes widened. 'So, you want me to be nicer to her? She never has a pleasant word to say about you.'

Coco shrugged her shoulders nonchalantly. 'Nor do you, but I still let you hang around, so quit busting her chops and she might, just *might*, let you ask her out.'

Cedric opened his mouth to respond, but before he could, a man appeared behind them and cleared his throat. 'May I join you?' he asked.

Coco did not need to turn around to know who it was. 'Sure you can, Frère Moreau.' She stepped back, gesturing for the young monk to join them behind the safety fence. 'I must say, I'm surprised to see you here.'

Mathieu Moreau's smooth forehead crinkled. 'Pourquoi? I've lived in this neighbourhood all of my life and I've seen this building pretty much every day.'

'Then you must be sad to see it go,' Coco replied.

Mathieu turned away from her to face the building. 'I've been waiting for this day for a very long time,' he whispered.

'What do you mean?' she asked.

'Frère Moreau, Frère Leroy has asked you to return to the monastery immediately,' a woman's voice called from the crowd.

It took Coco a few moments to ascertain who was speaking, but when she did, she knew who it was. Ebba's description of Estelle Grainger had been more than accurate. The monastery housekeeper was a slight woman, dressed in a drab beige skirt and matching cardigan. Thin hair hung limply around a thin, pale head, and her eyes were cold. Coco noted, however, that despite the cardigan, Estelle Grainger was hiding a rack that would make a topless model jealous.

'Mademoiselle Grainger,' Mathieu called out, his voice soft and subservient, 'I had permission to attend.'

'That was... *before*,' she snapped, fixing Coco and Cedric with a glare which was so icy it made Coco want to shiver.

'All the same,' Mathieu said calmly, 'I am here with the police. We did promise to cooperate, did we not?'

Estelle's face contorted, and she could not hide her irritation. Her eyes narrowed as if she was wrestling with what she should do or say next. She clicked her shoes together. 'Very well, I shall relay the message.' She glanced at a slim, plain watch on a bony wrist. 'I should remind you that supper is at 16H00 today and if you are not there, the kitchen will be closed until morning.'

Mathieu smiled at her. 'I wouldn't miss it, Mademoiselle Grainger.'

She stared at him, clearly assessing whether his cool, calm voice was patronising. She turned away abruptly, dashing through the crowd and back towards the monastery.

Coco watched her leave and chuckled. 'She really hates you, doesn't she?'

Mathieu watched the diminutive woman's retreating figure. 'I suppose she does,' he answered softly.

'And why is that?'

He considered his answer. 'For many reasons, I'm sure,' he

began, 'not least of which because my family owns the land the monastery is built on,' he explained. 'I imagine she thinks they should have donated it to the Church, not just letting them live there rent free. My family is pious, but they're also rich for a reason - they're not stupid. My grandfather realised if he signed over the land, the church could technically sell it whenever they wanted and keep the money, which lets face it, they probably would because it's likely worth millions. So, he made a deed stating the Church could have the land so long as the monastery remained on it, and if anything were to change, then the land would go back to my family.'

Coco stared at him. 'Then you're rich?' she asked without trying to sound impressed.

Mathieu laughed. 'Well, technically I'm a monk, so I don't have a cent, mais...' He trailed off, leaving the implication of his words to hang heavy in the air. He looked away again, staring at the monastery. 'I hate doing what Estelle tells me, but all the same, I suppose I should go back.'

'I thought you wanted to watch the demolition?' Coco asked.

'I do,' he tugged at his robe, 'but I still have to listen to my brothers.' He stepped away, but stopped abruptly. 'However, I do need to speak to you, Captain Brunhild.' He stole a sneaky look at Cedric before adding. 'Alone.'

Coco could not stop herself from grinning. 'That's my favourite way to talk,' she said in a way she meant to sound sexy, but she was sure made her sound as if she had constipation. Behind her, Cedric tutted. She glared at him, sending the obvious message. *Will you stop doing that every time I'm talking to a man?*

Mathieu smiled back at her. 'It's my favourite way to talk, too,' he exhaled, before looking away again. 'Later, okay?' he asked before moving away from them.

Coco watched his long brown robe disappear into the crowd. 'Lieutenant Degarmo,' she began. 'Can I ask you a question?'

Cedric rolled his eyes. 'Non, you absolutely cannot,' he sighed.

She stuck out her tongue. 'I realise it's been a while for me, and even when it wasn't… well, I was never good at boy things, mais…'

'And you think I am?' he interrupted.

She pointed at him. 'Well, you're a boy, aren't you?' She frowned. 'I mean, I assume you are. I realise I have no proof one way or another, mais, I've always assumed you to be a boy…'

Cedric held up his hands. 'Oui. I can confirm, I AM a boy. Your point?'

Coco gestured toward the monastery. 'Monk boy was flirting with me, wasn't he?'

Cedric sighed again. 'Don't you have someone other than me you can talk to? Like a shrink, for example?'

'Why would I talk to a stranger?' Coco retorted. 'You've literally been inside of me. We have no secrets…'

'I have not been inside of you!' Cedric hissed, louder than he intended, immediately realising several people had turned to them upon hearing his words.

Coco ignored the looks. 'And because of that, you have a responsibility to be my girlfriend…'

'Coco,' Cedric wailed desperately.

'Was he, or was he not flirting with me?' Coco pushed.

Cedric exhaled a long breath. 'I'm not an expert, mais… yeah, I suppose you could say it sounded like he was flirting with you,' he said.

Coco lit a cigarette. 'Then the question is. Why is he flirting? I mean, he's a monk. He shouldn't be flirting. Especially with me.' She looked down at her chest. 'I mean, I know I've got it all going on, but even I have to admit that he is "probably" a little young for me…'

A little? Cedric mouthed.

Coco ignored him and continued. 'Anyho. My point is - Monsieur Sexy Monk is flirting with moi, a woman old enough to be his...' she stopped, considering what to say, 'his middle sister. However, putting that all to one side, the fact remains it seems someone in that monastery was involved in how those coffins ended up in that building over there. Which makes me wonder - is our young monk flirting with me just to distract me? I mean, has he heard something about me?'

Cedric laughed. 'Well, I'm sure he could have read something about you on a bathroom wall in a truck stop, or something...'

Coco blew a raspberry. 'You make a good, if slightly nasty and judgemental point,' she replied, before wagging her finger, 'and don't knock truck stops, give it a few years, and I'm sure you'll find yourself hanging out in one of them. Non, my point is, he could easily have read up about me and my... *past*, and decided that if he wants me to stop looking too closely at him and the monastery, then he would try to distract me.' She stubbed out the cigarette. 'I mean, it's a bit of an assumption, but what are the alternatives? He really likes me?' she asked, trying to hide the hope in her voice.

Cedric sighed. 'This isn't high school, you know?'

Coco lit another cigarette. 'And then if he is only flirting to stop me from looking at his involvement, then it begs the question - how far is he prepared to go? I mean, how far *can* he go?'

Cedric clenched his fists. 'Again, not a shrink, nor your girlfriend.' He puffed out his cheeks. 'However, the fact is, just because he's a monk, doesn't necessarily mean he's dead below the waist...'

Coco raised an eyebrow. 'Then you really do think he has the hots for me?'

Cedric laughed. 'Non, but if he does it makes him blind, et...' his nose crinkled, 'with no sense of smell.'

Coco sniffed herself. 'I don't know what you're talking about. I had a shower this morning.' She paused, her brow creasing. 'I think…' she added pensively.

Aaron Cellier stepped onto a podium in front of the crowd and tapped a microphone. 'It's time to begin,' he announced proudly.

15H00

Coco and Cedric watched wide-eyed as the building crashed to the ground, sending a plume of dust and debris into the air. They were at a safe distance away from it; the site encased by a tall fence and all intently watched by a crowd, many of whom were holding camera phones high in the air. Coco watched Aaron Cellier shaking hands with several men, who she assumed were his employers, the new owners of the land. She caught his eye and waved, and he made his way quickly over to her.

'I'm so grateful you allowed this to go ahead,' he said gratefully. 'You do not know how much aggro you saved me.'

'This isn't over,' Cedric replied hastily.

Cellier gave him a quizzical look. 'I don't understand…'

Coco pointed over his shoulder to what remained of the building. 'We still need to figure out what happened over there.'

He shrugged. 'It was kids. Everyone agrees it was just kids messing around.'

Coco shook her head. 'I don't agree. At least not until we figure out who died and why.' She scratched her head. 'Tell me, did you know what the was building used for?'

Collier nodded. 'It was a drop-in centre for teenagers,' he replied. 'You know the kind of thing. Ping-pong, café, all dressed up to look like fun when really it's just do-gooders trying to keep them off the streets and out of trouble.'

'That's not necessarily a bad thing,' Coco reasoned.

Cellier scratched his jaw. 'I'm all for keeping kids out of trouble. I have one of my own and believe me, he tries my patience.' He looked off towards the monastery. 'I've nothing against the monks, because I think their hearts were always in the right place. I never bought into the belief that all kids needed was

Dieu to keep them on the straight and narrow. I'm just not sure feeding them doctrines from a book which is most likely fiction does kids as much good as they say it does. In fact, I'd say it makes them worse.'

Coco frowned. 'You sound as if you speak from experience.'

He turned back, staring at the rubble of what was only minutes ago the youth centre. 'Keeping kids off the streets is a good thing, don't get me wrong, I'm all for that. Mais, as I said, feeding them religious mumbo-jumbo will not get them to change their ways.'

Coco smiled. 'Not much of a churchgoer, eh?'

Cellier laughed. 'Not at all, but you were right. I do speak from experience,' he added, his tone laced with anger. 'All I know is that my boy was a handful. I'll be the first to admit to that. There were times I thought the only thing which would work on him was a damn good thrashing, but you're not allowed to do that sort of thing these days, more's the pity. So, my wife said, "send him to the youth club, they'll sort him out and put him on the right track."' Cellier clenched his fists. 'I should have never listened to her.'

Coco felt her blood run cold. 'What happened?' she asked softly.

Cellier shrugged again. 'Who knows? All I can tell is you that my son went from an, admittedly, arrogant, annoying swine, to a kid who is afraid of his own shadow.'

Cedric stepped forward. 'You think he was abused?'

Cellier stared at him before shaking his head. 'I don't think so. Not like… *that*, at least.' He pronounced the word *that* as if it caused him a great deal of pain. 'Mais, all the preaching changed him and the truth is, I don't know if it was for the best.'

'What do you mean?' Coco pushed.

'I don't really know how to explain it,' he answered finally. 'Only that my bright, outgoing kid now only talks about Dieu these days and how he has to serve him. My wife says it's not such a bad thing, mais, I don't know…' He stared again at the direction of the monastery. 'The fact is, he's judgmental about me, people who don't follow Dieu. He was never like that before. I certainly never raised him to be like that.'

Coco raised an eyebrow, following his gaze. 'And you believe the monks are responsible for the change in your son?'

Cellier nodded. 'Yeah, I do.'

'How did the monks get involved?' Cedric asked.

'The monastery owns all the land, or at least they did,' Cellier replied. 'The monks do a lot of work with the homeless, but they weren't really connecting with the younger generation, which I suppose is the why the outreach program came to be. A chance for the Catholic Church to interact with all parts of the community.'

Coco stared at the rubble that now replaced the building she had walked through yesterday. 'Then what went wrong?'

Cellier shrugged. 'A lot of things. You know what kids can be like. Some of them just don't really respect things as they should. The centre became more and more rundown and people just stopped caring. They had no damn respect, and then finally there was a fire and…' he trailed off and shrugged again. 'I suppose the Church just had enough of paying for it to be repaired, so they sold it to my employers, a bunch of property developers who plan on turning the land into apartments.' He turned back to what remained of the demolished building. 'I can't say I'm sorry to see it go.'

'And the monks. Are they happy?' Coco inquired.

'Who gives a shit what they think? After what they did to my son, they can go to hell as far as I'm concerned.' Cellier snapped. He bit his lip, his face clouding as if he had just said too much. He glanced over Coco's shoulder toward a crowd of people. 'Listen, I have to get back to my guests. There are a lot of important potential investors here today and I can't afford to piss anyone off more than I already have.'

Coco and Cedric watched him leave and then looked at each

other. There was something off, Coco was sure of it, but she could not figure out what it might be. The starting point had to be the coffins and how they ended up in the soon-to-be demolished building and the only person she could think of that might be willing and able to help with that was the young monk Mathieu Moreau. Talking with him again was a prospect which she did not find entirely unpleasant.

16H00

Dr. Bernstein tucked an abundance of wild, black curls under his skullcap and placed the visor over his face. Coco and Cedric watched in silence, knowing this was his way of preparing himself for what he was about to do. The unnamed corpse lay on the gurney in front of him, his lower half covered in a thin blue sheet. He had been washed and they could now get a much better look at him.

He was, Coco imagined, probably more or less the same age as her, nudging just past forty and he was reasonably handsome, she supposed. Quite tall, with a thin, athletic body and now she could see his face without the blood, she could make out he had a smooth, unlined face with a high forehead and brown hair swept over his skull. One of his eyes was slightly open, a pale blue pupil staring into the room. Even after being cleaned, his face was already showing signs of the beating he had taken. 'Sorry this happened to you, man,' Coco whispered. She looked over the rest of his body, but there did not appear to be anything which would give a clue as to his identity or what may have happened to him. There were also no tattoos or piercings.

Sonny cleared his throat and moved slowly around the body. 'The liver temp confirms he died less than twenty-four hours ago,' Sonny began. 'I'd pinpoint it so far as between 20H00 hours and midnight last night.' He paused. 'As for identification, all I can tell you is that his fingerprints and dental records haven't shown up in any of the usual databases.'

'And I've checked missing person reports,' Cedric added, 'and there's nothing there, certainly nothing matching his appearance.' He sighed. 'If he only died last night, someone may not have noticed him missing yet.'

Coco moved around the gurney. She pointed at the bruising around the neck. 'You can see the bruises forming in what looks to me like the shape of fingers.' She extended her own hand and placed it near the neck. Her fingers were shorter than the bruise pattern. 'And I'd go so far as to say that it appears to be a bigger hand than mine. A man's hand, par example.'

Cedric snorted. 'You hardly have delicate little fingers,' he quipped.

Coco stuck out her tongue in his direction. She turned back to Sonny. 'My point is, does that tell us anything?'

He shrugged. 'I don't think so.' He picked up a scalpel. 'But let's see if does have anything to tell us.'

'Well, there are clear petechiae in the eyes,' Sonny began as he removed his gloves and began washing his hands. 'What's interesting, however, is that I don't believe he was strangled by a hand.'

Coco frowned, staring at the exposed throat. She pointed. 'You can see the bruises.'

Sonny nodded. 'I agree. However, I don't believe it was the cause of death, not completely, at least.'

'What do you mean, doc?' Cedric asked.

Sonny finished washing his hands and began drying them. He moved back towards the body. He pointed at the neck. 'Let's begin with the fact there are no obvious signs of fingernails around the bruises…'

Coco stared at her own stumpy fingernails. 'Perhaps they bite them, like I do.'

'Peut être,' Sonny reasoned, sounding as if he was anything but convinced.

Coco stared at him. 'Then what are you suggesting?'

The doctor did not answer instantly, instead he continued to stare at the dead man. 'I can't be sure,' he began, caution clear in his voice, 'but I would suggest that whatever happened to this man, the fingernail marks we would see would be his.' He lifted the hand. 'And as you can see, his nails are reasonably well manicured.' He moved towards Coco and extended his fingers around her throat. 'What would you do if I did this to you?'

Coco smiled and pressed her knee between Sonny's thighs. 'I'd make sure you'd been speaking with a very, *very* squeaky voice.'

Sonny stepped backwards, moving towards Cedric, placing his hand around his throat. 'What about you, Lieutenant?'

Cedric considered his response for a moment before placing his own hand around Sonny's and squeezing. Sonny did not remove his hand, forcing Cedric to press even harder with his fingers before finally pushing the hand away from his throat.

Sonny smiled. 'As Lieutenant Degarmo so clearly showed,' he said, winking at Coco. 'If someone tries to choke you and you're conscious, you'll do whatever you can to get them off, usually by using your fingernails to force the hand away. There is no evidence of that.'

Coco ran her finger through her hair, pulling frizzy blue hair into a ponytail. 'Then what are you suggesting happened?'

'Well,' he said, clearing his throat, 'the hyoid bone is clearly fractured. My examination of the neck and the dissection and removal of the larynx and the examination of the hyoid bone and the tongue allowed me to pinpoint the superficial and deep musculature to confirm contusion haemorrhage. Additionally, when I exposed the laryngeal skeleton, it showed clear evidence of fracture, as did the cervical spine.'

Coco clapped her hands together. 'Alright, you've impressed me, Sonny. Cut to the chase.'

He smiled. 'You know I don't like to talk in suppositions, and in layperson's terms, you can safely consider this as a homicide, mais my belief is that there were at least two people involved in what happened to this poor man.'

Cedric flashed him a surprised look. 'How do you come to that conclusion?' he demanded.

'It's a common enough thing,' Sonny replied. 'Even the police use it.'

'You're talking about choke holds?' Coco interrupted.

'Oui,' Sonny replied. 'It's a pretty effective way of subduing someone. You stand behind someone, place your arm around their throat, and the pressure on the carotid artery can very quickly render them unconscious. However, it's very dangerous and if the pressure is applied for too long, it can easily result in death, whether or not that was the intention. It would also leave practically no external marks on the body.'

Coco stepped away. 'Why do you think there were two perps?'

'I can't say with any certainty,' Sonny replied. 'Mais, if we extrapolate the two injuries, first the bruises around the throat, we might presume that was the cause of death, however my examination of the larynx and hyoid don't fit with that, but it would with someone standing behind him and subduing that way. The damage to the bones are spread out, rather than focused.'

'Interesting,' Coco mused.

Cedric turned on her. 'I don't see how. It tells us nothing.'

'I know that!' Coco exclaimed. 'I was trying to sound smart. Would you rather I said it told us bugger all?'

'That's what Commander Demissy is going to say,' Cedric reasoned, his mouth extending into a smile.

'What about the injuries to the face?' Coco continued, suddenly feeling exhausted.

'Well, as you can see, he took quite a beating,' Sonny confirmed, pointing at a row of images on the screen above them.

Coco walked slowly between them, her face tilted. The images were shocking, showing various stages of the last moments of a man's life. 'They didn't kill him?'

Sonny shook his head. He pointed at one of the photographs. 'This blow here fractured his cheekbone, and this one, his eye socket. That's why that eye doesn't close properly.'

Coco winced. 'Ouch. So, he was beaten and then choked?'

Sonny shrugged, but did not answer immediately. 'That is a logical assumption,' he said finally. 'I can certainly tell you that this part of the attack was pre-mortem, and I imagine it subdued him enough for what came after.' He paused. 'And that got me thinking.' He stepped in front of the screen and pointed at one of the images. 'Do you see the face where I have cleaned it up a little? Look in the middle. There are what appear to be two circular burns, about an inch apart.'

Coco narrowed her eyes. 'Yeah, I think I see it. What does it mean?'

Sonny pondered. 'I can't be completely certain, but it looks to me like the sort of burn that might come from something like a Taser or electroshock weapon.'

Coco raised an eyebrow. 'Interesting. So, he could have been Tasered to subdue him enough to finish him off?'

Sonny nodded. 'It's certainly possible.'

'Did the beating come before or after the Taser?' Cedric questioned.

Sonny considered his answer, staring at the image and then at the face of the unknown man. 'I'm almost certain the Taser, if that's what it is, came before the beating.' He shrugged. 'As to its relevance, or whether it is important, I can't really say. Attacks such as these are often frenzied, and it can be difficult to pinpoint exactly what happened when.'

'What about the body?' Cedric asked. 'Is there anything which might point to who did this to him?'.

'Not really,' Sonny replied. 'We've swabbed for DNA, so that might bring something back. But I didn't find any stray hairs.

Désolé. Let's hope the DNA and blood samples bring something back.'

Coco moved to the evidence table, her fingers tracing across the bags. 'What about the clothes he was wearing? Anything there?'

'I don't believe so,' Sonny replied. 'Ebba examined them. There was nothing in his pockets. No wallet, no cell phone. Nothing which might give us a clue who he was, or how he ended up where he did.'

'We could always use the photo of his cleaned up face to appeal for witnesses,' Cedric suggested.

'I hate doing that,' Coco grumbled. 'The thought of someone turning on the news and seeing a picture of their dead loved one pisses me off.'

Cedric shrugged. 'If we have no other choice, what else can we do?'

'Je sais, je sais,' Coco exhaled

Sonny glanced at his watch. 'Désolé, I don't have more for you, mais…'

Coco took a deep breath. 'You've got a hundred and one more things to do before you day is over. I get that.' She gestured to Cedric. 'Come on, Lieutenant, let's at least try to find something before Demissy has one of her hissy fits.'

'And how do you propose we do that?' Cedric questioned. 'We have nothing.'

She smiled. 'I'm going to find me a handsome monk. It seems a good enough place to start, non?' She blew Sonny a kiss. 'Bissous, Sonny et merci.'

17H30

Coco pulled the car to a halt but kept her hands on the steering wheel. The text message kept playing in her head. *Meet me at Café Beau on Rue de Jeann at 17H30. Mathieu.* There was nothing wrong with it, she supposed, after all, she had made it clear she needed to speak to him, but again she was troubled by the familiarity of him using his first name.

She shook her head, realising she was being ridiculous, imagining things that were not there. She lit a cigarette and checked her appearance in the rear-view mirror, sticking her tongue out at herself. Her hair was unkempt, bordering on frizzing, but was she really so bad? She wore little makeup, just eyeliner and mascara and a red lipstick and she reasoned that despite the life she had led, she was not in such terrible shape after all. As she had walked into her fifth decade, Coco had realised one thing and one thing only. Relationships were not for her. She could not be trusted in one. Her choice in men had proven to be nothing short of disastrous and the realisation had slowly dawned on her she could not risk it again, not just for her sake, but for her four children. There could be no more mistakes when it came to men. She would not allow it.

'Are you going to sit there forever?'

Coco did not need to turn around to know who it was. She already knew his voice and the sixteen-year-old girl who still shared space in Coco's brain had already picked out china patterns. The only patterns in Coco's dinner sets were the chipped *Charlie's Angels* plates she had found for a euro a piece at a flea market.

Coco pivoted her head, exhaling a plume of smoke directly into Frère Mathieu Moreau's face. He wafted it away and grinned at her. His smile barely creased his smooth face. Coco pushed open the car door, smashing it into his knee, causing him to wince in pain and move away.

Coco's face reddened, and she dashed towards the café door. 'It's about knocking off time. I'm having a beer.'

Coco watched as Mathieu sipped the top of his beer. Her eyebrows knotted. 'Are monks even allowed to drink alcohol?'

Mathieu took a gulp of the beer. 'Sure. Rumour has it we do a lot of stuff we're not supposed to do…' he trailed off, allowing the words to dissipate into the air.

Coco swigged her own beer. 'Well, I'm fairly sure they're not supposed to be such terrible flirts.'

Mathieu smiled, cocking his head and studying Coco with a clear burning curiosity. 'I'm confused. Are you saying I'm terrible at flirting, or that I flirt a lot?'

Coco turned her head away from him. 'Both,' she whispered. Suddenly she hated his voice and she could not be sure whether it was because he was a liar, or worse that he was being straight with her. 'Why the hell are we here, anyway?' she grumbled.

Mathieu stared at her, his face turning slightly to the side. His eyes widened. 'You told me to be here,' he stated simply.

Coco gestured to the waiter for two more beers. 'You're rich, you can pay for them,' she mumbled to Mathieu.

'I shouldn't…' he began.

Coco tapped her chin. 'I have a feeling this isn't the first time you haven't exactly been as "monkly" as you should have been.'

He gave her a surprised look. 'What's that supposed to mean?'

Coco shrugged. 'It means a lot of things, I suspect,' she answered cryptically. 'Mais, let's start with how three coffins made their way from your monastery to the building next door that was about to be demolished.'

'I'm sure I don't know,' he responded huffily.

'*I'm sure I don't know,*' Coco repeated mockingly. 'Mais, someone does, non? I mean, if I'm supposed to believe everything you and your brothers have had to say, then it appears that these damn coffins somehow or other materialised from one place to another with no one knowing how and all the doors and gates being locked.' She stared at Mathieu. 'Now, I believe in a lot of crazy shit, but I don't believe in that.'

Mathieu nodded, emitting a long sigh. Coco leaned forward, forcing herself to resist inhaling his scent. 'Let's cut to the chase, Frère…'

'I wish you'd call me Mathieu, or Matt,' he interrupted.

Coco narrowed her eyes. 'As I was saying, *Frère* Moreau, I can't see anyway around it other than one of your frock wearing homies somehow or other helped someone steal three coffins and,' she paused as if for dramatic affect, 'as far as I can tell, helped to cover up a murder.'

Mathieu raised an eyebrow. 'You know nothing of the sort,' he snipped, before adding with a faint smile, '*Captain* Brunhild.'

Coco stared at him. She pulled back her shoulders and wished she could slap her own face for being so ridiculous. 'I'm all ears if you have another explanation.'

Mathieu moved the beer between his hands. He lifted his head slowly. 'It was only supposed to be a joke,' he said finally.

Coco gawped at him. 'A joke? To steal three damn coffins?'

He shook his head quickly. 'Non, that wasn't… that wasn't the plan.'

She leaned forward, acutely aware that whatever was coming next was important. 'The plan?'

Mathieu sighed. He gestured out of the window onto the busy boulevard. 'Do you know I've spent my whole life in this neighbourhood? For twenty years, I've never even been out of this arrondissement. Not for a holiday, not for a day trip. And yeah, you're right, my family is rich. Filthy rich, you might call it.

However, the one thing they don't like to do, or at least be seen to be doing, is spending money. At least on anything other than good causes,' he added. 'That's why I know these streets so well, and why I know everyone here and everything about them.'

'Sounds boring,' Coco interrupted, before quickly bowing her head and mouthing an apology.

Mathieu smiled at her. 'Don't apologise, it's true. It's boring, in fact,' he looked around as if satisfying himself there was no one in earshot, 'it's *fucking* boring.' He beamed at her again. 'See, monks can even swear sometimes, too!'

Coco fought the urge to reach across the table and plant a smacker on his lips.

'My family has always held court, as if they are royalty or something,' Mathieu added with a sad laugh. 'And the really depressing thing is that I never honestly thought about leaving, because it was just my life. It was what they expected of me. Holidays and foreign countries were things other people did. For me, it was just fantasies. Things to watch on the television. My father was never around, so my mother and my grandfather were the only two constants in my life, but as I told you earlier, religion is very important to them. It always has been in my family.'

He stared at his feet. 'My life, my journey to the brotherhood, was decided before I was even born, I expect. I didn't even know there was an alternative, and I suppose I never wanted one. My grandfather is dead now, but it was his dying wish to see me join the Church. It was all he wanted from me and I suppose I never thought to disappoint him. He got to see me join the order, and it was the happiest I'd ever seen him. He'd been waiting for it all of his life, I think. I've never seen such happiness on anyone's face. How could I not do something that would make someone I loved so happy?'

'What about your life? Didn't you deserve the chance to live your own life the way you chose?' Coco blurted. She bit her lip.

'Désolé, it's none of my business.'

He smiled at her. 'I understand what you mean, but to put it in context, you have to know my family. I was literally born to do what I'm doing. I guess it's a cliché, but you could say it was my destiny. And I'm sure you're wondering how I feel about having no real choice about how my life was going to be, then all I can tell you is that I'm doing what I can for my family, because that's all I know how to do.'

Coco fought the urge to touch Mathieu's arm. There was a deep sadness in his eyes, and the tone of his voice made him sound much older than he really was. She understood something about expectations. Her parents had installed their own beliefs onto her as a child. She had understood what was required of her. There was even a time she might have conceded to their wishes and become the nice, polite Jewish wife they desired her to be. It was, however, not a life she could have lived, she was sure of that, not just for her sake, but for the sake of anyone around her. She had left her hometown alone, a child growing in her stomach, and she had never looked back, not really. She had disappointed her family and caused a rift which had resulted in nothing but decades long forced politeness and thinly veiled passive aggressive digs. It was a relationship Coco had made peace with a long time ago.

She sought another look at Mathieu and she saw him for what he was - a young man barely out of adolescence who had not yet had the chance to experience anything of a life of his own choosing. She was sad for him, but she knew she could not be the one to change anything for him.

Coco sipped her beer. 'What happened yesterday?'

Mathieu took a deep breath. 'When I was growing up, I had five friends. We all lived in the same neighbourhood. We went to the same school, the same gym, the same everything. We were inseparable - we did everything together, until we didn't.'

Coco frowned. 'What do you mean?'

'We were playing,' Mathieu continued. 'We were nine, almost ten years old, and Paul fell, smashed his head on the ground. At least that's what they said. Nobody actually saw what happened.'

'And where was this?' Coco asked.

'I think you can guess,' Mathieu replied.

Coco nodded, lighting a cigarette. 'The youth club.' She inhaled. 'Are you suggesting there was something suspicious about his death?'

Mathieu shrugged. 'I don't know, and as far as I remember, everyone just thought this was just a horrible, horrible accident.'

Coco stared at the cigarette smoke, wafting it slowly with her hand. 'What does this have to do with yesterday?' she demanded again.

'It happened exactly ten years ago today,' Mathieu whispered.

Coco shook her head irritably. 'I'm sorry about that, but I can't imagine what it has to do with someone dumping three coffins on a demolition site, and not just that, murdering someone else, unless… unless…'

'Unless?' he repeated.

'Unless there's a connection,' she responded. 'Which means you have to be honest and tell me exactly what happened.'

'There is no connection.'

Coco slammed her glass on the table, splashing beer onto her hand. 'I'll be the damn judge of that,' she hissed.

Mathieu smiled, pulling a handkerchief from his pocket and wiping her hand. She pulled it away. 'Your nostrils flare when you get angry,' he whispered. 'It's very cute.'

'And stop flirting with me,' Coco snapped. 'It's… it's…'

'It's nice?' he asked.

'It's weird, that's what it is. You're wearing a dress…'

'It's called a cassock,' he interrupted.

'Whatevs,' Coco retorted. 'I tend to prefer my men in trousers… well, apart from that one time, and that was part of his job.'

Mathieu's eyebrows knotted in confusion.

'I dated a drag queen once,' Coco explained. 'A bit weird to start with, but once you get the hang of it, it's not so bad, y'know?' She sighed. 'Shame he had to go, but when your man looks better in your clothes than you do, it's time to move on.' She cleared her throat, irritated with herself for getting distracted by the handsome monk. 'Anyway, no more trying to distract me. Spill the beans and spill them now.' She gestured for the waiter to bring more beers. 'I'm not averse to dragging you to the commissariat and pounding the truth out of you!'

Mathieu smiled at her. 'I'm not sure I'd be averse to that either,' he laughed.

'Arrête!' Coco cried. 'You gotta stop flirting with me,' she commanded.

'Why?' he countered.

She reached across the table and began slowly tracing her finger across his chest in her best seductive manner. He pushed himself back in the chair. 'What are you doing?' he asked, flustered.

Coco smiled. 'I'm not sure what game you think you're playing with me, Frère, but I'm here to tell you stumbled across the only woman who is likely immune to game playing.'

'I'm not playing games,' he blurted, clearly embarrassed.

'The hell you are,' she snapped. 'Men always do.' The waiter appeared and placed two more drinks in front of them. Coco gratefully took a slug, happy for the distraction. 'So, back to the point of this conversation. The ten-year anniversary of the death of your friend, Paul. Tell me about him.'

Mathieu lips pressed against the top of the beer glass. 'He was a sweet kid and I remember I liked him a lot. I don't really remember a lot about him, other than someone in the neighbourhood adopted him. They were a rich couple, they'd never been able to have children of their own, I think, so they took in kids all the time and Paul was one of them.'

Coco nodded. 'Did you ever think there was something untoward about his death?'

He considered his answer, long fingers trailing around the beer glass. He wiped away the condensation and placed the finger against his lips. 'There was talk,' he said finally. 'I was only a kid, though, so I paid little attention to it. I was just sad to lose a pal.'

Dozens of thoughts whirled around Coco's complicated and frazzled brain at the same time. However, she knew first and foremost that the biggest part of her job was separating the wheat from the chaff, and whatever had occurred ten years ago did not necessarily lead to what had happened the day before. She stared at Mathieu. 'You gotta level with me, kid.'

He leaned forward. 'I'm trying.' His voice appeared earnest and sincere.

Coco touched his hand. His skin was warm and smooth and it made her feel sad in ways she did not quite understand. Her own hands were rough and dry from the cheap detergent she used to wash her clothes and dishes.

'You've nothing to worry about with me,' she offered. 'Just tell me what happened. I'm guessing you're the one who left the gate unlocked.'

His eyes connected with hers. 'Am I in trouble?'

Coco found it difficult to hold his gaze. 'Depends what you've done, kid. Spill your guts and then I'll tell you.'

'I'm scared,' he blurted.

Coco sucked in a breath. Mathieu suddenly appeared younger, a child who did not understand what was happening to him. 'Did you murder anyone, Mathieu?' she asked abruptly.

His eyes widened in horror. 'Bien sûr, non!'

Coco smiled at him. 'Bon. Then let's move on. Be honest with me and I promise you I'll do what I can to help, mais I can't do a thing unless you tell me what happened.'

For the longest time, he remained silent, his finger moving slowly around the glass. 'All I do is leave the gate unlocked at a certain time for them. That's it, that's all I do,' he said finally.

'For them?' Coco questioned.

He took a long breath. 'My friends. Well, at least they were back in the day. I'm not sure what I'd call them now. I guess they've never really forgiven me for choosing such a different path to them.'

Coco pulled a notebook from her bag. 'Give me the names.'

Mathieu sipped his beer. 'Sofia Charton, Idris Cellier and Jericho Martin,' he answered with obvious reticence.

Coco wrote down the names. 'Why did they want to come into the monastery?'

Mathieu flashed a sad smile. 'You might say it's a habit. We used to do it when we were kids. We'd sneak in and hang out in the crypt. It was always boring in the centre and it just felt like we were being grown up to sneak off when the monks were occupied. The gates didn't always used to be locked, you see. I suppose it was like a dare or something, but it carried on and as we got older, it was just a cool place to hang out, get drunk, get high, get...' He stopped, hair falling over his face covering his reddening cheeks.

'And you go with them still?'

'Non,' he answered. 'Not since...' he tugged at his cassock. 'But I let them in,' he added with a sad sigh. 'I suppose it seems a way of still hanging out with them from a distance.'

Coco sucked in her breath, suddenly feeling very sorry for the twenty-year-old not being able to spend time with his friends, but not entirely understanding why he could not. 'So, last night. Was it normal? I mean, was there anything out of the ordinary about it?'

Mathieu considered his answer. 'I don't think so. The truth is, I unlocked the gate as normal and went back into the *Abbaye* for evening prayers.'

Coco lit another cigarette. 'And do your brothers know about any of this?'

Mathieu hid a smile. 'Non. My *brothers* know nothing about it. We exist in our own little world most of the time and pay little attention to what may happen in the world outside. That's kinda the whole point.'

There was something about the way he pronounced brothers which caught Coco's attention, but before she could question him, he continued talking.

'It is all perfectly innocent, I assure you,' he said. 'Teenage rebellion, nothing more. My friends like to think they're living dangerously, but really there is no danger. It's just a place to hang out, that's all.'

'And yet something changed last night,' Coco stated. 'Three coffins were removed and somebody was murdered, all on the eve of the death anniversary of one of your friends.'

He shook his head. 'We don't know it has anything to do with that,' he suggested.

'And we don't know it doesn't,' Coco countered, 'which is why I need to speak to them pronto. When was the last time you spoke to any of your friends?'

Mathieu considered his answer. Coco watched him as did because she wanted to see if he was lying. After almost two decades as a police officer, she had slowly come to be able to spot the signs, often a glance to the left, a shuffle of a foot. It was often subtle, but easy enough to spot after a while. As far as she could tell, Mathieu did not appear to be searching for a lie, rather simply trying to remember.

'Not for a while,' he answered finally. 'A few weeks, maybe longer. Désolé, I'm not trying to be obstinate. It's just, well, I suppose you could say most of my days just seem to melt into one.' He smiled. 'We have our routine in the monastery, you see, and we don't tend to deviate from it. I suppose it might be one of the reasons I let my old friends in. Every Saturday I leave the gate unlocked. I can't be part of it, not like I used to be, but it means something to me. I'm close to the party, you might say, and most of the time that's enough.'

Coco smiled at him. She wanted to say something but could think of nothing, which for her was a surprise because her instinct was usually to say the first thing which popped into her muddled brain, more often than not something entirely inappropriate. Instead, she thrust forward her notepad. 'I want their addresses and cell phone numbers.'

Mathieu nodded, stretching out his hand and taking the notepad from her. He moved the pen slowly across the paper. 'Will they get in trouble?' he asked.

Coco gave him a quizzical look. 'Only if they've done something wrong,' she replied. 'Tell me, do *you* think they've done anything wrong?'

Mathieu smiled. 'Only for most of their lives,' he conceded. 'Mais, not this… not whatever *this* is.' He stopped and glanced at his watch. 'I really have to get back to the *Abbaye*,' he said, pushing the notepad back to Coco. 'I don't know what happened last night, but I hate the thought my friends could be involved.'

Coco stood. 'Then let's hope they're not.' She tucked the notepad back into her bag. 'Merci for this, and I'll leave you with your prayers,' she said in a harder tone than she intended.

He reached out to her. 'You don't have to do that, you know,' he said.

Coco frowned. 'Do what?'

'Imagine that all men are the same. We're not.'

She nodded and moved towards the exit. 'Yeah, you are,' she whispered. 'You all look different, but you're all the same, really.' She stopped. 'Don't get me wrong. I'm as bad, but the one thing I'm not is a liar. What you see is what you get.' She moved her hand around her body. 'My hair is a weird colour and tends to frizz dependent on the weather. My clothes are mostly second-hand and my shoes are held together by tape, but I have my pride and I can tell you this: I don't hide behind anything, least of all a monastery. Au revoir, Frère Moreau,' she added, moving out of the café without looking back.

18H30

Cedric stepped into Coco's office. Her head was resting on the desk, loud snores emitting from beneath wild blue hair. He stopped, his mouth twisting into a mischievous smile. He slammed a pile of files onto the desk, causing Coco's head to jerk upwards, leaving a trail of spittle behind her.

'Jeez-us!' she cried. 'I nearly shi…'

'Captain Brunhild,' Commander Demissy interjected, appearing in the doorway behind Cedric.

Coco wiped her mouth with the sleeve of her jumper. 'That's my name. Don't wear it out,' she quipped.

Demissy stepped into the office. 'I don't appear to have received an update from you regarding our murder yet.'

Coco was about to respond but thought better of it. 'We're homing in on suspects as we speak,' she said instead.

Demissy raised an eyebrow, demonstrating her doubt. She tapped the watch on her wrist. 'It's now 19H00, and as far as I'm aware, we are no further forward in understanding how three coffins from a monastery ended up in a building that was about to be demolished.' She counted them off on her fingers. 'In addition, we are no further forward in understanding what happened to one corpse, and more importantly, who was murdered yesterday and placed in the recently vacated coffin.' She paused. 'Am I missing anything?'

Coco wrapped her knuckles together. 'Nah, I think you about covered it. Your tone may have been a little sarcastic, but I'm not one to judge… And actually,' she countered, 'it's not true to say we're getting nowhere. We think we know how the coffins were removed and by who.' She gestured to Cedric. 'Lieutenant Degarmo was about to give me an update on their location.'

'I tried the cell phones, but they're all turned off. I've left messages, but no response yet,' Cedric said. 'I've sent officers to their addresses, but they don't seem to be in and their parents don't know where they are.'

'Who are we talking about, exactly?' Demissy demanded.

Coco exhaled. 'As far as I can tell, just three punk kids who liked to mess around in the monastery. One of the monks let them in.'

'One of the monks?' Demissy asked in surprise.

Coco took in a deep breath. 'Yeah, it appears he grew up with them and didn't think too much about turning a blind eye to their fun and games. He swears he had nothing to do with happened, and for that matter, he doesn't believe his friends do either.'

Demissy flopped into a chair. 'And do you believe him?'

Coco considered her answer. 'I don't believe a thing most people say, but what do I know? The monk claims this was a regular thing, which if true begs the question - why now? Was this just about the demolition? If so, why arrange the coffins in that way?'

'It could be connected to the dead kid,' Cedric suggested.

Demissy gasped loudly, a hand flying to her mouth.

Coco hid a smirk. 'Don't get your panties in a bunch,' she laughed. 'This happened ten years ago.'

Demissy turned to Cedric. 'Then how could it be connected?'

'Because it happened exactly ten years ago today,' he responded.

Demissy's eyes widened. 'What happened exactly?'

'We don't really know. Frère Moreau just told me about it,' Coco answered. 'And the date thing might be interesting, I'm not entirely sure.'

'Well, don't you think you should find out?' Demissy asked witheringly.

Cedric turned the computer monitor around and grabbed the

keyboard. Coco had already filled him in on the details, as scant as they were. 'You said he was a foster kid called Paul, aged nine or ten, right?'

'Yup,' Coco confirmed.

Cedric's fingers worked quickly, his eyes scanning the screen. 'I'm not seeing anything.'

'I guess if they ruled it an accident, there might not have been much of an investigation,' Coco suggested.

Demissy shook her head. 'All the same, I'd like it ruled out.'

Coco sighed. 'Lieutenant, have Ebba see what she can find?'

Cedric nodded and left the office.

Demissy turned back to Coco. 'What's your feeling about all of this?'

Coco flashed the commander a surprised look. She was not used to Demissy valuing her opinion, or anything else about her, for that matter. 'This shit stinks, that's what I think,' she answered, immediately regretting her choice of terminology.

Demissy closed her eyes, slowly shaking her head. 'I know I'm going to regret asking this,' she said finally, 'but what do you mean by that?'

Coco took a breath, fighting the urge to say the first thing that came to her. Her ability to filter her thoughts as they were about to become verbal was lacking and it was a situation which only appeared to be exasperated when she was dealing with someone like Commander Imane Demissy. 'Let's take the ten-year-old death out of the mix for the moment, at least until we know more or have something to go on,' Coco began slowly. 'What we have is something which was either a prank, or something else made to look like one.'

The commander pursed her lips. 'Although your language was colourful, I concede you may have a point.'

Coco widened her eyes. 'That almost sounds like a compliment.'

Demissy sighed. 'Don't push it, Captain. What I have to wonder is, do you believe the monastery to be involved?'

Coco shrugged. 'I can't be sure of anything. I think the young monk who left the gate open is on the level. I don't see him being involved…' She stopped, unsure whether she was actually telling the truth, or if she was being led by some other emotion. She hoped beyond hope it was not the latter. 'But he knew they were coming into the crypt and whatever happened next resulted in the removal of three coffins and a murder.'

'Then you need to find those three people. They are our prime suspects,' Demissy interjected. She looked at her watch again. 'Dammit, I have to go.' She sighed. 'What's the plan?'

Coco shrugged again. 'There's not a lot we can do. I can place some officers outside the suspect's houses. We could lean on the parents to see if they're lying to protect them, or we could have Ebba trace their cell phones.'

Demissy shuddered, her hand shaking as she touched her face. 'It's Sunday evening. My budget can't take it.' She stood. 'All the same, unless we have some answers by morning, there's going to be a lot of people breathing down my neck, not just the press. I've already been fielding calls from the Catholic Church.' She stopped, tapping her chin. 'Have officers drop by the houses this evening. Wherever these kids are, they're going to have to surface, eventually.'

'Unless they're on the run already,' Coco suggested.

Demissy looked at her watch again, clearly flustered. 'D'accord. Give it an hour. If you don't find them, call Ebba and have her track their cell phones.' She moved to the door. 'I really have to go, but text me when there's news. And make sure it's good news.'

Coco smiled. 'Sure, I can do that,' she muttered wistfully.

19H25

Cedric appeared in the doorway of Coco's office, stopping abruptly, causing Ebba to crash into him. She immediately began uttering a string of what sounded like Swedish curses. Coco lifted her head quickly, her eyes widening in surprise. She had been enjoying another rather pleasant forty winks in an entirely debauched fashion.

'Ebba found our mysterious dead kid,' Cedric stated, throwing himself gamely into the chair opposite Coco's desk.

Coco nodded, extracting a cigarette and lighting it. 'Grab a pew, sweet chops,' she instructed, pointing to the other chair.

The small, slender forensic technician sat, fixing Coco with an irritated look. 'I understand nothing about you,' she complained.

Coco shrugged. 'Not my problem, kid. You've been in France a while now, your command of the language should really be better.'

Ebba snorted. 'I speak eight languages fluently,' she proffered. 'And my French is better than yours,' she added huffily.

'Anyho,' Coco pressed. 'Tell me about the boy.'

Cedric passed Coco a printout. 'His name was Paul Lecourt,' he stated, before adding, 'sort of.'

Coco sighed wearily. 'What on earth is that supposed to mean?'

He smiled. 'He was found on the steps of the monastery in 2002, barely a day or two old.'

'Does that sort of shit really happen?' Coco asked.

'More often than you would imagine,' Ebba retorted. 'And actually, it's kinda poetic that the Catholic Church is where they end up. If they weren't so fucking archaic in their opinions about abortion, then more kids wouldn't end up having babies they didn't want. If the church is so determined they have the right to legislate a woman's body, then they should also have to pick up the pieces, don't you think?'

'Oookaaayyy,' Coco drawled. She turned back to Cedric. 'What did you mean, "sort of?"'

'When there is no evidence of the birth parents, it's customary when a baby is abandoned to name them after the person who found them. In this case, the baby was discovered by one of the monks.'

'Paul,' Coco concluded. 'And the surname?'

'A foster family took the kid in, they eventually adopted him when no one came forward to claim him,' Ebba answered.

'What about his death?'

Cedric pointed at the paper he handed Coco. 'That's the police report. He died ten years ago today. There was an investigation, but it seems to indicate there was nothing untoward. The kid was just playing and fell, banged his head. The autopsy confirmed it, and there were no other signs of trauma, so the investigation didn't really go anywhere.'

'Hmm,' Coco pondered. She closed her eyes, reminded of a time when she was a young mother, barely in her twenties and already with two babies under the age of two. They had been in a park and her son, Julien, had just begun walking and while Coco was dealing with his sister, Barbra, he slipped away. He was only out of her sight for a few seconds, but it was enough for the unsteady on his feet toddler to fall forward, smashing his head against the concrete pavement. The following days had been traumatic for Coco, consumed with guilt and regret as she waited for his prognosis. Julien had survived with little more than a bump and a small scar from the stitches, but Coco had never forgotten it and how close she had come to a very different result.

'Accidents do happen,' Coco said finally. 'And there's no reason to suggest this was anything but an accident.'

'Then what about the connection with the dates?' Cedric demanded.

'It might have nothing to do with it,' she reasoned. She turned to Ebba. 'What about his adopted family?'

'As far as I can tell,' Ebba replied, 'they left the area after his death. I believe they now live in Switzerland. Do you want me to track them down?'

Coco considered for a few moments. 'I don't really want to drag up painful memories like these unless I really have to. But all the same, find out their address and telephone number and see if there's anything about them we should be concerned about, just in case we do need to contact them.' Her eyes scanned the police report Cedric had handed to her. 'There really isn't a lot to go on,' she mused, flicking through the pages. She halted, her eyes locking on a school photograph of Paul Lecourt. He was smiling at the camera, but she could see the sadness in his eyes. He was cute, with thick blond hair and a rosebud nose. 'Poor kid. You didn't have much of a life, did you?'

Ebba shrugged. 'Who's to say that? He was too young to know about it when he was dumped and it looks as if landed on his feet with a rich couple. If the report is correct, he was probably just having fun, playing around and banged his head. He probably didn't even know what hit him.' She narrowed her eyes, her jaw flexing. 'I don't need to tell you what sort of shit we see in this job, day after day. What some kids have to endure in their lives, whether they live long or short. There's nothing to suggest Paul Lecourt went through anything like that.'

Coco turned away, staring at the photographs on her crowded desk. She wanted nothing more than to pull one of her children to her nose and inhale their scent. She pulled back her head, widening her eyes, which had watered. She pointed at the clock. 'Anyway, I have to get home and see the kids before Helga does a full-on exorcist on me. What about you?' she asked Cedric.

He sighed. 'I don't have plans tonight, so…'

'You could hang around and try to track down our witnesses-slash-suspects?'

He nodded reluctantly. 'Yeah, I can do that, for a while at least.'

Ebba glanced down at her feet. 'And I can monitor their cell phones.'

Coco grabbed her coat and edged towards the door. 'Brilliant! Call me if you must!' she called out cheerfully as she disappeared into the hallway.

23H00

Coco awoke with a start, knocking the wine glass she had been nursing onto her pyjamas. A string of curses followed as she tried to assess where she was. The flickering light of the old black and white portable television at the foot of her bed told her that and the gentle snores of her two youngest children, Cedric and Esther, confirmed it. On her rollout bed was Helga, the mature German nanny, who was as surly as anyone Coco had ever met, but she was, Coco had no doubt, completely indispensable.

'This film is shit,' Helga grumbled. She spoke in broken English, although she had been in France for over a decade. Somewhere along the way, she had decided that of all the obstacles she had faced in life, properly learning a new language was not something she needed to do. 'There are no sex scenes,' she added irritably. 'What is the point?'

Coco murmured her agreement, irritated that they had awoken her during a rather wonderful dream before she had succeeded in her mission of removing a pesky cassock from a rather handsome young monk.

'Your phone has been ringing,' Helga stated, stretching her arms nonchalantly. 'I didn't answer it, because I am not your damn secretary.'

Coco stuck out her tongue. 'I don't know why on earth I keep you around,' she muttered.

Helga snorted. 'Because no one else would work for peanuts and a stinking bed on the floor.'

Coco dropped her feet onto the ground, draining the remnants of the wine while studying the diminutive woman. Concerns regarding Helga were always in the back of her mind, but she would take great pains to avoid thinking about it. She could barely afford to pay Helga as it was, let alone paying her or someone else more. Their relationship worked primarily because, for Helga, life with Coco was better than the life she had escaped from. They did not talk often but once, one New Year's eve, after Helga had consumed a few glasses of the cheap out-of-date champagne Coco had "found" in an evidence locker, she had touched Coco's face and whispered in her ear, *Danke, I feel safe here.* Coco had to leave the room for fear of crying at the rare show of emotion between the two of them. The fact was that Helga was probably the only person in the world she trusted her children with.

'If you're going to start yapping, do it in the other room,' Helga said, pointing towards the door, without removing her eyes from the direction of the television screen.

Coco moved slowly out of the bedroom, tiptoeing so as not to wake the children. She stared at her cell phone at a text message from Cedric. *I'm downstairs. Come down, I have news.*

'It looks like I have to go out,' Coco called back to Helga.

Helga stuck two fingers up at her.

Coco stepped out of the vestibule into the boulevard, wrapping her trusty green and blue wool coat around her body. She stopped and lit a cigarette, her eyes scanning the darkened street. Cedric flashed his car lights and jumped out.

'What's up?' Coco called out, blowing smoke in his direction.

Cedric stared at her, his eyes widening. Coco had put her coat over her Spiderman pyjamas. 'What on earth are you wearing?'

Coco looked down. 'What's wrong with them? They used to belong to Julien. He grew out of them but they were perfectly fine still, so I kept them.' She looked at her leg. There was a hole above her knee and it instantly reminded her of the time Julien, her second oldest child, fell down the stairs and ripped the pyjamas. He cried for an hour because they were his favourite and the whole time he held her hand. It was one of the last times he did so before he decided she was no longer his mother, rather the anti-Christ.

Cedric shook his head in disbelief. 'I'm amazed your kids aren't in therapy,' he paused, 'or jail.' He stopped suddenly and bit his lip. 'Désolé. I have such a big mouth.'

Coco sucked on the cigarette. 'Lucky you've got a fat neck to hold it up then, isn't it?' she quipped, knowing he had meant no malice. 'Anyway, what's going on? Have you found the kids?'

'Not yet,' he replied. 'They haven't gone back to their houses yet, mais Ebba has tracked their cell phones to the Seine.'

'They're on the Seine?' Coco asked, confused.

He laughed. 'Yeah, literally. We checked their Instagram accounts, and it seems that right now they're kicking up their heels on a boat party sailing up and down the river.' He looked at his watch. 'The boat's not due to dock for another two hours, so I thought I would hang out at the docks and wait for them.'

Coco's eyes widened. 'Not the first time you've been hanging out at the docks, I'm sure,' she laughed.

'Nor you, but I suspect for very different reasons,' he retorted. 'Do you want to come or shall I go on my own?'

Coco considered. 'Two hours, you say?'

Cedric nodded.

'Then bugger that. Call the Préfecture de Police,' Coco said, stubbing out her cigarette. 'They can give us a ride.'

'The boat cops?' Cedric asked. 'They will not like that, especially at this time of night on a weekend.'

Coco shrugged, moving towards his car. 'We've got a murder to investigate and I've no intention of cooling my heels at the dead of night on a dock.'

Cedric sighed. 'Well, aren't you at least going to get changed first?'

Coco looked down at her pyjamas. 'Why? There's nothing wrong with these, they were new on last week. Now c'mon, hurry up, we've got a boat to catch!'

23H45

The officer in charge of the police patrol boat eyed Coco and Cedric, his eyes flicking between their ID cards. He was clearly assessing what he should do next. Coco cleared her throat and irritably extracted a cigarette and lit it, blowing smoke in the young officer's direction.

'Are you going to make us stand here all night?' she demanded.

'The patrol boat isn't used for giving people lifts,' he answered in a shaky tone, lacking in any sort of confidence.

Coco suppressed a smile. 'Well, luckily I'm not asking you to take me on a secret tour of romantic Paris by night, isn't it?' She stopped, giving the young man a wink. 'However, maybe later, if you play your cards right, you might just get lucky…'

Cedric glared at Coco and pushed in front of her. 'We realise this is slightly unorthodox, but we are actively pursuing three witnesses-slash-suspects in a murder investigation.'

The officer frowned. 'This sort of thing has to be booked in advance…'

Coco tutted. 'When I catch the perp, I will ask him to give us notice next time he murders someone so we can book our boat trip…'

The officer gave her an irritated glare. 'You said you wanted to board a party boat. I can't imagine that's the sort of place a murderer would hide out,' he added sarcastically.

Coco glanced around. 'Oh, then if that's what you imagine, we can go home, eh?'

The officer looked anxiously at Cedric. Cedric nodded. 'I find it's best not to argue with her too much. She seems to become more powerful when you do.'

The officer sighed. 'I can't just take you out, I have to call it in, but at this time of night, my commander is gonna be pissed…'

Coco yanked out her cell phone and scrolled through it. She held it up in front of the officer, his eyes widening in horror.

'Jean Lenoir?' he spluttered.

Coco nodded proudly. 'A close, personal friend of mine,' she replied with another wink, 'if y'know what I'm saying…' She trailed off, digging Cedric in the ribs. 'Now, if you like I can call him, but a big, important man like JL needs his beauty sleep and I for one know how pissed off he gets when it's disturbed for something mundane, mais, if you feel aiding two fellow flics apprehend a murder suspect is less important than your rules and regulations…'

The officer sighed. 'I'll start up the boat,' he said, trudging wearily down a gangplank.

Coco screamed into the air, blue hair flailing madly around her as the police boat bounced across the Seine. She waved her hands in the air and roared into the night. 'This is better than sex!' she yelled. 'The only thing that would make it better is to be having sex at the same time.' She winked once more at the officer, who turned quickly away, concentrating on steering the boat.

'Leave him alone,' Cedric groaned, 'or he'll crash the boat.'

'Do you know what the boat's called?' the officer yelled above the roar of the wind.

'*Le bateau de fête,*' Cedric replied. 'The organisers couldn't tell me exactly where it would be though…'

'It can only go two ways, back and forth,' Coco gestured in front of her, the spray from the river dampening her face. 'And besides, I don't think it's going to be too hard to spot a boat filled with young revellers.'

The officer pointed ahead of them. 'I think we may have found them.'

Coco narrowed her eyes, peering into the darkness. It was hard to see, especially with the spray in her eyes but it did not take her long to spot the boat in the near distance, the sound of pulsating music soon reached her ears, along with the vision of a crowd of youths bouncing to the beat on the top deck. 'How are we going to get on board?' she asked, realising she had not entirely thought it through.

'I'll get in front and signal to the captain and get him to follow me to the next terminus,' the officer responded.

Coco clapped her hands together. 'Bon, let's go and join the party then!'

LUNDI /
MONDAY

00H05

Coco moved gingerly up the gangplank from the dock, reluctantly steadying herself on Cedric's arm. The captain from the party boat was standing at the top, fixing the approaching police officers with a furious look. Coco noticed this and spread her mouth into what she considered to be her most charming smile.

The captain stared at her as if he was concerned she was in pain. 'What the hell's going on?' he demanded, thumbing upwards. 'I've got a hundred rich, spoilt brats up there who've paid for a cruise and they will not be happy about being grounded by the cops.'

'We're not grounding anything, Monsieur,' Cedric replied. 'We're just here for three of your passengers. Once we find them, we'll be on our way and you can get the rest of them back to their partying, isn't that right, Captain…' he turned around, his face crumbling in confusion when he did not spot Coco. He glanced around, sighing when he noticed her retreating figure boarding the boat. 'Dammit,' he mumbled, running after her.

Coco yelled at the DJ on the top deck of the boat. He pulled back sharply, giving her an incredulous look and vigorously shaking his head. She regarded him in surprise and pushed him out of the way, stepping onto the raised platform he was on, her eyes flicking over the computers and turntables in front of her before realising she did not know what to do with any of it. Instead, she moved around the platform, looking for something to help.

'Ah-ha!' she cried triumphantly before grabbing the electric plug and pulling it from the socket, immediately plunging the entire top deck of the boat into silence, shortly followed by a hundred or so teenagers swiftly and loudly voicing their anger.

Coco raised her arms in an attempt to pacify the crowd. She grabbed the microphone from the DJ and tapped the side, causing a loud, shrill feedback. 'Désolé for the slight interruption to your bopping,' she stopped, noticing a young couple necking in the corner, 'and anything else you might be up to. I promise I won't keep you away from it for too long. I am Captain Brunhild from the Commissariat de Police du 7e arrondissement and as long as I leave the boat within the next five minutes with Sofia Charton, Idris Cellier and Jericho Martin, I won't feel the need to drag you all to the commissariat and search you. None of us want that, now do we?' She stopped and smiled sweetly, waiting a few moments for the realisation of what she was saying to sink in. 'So, if the three individuals I have just mentioned step outside right now, then the rest of you won't have to spend the rest of your night in a jail cell.' She handed the microphone back to the DJ and stepped from the stage, moving past Cedric onto the balcony at the bow of the boat.

'Do you think they'll come?' Cedric asked.

Coco shrugged. 'You know what rich kids can be like, it could go one of two ways - righteous indignation or blind ignorance, either way it doesn't really matter, just so long as we see their reactions, because that will tell us all we need to know.'

Cedric looked onto the crowded dance-floor. 'The officer had a point, though,' he began. 'I just can't see three kids offing someone and then going to a party, not unless they're all sociopaths.'

Coco pointed into the crowd at three people striding determinedly toward them. She rubbed her hands together. 'It looks like we're about to find out.'

00H30

Three figures emerged from the dance-floor, stepping out of the neon flickering lights. Coco could tell immediately by their gait that they were, at the very least, drunk, most likely wasted. She cursed, realising that she was likely to get nothing out of them that night. She stepped towards them. 'Are you Sofia Charton, Idris Cellier and Jericho Martin?' she asked.

'I'm Sofia,' the young woman added. She was small and thin, with black hair cut into a spiked pixie style.

'I'm Idris,' a tall, blond young man chipped in. His voice was deep, but he appeared anxious and relatively more sober than his friends.

'And I'm Jericho,' the third of the group stated. He was black and his head was shaved. Coco recognised the cocky sneer on his face. She had seen it a hundred times before, and it irritated her. Jericho's eyes flicked over Coco's coat and pyjamas. 'And what the hell are you wearing?' he laughed, throwing back his head and cackling.

It was a cruel cackle, and one which made the hairs on the back of Coco's neck stand on end. She glanced down at the worn pyjamas and puffed out her chest. 'You know nothing about fashion. This is a Jean Paul Gaultier jumpsuit!' she bluffed.

Jericho scoffed. 'If that's a Gaultier, then he must have been on crack when he designed it, that's all I can say.'

Idris pushed past Jericho. 'What is this about, officer?' he asked Cedric.

'Where were you all yesterday evening?' Coco demanded.

The three suspects exchanged a look. 'Who the fuck knows?' Jericho answered with a snarky sneer.

Coco grabbed his t-shirt and pulled him towards her. 'Hey,

you listen here, punk. I'm a cop and you answer my questions, or…'

The three of them giggled. Sofia pointed at Coco's pyjamas, muttering incoherently before covering her mouth. 'I think I'm going to hurl,' she cried.

'We can't interview them like this,' Cedric whispered in Coco's ear.

Coco tutted in disgust. 'C'mon you lot, you can sleep it off in the cells back at the commissariat and then we'll talk.'

Jericho rounded on her. 'The only place we're going, old lady, is back into the party.'

Coco tapped the gun on her hip. 'We can either do this the easy way, or the hard way. Choice is yours, punk.'

'Is this about breaking into the monastery?' Idris asked, gently pulling Jericho away from Coco.

'Shut your damn mouth, Idris,' Jericho hissed.

Coco gestured for them to head towards the stairway. 'We'll start with that,' she stated, 'and see where it leads us. Now let's go.'

09H00

Commander Demissy moved slowly backwards and forwards along the stone corridor outside the detention cells in the bowel of the Commissariat de Police du 7e arrondissement. Sofia Charton, Idris Cellier and Jericho Martin had been placed in separate cells and appeared to be sleeping, huddled under blankets and their coats. The door to the end of the hallway opened and Coco walked in.

After signing in the suspects, Coco had returned home and slept fitfully for a few hours before rising, sorting out the two younger children for school and arguing with the two older ones. She had finally thrown herself under the shower, savouring the last few remaining trickles of hot water before trudging wearily to the métro at the end of the street, facing another cramped commute to the commissariat.

Coco stopped, immediately spotting the pinched, pursed blue lips of the commander, dark eyes trained angrily on her. Coco felt her shoulders hunch, knowing that she was most certainly about to be chastised yet again.

'Care to explain yourself, Captain Brunhild?' Demissy hissed through gritted teeth, stiletto heels stabbing angrily against the concrete as she strode towards Coco.

'Well, I couldn't begin to explain myself, really,' Coco said with as much bravado as she could muster without having had any café or cigarettes yet. 'You might say I'm a riddle, wrapped in a mystery, inside an enigma,' she added with a flourish.

'The only mystery to me is how you still have a job,' Demissy retorted with a weary exhale. She thumbed behind her. 'Care to explain why we have three people in custody?'

Coco made her way to the cells, noticing one figure was

moving. She narrowed her eyes and could see Jericho Martin glaring at her from beneath a slit in his hoodie. She turned back to face Demissy. 'These are the three kids named by the monk,' she said in a whisper. 'And therefore, the last people we know were in the crypt before the coffins disappeared.' She paused, a wry smile appearing on her face. 'And you instructed me to find them, did you not?'

Demissy glared at her. 'And why are they in cells?'

'Because they were too wasted to talk last night,' Coco replied. 'They were at a boat party, you see.'

Demissy fixed her with a steely look. 'Oui. I understand you commandeered a police water patrol boat. The commander in charge left me a charming little voicemail reminding me of the need to follow proper protocol in such matters.' Her lips pulled into a tight, angry smile. 'I was delighted to have him mansplain my job to me like that, as I'm sure you can understand,' she added in a sweet tone that was laced with venom.

Coco shrugged as if she could not care less. 'You knew the score. In fact, it was your words that we had to have something to tell the Minster, the press and the Catholic Church by this morning. Well, now we do have something to tell them. Once we knew who they were. I couldn't really take the risk that three murder suspects might be on the run. That would have been foolish. I'm sure you'll agree…'

'They were hardly on the run, they were at a dance party,' Demissy interrupted.

Before Coco had a chance to respond, the door opened again and Cedric entered, a cloud of irritation clear on his face. 'I have an avocat here for one of the suspects,' he blurted.

Moments later, a tall, thin man pushed past the lieutenant, stepping into the dimly lit corridor. He glanced around, tilting his head and peering down his nose as if it was all beneath him. Coco noted the cashmere coat that probably cost more than her annual salary, but then she saw the face. The cold sneer on a too-tight, much too wrinkle-free face. He caught the change of expression and touched his head, smoothing thick grey hair as if he was reassuring himself it was all in place.

Commander Demissy swept forward. 'Maître Duchamp,' she said breathlessly. 'It is good to see you again.'

He analysed her, clearly deciding if he knew who she was and whether she was worth remembering. 'Commander Demissy,' he said after a few moments. His voice was light, but it was cool and seemed to hide a harsh undercurrent, as if he was used to delivering blows with his words, not his fists. 'My regards to your husband. I find his Chopin to be, by far, one of the best I have heard in a very long time.'

Demissy lowered her head. Coco could not decide if it was because she was embarrassed, or rather fed up with living in the shadow of her famous, classical violinist husband. 'Merci,' Demissy said in a tone which Coco instantly recognised. *I defer to you, but I hate you as much as you look down at me.* It was one of the things Coco liked most about her boss. It was also one of the many things she hated because she knew she could never be like her. Whatever filter Demissy had, Coco had never managed to find one of her own.

Maître Duchamp cocked his head in Coco's direction, cold eyes appraising her with lazy flicks of his eyelashes. 'It's Captain Brunhild, is it not?' he asked. 'I believe you are a friend of my son?'

Coco brushed past him, heading towards the exit. 'I most certainly am,' she snapped, 'mais, I'm not a friend of you, the sperm donor that created him.' She pushed the door open, disappearing into the darkness.

Cedric looked desperately around, and then at his feet.

Pierre Duchamp gave a low laugh. 'I forgot how "colourful" Captain Brunhild could be.'

'I must ap...' Demissy began.

Maître Duchamp raised his hands. 'Don't apologise,

commander. I am used to the more...' he paused, searching for the words, '*colourful* aspects of my son's life and the people he calls friends. It does not surprise me.' He stopped and cleared his throat. 'However, I am here at this hour because I have been informed by one of my own very dear friends that you dragged their child from a party in the dead of the night and dumped them in a cell along with all the other vagabonds arrested in Paris last night.' He clasped his fingers together. 'I am sure we will discuss that particular issue for some time, but in the meantime I must tell you that unless my client and his friends are released immediately, then you and I are going to have a very, VERY substantial problem.'

Demissy took a deep breath. 'Follow me, Maître Duchamp.'

09H30

Coco flopped heavily onto the seat outside the interview rooms. She watched a police officer walking past her, and noticing a packet of cigarettes in his shirt pocket, she jumped to her feet and grabbed them. 'Don't ya know smoking is banned in a government building?' she demanded, shooing him away. She waited for him to leave and then pulled one from the pack and deftly lit it.

Demissy's eyes widened. She pointed at the no-smoking sign above them. Coco blew smoke rings towards it. Demissy sighed, staring through the one-way mirror. Pierre Duchamp was standing with his back to them, engaged in a seemingly intense conversation with Jericho Martin. 'You should apologise to Maître Duchamp.'

Coco rounded on her. 'Never in this lifetime. He's a prick, in fact, he's an insult to men who are pricks, because he's worse than that, he's like a mosquito on a really tiny penis that nobody cares about, so they just let the big mosquito suck the blood out of the really tiny penis until it gets smaller and smaller and smaller until finally it's so small it's like the leaves you peel off a sprout…'

Demissy shook her head in disbelief. 'As usual, I have no idea what you are talking about. However, my point is, you can't afford to make enemies of a man like Maître Duchamp.'

Coco snorted. 'I disagree. Men like that idiot are designed to be enemies of all of us with half a brain and I don't intend on bowing and scraping to him…'

'We don't have a choice, Captain,' Demissy snapped.

'The hell we do,' Coco retorted. 'Believe me, every time Pierre Duchamp raises a bitchy point, we just mention Jean Lenoir. The Minister of Justice hates him as much as I do, trust me, and Pierre knows it, and most likely hates it, because so long as JL is Minister, Pierre can't get away with half the shit he'd like to.'

Demissy looked into the room. 'What's so bad about him? I mean, I know he's an arrogant asshole, mais…'

Coco stared at the man behind the mirror. 'You haven't met his son. Hugo Duchamp is one of the finest men I think I've ever met. He's honourable, an amazing flic, and one of the sweetest, sexiest men you could know.' She pointed at Pierre. 'The reason I called him the sperm donor is that I do not know how someone like him produced something as amazing as Hugo Duchamp.'

Demissy shrugged. 'He has a hell of a reputation though, Captain. And more than that, he probably has just as many important friends as Jean Lenoir.'

Coco nodded. 'Which begs the question, what the hell is he doing here?'

Demissy pointed into the room. 'He seems to represent this one. Who is he?'

Coco stared at the dark-skinned, shaved headed young man and sighed. 'His name is Jericho Martin. And he's a problem.'

'A problem?' Demissy questioned.

'Yeah,' Coco replied. 'Seems to me to be a rich, arrogant punk who knows he can pretty much do as he wants because his parents will bail him out of whatever trouble he gets into. Hence them pulling sperm donor Duchamp out of the wrapper.'

Demissy pressed her fingers against her chin. 'We see people like this all the time, Captain Brunhild. What we need to understand is this - are they hiding something and is it worth threatening our careers to find out?'

'Always,' Coco retorted, 'or what the hell is the point of being here?'

Demissy turned to her. 'I need to talk to you later about something,' she blurted.

Coco raised an eyebrow. There was a reluctance to the commander's tone, which alarmed her. It was almost as if she was afraid to speak about something. 'About what?'

Demissy turned away again. 'That will have to wait. Right now, we have this to deal with. So, tell me, Captain - how *are* we going to deal with this?'

Coco knocked on the window. 'We make sure that the old idiot in there doesn't think we're afraid of him.'

'Even if we are?' Demissy countered.

Coco pushed open the door. 'The day I'm afraid of men like Pierre Duchamp is the day I give up. C'mon, Commander. Watch Captain Coco at work and you might just learn a thing or two.' She stopped. 'But for once, just be quiet. Let me talk and don't interrupt worrying about the bigger picture, and if you do, we might just make headway. D'accord?'

Demissy flashed her a doubtful look. 'We'll see,' she agreed with obvious reluctance.

Coco knocked on the door of the interview room and pushed it open. The four suspects had been removed from the cells. Pierre Duchamp was huddled in a corner in an intense discussion with a bored-looking Jericho Martin. Sofia Chorton and Idris Cellier appeared alert and with an expression of wariness and fear etched on their faces. Coco stubbed out the cigarette on the floor, ignoring Demissy's irritated expression, and she cleared her throat.

Pierre Duchamp's head jerked around. 'I don't recall giving you permission to enter the room,' he hissed, causing Jericho Martin to snigger in a way that made Coco want to slap the silly from him.

Coco looked around. 'Who died and made you Dieu, Monsieur?' she retorted, gesturing to the empty seats. 'Now take a seat and let's get on with the show, eh?'

Pierre pressed Jericho's shoulder, indicating for him to take a seat. He followed behind him, standing stiffly behind the three suspects.

'I have instructed my client to remain silent to your questions,' Pierre stated. 'And while I do not represent his friends, I have given them the same advice until they can make their own arrangements regarding legal counsel.'

Coco nodded, flopping onto a chair. Demissy hovered above her, appearing as if she wanted to be anywhere but in the interview room.

Jericho laughed loudly, slapping his hands on the table, his cocky expression fixing on Coco. She was wearing her usual woollen coat over a pair of ripped jeans and a badly creased blouse. 'I see you've gone for even more haute couture than you did last night. Who's the designer this time?' he asked, his voice thick with sarcasm and arrogance.

Coco met his gaze. She had dealt with enough punks like him to not let it bother her, but it did not stop her from wanting to forget she was a police officer for a moment or two. She patted her thighs. 'It's by the same designer who created the lovely orange jumpsuits you'll become accustomed to wearing for, say, the next ten to twenty years.'

'Captain Brunhild,' Pierre Duchamp interrupted with a bored tone. 'I'll say this only once. Unless you have specific charges to level against my client and his friends, then you holding us here is entirely inappropriate and will cost you dearly unless you rectify it immediately.'

Jericho thumbed towards Duchamp. 'What he said,' he laughed.

Coco's lips twisted. She wanted Jericho to be guilty just so she could see the dawning of panic creeping onto his face. 'Let's start with what we know,' she began. 'And that is two nights ago, your client and his friends illegally entered the crypt beneath *Abbaye Le Bastien…*'

'You have proof of this?' Duchamp demanded. 'A witness statement I can examine, par example?'

'We have a witness and he will make a statement,' Coco retorted.

He chuckled. 'We'll see about that.' He entwined his fingers in front of his chest. 'And let me further say that even if this is true, it would be youthful hijinks at worst, because unless you have evidence to the contrary, you have no evidence when the coffins were removed from the crypt. They could have been removed then, or last week, or last month even.'

'Then if they were removed before, where have they been?' Coco demanded. 'Because people were in and out of the demolition site. They would have spotted them.'

Pierre Duchamp sneered. 'I am not here to answer your questions, Captain Brunhild.' He gestured for Jericho to stand. 'Now, bring me some evidence, such as a witness that directly implicates my client in a crime and then we'll talk further, but for now, I am taking my client home.'

'The hell you are…' Coco snapped. Demissy touched her shoulder and quickly shook her head.

'I would ask your client to remain in Paris while we continue the investigation,' Demissy spoke to Duchamp, 'and that you make him available to us when requested.'

'Bien sûr,' he said smugly. 'So long as all the correct protocols are followed.' He gestured to the three suspects. 'Mademoiselle, Messieurs, follow me.'

Coco opened her mouth to speak but thought better of it, instead biting her lip. Jericho walked past her and blew her a kiss. 'This isn't over. You'll be back in the cell before you know it.'

'Try your best, old lady,' he challenged.

Coco and Demissy watched in silence as Pierre and the others left.

'As much as I hate to say it. Maître Duchamp might have a point,' Demissy grumbled. 'I mean, what evidence do we have linking the three of them? And he seems pretty sure the monk will not give a statement.'

Coco smiled. 'Don't worry, I'll get a statement from him, one way or another.'

'That says what?' Demissy demanded. 'From what you told me, even if the monk makes a statement, he can't say more than he left the door open for them. Maître Duchamp will tear the statement to pieces, as he probably should, because all he has to say is that if the door was left open, then anyone could have gained access to the crypt and removed the coffins.'

'I don't care what he says,' Coco snapped. 'Those punks are up to their eyes in this mess.'

'Well, of course they are,' Demissy agreed. 'Mais, he was right about one thing - it is not for Maître Duchamp to prove their innocence, rather for us to prove their guilt.' She smoothed her hijab, pursing purple painted lips. 'We keep coming back to the same point. Removing three coffins seems to be the start of a prank, but why take it so far? And what was its purpose? And more importantly, where the hell is the missing corpse and who was murdered? Find the answers to those questions and we might just be able to build a case. Until then, I'm afraid we have nothing. In fact, we have less than nothing.'

'Yeah, why didn't I think of that?' Coco grumbled. Her nose crinkled. 'Dieu, I hate that scent Duchamp wears. It's probably a zillion euros a bottle, but it still can't mask the stench he emits.'

Demissy regarded her with surprise. 'You *really* hate him, don't you?'

Coco nodded. 'Yeah, I do. And not just for what he did to Hugo, although that's enough as far as I'm concerned. He's a man who has made his entire career about saving shit heads from their crimes just so long as they're rich…'

'He's a defence avocat,' Demissy reasoned. 'It's sort of his job, you know.'

'Je sais, je sais,' Coco reasoned. 'It still doesn't mean that I don't want to wipe the smug grin off the creep's face. That would make me a VERY happy woman.'

Demissy smiled. 'I can't say I disagree with you,' she paused. 'I know you don't like my advice, mais if I could suggest at least trying to proceed cautiously whilst dealing with men such as Pierre Duchamp. Believe me, I meet them all the time and I see the same blank expression on their faces when they see me, the questioning look - why is she here? She doesn't belong with people like us.'

Coco exhaled. 'Then why do you put up with it?'

Demissy shrugged. 'Because I love my husband, and my husband loves me. Men such as Duchamp, in the end, are inconsequential to me. Smiling as they politely insult me is what I must do, because the one thing I have learnt is men like him are not frightened by the fact I wear a hijab, or that I'm black and a Muslim, it's not even about the fact I'm a woman. They are frightened because if I walk through their lives I will see their truths, and for men like that, the truth they hide is something they can not bear to be revealed. So, when I smile at men such as Pierre Duchamp, I am able to do so because I am thinking only one thing. I know your secret.'

Coco flashed her with an impressed smile. 'And what is Duchamp's secret?'

Demissy shrugged again, this time as if she could not care less. 'What does it matter? Rich, white men like him always have the same tedious problems. Small penis, dwarf fetish, golden showers, things such as that.'

'I never thought I would ever hear you say the word penis,' Coco laughed.

Demissy slid away. 'You have no idea what I am capable of, Captain,' she called back. 'You, like those men, have made the same mistake in viewing me in a particular way. You see what you see and you assume what you assume. I may be all the things you assume, but I am also so much more.'

Coco cackled and lit a cigarette. 'Hey, you said you wanted to speak to me about something else. Do you want to do that now?'

she called after the commander.

Demissy stopped dead in her tracks. 'Non,' she answered after a lengthy pause. 'Not now, at least. I need to speak to someone first.'

Coco coughed, pushing smoke from her lungs. 'What is this about? Should I be worried?'

Demissy turned her head. 'Non, I don't think so. Mais, when we do speak, I ask one thing of you. Remember, you are a police officer, first and foremost, so that when we discuss what we must discuss, your reaction will be entirely grounded in that. Now, go find me some evidence and a corpse.'

Coco watched Demissy walk away. She did not look back and as Coco sucked on her cigarette, she instinctively knew what Demissy needed to talk to her about. *Mordecai Stanic.* The former commander of the commissariat and the father of Coco's two youngest children and a man now serving a life sentence in prison. Coco had hoped he would disappear from her life completely, but she knew he never really would. She had so far refused to see him because she did not know how she would react. Would she feel a pang for the man she had once loved, or would she forget everything and stab him through the heart just as he had to her? Either way, she was sure of only one thing. She did not want to test herself in his presence, but she had a feeling that decision was about to be taken out of her hands.

10H30

Coco stared at the telephone on the corner of her desk, her hand inching towards it. She knew she should call the *Abbaye Le Bastien* and ask to speak to Frère Mathieu Moreau, but she could not bring herself to, and that fact angered her in a way she did not quite understand. She had been attracted to men before, even *slightly* younger men, but something about him had unnerved her. She supposed it might have something to do with the ongoing uncertainty regarding Mordecai, she hoped that was all it was.

Cedric stepped into her office, his face crinkling when he saw her. 'Your face looks like you've either got constipation or were in the middle of an erotic fantasy.'

Coco considered, spreading her hands in front of her as if she was weighing up her options. 'A bit of both, actually,' she replied. 'What's up?'

'I got a call from the *Abbaye*,' he said, with obvious irritation. 'Frère Leroy said they weren't willing to make a statement about the apparent theft of the coffins two nights ago.'

Coco snorted. 'Sounds exactly like the words of Pierre Duchamp. I knew that creep would get to them in one way or another.'

Cedric shrugged. 'Even if he did, he has a point. There is no evidence, one way or another. And I suppose they don't want to implicate Frère Moreau in something which they can't be sure resulted in a crime being committed. They've probably been told to keep their mouths shut.'

Coco sipped her café before spitting it out because it was cold. She wiped her shirt. 'Aren't they worried at all about the missing corpse and the dead man with no name?'

He shrugged again. 'He said something about they're praying

to Dieu for a speedy resolution.'

Coco frowned. 'Or they don't want a resolution at all.'

'What do you mean?' Cedric countered.

She tapped her chin. 'I don't know really, other than it all seems terribly convenient. No one seems to care about what happened and I have to wonder why and what it might mean. What are they hiding?'

Cedric shook his head. 'You can't really think a bunch of monks are caught up in some grand conspiracy?'

'Why not?' Coco rounded. 'Need I remind you what happened to this department two years ago?' She stopped, closing her eyes and pressing her fingers against her temples as if the thought was painful to her. Her eyes snapped open again. 'The only thing I know for certain about people since I became a police officer is that no matter what they say, no matter how they dress, everyone has demons. It's just some people are better at keeping them buried.' She grinned impishly. 'Pardon the pun. Non, I don't believe them. That's not to say they did anything wrong, but keeping their mouths shut just makes our lives more difficult and because of that, we're going to have to make their lives more difficult.'

Cedric raised an eyebrow. 'You just want to interrogate the young one, don't you?'

Coco smiled sweetly at him. 'The thought hadn't entered my mind...' she answered innocently. She tapped her fingers on the desk. 'If only we could have gotten those damn kids in an interview room, we'd soon knock the truth out of them, and then at least we'd know if we were on a wild goose chase.'

'Peut être,' Cedric reasoned, 'mais, as that's not an option. What do you propose in the meantime?'

She considered. 'What about missing person reports? It's crazy no one has missed our dead guy yet.'

'Rien,' Cedric replied. 'I've searched all arrondissements and

I've even extended it nationally. Ebba's dealing with Europol and Interpol. I suspect unless someone reports him missing, we're going to have trouble identifying him.'

The telephone began ringing and Coco snatched it irritably. 'Allô. Brunhild here.' She stopped, listing intently. 'In a damn skip?' she exclaimed, her voice rising sharply. 'Okay. I know where that is. We're on our way.' She threw the telephone back onto its cradle and jumped to her feet. 'Someone just found what looks like, and I quote, "a mummified corpse" in a rubbish skip downtown. Let's go. We'll call Sonny on the way and have him meet us there.'

11H15

Coco stared at the skip and pursed her lips. She lifted her left leg as far as she could, but she could not stretch far enough to peer over the top. 'Hey, Cedric,' she called out. 'Grab my ass and boost me up so I can get a peek.'

Cedric climbed out of the car, his eyes widening. 'I've had this discussion with you before. I will not, not now, not ever, touch your ass, no matter how much you beg.'

She tutted. 'I'm not begging,' she complained, 'merely requesting as your superior that you, my inferior, assist me in the way I have just requested.'

He laughed. 'You know, that's like probably illegal...'

'Oh, don't #metoo me, Lieutenant gym-bunny, I'm not asking you to cop a feel,' she snapped before shrugging, 'although admittedly with an ass as fine as mine, it would probably be criminal of you not to enjoy it a little, mais...'

Cedric shook his head. 'You really are delusional, aren't you?'

Coco tutted again. 'My point is, boost me up so I can see our mummy.'

'Oh merci Dieu!' Cedric exclaimed upon seeing Sonny and Ebba approaching. Ebba was carrying a pair of ladders, which she placed against the skip. She clambered up quickly, launching herself into the skip, landing with a thud on the other side.

'She's braver than I would be,' Coco mused. 'You've no idea what could be in there.'

Sonny tucked the abundance of curls on his head underneath a cap. 'Ebba isn't afraid of anything,' he reasoned.

Coco moved around the alleyway. 'I don't see any cameras.'

'There aren't any, not here or in the next street and it backs onto a dead end.'

Coco pointed to the wall. 'What's behind there?'

'It used to be a Chinese restaurant, but it went out of business a few months ago,' Cedric confirmed.

Coco moved into the street. As far as she could tell, there were no other occupied buildings or houses. 'Whoever dumped the corpse chose a pretty good place away from prying eyes.'

Cedric pointed into the distance. 'The boulevard over there is pretty busy, but I doubt anyone would notice someone coming down here, especially when we can't be sure when the body was dumped.'

'What about the person who found him?' Sonny asked.

'A prostitute,' Cedric replied. 'She often brings her tricks here when they have a car and want a little privacy. We're lucky she decided to dispose of her... er... "work product" or we may never have found the corpse at all.'

'And she's on the level?' Coco demanded.

Cedric shrugged. 'I don't see why not,' he murmured. 'I checked her records, a few busts, but nothing major. I can't see her being connected, and her trick was a German businessman who is only in Paris for a few days and no doubt gave his hire car a little extra mileage when he's away from home.'

'Then we're back to square one,' Coco grumbled. 'Have you found anything, Ebba?' she yelled.

Ebba's head appeared over the top of the skip. 'Not really. It looks like it hasn't been emptied in a while, but there's not a lot in it. Give me a hand and we'll get the corpse out.'

Coco gestured to Cedric. 'Well, go on, you heard her.'

'You do it,' he whined.

'I've just had my coat cleaned,' Coco countered.

Cedric pointed at the fresh ketchup stain on the lapel. 'Not very well, obviously.'

Sonny sighed and finished laying a sheet on the ground before climbing the ladders. Ebba lifted the corpse and between the two of them they manoeuvred him upwards and finally over the top of the skip before carefully lowering him to the ground.

'Thanks for the help, you two,' Ebba complained.

Coco lowered herself onto her haunches, attentive eyes drifting over the remains. She inhaled deeply.

'What are you sniffing him for?' Cedric demanded.

She shrugged. 'I dunno. I've never smelled someone who has been in a coffin for a while.'

'What does he smell of?'

'Shit,' she answered. 'Mais, nothing unusual.' She clambered back to her feet. 'So, this is our John Doe?'

'John Doe?' Sonny interrupted.

'Oui,' Coco replied. 'Some kind of big wig who wanted to be buried in the crypt and paid handsomely for the privilege.'

Sonny shook his head. 'He can't be a John Doe. I mean, there has to be a death certificate somewhere. Someone would have had to examine him and sign it off.'

'I don't know what to tell ya,' she retorted. 'Other than it's the Catholic Church we're dealing with.' She stared at the body. It reminded her of a waxwork and gave her the creeps. The wind caught a wisp of his fine straggly hair and blew it over his face and it made her shudder. 'He doesn't seem to have been affected by his slight detour,' she quipped.

'Well, he was already dead, so I don't imagine he minded too much,' Ebba reasoned.

Coco sniggered. 'You may have a point.' She touched his robe. It was dusty and brittle to the touch. 'He doesn't seem to have been damaged, or mutilated in any way.' She turned to Sonny. 'Could this be about necrophilia?'

Sonny's eyes widened. 'I'd have to check,' he whispered, before shaking his head. 'Mais, what I said about there had to have been a death certificate for him, also applies to me. I can't perform any invasive actions on him, not until I know who he is.' He considered. 'Look, I'll take him back to the morgue and run some preliminary tests - fingerprints, dental, that sort of thing. I'll even track down a local Catholic chaplain I know, who is also a pathologist. We went to school together and have remained pretty good pals. He may be able to help.'

Coco nodded. 'D'accord, so long as the Catholic Church doesn't swoop in and reclaim our John Doe before he gives us some answers.'

'I'll try,' Sonny responded. 'Though I can't really hide a corpse unless I have a good reason to.'

'Then we'd better give you a good reason,' Coco suggested. She lowered herself again, turning her head to the side and studying the ground. She stood again and took a deep breath. 'There's a lot of tyre tracks, but I don't think we're going to be able to easily tell which is new, are we?'

Ebba looked around. 'I could try, but even I'm not a miracle worker.'

Coco turned to Cedric. 'We're missing something here. I don't know what, but I can just tell we are.'

He shrugged. 'I don't know what to tell you.'

Coco began pacing. 'This ended in a building that was about to be demolished and, by the very definition of what we found, we have to assume there was some kind of pattern to it.'

'I'm not sure that's true,' Cedric stated.

'It's all we have, so let's just hope it is,' Coco said forcefully. 'Which gives us a starting point. Frère...' she stopped, her cheeks flushing, 'the monks told us it used to be some kind of after-school youth club for adolescents.' She tapped the side of her nose. 'And I smell trouble.'

'Abuse?' Sonny asked.

She shrugged. 'Peut être. In one way or another, at least. D'accord,' she glanced at her watch. 'Sonny, Cedric and I will go back to the commissariat and try to figure out what went on in that building. Can I leave you to figure out who our mummy is and what happened to him?'

Sonny nodded. 'Absolutely.'

She touched his shoulder. 'What would I do without you, Sonny? C'mon, Cedric, let's hit the road.'

Sonny watched them leave, his eyes locked on Coco. Ebba stepped next to him, staring at his sad face. 'You really oughta get better taste in women, boss,' she mumbled. 'Even if she knew you existed, she'd only end up crushing you to death, literally AND figuratively,' she added with a laugh, as if she had impressed herself with her quip.

12H30

Coco's eyes scanned the computer screen. She had spent ten minutes searching the Internet and police database for any mention of the youth centre, which had once inhabited the recently demolished building. To her chagrin, she could find nothing to suggest anything untoward, not in the press, nor in the police records. She pushed herself back into her chair and lit a cigarette.

'I don't know what you were hoping to find,' Cedric said after a few moments. 'But surely it's a good thing if there isn't any record or suggestion of a crime.'

'Well, it would be a good thing,' Coco responded, 'if I believed it. Someone hated it enough to go to such extreme measures…'

'We don't know that,' he interrupted.

Coco ignored him and leaned forward. 'The youth centre finally closed last year because of problems with the building,' she said, reading the screen. 'There's another reason why I don't believe all the good press.'

'Your friend, the flirty monk?'

Coco suppressed a smile. 'Yeah. He said, and I can't remember the exact words,' she added, not sounding entirely convincing, 'but it was something along the lines of he was quite happy to see the building being knocked to the ground.'

'That could just be because of what happened to his friend, Paul,' Cedric suggested.

'You're probably right,' she agreed. 'I mean, I got the idea he was sad about losing his friend, and then seeing the building about to come down, it probably brought it all back and he was just pleased to see it gone.' She shrugged. 'Who knows?'

'Then we should ask him. Oh wait, I forget, nobody wants to

talk,' Cedric grumbled. 'This, like every investigation, is hampered because people with power or money behind them decided to keep their damn mouths shut.'

Coco spread her hands in front of her. 'That's never going to change, lieutenant. However, it doesn't mean we have to listen. Have I taught you nothing?'

'Then what do you propose we do?'

'We keep digging and digging until we hit the dirt,' she reasoned. 'People always think they bury their secrets, but they never really can, not truly.' She stared again at her computer screen. She pointed at the screen. There was a grainy newspaper picture of several men and women, two of whom she recognised as Frères Gerard Leroy and Henri Aries. The caption below the photo read: *Abbaye Le Bastien Youth Centre, now open.*

She mused as her eyes scanned the text. 'It says the man in charge was called Odilon Sander. Seems a good place to start asking questions, non? I mean, if there are secrets to be found in that place, then we start at the top, don't we? Let's go and shake the tree and see what we find.'

13H25

Chantel Sander moved slowly across the living room, each step deliberate and nuanced as if she was used to treading the same path day in, day out.

To Coco, it appeared forced, like someone focussing on a path to avoid thinking about whatever thoughts were invading her consciousness. She did not appear to be worried, but it was hard to tell. She had opened the door and invited Coco and Cedric into her home with a stoic expression on her face, as if it were perfectly natural for the police to call and ask to speak to her. Before they had left the commissariat, Ebba had confirmed she had checked the police database and had found no criminal record for anyone who appeared connected to the youth centre, nor any crimes reported. The news had disappointed Coco, as she was hoping for something which would make sense of the situation.

'Can I get you anything? Thé? Café?' Chantel asked, gesturing for Coco and Cedric to sit. Her voice was thick, as if she smoked too much, and her face was one Coco could only describe as being plain and nondescript, encased in loose brown curls. Chantel looked up at Coco and Cedric with tired, watery eyes. There was something about her demeanour which seemed out of place. Again, Coco reasoned, she did not appear worried. It was something else, something different.

Coco and Cedric both shook their heads. 'Is your husband home?' Coco enquired.

Chantel flashed a confused look. 'Odilon? Non, he is away on business. What is this about?' she demanded. This time, Coco noticed a faltering in her tone.

'The *Abbaye Le Bastien* youth centre,' Cedric answered.

Chantel tutted loudly and turned her head. 'I might have

known,' she snapped. 'Even razed to the ground, the damn place is still causing trouble.'

Coco stole a look at Cedric. 'Were you at the demolition this morning?' Coco asked.

Chantel smiled. 'I was, if only to make sure it finally happened.'

Coco leaned forward. 'There were problems at the centre?'

Chantel sat, crossing her legs in front of her. 'There were always problems. Too little money, too many children, too few children, too many problem children. Too few staff. I used to work there too, mais I can't say I ever enjoyed it. My husband worked sixty, seventy hours a week, more if he could and I would let him. Even when he was home, he was never really here, always dealing with problems, paperwork. And he had no help. Whenever he asked the Church or the monastery, they always said the same thing - *pray to Dieu and he will give you the answers you need and the help you seek.* What they actually meant was, if you want more money, use your own.'

Coco looked quickly around the room. It did not appear to her as if Chantel and Odilon Sander were short of money. The house was in an exclusive neighbourhood, a short walk from the former youth centre.

Chantel noticed Coco apprising her home. 'The money comes from my family, not Odilon's,' she stated brusquely. 'And I was determined that my families hard earned money was not going to be squandered on Odilon's pet project, especially not when the damn church could have easily dipped into their own expansive pockets.' She shook her head determinedly. 'Non, a line had to be drawn, and that was it. It might sound selfish of me, but that place destroyed my marriage.'

Coco raised an eyebrow. 'In what way?'

'Some men have mistresses. Odilon was no exception, only his mistress was the youth centre.' She shook her head. 'And non, before you ask, there was none of that. There was no child abuse. Odilon might be many things, a weak man, par example. However, he is a good man with a good heart, and he would never have tolerated such behaviour, and as he spent most of his life there, I feel certain he would have noticed anything untoward going on.'

Coco nodded. She was not sure she shared Chantel's confidence. It had always been her experience that the devil often hides in plain sight. It had happened to her. She had woken up next to Mordecai Stanic on more occasions than she could remember. She had been lost in his arms and his eyes and she had never, not once, seen the monster hiding right in front of her. Coco coughed, blinking rapidly in an attempt to push the dark thoughts away. 'You said your husband was away on business?' she asked.

'Oui,' Chantel replied. 'He's in the Far East. He travels there several times a year. After the centre closed last year, he took a position in my father's company. He is in charge of the Chinese office and spends a lot of time there,' she added, in such a way it told Coco that Odilon Sander's wife did not mind her husband being away from home very much at all. 'My father, like Odilon, is devout, and therefore divorce was out of the question.'

She laughed sadly. 'The Chinese job was, I suppose, my father's way of allowing us to separate and lead our own lives without having to actually make it formal.' She narrowed her eyes, biting her lip as if she had suddenly realised she had spoken out of turn. 'You still haven't told me what this is all about,' she stated.

Coco cleared her throat, giving herself a few moments to consider how much she should tell Chantel. 'Shortly before the demolition, we discovered a crime had been committed on the site of the old youth centre.'

Chantel moved her shoulders quickly. 'And why would you think that is anything to do with my husband or I? I told you, the centre has been closed for some time now.'

Cedric interjected. 'We are trying to speak with anyone who

had been involved in the youth centre, to see if we can make some sense of what happened there.'

'And what sort of crime was committed?' Chantel demanded.

Coco met her eyes, and she reasoned that the likelihood was the press would soon report what had happened. 'We discovered three coffins had been placed inside the building.'

'Three coffins?' Chantel cried, her deep voice rising sharply. 'From the monastery?'

'What makes you say that?' Coco interrupted.

She shrugged again. 'I don't know. Just that the crypt was just next door, and as I recall, there were rumours that some of the children used to sneak into the crypt and do whatever it is rambunctious, undisciplined children do.' She stopped, pursing her lips and tapping her chin. 'How curious,' she murmured.

Coco studied her face. 'And it means nothing to you?'

'Why would it?' Chantel snapped. 'Other than it sounds like a macabre prank some brat would play, don't you think?'

Coco was not sure she could disagree. 'Nothing like that happened when the centre was open?'

Chantel chuckled. 'I don't believe so. I think I would have remembered something like that!'

'When is your husband due back in the country, Madame?' Cedric asked. Coco could tell by the way he was tapping his foot against the carpet that he was getting impatient and itching to leave. She could almost hear him saying - *this is a dead end. Let's move on.*

'I'm not sure,' Chantel retorted, her voice wavering. 'My husband and I… we don't talk very often. He emails once or twice a week.'

Coco nodded. She could not imagine the problems in the Sander's marriage had anything to do with her investigation. All the same, she wanted to at least speak to him so she could remove it from her 'to do' list. And it appeared that Odilon Sander had been on the front line for whatever had happened at the youth centre.

'When was the last time you heard from him?'

'He sent me an email yesterday,' Chantel smiled. 'He wanted me to record the demolition for him. You see, he was very sad about it.' The smile broadened. 'I told him it would be my pleasure.'

'D'accord. Well, next time you are in touch, could you tell him we were here, and we would like to speak to him regarding the centre?' Coco asked. She stood and handed her card to Chantel. 'It's purely a formality.'

Chantel took the card. 'I'll ask my son to pass this on. He speaks to his father regularly.'

Coco moved towards the door, closely followed by Cedric. She stopped in the doorway. 'Did your son attend the youth centre also?'

Chantel nodded, clearly irritated. 'Oui, he did,' she snapped, as if the memory clearly bothered her.

'Is he here? Could we talk to him?' Coco asked. 'What happened may mean something to him.'

'I don't see why,' Chantel retorted. 'In any event, he's not here. He's at college.' She waved the card. 'I'll give this to him and have him and my husband call you. Is that all?'

Coco nodded. 'Merci for your time. Au revoir.' She stopped dead in her tracks, noticing an ornate silver frame on a bureau. She picked it up. The photograph was of Chantel, with a man in his forties and a younger boy. 'Is this a photograph of you with your husband and son?'

Chantel moved slowly across the room and took the frame from Coco. 'Oui. That's Odilon and our son Vichy on the day Vichy graduated from school. We had a big party for him,' she added with a proud smile.

Coco gestured for Cedric to look at the photograph. His eyes widened. 'When was the last time you say you heard from your husband?' he asked.

'As I said, yesterday. Why?'

Coco stared at the photograph of the man called Odilon Sander and she was almost certain he was lying on a slab in Sonny Bernstein's morgue. She turned back to Chantel. 'Can you write down the name of the hotel your husband is staying in and forward me the email he sent you?'

Chantel's cheeks flushed, the calmness seeping away. 'What's going on?'

'I'm not sure,' Coco answered, her mind a whir of thoughts, 'just please do as I ask, as soon as you can.'

14H00

Coco stared at the image of Odilon Sander on the computer screen. She moved her head between the photograph in her hand and the picture on the screen. 'I just can't be certain,' she said glumly. The image on the screen, despite being cleaned up, still bore the tell-tale signs of the beating he had taken, whereas the photograph was different. Odilon Sander was smiling, his eyes twinkling and full of life.

'Then we've gotta get his wife to ID him,' Cedric reasoned.

'What if it's not him?' she replied. 'I really don't want to put her through that if I don't have to.'

He laughed. 'I got the impression Chantel Sander would be more disappointed if it wasn't him.'

'You're right, still…' she trailed off. 'I just want to be sure, and as far as she's concerned, he's off somewhere in the Orient. Ah,' she jumped to her feet, waving wildly. 'Ebba, Ebba!' she yelled. Ebba ignored her and continued walking. 'Hey, the chicks ignoring me. EBBA!' she screamed at the top of her lungs, before coughing wildly. 'That hurt,' she croaked.

Ebba appeared in the doorway. 'You bellowed, Captain?'

'I guess you didn't hear me…'

'Oh, I heard you,' Ebba responded cheerfully. 'I just chose to ignore you because I've already had my fill of crazy today.'

Cedric guffawed. Coco shot him a disparaging look. 'Don't make me slap the silly out of you, young man,' she warned. She turned her attention back to Ebba. 'We need your very particular set of skills and we need them pronto.'

Ebba flopped heavily onto the chair opposite Coco's desk, pulling out her laptop and opening it. 'I don't get paid enough for this.' She sighed. 'What do you want?'

'Odilon Sander,' Coco replied. 'He might be in China, or he might be in the morgue.'

Ebba raised an eyebrow. 'Now you got my attention.' She began typing rapidly, her face illuminated by the screen, her eyes flicking quickly from side to side as she read. 'Where is he supposed to be?'

Coco slid a piece of paper across the desk. 'In this hotel.'

Ebba snatched the paper and continued typing. 'I'm accessing the hotel records now,' she said after a few minutes had passed, before finally shaking her head. 'Non, it appears he was meant to check in two days ago but never arrived.'

'Are you sure?' Cedric asked.

'As I keep telling you, I speak eight languages fluently, Chinese is one of them, so yeah, I'm sure,' Ebba quipped. 'The room was paid in advance via a standing order, so I imagine they just assumed his plans had changed and kept the room vacant in case he turned up late.'

Coco bit her bottom lip. 'Mais, according to his wife, everything was as normal and he sent her an email yesterday.'

Ebba shrugged nonchalantly. 'I don't know what to tell you, perhaps he's off with his lover or something. I mean, isn't that what married people do when they've become bored with shagging the same person?'

Coco covered her mouth, hiding a smile. 'Only if they're doing it wrong,' she answered. 'Besides, I got the impression that Madame Sander couldn't care less if her hubby was shacked up with a bimbo somewhere. I think it was rather the point of his trips abroad.' She frowned. 'The trouble is, if Odilon Sander is our dead guy, then he actually died two nights ago, so unless he knows something that we don't about the afterlife and the internet connection in heaven, then he's not likely to be emailing his wife and asking her to video something for him, is she?'

'We only have the wife's word he sent an email,' Cedric

interrupted.

Coco pointed at her screen. 'Here's the email. Chantel Sander sent it over.'

Ebba stood up and moved to Coco's computer. 'Give me a minute,' she said.

'What does it say?' Cedric asked.

Coco narrowed her eyes and read from the screen:

Cher Chantel. Hope all is well. Life here is the same as normal. Busy. One polite meeting after another and food I can barely stand. I'll call Vichy in a day or two, just explain to him the time difference again as I'm sure he thinks I'm just ignoring him. Thinking of Paris today and the end of an era. I wish I was there, but I'm actually pretty glad I'm not. So much happened there, good and bad, and we all paid a price for it, didn't we? As I can't be there, I need to ask you something. Can you video the demolition with your phone? I'm not even sure I want to see it, I mean, it was part of my life for so long, but I just know that if I don't, I'll probably end up regretting it. Anyway, I'd better go, got a meeting in half an hour to prepare for. Love to you both. Odilon, X.

Coco pursed her lips again. 'Seems a nice enough email, except...'

'Except?' Ebba queried.

Coco shrugged. 'Chantel Sander didn't really hide the fact that the blossom had fallen from the love bloom of their marriage and this email seemed rather... *nice*. I'd even go so far as to say it sounded pretty loving.'

Ebba turned the screen around. 'Well, if Odilon Sander sent it, he certainly didn't send it from China.'

Coco pulled back her head. 'Quoi? How the hell do you know that?'

Ebba pulled back her shoulders. 'You want the real answer, or the one you can live with?'

Coco laughed. 'What you got, kid?'

Ebba turned her laptop around and pointed at a map. There was a large blinking circle in the middle of it.

Coco narrowed her eyes and stared at the screen. 'What am I looking at?'

'A map of Paris and the area where the email was sent from,' Ebba replied.

Coco could not hide her surprise. 'Paris? Are you saying the email was sent from Paris?'

'I am,' Ebba confirmed.

Coco scratched her head. 'Are you sure?'

Ebba nodded. 'Unless whoever sent it has mad kung fu with proxies, the server route it came in on covers this area,' Ebba snapped. 'And before you ask, I can pinpoint it to a radius of a few kilometres, but probably not more specific than that. But yeah, the likelihood is it was sent from Paris.'

'I've no idea what you just said, but are you saying it was definitely sent yesterday from Paris?'

Ebba nodded again, suppressing a yawn.

Coco turned to Cedric. '<u>After</u> he ended up stuffed into a coffin,' she pondered. 'It makes no sense.'

'What do you want to do?' he asked.

'There's nothing we can do until we have a positive identification. Let's go ask Madame Chantel Sander what she knows about her husband's current whereabouts.' She pulled on her coat. 'I think we may have just caught a break.'

15H00

'This is my son, Vichy,' Chantel Sander stated briskly. Despite her tone, Coco noticed the way in which the other woman lifted her hand to gently stroke her son's hair was tender and loving. Coco also noticed, that unlike her own children, Vichy Sander did not recoil as if he had just been touched by a red-hot poker.

They were stood stock still in the foyer of the hospital, waiting for Dr. Bernstein to arrive. Coco and Cedric had returned to the Sander family home and asked Chantel to accompany them to the hospital. Chantel had insisted on bringing along her son, who had just returned from college.

Vichy Sander was tall and thin, with coarse red hair and a face lined with angry red spots, but his eyes were bright and gave him more of an air of maturity than other people in his age group. Coco had not told them why she wanted them to accompany her to the station and they had not asked, which she considered odd.

Vichy cleared his throat. 'Is this to do with what you found at the old building?' he asked. His voice was deep and cracked as he spoke. Coco imagined him to be about twenty-years-old, around the same age as Frère Mathieu and the three suspects, but his demeanour and his physical appearance made him seem much younger.

'What do you know about that?' Cedric asked Vichy.

Chantel pressed her hand on her son's shoulder and moved him to the side. 'He knows nothing,' she spoke quickly.

'Everyone's talking about it,' Vichy added with a bored shrug, 'and it's all over the internet.' He paused, a curious expression passing across his face. 'Is it true there were coffins?'

Coco had hoped the situation could be kept under wraps, but

she knew that was an unreasonable assumption. She nodded slowly.

Vichy looks away. 'That's bizarre. It doesn't make sense,' he added distantly.

Chantel sniffed, her face wrinkling with anger. 'It was only a matter of time before something like that happened. The youth club has been nothing but an attractive nuisance the whole time it's been there, as far as I'm concerned.' She stole a sly look at her son. 'Young people with nothing better to do and no one at home who cares enough to question what they might be up to when they are outside the home. It only got worse when it closed because there was no one to stop them from doing what they wanted. Blowing the damn thing up is the best thing that could have happened.'

Coco pursed her lips. 'You sound as if you know what you're talking about.'

Chantel stared blankly at her. 'I told you. I spent a great deal of time there. I thought it was good for my marriage, but of course, it wasn't. Every time I tried to speak up about what I saw, I was shut down.'

'And what sort of things did you see, exactly?' Coco asked keenly.

Chantel continued staring at her as if she was assessing if she should continue. Finally, she shrugged. 'The whole damn place was built and run by do-gooders who saw fit to turn a blind eye to bad behaviour because they thought they could,' she paused, visibly shuddering before continuing with a sarcastic tone and raising her fingers into air quotes, '"pray out the badness."' She snorted. 'The only thing I know for certain about children is that praying is the last thing on their minds, and most certainly the least effective thing to temper their behaviour.' She stared at Coco. 'If you're asking me, am I surprised about this latest ridiculous tomfoolery? Then non, I'm not. They are brats who were bred from brats, and that is a fact.'

'*Maman*,' Vichy cried wearily.

Chantel's head jerked towards her son. 'You of all people know exactly what those,' she stopped, her forehead creasing as if she was searching for what else to say, before finally adding, '*juveniles*, are capable of.'

'They were my friends,' Vichy snapped, before biting his lip. 'They ARE my friends.'

Chantel cackled. 'Are they? Are they really?' she demanded sarcastically. 'Do I need to remind you of the times you came home from school crying for one stupid reason or another?' Her mouth contorted as she continued. 'Do I need to remind you what they did to you?' She pulled her son close to her, rubbing her hand across his hoodie and with evident irritation removing pieces of fluff from it. 'Because I'm telling you, I remember it all. The tears, the tantrums, the desperate pleadings, *why do they hate me, maman?* All the time covered in bruises and every time I begged your father to step in and deal with the damn monks and the ignorant parents, he always refused. It was always the same. *Leave it to the Abbaye*, was all he said. Your father put his faith in those people and look where it got him, thrown out on the street the one time he chose to stand up to them.' She stopped abruptly, biting her lip as if she realised she had said too much. She turned to face Coco and Cedric, her eyes scanning their faces to see if they had been listening.

Coco flashed her a knowing look. 'What do you mean about your husband being thrown out because he stood up to the monks?'

'Nothing,' Chantel answered quickly.

'It could be important,' Coco retorted.

'What is this about?' Chantel demanded defiantly. 'My husband isn't even in the country. He can't have anything to do with what you found in the old building.'

Coco turned to Vichy. 'When was the last time you spoke to your father, Vichy?'

Vichy bit an already nibbled fingernail, before shrugging.

'Dunno. Saturday?' he stated as if it was a question.

The day he died, Coco flashed the thought to Cedric. 'And what did he say?'

Vichy's eyebrows knotted. 'What do you mean?'

Coco took a step closer to him. 'Oh, I don't know. How did he seem? Happy? Anxious? Sad? Worried?'

Vichy shrugged again. 'Dunno. He seemed like Papa. Like he wasn't here, for a change,' he added with evident bitterness. 'He was on his way to the airport.'

'And did he say anything about his plans in China?' Cedric interrupted.

Vichy shook his head. 'Non, why would he?' He sighed. 'Look, when he's away we have these calls two or three times a week. They last exactly ten minutes, most of which is filled with awkward silence and amounts to the same script. *How's school? Did you meet a girl yet? Are you helping Maman around the house?* I'd grunt a response and that would be that.'

Coco suppressed a smile realising Vichy had just explained the conversations which took place between most parents and their surly late-adolescent children.

'Vichy, how many times have I told you not to speak like that?' Chantel snapped. She touched his hoodie again, pressing her fingers and irritably rubbing a stain. She glanced over her shoulder. 'Especially in front of strangers.' She pushed back. 'Now, stand up straight and talk as if you have had the decent education your father and I paid for you to have.'

Coco watched as the young man visibly shrunk in response to his mother's chastising.

Chantel stepped in front of her son. 'You still haven't told me what this is about,' she snapped.

Coco studied the other woman's face to see if there was any trace of fear and realised that either Chantel Sander was a damn good liar, or she thought she had nothing to worry about. 'How sure are you that your husband is in China?'

Chantel pulled back her head. 'What kind of stupid question is that? If you're asking me, did I see him get on the plane? Then, non, I didn't. As I told you, my husband gets on such a plane several times a year and that's it…' She trailed off, a cloud sweeping over her face. 'Oh, wait. Is that what this is about?' She stepped forward, lowering her voice away from her son. 'Are you saying my husband is fooling around? Is that what this is about?' she demanded again, before dark, tired eyes narrowed into angry pinpricks. 'And if so, what the hell does this have to do with the police?'

Before Coco had a chance to respond, Sonny appeared from the shadows. He had changed into a suit Coco assumed had been stuck in the back of his locker for several years. It was plain and sombre and did not match the zealousness of his nature, but it was what he brought out when he was about to do something which he suspected would forever live in the memories of the person he was escorting into his morgue. It had always reminded her of a child wearing a suit for a wedding or a funeral, seemingly at odds with their natural demeanour. He nodded an acknowledgment at Coco.

Coco gave him a sad smile. She glanced at Vichy Sander and wondered what she should do, before realising he was most certainly a legal adult in his own right. Sonny stepped forward and handed her a folder. Coco touched his hand before turning back to Chantel and her son. 'I need to show you something,' she said softly.

Chantel studied her face, a shadow passing across it. 'Very well,' she whispered before turning to her son. 'You stay here, Vichy.'

Vichy opened his mouth, seemingly to object, but he quickly lowered his head as if he realised how futile it was. 'Oui, maman,' he responded softly.

15H30

Chantel stepped into the chapel and moved slowly towards the table. Sonny had folded the shroud down over the chest, leaving only the face of the deceased exposed.

Coco fell into step behind her. She had left Cedric on the ground floor with Vichy Sander and accompanied Chantel in silence in the elevator to the depths of the hospital. Chantel had taken one look at the photograph Sonny had handed to Coco, and she had instructed her son to take a seat, before moving in silence towards the elevator. Coco had watched her carefully as the other woman moved swiftly in front of her. Chantel had said nothing, merely grabbing the photograph and handing it quickly back to Coco.

'That is my husband,' Chantel exhaled, her voice cracking as she did. 'Why is he here?'

Coco took a tentative step towards her. 'I was rather hoping you might be able to answer that question.'

Chantel turned her head. 'He was supposed to be in China. He WAS in China,' she stated, her voice cold and filled with irritation. She turned to Coco. 'Apparently, you know otherwise.'

Coco shrugged. 'Sadly, I know very little,' she replied, 'other than the email you forwarded from your husband suggests it was sent from Paris, not China.'

Chantel frowned. 'That makes no sense.' She stared at her husband's body again. 'How did he die?' she asked Sonny.

Sonny looked to Coco. Coco nodded for him to continue. 'We suspect he was murdered,' he said after a few moments.

'In Paris?' Chantel snapped.

Coco nodded.

'Murdered?' Chantel repeated.

'We believe so,' Coco confirmed. 'We aren't sure exactly what happened yet, mais…'

'He was in the youth centre?' Chantel asked with a frown. 'Is that what you're telling me?'

Coco nodded.

Chantel touched her head. 'Was this to do with the coffins?'

Coco nodded again. 'Oui. I'm afraid we found your husband in one of the coffins.'

Chantel screamed. 'Oh, I don't believe this, it's just too… too… sinister.'

Coco found herself unable to disagree. She was finding Chantel difficult to read. She had stared at her husband, all the time her face remaining stoic. She did not cry, nor did she look happy or relieved. It was almost as if she had no feelings one way or another regarding her husband and it troubled Coco. Grief, relief, happiness were all emotions Coco could get behind when considering response to such a loss, but she was seeing none of them in Chantel Sander. If anything, there was only indifference.

'You said the email was sent from Paris? What about the phone call to Vichy?' Chantel asked.

'We'll have to check his phone records, but I think it's clear your husband was in Paris when he made the call,' Coco responded. 'There's so much I don't understand yet, I'm afraid.'

Chantel snorted. 'That makes two of us.' She looked towards the elevator. 'I need to inform my son,' she said. 'He will take this very badly.'

Coco stared at her. 'Bien sûr. I am sorry, but we do need to talk more about this in order to try and understand what might have happened to your husband and where he has been.'

'Can it wait?' Chantel asked softly. 'There is so much to do. I need to be with my son, but I would like to tell our family and friends, I'd hate for them to find out from someone else.' She noticed Coco's reticence. 'Give me an hour and I'll come to the commissariat and I will answer all of the questions you might have, though I'm afraid I'm not sure how much help I will be considering as far as I knew my husband wasn't even in the country.'

'That's fine,' Coco agreed. 'I think if we're to understand what happened to your husband, then I'm going to need your help to try and piece it all together.'

Chantel strode away. 'I was married to the man for over twenty years, and I can't say I understood him at all.' She stopped and looked over her shoulder. 'Ask the damn monks, they probably knew my husband better than anyone, and it wouldn't surprise me if they're up to their necks in this.'

16H00

'Ask the damn monks, they probably knew my husband better than anyone,' Coco repeated the last words spoken to her by Chantel Sander. She had returned to the commissariat and was sitting in her office, with Cedric and Ebba. 'What do you think she meant by that?'

'Probably nothing much,' Cedric responded. 'Odilon Sander worked with the monks for a long time at the youth centre, so they probably did know him well. And plus, there wasn't much love lost between the Sander's.'

Coco flashed an unconvinced look. 'Still…' She stopped and sighed. 'There was something off about her, don't you think?'

He laughed. 'You always think there's something off about people.'

She nodded her agreement. 'In our jobs, it would be foolish not to. Most people lie to our faces and many of them do it quite convincingly. However,' she conceded, 'I'm sure she was surprised by the news her husband wasn't in China after all.'

'Speaking of that,' Ebba interjected. 'I checked further back. Of the last four times Odilon Sander claimed to be in China, he wasn't. He sent his deputy instead, but there are emails between Odilon and his son and wife which seem to suggest he was in China each of those times.'

Coco tapped her fingers on the desk. 'Then it appears our dead man was doing the dirty.'

'You think?' Ebba responded.

'It's a tale as old as time,' Coco exhaled. 'Husband tells the wife he's off on a work trip while all the time he's schlepping someone else. So, it begs the question - who was Odilon Sander schlepping?'

'I've requested a mandate for his bank records,' Cedric stated. 'Mais, these things take time, and unless he was stupid, the chances are we're not going to find where he has been and who he was with, not unless he wanted to risk his wife finding out. He probably paid cash, or had his lover pay for it all.'

'Then we interview his friends, his colleagues. Someone has to know something about what the dirty dog was up to,' Coco reasoned. She turned to Ebba. 'Start with his deputy, the one who is in China. They might just know what he was really up to, and go through his phone records with a fine-tooth comb - see if there are any numbers he rings a lot. It might also help us pinpoint where he has been all the times he was supposed to be in China.' She tapped her chin.

'What's bothering you?' Cedric demanded.

'The monk thing still bothers me,' she said after a moment. 'And I don't know why, other than they seem to have their paws all over this and they're being awfully tight lipped, and you know how much I hate that.'

'You just want a chance to get up close and personal with your boy-toy in a smock again, don't you?'

Coco suppressed a smile. 'The thought never even crossed my mind,' she responded. The fact was Mathieu Moreau had been on her mind and it bothered her. She had no time for relationships, let alone one with a man-child barely out of his teenage years. And yet. *And yet.* Every time she closed her eyes she saw his face, dark hair falling over even darker eyes and the full lips which, as far as she was concerned, begged to be kissed.

'Anyway, Monsieur Rude,' she said in a mock scolding tone, 'I think the main reason I keep coming back to it is because it was the first time I noticed a change in Chantel Sander's demeanour. In comparison to her reaction to seeing her husband dead, she only became animated when she was talking about the monks and I'd love to know why.'

Cedric pointed into the main office. Chantel and Vichy Sander had stepped out of the elevator. 'Well why don't we ask her?'

16H30

'There's no easy way to say this,' Coco began, 'mais, it appears that Odilon didn't just miss the last trip to China, but also several before.'

'What are you talking about?' Vichy Sander demanded. 'I spoke to him every time he was away…'

Chantel tapped her son's arm. 'Vichy, I want you to wait outside.'

He snatched his arm away from her. 'I'm not going anywhere, not until I find out what happened to my father.'

Chantel crossed her legs, fixing Coco with an antagonistic look. 'Then you believe my husband was having an affair?'

Coco shrugged. 'I can't answer that, not yet at least,' he replied. 'That's why we need to try to understand where he was and what he might have been up to. Earlier, you suggested I should speak with the monks. Why was that?'

Chantel gave a cold laugh. 'Because they controlled everything my husband has ever done.'

'Controlled?' Coco interrupted, confused by her choice of word. 'What do you mean?'

'What does it matter now, Maman?' Vichy wailed desperately.

'It matters,' Chantel hissed through gritted teeth, 'because this stinks of them and their pious sanctimoniousness. I know, I just KNOW that whatever your father was up to, they knew about it.'

Cedric cleared his throat. 'Madame Sander - when was the last time you saw your husband?' he asked.

Chantel considered her answer. 'Saturday morning, when he left to go to the airport,' she stopped, emitting a low, sarcastic laugh. 'The airport, ha!'

'And what time was that?'

She shrugged. 'His flight was at 12H00, but he left early, around six. I sleep lightly, so he woke me when he was getting ready to leave.'

Coco made a note. 'And did you speak with him?'

Chantel nodded. 'Briefly. I don't recall what about…' She paused as if remembering something. 'Ah of course, he told me he had to stop off to see *them* before he left.'

Coco and Cedric exchanged a look. 'Are you saying your husband went to the Abbaye after he left your house?' Coco asked, realising that the monks at *Abbaye Le Bastien,* were likely some of the last people to see Odilon Sander alive.

'Oui,' Chantel replied. 'He said he was stopping off on his way to the airport as he had something to discuss with Frère Leroy.'

Coco raised an eyebrow. 'Something to discuss? Did he mention what it might be?'

She shrugged again. 'Not really. They've been meeting a lot lately. I always assumed it was about the demolition. I think Odilon was hopeful the youth centre was going to be rebuilt, but it was never going to happen. The land had been sold and that was that. It was all about money. Odilon was praying they would change their minds, mais I think he had begun to realise it just wasn't going to happen. As I said earlier, the damn place should have been closed a long time ago, if it had…'

Coco leaned forward. 'If it had?' she asked keenly.

Chantel stole a sly look at her son. 'If it had, things would have been different for us all.'

Coco frowned. 'You're going to have to level with us, Madame Sander. We've been getting lots of mixed messages about the youth centre, and it seems to me that whatever went on there, it wasn't great. That's why we need to understand what that was if we're to stand a chance of figuring out what happened to your husband.' She stopped and turned to face Vichy. 'And your father,' she added hoping her words would have more affect on the child than the wife.

Vichy looked at his mother. Her lips tightened and she moved her head slowly as if she was instructing him not to speak. He turned back to Coco. 'I don't know what answers you're looking for at the Abbaye, but I don't think it has anything to do with my father, not really.'

Coco took a deep breath. 'What sort of things are we talking about here, Vichy?' she asked. 'I'm not looking for you to betray confidences, but I do need you to tell me what you know, no matter how inconsequential you might think it is. It really is important, for your father, but also to make sure whoever hurt him is punished. Do you understand what I am saying to you?'

'Nothing good will come from this,' Chantel warned. 'Nothing ever does.'

Coco continued staring at Vichy. 'Was there abuse at the youth centre, Vichy? Did the monks abuse children?'

'Oh, Dieu, non,' he spat distastefully, 'nothing like that. That's gross.'

'Then what happened there?' Coco pressed.

Chantel raised her hand in front of her son's face in an attempt to keep him from talking. 'The youth centre was nothing but a clique for rich, spoilt children who had nothing better to do than terrorise other children, and they did so without fear of recrimination because the monks and the staff did little to stop them for fear of upsetting their parents.'

Coco kept looking at Vichy. He had lowered his head and was staring at his feet, his cheeks were red.

'You're talking about bullying?' Cedric asked.

'Hazing is what they call it, so I understand,' Chantel responded. 'And,' she paused, moving her fingers into air quotes, before adding, '*apparently* it's harmless and perfectly normal.' She touched Vichy's shoulder and he immediately recoiled, pushing it away as if her touch hurt him. She continued. 'Some of the children were relentless in the way they bullied the other children and because of who they were, they got away with it, time after time.'

Coco nodded. She could not help but wonder if it had anything to do with her three suspects. She could certainly imagine Jericho Martin to be a bully who was confident he could always get away with his actions. 'Was there anyone in particular?' she asked.

Chantel's eyes widened. 'Oh, who knows? And what does it matter now?'

Coco decided to try another tack. 'You talked about hazing. What form did that take?'

Chantel shrugged, but said nothing. Coco leaned forward. 'Vichy?'

Vichy lifted his head slowly. 'They called them games. Par example, if you wanted to become part of their clique, you had to pass three separate trials.'

'And what exactly did you have to do in these trials to pass?' Cedric asked.

Vichy's mouth twitched. He looked slyly at his mother. Chantel did not look at him. He coughed. 'Once they made me run through the youth centre naked,' he stated matter-of-factly, 'and took pictures of me and posted them all over social media.' He laughed. 'That was "fun,"' he added bitterly. 'And then they said I had to steal something very specific, like a pair of monk's underpants from the washing line, something stupid like that. And then, finally...' He stopped abruptly.

'Finally?' Coco pushed.

'Finally,' Vichy said after a minute had passed, 'you had to spend a night in the crypt.'

'That doesn't sound so bad,' Coco reasoned, although she could scarcely imagine anything worse, even the thought of it gave her the creeps, unless of course, she had someone to snuggle up with.

Vichy clasped his hands together. 'That wasn't all you had to do. You had to spend the night inside one of the coffins.'

'What?' Coco cried, her voice rising sharply. 'You're kidding?'

'I told you they were monsters,' Chantel interjected. 'They forced my son to spend the night in a coffin just so he could join their damn clique. And what's worse, my husband, Vichy's actual father, not to mention the monks, all knew this sort of thing was going on, and did nothing.'

'They knew children were accessing the crypt?' Coco questioned.

'Bien sûr,' Chantel retorted, 'there wasn't a single thing that went on they didn't know about, any of them. And I hated my husband for turning a blind eye to what our son was going through…'

'Maman…' Vichy cried. 'It was harmless…'

'Harmless?' Chantel screeched. 'Need I remind you of the weeks of nightmares that followed? How you'd wake up screaming night after night after night. And in the end what good did it do you? They still treated you like you were beneath them. You went through all of that, and where are they are now? Because I don't see them calling you up or inviting you to any of their parties.'

Vichy's head dropped again.

Coco saw the pain on Vichy's face and she wanted to tell him that it would be alright. Bullies were bullies for their own reasons, but they were never happy people. Success and happiness were the best antidotes and revenge to show a bully that they had not ruined you. She vowed to find a time where she could speak with Vichy in private and tell him just that. But now was not the time, not in front of his mother and Cedric, because she felt sure it would just embarrass the young man and make him feel worse. She tapped her fingers on the desk, facing Chantel again. 'Are you really telling me the monks knew about what was happening in the crypt?'

Chantel nodded quickly. 'Not only did they know about it, they actually sanctioned it,' she added with bite. 'Odilon said it was harmless enough. A rite of passage was what they called it. A rite of passage they all had experienced and was character building.' She snorted. 'Have you ever heard anything so ridiculous?'

Coco and Cedric exchanged a look. 'We'll certainly discuss it with Frère Leroy,' Coco said.

Chantel frowned. 'I should hope you would, but do you think it could have something to do with what happened?'

'We certainly can't rule it out,' Coco responded. 'Especially after finding the coffins. There could be a link there. We'll see what they say.' She took a breath. 'Do you remember a boy called Paul Lecourt?'

Vichy's head jerked upwards, his eyes widening. Chantel sighed. She patted her son's knee. 'Paul. I haven't thought of him in some time. He was a delightful child. Sweet and kind, and innocent. Whatever life he had been saved from had not affected his nature. He was my son's best friend.'

'Oh, I'm sorry, Vichy,' Coco blurted.

He shrugged. 'It was a long time ago,' his voice cracked.

Chantel frowned. 'Why are you asking about Paul? As my son said, it was a long time ago and it was nothing but a horrible accident.'

'So I understand,' Coco responded. 'It just came up as part of our investigation because today is the tenth anniversary of his death.'

Chantel took a sharp breath. 'Ten years. Oh gosh, it seems so long ago and yet like it was yesterday.'

Coco nodded. 'You said it was nothing but a horrible accident. What do you recall about it?'

Chantel considered her answer. She clasped her hands together, her fingers entwining and circling one another. 'Very little,' she said finally. 'I was inside the centre and heard an almighty commotion. I ran out and saw him lying there. Well,' she stopped abruptly, her bottom lip quivering. 'I saw his trainer and the bottom of his jeans. There was already a crowd gathered around him you see. And I'm sorry to say that my first thought was relief. You see, he had the same shoes as… as Vichy.'

Vichy muttered something indecipherable under his breath.

'He fell,' Chantel continued. 'A tragedy. And while it was awful, I can't think why you would bring it up now. We'd forgotten all about it.'

'I haven't,' Vichy whispered. 'He was my best friend. And I haven't forgotten him at all, nor what happened.'

Chantel patted his knee. 'Bien sûr, he was darling.'

Coco and Cedric looked at each other. 'You were there when it happened?' Cedric asked.

'We all were,' Vichy gave as an answer.

'You all were?' Coco spoke quickly.

Vichy turned to his mother. 'I'd like to go home now,' he said monotonically.

Chantel jumped to her feet, seemingly pleased to be able to do something for her son. 'We're leaving,' she snapped at Coco and Cedric. 'My son has just lost his father. We need to be at home together.'

Coco nodded her understanding. 'We are doing our best to understand what happened to your husband. If you think of anything, please let us know right away.'

Chantel considered, her fingers playing with the zip on her jacket, her mouth twisting as if she was wrestling with something. Finally she shook her head. 'I don't think I can help you. I don't know where my husband was, or what he was up to. I'm not even sure I want to know. I foolishly believed what he told me, although in hindsight I really ought to have known better. Odilon cared only about himself and the Church. Not me, not his son, and what did it get him in the end?' She tugged on her son's sleeve. 'Let's go,

Vichy.'

Vichy stood and shuffled behind his mother, stuffing his hands into the pockets of his jeans. He flipped his hood over his head.

Chantel stopped in the doorway and turned back to Coco. 'If you are going to see Frère Leroy you can give him a message for me. Tell him he's not going to get away with it. Whatever he did. Whatever happened, if I find out he is involved, he will pay, one way or another, he will pay.'

17H15

Coco weaved the car through the busy Parisian streets, deftly moving between stationary and slow-moving vehicles. The night was descending, bringing with it the twinkly hue of busy cafés and theatres. As usual, Cedric was to her right, gripping tightly onto the seat, switching between irritated tuts and concerned gasps. 'You nearly hit that pedestrian!' he complained.

Coco glanced over her shoulder, noticing for the first time the man who had just fallen onto the bonnet of a parked car. 'The man's obviously blind, or drunk,' she reasoned.

Cedric appraised her. 'Are you sure you actually passed your driving test, cos I've gotta tell you, I'm not entirely convinced.'

'Psssh,' Coco sniffed. 'I'll have you know, not only did I pass my driving test on my first attempt, but my instructor said it was the happiest hour he had ever spent in his car.'

Cedric grabbed the handrail. 'Well, either he didn't get out much, or he was relieved because you never actually got out of the back seat and into the driving seat…'

Coco flashed him a mock-offended look. 'How dare you!'

'So, what did Sonny say exactly when he called?' Cedric asked.

'Not a lot,' Coco replied. 'Just that he'd spent the day trying to track down the Catholic chaplain slash pathologist he went to doctor school with and that he finally had, and we really should meet him.'

Cedric's eyes widened. 'Oh, wait, this isn't another one of your dates, is it?'

Coco chuckled. 'I wished. It's been so long I think I may have forgotten how to do it, and I've most probably healed over,' she pointed down in the direction of her groin, 'down there, by now.' She shook her head. 'Non, Sonny said his frock wearing friend had something to share, something he would only do off the record and in private.'

'What do you think that means?' Cedric asked.

Coco narrowed her eyes, staring at the traffic ahead of her. They had dealt with the Catholic Church before and she still bore the bruises from it and the only thing she knew for certain was that she was not ready to lock horns with them again. 'All I know,' she said finally, 'is that I hate anyone who hides behind something - religion, law, whatever, because they use it as an excuse to browbeat other people into accepting what they're selling. I won't allow it to happen again. Let's see what Sonny's friend has to say and just hope it gives us the break that we need.'

'And then what?'

She shrugged. 'We go and see the monks again like we planned. They have a lot to tell us, I'm becoming more and more certain of that, but I also want to be ready. I don't want to give them the chance to bamboozle us and brush us off anymore. If they're lying, I want to know why and what they are lying about.'

'And if they don't want to tell you?'

Coco laughed. 'Then they'll feel the wrath of Coco,' she smiled sweetly. 'And we all know how brutal that can be.'

17H30

Dr. Joël Allard extended his hand, thin lips pulling into a warm smile. Coco shook it. It was small and cool against her own. Allard was a slight man, with a pinched face and large round glasses perched on the edge of his nose. 'It's a pleasure to meet you, Captain. Sonny has told me a lot about you.'

Coco winked at him and nudged Sonny. 'Don't believe a word of it, unless of course, he told you I was fabulous and *quite* the catch.'

Allard rubbed Sonny's shoulders. 'Something like that. In fact, I'd go so far as to say if I didn't know better, I'd say my old pal here has quite the crush.'

Sonny jerked his shoulder away, his face flushing with embarrassment. Coco stepped back, mouthing *awkward* in Cedric's direction.

'We were on our way to *Abbaye Le Bastien* before you called,' Cedric began, staring directly at the Catholic chaplain and pathologist. There was a harshness to his tone Coco did not recognise, though it appeared to her it was laced with contempt and irritation. He had been by her side during the investigation which had torn a hole through her private and professional life. However, Cedric had appeared unaffected by it. They had never really talked about it in any real sense, and in that moment she wondered whether they should, even if she had no idea how that kind of conversation might happen, nor what it might entail.

Sonny gestured for them to take seats in his small, cramped office, hurriedly removing files and boxes from the chairs. 'Take a seat everyone,' he said.

Coco flopped down and immediately lit a cigarette, despite the no-smoking sign. 'So, priest, what's the low-down?'

Dr. Allard's eyebrows knotted in confusion. 'Low-down?' he asked with evident confusion.

Sonny smiled. 'I warned you about Coco, Joël, and as I said, her bark is most definitely worse than her bite.'

'Only when it suits me,' Coco quipped in response, before winking again, 'and it depends on the man.'

'Anyway,' Sonny exhaled, moving across the small office and taking a seat. 'Let's get to the reason why I called you over. I told you I was going to reach out to my old school friend because I thought he might be able to assist with making sense of what happened yesterday.'

'You're familiar with the Abbaye?' Coco asked Dr. Allard.

He nodded. 'Very much so,' he responded. 'And I also knew the youth centre,' he added. 'In fact, I spent a great deal of my internship ministering there.'

'Ministering?' Coco interrupted.

Joël Allard raised his hands. 'I know how that sounds in the modern world, and as much as I understand the reticence attached to what I do, I also am conscious of the good work we do, and the fine intentions of the people involved. There are issues, as I'm sure you know on all sides of this spectrum.' He stared at Coco. 'Good cops, bad cops, that sort of thing.'

'Good priests, bad priests,' Coco snapped through gritted teeth.

Allard nodded his agreement. 'I can't say I disagree with you, necessarily.' He coughed. 'However, we're talking about one issue, and that is *Abbaye Le Bastien* and the youth centre. I can speak of problems, but they are not the problems you imagine them to be.'

'You mean bullying?' Coco interrupted.

He took a deep breath. 'The centre was created to help children. To teach them not just the way of the Lord, but to prepare them for the path that lay ahead of them and give them the tools and the necessary encouragement they might need to forge a good, Christian life.'

Coco stifled a yawn. 'Merci for the Catholic pamphlet recital, so how's about spilling the real tea? What went on at the damn place? We already know there was some kind of ridiculous hazing going on. Kids having to spend the night in coffins with corpses? Did you know about that?'

Allard stole a look at Sonny. 'Did you?' Sonny demanded.

'It was what you might call a common secret,' he finally answered after a few moments had passed.

Coco leaned forward, pressing her elbows on her knees. 'And who exactly was privy to this common secret?'

'I don't like speaking on behalf of others,' Allard retorted.

'Try,' Coco pushed with a tight smile.

A moment passed. 'I grew up in the neighbourhood,' Allard said finally. 'In fact, I was one of the first kids who went through the door of the youth centre. It was a great place. We had a whale of a time, and it was a lot of fun. We all went to private school, you see, and it was pretty dull and unimaginative. At the youth centre we could play, but it was also a place to feel safe. The brothers were there watching over us, offering us advice, guiding us and it was nice.'

Coco stifled a yawn. 'You really did write the brochure for them, didn't you?'

'Coco,' Sonny sighed.

Allard raised his hand. 'She has a point, Shlomo. These places aren't for everyone. They can be oppressive sometimes and just because I believe in Dieu and His power, I'm not blind to how He presents to others. I do the same job as you and I see the same sort of things and it is both tragic and heart-breaking and infuriating and completely without understanding, and yet...'

'And yet? Coco demanded. 'There's a "and yet" at the end of that sentence.'

He smiled at her. 'Oui. There is a "and yet" and that is my

belief. Dieu is there for me and that is enough for me.'

Cedric cleared his throat. 'As enlightening as this is... can we cut to the chase?'

Coco smiled at her lieutenant. 'What he said,' she added.

Allard took a deep breath. 'It's no different to schools, sororities, universities all over the world. Whenever you put young people together in any sort of environment, particularly when adult involvement is minimal, then the sort of ritualistic handed down behaviours become prevalent. It's not unusual and it's not always a bad thing.'

Coco tried hard not to snap. She wanted to understand Allard and his reasons, but she was not sure she could. 'Then you're saying you all thought this sort of behaviour was a good idea?'

Allard shrugged. 'A good idea is a stretch, but I think the general consensus was that it was harmless enough.'

'Harmless enough?' Cedric interrupted wide-eyed.

'These are rituals, nothing more, nothing less,' Allard reasoned, 'and because of that, they are regulated. The Frères always kept a distance, deniable liability you might say, mais it didn't mean they didn't keep an eye on what was going on.'

'And that was the extent of it?' Coco asked. She watched Allard's reaction, he turned his head quickly, his left eye twitching. It told her everything she needed to know about him. He was about to lie to her. 'Loyalty to the Church is one thing,' she stated, 'however, loyalty to the Republic is more important and dare I say more dangerous. Lies can make sure you end up in jail.'

'Charlotte,' Sonny cried. 'S'il te plaît.'

Coco gurned at him. She had just about had her fill of men lying to her, particularly those who hid behind their jobs or their religious calling. It seemed to her it was a luxury not afforded to women. She cleared her throat. 'I'm sure Sonny has already explained the situation to you, but I'll just add my own two cents worth. Whatever games went on at the *Abbaye Le Bastien* youth centre, I have a lot of cases on my desk, all of which need closing. Not least of which is a murder, and I have to warn you my tolerance of anything to do with the Catholic Church rubs me up the wrong way…'

'What happened to you, Captain Brunhild?' Joël Allard interrupted. 'Sonny didn't mention anything, but I sense you have had some bad experiences.'

Coco snorted. 'Have you got a spare few hours?' She stood, pacing along the narrow stretch of carpet in front of Sonny's desk, before finally collapsing back onto a chair, her body crumbling.

Allard clasped his hands in front of him. 'When Sonny called me and mentioned the Abbeye, I have to admit, my first thought was just to deny all knowledge of it and tell him I couldn't help.'

Coco raised an eyebrow. 'And what changed your mind? Dieu spoke to you and sent you to confess at the alter of Coco?'

He laughed. 'In a way, I suppose. You might say I left the Catholic Church to pursue my career in medicine, but of course that's not really true. I never left it, not really, that's not how it works. You might say I became disillusioned with it, but never enough to truly walk away from it. Dieu told me I could serve both masters, so that's what I did.'

'Lovely, I'm sure, but let's get back to the youth centre,' Cedric snapped, tapping his watch.

Allard nodded. 'Even when I was at the centre, there were always children who pushed the boundaries, and that never really changed. The children of prominent families in the area, all very involved in the Church. That afforded them a little leeway.'

'It always does,' Coco snapped. 'But not as far I'm concerned.'

'Sometimes youthful indiscretion is just that, the folly of youth,' Allard explained. 'We've all experienced it, I'm sure.'

Coco snorted. 'I think I wrote the book,' she quipped. 'However, Dr. Allard, I was always held responsible for my actions, no matter how old I was. And don't hide behind the church. My father is a Rabbi, which only meant he held me to a higher standard, but it wasn't just me, it was everyone else.' She stopped abruptly, muttering under her breath, 'apart from himself, of course.'

'These children are different,' he responded.

'You mean they could do what the hell they wanted, and no one interfered, presumably because their parents were regular contributors to the Church coffers,' Coco interrupted.

'That's not fair,' Allard snapped. 'Mais, you do have a point, at least on some occasions,' he added with clear reticence.

'Bon. So, tell us what you know and if it makes you feel any better and loosens your tongue, we won't say it came from you,' Coco offered.

He smiled at her. 'I can't say I understand what happened yesterday, or even if there is any connection to what happened when I was involved with the Abbaye. Mais, I do know something about the missing corpse and his true identity.'

'Ah,' Coco replied. 'The dude with no name.'

'Oui,' Allard agreed. 'Although of course Sonny was right. You can't bury someone without a death certificate, it's just not allowed.' He took a breath. 'However, there were reasons for it, and reasons which were accepted by the authorities.'

Coco flashed him a doubtful look.

'His name was Gasper Peron,' Allard continued. He swallowed, as if his mouth was dry. 'He was a major contributor to the Abbaye, not just financially, but also with his time. And not just the Abbaye and the youth centre, he was a benefactor to many other charitable causes throughout France. By all accounts, he was a very fine man.'

Coco scratched her head. The name was familiar but she could not place it. '*By all accounts?*' she repeated.

'You caught that,' he answered with a grin. 'Mais, don't read too much into it. Gasper was a…' he searched for the word, 'an acquired taste, you might say. An eccentric. A man who devoted his life to Dieu after he made a whole lot of money off the back of some very, let's say, unusual activities.'

'Illegal?' Cedric interjected.

Allard shrugged. 'All I can say is that I believe he was a man who came to the Lord to repent his past. I was not privy to it, nor did I ask.'

Cedric's nostrils flared. 'Yet he was allowed to be around children?' He pulled out his cell phone and being sending a message. He looked at Coco. 'I'll have Ebba look into Gasper Peron,' he stated.

'I never suggested for a moment anything untoward went on,' Allard snapped. His tone was hard and he bowed his head afterwards as if he was ashamed. 'Gasper was a man used to doing things his own way. He had no family of his own, not close family at least, and I think he just wanted to distance himself from his past, and I suppose create a little mystique.'

'He wanted to be a legend,' Coco said. 'A star who would have people talking for decades, even centuries to come. Who was the mysterious benefactor who lies unnamed in the crypt? He wanted to live in immortality, an unnamed hero, rather than some rich dude who had made his fortune from one sordid way or another. Have I hit the nail on the head, or not, sailor?'

Allard looked to Sonny. 'She is exactly how you described her, old friend. I see why you like her so.'

Coco turned her head. It bothered her that Sonny and Allard had obviously discussed her in depth, and she was not sure why. It almost felt as if she was part of joke she did not understand, and that had never sat well with her. 'I asked you a question,' she snapped in a harsher tone than she had intended.

Allard appeared taken aback. 'Désolé, I wasn't trying to be evasive. I suppose I've spent so long deferring to what I am told is for the best, that sometimes I forget that I serve more than one master. To answer your question, Gasper Peron was a self-made man who undoubtedly made his fortune by nefarious means.' He stopped and raised his hands. 'The extent of which I cannot be sure. All I know is that as he grew older he wanted to atone for his past. He had codicil in his will stipulating exactly what he wanted.'

'And in return he left the Church a hefty sum?' Coco enquired.

Allard nodded. 'His entire fortune was left to the Church and his only stipulation was that he be interred into the crypt and his identity withheld.'

Coco scratched her head. 'And didn't you think it was odd? I mean, what did he die of?'

Allard watched her. He took his time as if he was carefully considering his response. Finally he spoke. 'I suppose I did think it odd, but again, this was not my decision and certainly not one I was involved with making. What I was involved with, however, was his autopsy, and for that I can assure I acted as a doctor, not a Chaplain.'

'How and when did he die?' Coco pushed.

Again, Allard did not answer immediately. 'Monsieur Peron died two years ago and he was suffering from terminal cancer.'

Coco and Cedric exchanged a concerned look. 'Suffering from and died from are two different things, Dr. Allard,' Cedric stated.

Allard took a deep breath before slowing exhaling. 'Monsieur Peron died from a morphine overdose,' he said quickly. 'I realise that may give you concern, but let me assure you it shouldn't. I performed the autopsy myself and I was satisfied that he took his own prescribed medication. He also left a letter detailing why he was doing it. He wanted to go before the pain became any worse. The letter was independently verified by several people including his avocat who all confirmed the letter was in Gasper Peron's own handwriting.'

'That doesn't mean he wrote it willingly,' Coco stated.

'Coco, I checked the autopsy report myself,' Sonny chimed in. 'And I agree with Joël. Gasper Peron was very ill. The cancer had spread through most of his body and had invaded all of his vital organs. He would have been in a great deal of pain and his prognosis would have been weeks, if not days. We've seen cases like this before. People simply choose to go of their own volition when they are ready because cancer is cruel and it often takes its time.'

'All the same,' Coco grumbled. 'There's something about all this that I don't like.'

Allard leaned forward. 'Sonny filled me in on your case. And while I agree there is something very odd about it, it does seem to me you are most likely looking at another terrible prank. If there was any connection to Gasper Peron, then why was his corpse simply removed and placed in a skip. I don't believe it is connected.'

'A prank or not,' Coco explored, 'it doesn't explain how or why Odilon Sander ended up murdered. Tell me, did you know Sander as well?'

'Oui,' he nodded. 'I knew Odilon very well indeed. He was a good, honourable and decent man. I am at a loss to understand why anyone would want to hurt him.'

'Did you ever hear or see anything untoward about him?' Cedric asked.

'In what way?'

'Oh, I don't know,' Coco pursed her lips suggestively. 'Maybe he got a little handsy with the kids, par example?'

Allard's eyes flashed with irritation. 'Nothing, *nothing* like that went on in the Abbaye or the youth centre. These were good men with a common goal to do nothing but good. I don't believe any of them have a single bad bone in their bodies or bad thoughts in their heads,' he stated forcefully.

Coco held his gaze, not at all sure she agreed with him. 'Do you know Sofia Charton, Idris Cellier and Jericho Martin?' she asked.

He nodded again. 'Oui. They spent a great deal of time at the centre.'

'And were they involved in the hazing?'

Allard turned his head. 'I don't know.'

Coco stood and stepped in front of him, blocking him from turning away again. 'Oh, I think you do,' she said. 'Were they involved in the hazing?' she demanded again.

He sighed. 'I believe so. They were certainly the more popular in the group, and I believe the other young people looked up to them and sought to gain their approval. If you are asking me do I believe they are involved in what happened yesterday then I cannot say. I have had nothing to do with the Abbaye since the centre closed. My work at the hospital and my volunteer work in another arrondissement keeps me busy.'

'Is there anything else you can think of that might help us?' Coco asked in a defeated tone. She was not sure if the information he had provided was helpful in any way, or if he was telling them the whole truth, for that matter.

'I don't believe so,' he replied. He looked at watch. 'I'm very sorry, but I really have to get back to work.' He rose to his feet. 'All I can tell you is Odilon Sander was a good man, of that I am sure.'

'A good man with a very big secret,' Coco interjected.

Allard shrugged, a wry smile appearing on his thin face. 'We all have our secrets, Captain Brunhild,' he responded. 'Often, they're not as important to others as we imagine they would be.'

'What do you mean by that?' Cedric demanded.

Allard continued to the door. 'Only that just because you believe Odilon had a secret, that secret need not be important. It could have nothing to do with what happened to him, and it could have no importance. It could be, what you police call, a red herring, non?' He waved to Sonny. 'See you old pal, let's not leave it so long next time, d'accord?'

Coco watched Dr. Allard leave and turned to Sonny. 'Well? Is he on the level?'

Sonny laughed. 'I don't know how to answer that. All I can tell you is I think Joël is a decent man. A great doctor who doesn't seem to let his religious beliefs interfere in his work. If you're asking me if he's telling you the whole truth about the Abbaye, then I can't say other than to reaffirm my own assumptions that I don't believe he was lying to you. And as for the death of Gasper Peron, as I said, I read the autopsy report and I agree with Joël there was likely nothing suspicious about his death. Even if someone did murder him, they only brought his death forward by a matter of days. Why would they do that?'

Coco shrugged. 'Oh, I can think of one reason right off the bat,' she answered. 'Par example, what if old Monsieur Peron had changed his mind and decided against leaving his money to the Church? Someone might have got pissed off about it and decided to finish him off before he had a chance.'

Sonny looked doubtful. 'I don't think the Catholic Church is in the business of killing off their parishioners just to make some money.'

Coco pulled on her coat. 'That's where you and I differ, Sonny. I think everyone is capable of doing anything under the right circumstances, especially when it comes to money. Merci for your time and assistance.' She looked to Cedric. 'Let's go, Lieutenant.'

18H00

'It appears, Gasper Peron was up to his neck in a lot of shady things,' Ebba Blom stated.

Coco weaved the car through traffic. They were on their way to *Abbaye Le Bastien* and her mind had been elsewhere, focused on a certain young monk and his muscular calf. 'He has a record?' she called out to the cell phone on the dashboard.

'A long one,' Ebba replied. 'Including two rather lengthy stints in jail.'

'What kind of crimes?' Cedric asked.

'Mainly drugs. It looks like he started off dealing but worked his way up, because one of his jail sentences was for trafficking,' Ebba explained. 'Odd thing is, after he got out the last time, over twenty years ago, he appears to have gone clean because there were no further arrests and as far as I can tell, no suspicion of any crimes.'

'Maybe that's when he found "Dieu,"' Coco stated using quotes. 'Anything else?'

'Not really,' Ebba continued. 'No family to speak of, a couple of cousins in the North of France, but that's about it. He was rich, very rich. I found a couple of newspaper articles and it seems he might have made his fortune from drugs but he ploughed it into legitimate businesses that the cops couldn't touch.'

'You said one of his jail sentences was for trafficking - what was the other?' Coco asked.

'He was involved in a murder investigation. Some fifteen-year-old kid died of a drug overdose and the batch was traced back to Gasper Peron's cartel.'

Coco frowned. 'And he was convicted of it?'

'According to the newspaper he plead guilty because he was

ashamed of what he had done,' Ebba answered. 'The court didn't buy it, thought he was just laying it on to get a lighter sentence. He got ten years and that was his last bust as far as I can tell. He came out of prison twenty-one years ago and it seems like he went straight.'

'Maybe he did find Dieu,' Cedric mused.

Coco shook her head. 'Or he just got better at covering his tracks.' She frowned. 'If he really was some big kingpin, would he really take the fall himself? Why not pay one of his minions to do the time for him?'

Cedric shrugged. 'Because that wouldn't be paying penance for his sins, would it? Maybe he was on the level.'

'Find out what else you can on him, Ebba,' Coco continued. 'Especially about the death of the teenager.'

'You think it's important?' Cedric asked.

'Dunno,' Coco replied. 'All I know is that we've got a whole mess of a case and no answers. And I really don't like this whole buried without a name business. What if he was deliberately removed from his coffin?'

'Why?'

Coco pursed her lips. 'Well, if we ever get to speak to the idiots who did it, I'll be sure to ask. Merci, Ebba. Talk to you later.'

'Yeah, whatever,' Ebba muttered and disconnected the call.

Coco smiled at Cedric. 'I think she's warming to me.'

18H30

Coco and Cedric shuffled into the icy cold room. They had not been there before, and Coco assumed it was the office of Frère Gerard Leroy, the monk in charge of the Abbaye. She looked around. The room was sparse, with only a long table along the middle of it, a pair of tall ornate candlesticks positioned at either end of it, and a large marble fireplace in the centre of the far wall.

She stopped. There were no seats, other than the three occupied by Leroy and Frère's Henri Aries and Mathieu Moreau. Coco found herself unable to look at any of them, so she pressed herself against the wall, smoothing down the crinkles in her skirt. She quickly realised it was pointless because the creases had folded themselves into the fabric and seemingly had no intention of leaving it.

Frère Leroy watched Coco in a way which irritated her. It was as if he was judging her, and as far as she could tell, she had far more to judge him on than he did her. 'I'm not sure why you insisted on seeing us again, Captain Brunhild. Whilst I realise you are struggling with your investigation…'

'I've never struggled with an investigation in my life!' Coco exclaimed with as much conviction as she could muster. 'The *only* thing I've struggled with is assholes who think they're smarter than me and have more important pals and see fit to lie to me and think that I'll just go away.' She winked at him. 'That's one thing I don't do. I don't go away. I'm like a dog with a bone. Capeesh?' She stared at Leroy, all the time avoiding Mathieu who was staring at her, big black eyes boring into her in a way which bothered her. Still, she could not bring herself to look at him, or to tell him to stop.

'I'm not sure what your point is,' Leroy continued.

'Story of my life,' Coco retorted. Mathieu spluttered and quickly covered his mouth, dropping his eyes when he noticed the withering looks coming in his direction from his fellow monks. Finally she turned her head, smiling in the vague direction of the young man. She faced Leroy with determination. 'What can you tell me about the murder of Odilon Sander?'

Leroy bowed his head, quickly muttering a prayer. Mathieu and Henri Aries did the same. After a while, they slowly lifted their heads in unison.

'Odilon was a dear, dear friend,' Leroy said finally. 'And frankly, I'm struggling to make sense of his death.'

'As am I,' Aries added.

'And more importantly why anyone would want to hurt him,' Leroy continued. 'Odilon was not only a fine man, he was a dedicated avocate for the young people he ministered.' He raised his hand. 'Before you ask the question I am sure you are poised to ask, I will stop you. Odilon Sander was not capable of hurting a child, not in any way, and that is all I will say on *that* subject, other than to counsel you that I will not allow blemishes and unfounded accusations to be made against his character.'

'That's me told,' Coco quipped lightly. 'So, he was a Saint, I get that. Then answer me these two questions. He came here to see you on Saturday morning, the day of his murder.'

Leroy and Aries shared a look. It was only fleeting, but Coco caught it. 'That is correct,' Leroy confirmed.

'And what happened?' Coco asked.

He frowned. 'What do you mean? He came to pray with us, as he often did, especially when he was going to be away for a while. We talked a little. He was upset about the demolition but was pleased he was not going to be around to see it. I agreed with him, stating that I myself would not be watching it either. And then he left for the airport.'

'Except he didn't,' Coco interrupted. 'He wasn't going to the airport and it seems his whole Asian side-line was nothing but a smokescreen and the burning question is - for what?'

Frère Leroy moved his shoulders, his head tilting to the side. 'As I have explained to his wife, I have no knowledge of anything to do with that.'

'And did she believe you?' Cedric asked.

Leroy flashed the lieutenant a sad smile and shook his head. 'I think Chantel would think me lying if I told her the sky was blue.'

'Well, it isn't always, is it?' Coco smiled.

Leroy looked wearily at her.

'Why does Chantel Sander hate you?' Coco enquired. 'Because she does hate you, doesn't she? And despite the fact she also worked at the youth centre.'

'I believe,' Leroy answers finally, 'that Chantel blamed the Church, and by extension the monastery for the problems in her marriage.'

'And you think that was unfounded?' Coco countered.

'The Church is blamed for many things,' Aries stated, 'however, I don't believe we can take the blame for a man loving his job so much he neglects his marriage for it. Whatever problems were in the marriage, they were likely there before Odilon came to us. Even if they weren't, blaming us is just an easier way for Chantel to cope with the end of her marriage.'

'You said you had two questions?' Leroy interrupted impatiently.

Coco appeared confused. 'Ah, oui. I hear you talking about how good at his job Odilon Sander was.'

'That is correct,' Leroy conceded.

'Then why did you fire him?'

Leroy pushed himself back in his chair. 'What are you talking about?' he demanded.

Frère Aries tutted loudly. 'Is this coming from Chantel?'

Coco continued staring at Leroy. 'You didn't answer my

question.'

'Odilon was unhappy about the decision to sell the land,' Leroy said, his voice cracking. He looked across the room, his eyes focusing on the fireplace. 'I can see him standing there, arguing with me, over and over. I tried to make him see sense, mais…'

'What was he objecting to, exactly? Cedric interrupted.

The monk shrugged. 'He knew the building was beyond economic repair. I mean, he'd been badgering us for years about the repairs that were needed, and for a time we did what we could, but finally it became obvious it was just too much. Odilon knew that, he sanctioned it, but he had assumed it would be rebuilt.'

'And why wasn't it?'

Leroy shrugged again. 'Money. I suppose in this modern world it all comes down to that. It would cost too much to rebuild and by selling the land it was reasoned we would make a lot more money which would allow us to extend our mission and help many more people.'

Coco nodded. 'If that was the case, why was he so angry about it? I mean, if it was as simple as making a whole heap of money and moving on to a bigger and better centre, why was he so pissed about it?'

Aries winced when she cursed, fixing her with a scolding glare. 'He was,' he coughed, 'angry, because he believed the money had been allocated for the rebuilding of the centre by Monsieur Peron.'

'And had it?'

'Gasper was keen for the centre to remain where it was,' Aries replied. 'Mais, he was also a pragmatist. However he might have made his money originally, he was a businessman. He would have seen the sense in selling the land and moving our efforts elsewhere.' He narrowed his eyes. 'I realise it may be difficult for you to understand basic economics, but that's the truth of the matter.'

'Merci for the mansplaining,' Coco said cheerfully. 'I don't know if I'd ever have been able to come to that conclusion myself without your help.' She bit her lip and turned back to Frère Leroy. 'So, you fired Odilon Sander because he didn't agree with your decision?'

'It wasn't a question of dismissing him,' Leroy conceded. 'Rather he did not agree with the decision that had been made, and because of his strong feelings it was mutually agreed to terminate our involvement.'

'Bit harsh,' Coco mouthed.

'And yet it seems he successfully made other plans,' Aries said, his voice laced with irony.

'Plans which seems to have resulted in his death,' Cedric suggested.

Aries's lips twisted into a smirk. 'And I can't imagine what you might think that has to do with us? Odilon made his decision. He did not support the selling of the land, but in the end, it was nothing to do with him, and in any the event he moved on to another job, or whatever it was he was doing with his time,' he added, his jowls wobbling as he laughed.

Coco grimaced. 'He's dead,' she snapped. 'As far as I can tell, the last people who saw him alive were in this monastery.'

'You can't say that,' Mathieu interrupted. 'His murderer was the last person to see him alive.'

Coco moved her head slowly towards him. He smiled at her, pushing the hair from his face. 'Exactly.'

Aries sighed. He pointed at the clock on the wall. 'Are we done now?'

'Almost,' Coco replied. 'What can you tell me about Gasper Peron?'

'That sounds like a third question,' Frère Aries mumbled under his breath.

Leroy shrugged. 'Nothing that would help you.'

'Let me be the judge of that,' Coco shot back. 'Because as far as I can tell there's some shady shit going down.'

'Shady shit?' Frère Henri Aries repeated.

Coco giggled. 'You swore,' she laughed. 'I didn't know you were allowed.'

'We do a lot of things most people don't think we're allowed to do,' Mathieu interrupted, reminding her of what he had said earlier.

Coco continued to ignore him. He frowned at her, as if he was wondering what he might have done to offend her. She turned again to Leroy. 'I want you to tell me everything you know about Gasper Peron and work on the assumption that I am in charge of the investigation and I will decide what is or is not important. If you do that, then I think we'll all get along much better, non? And as for all that confidentiality shit, I think we can safely assume we've moved on from that by now. Peron ending up in a skip kinda cancels it out, don't you think?'

Frère Henri Aries pushed himself back in his chair, it groaned under his weight. He reached over and whispered something into Frère Leroy's ear. Coco could not hear what he said, but judging by the senior monks changing expression, it was something he did not like.

Leroy turned his head slowly to face Coco and Cedric. 'No doubt by now you know of Gasper's past.'

'Oui, we do,' Cedric replied.

Leroy nodded. 'Whilst I don't condone his actions, neither do I judge them. The Gasper I knew was a good man whose intent was to do good. It was his intention to atone for past indiscretions…'

'Past indiscretions?' Coco interrupted. 'People aren't given lengthy prison sentences for indiscretions,' she stated.

Henri Aries coughed. 'I think Frère Leroy was quite implicit. Our job is not to judge, but to accept people into our fold. Those who are repentant are entitled to forgiveness, are they not?'

Coco moved her shoulders quickly. 'I'm not sure it's so easy for everyone to forgive when they are the ones that find themselves on the receiving end of bad behaviour.' She took a deep breath. 'And I suppose you might say your forgiveness was tempered by Gasper Peron's deep pockets.'

'That's an outrageous thing to say!' Henri Aries hissed.

Gerard Leroy touched the other monk's arm reassuringly. 'I can see how it might look that way, Captain Brunhild,' Leroy said, his voice calm and soothing. 'What Gasper chose to do with his money was entirely his own affair, but I would be lying if I said I wasn't very grateful he chose to help us in our endeavours. His contribution was invaluable and will continue to be invaluable for some time. The centre was very important to him. He spent a great deal of time there. Gasper talked little of his past, and I certainly had no intention of prying, but on the few occasions he did speak of it, I saw how important it was for him to be a part of something good and constructive in the lives of young people.'

'Atoning for past sins,' Cedric mused.

Henri Aries narrowed his eyes, his jowls wobbling with irritation. 'Would you rather he didn't, young man? What would be the sense in that? None of us are perfect, it is what we do with repentance that matters. Frère Peron was intent on doing wonderful things with the remainder of his life.' He trailed off, his face twisting with sadness. 'Sadly, it was not to be a long life, mais his generosity will continue to do wonderful things.'

'Speaking of that,' Coco pondered. 'What was with selling off the land to the highest bidder if you had so much money?'

Leroy spread his hands in front of him. 'The decision, ultimately was not our own,' he threw a shady look at Mathieu who dropped his head as if he was ashamed or embarrassed. Leroy continued. 'Once it was decided that the building was no longer fit for purpose and was in fact dangerous, it of course made sense to sell the land to the highest bidder. The decision was made in all our best interests, really. There will be another centre built in another location and I can assure you it will be in honour of Gasper and his contribution, not just financial but also for all the fine work he did volunteering at the centre. He was an excellent mentor to many young people.'

Coco guffawed. 'Mentoring them in what? How to make a fortune selling drugs?'

Mathieu laughed, immediately receiving a scolding look from Frère Aries. Aries continued. 'As I said. His past was his past. Whatever he had done then was behind him and he had gone on to achieve many great things. Gasper was teaching the young people the value of reinvention and never giving up on yourself, no matter how many missteps you might make.'

Coco pulled out her notepad and scribbled something on it. It was nonsense but she wanted to take a moment to gather her thoughts because she was struggling to retain focus with the intent stares of three monks boring down on her. There was something they were holding back, she was sure of it, but what it was, and if it was important to the investigation, she could not be sure.

Henri Aries cleared his throat again. 'I'm not sure what Monsieur Peron's death and legacy has to do with any of this. I mean, there were three coffins taken, weren't there?'

Coco nodded. 'Oui. And we're looking at the other coffins, however, as far as I can tell, they didn't lead quite as interesting a life as your patron did. A monk and a spinster. And then there's the fact Monsieur Peron's corpse was replaced by an altogether more recently deceased person. Which makes me wonder. Did Gasper Peron and Odilon Sander know each other?'

'They were very good friends,' Leroy confirmed. 'Gasper was friends with both Odilon and Chantel, indeed he was godfather to Vichy, their son.'

Coco raised an eyebrow. 'Now, that is interesting. A small

world, indeed.'

'I don't see anything strange in it,' Henri Aries snapped. 'After all, they worked closely together at the youth centre. It makes perfect sense they would become friends.'

'Close enough to share a coffin,' Coco muttered.

'Excusez moi?' Aries asked leaning forward, cocking his head in her direction.

'Rien,' Coco said. 'I was just thinking out loud, that's all.'

Frère Leroy rose to his feet. 'Well, if that's all Captain Brunhild, we have evening prayers.'

Coco nodded. 'D'accord. One last thing. What can you tell me about Sofia Charton, Idris Cellier and Jericho Martin?'

Leroy shrugged. 'They are young people who used to come to the centre. Their families are fine members of our community.'

'Oui,' Coco replied. 'Mais we also have it on good authority these three rather charming individuals were up to their necks in what is commonly called hazing, which, as far as I'm concerned, is just bullying by another name. Rich kids exerting their authority over kids they deem to be lesser.' She stopped, noticing Mathieu Moreau was breathing quickly, his eyes dropped towards the table. She stared at Leroy. 'You were aware of what they were up to though, weren't you? And before you think of lying to me again, just know I have it on high authority, you might say, that you knew all about their shenanigans.'

Leroy exhaled. 'It was harmless enough,' he began. 'Hijinks, you might call it.'

'Not if you're on the receiving end of it, I'm sure,' Coco quipped. 'What can you tell us about them?'

Leroy shrugged. 'Very little, I'm afraid, other than they come from prominent families in the neighbourhood. Sofia's mother a fashion designer, and Idris's father is actually the developer in charge of the demolition site.'

Coco tapped her head, recalling Aaron Cellier. 'Ah, I knew I recognised the name. He was the one who discovered the coffins,' she mused, wondering what significance it might have. She also recalled a conversation they had where it had appeared that Monsieur Cellier senior was less than happy when talking about his son's experience and time at the centre. She made a mental note to seek him out and press him for more information. After their discussion, Coco had gained the impression he was troubled by what had happened to his son at the youth centre and she was fairly sure he had made no secret of the fact he was pleased it was to be demolished.

'And what about Jericho Martin?' Cedric asked.

Leroy's eyes narrowed. 'I believe his family run a very successful business.'

Coco pursed her lips. Judging by the monk's tone, she suspected he was not impressed with Jericho Martin and his family, which suggested to her it was because it was something less than impressive, which is also why she supposed someone like Pierre Duchamp was representing him.

'Were you aware they were still accessing the Abbaye crypt?' Cedric continued. His tone was direct and he appeared bored.

Leroy lifted his head. 'Non, I was not, but believe me, it will not be something that happens again,' he stated, his eyes flicking in Mathieu's direction. 'Anyway, Captain, as I said, we must get to evening prayers.' He pulled open the door, causing the monastery housekeeper Estelle Grainger to jump back, her cheeks flashing with embarrassment at being caught seemingly listening at the door.

Coco suppressed a smile. 'That's okay. We can have a word with your housekeeper, save us a trip back.'

'Very well,' Leroy replied, gesturing for Frères Mathieu and Henri to follow him. Mathieu rose slowly to his feet, all the time staring directly at Coco. Instead of looking at him, she gestured for the housekeeper to enter the room.

19H00

Estelle Grainger moved slowly into Frère Leroy's office, closing the door behind her hesitantly. She crossed the sparsely furnished room and pulled out a chair, positioning it directly in the middle of the table opposite Coco and Cedric. She toyed with the scarf around her neck, fixing Coco with a defiant look. Coco could not determine the age of the prim and proper woman, other than she appeared older than she most likely was. 'I've been expecting you,' Estelle sniffed.

Coco was surprised. 'You have? Pourquoi?'

Estelle pulled at the scarf. 'Isn't that what you do? Don't the police like to throw grenades into peoples lives just because they can?'

Coco and Cedric exchanged a look. 'So, this isn't your first time in front of a flic, then?' Coco enquired.

Estelle rang her fingers across drab, lifeless hair. She opened her mouth to respond but seemingly thought better of it. 'I don't know what you think I can tell you,' she said instead.

'Were you aware one of the monks was allowing people to sneak into the crypt?' Cedric asked.

She snorted. 'Bien sûr,' she laughed, her voice cold and sarcastic. 'However, Mathieu Moreau is no monk,' she added with bite. 'Not really, not like the other fine men who are here and devoting their life to Dieu.'

Coco dropped onto one of the vacant chairs. 'He isn't?' she asked cheerfully.

Cedric tutted before turning back to Estelle. 'What do you mean by that, Mademoiselle?'

Estelle folded her hands onto her lap, thin pale lips twisting. It was clear to Coco that Estelle was wrestling with what she should and should not say. It took her a minute to reach her decision, a sly smile appearing on her face.

'The Moreau family practically own this entire neighbourhood and they do as most rich people do, they use their money to control and exert their will.' She looked over her shoulder as if she was reassuring herself the door was still closed. 'Mathieu's grandfather created this monastery, though he saw no reason to become a monk himself, too difficult I suppose for a man with an eye for the ladies as he did, mais, he did the next best thing, he had his daughter sacrifice her own child because he never managed to have a boy of his own.'

'Mathieu,' Coco exhaled. 'I got the sense he wasn't… like… the other monks here.'

'It's not his fault,' Estelle said with obvious reluctance. 'Mathieu's not a bad boy, I suppose, but he has no business being here.'

'Then where should he be?' Coco demanded.

Estelle frowned as if she did not understand the question. After a few moments, she shrugged. 'He should be running with the pack of wolves he allows to sneak into the crypt. You think we didn't know what he was up to? It was pitiful, the brothers said nothing for fear of upsetting Mathieu's mother as she holds the purse-strings, and the other families who throw money like it's confetti. Mathieu gets to live vicariously through his friends. It's like he can still be part of it, without actually having to slip out of his cassock.'

Coco leaned forward. 'You really don't like him, do you? Why? I just don't get it. He doesn't seem a bad kid, even you don't say he is. He's a victim of circumstance if anything.'

Estelle looked around the room. 'For some of us, this place is sacred. It saved us when we needed it the most. It gave us sanctuary and hope when we had none.' She exhaled. 'My life was very different before I came here, you are correct about that. I was, you might say, a very different person before I walked through these gates, and because of that I resent anyone who takes advantage of this sanctuary.'

'Mathieu is hardly taking advantage,' Coco reasoned. 'He's doing what was asked of him by his family. I can't say I approve of it, but I do understand it.'

Estelle moved her shoulders nonchalantly.

Coco crossed her legs. 'You talk about the sanctuary of this monastery. Mais, it wasn't just for you, was it? There was also Gasper Peron.'

Estelle clenched her fists. 'I don't know what you're talking about,' she said defensively.

Coco shook her head. 'See, you're going to have to do better than that if you want to bullshit a bullshitter. Spill it, or me and my lieutenant here are going to have to assume you're up to your starch collared neck in all of the shady business going on here, and if we think that, we're going to have to take a real long hard look at your journey to this so-called sanctuary.'

Estelle picked a piece of fluff from her plain dress. It appeared to Coco to be made of the same material as the monk's cassocks. She slowly lifted her head. 'I won't have you, or anyone else for that matter, destroy what has been built here.'

'That sounds rather like a threat,' Coco retorted.

Estelle shrugged nonchalantly. 'You can take it any way you choose. I just know the way I intend it.'

'This isn't going to go away,' Cedric interrupted. 'Not at least until we figure out why three coffins were stolen from this Abbaye and one of them filled with a dead body of a man who, by all accounts, was loved by everyone.'

Estelle snorted.

'Not quite by everyone, it seems,' Coco suggested.

Estelle pushed back the chair, the legs scraping against the tiled floor. 'I have nothing else to say, other than this - you need to look elsewhere if you are going to get the answers you seek.'

Coco frowned. 'What is that supposed to mean?'

The older woman shrugged. 'It means look elsewhere.'

'I'm not sure you understand. We are police officers, and we are investigating a very serious crime,' Coco stated forcefully. 'I won't tolerate you playing games with me.'

Estelle laughed. 'I answer to a higher master than you, and I am scared only of him.' She folded her hands across her chest. 'Now, excuse me, I have to prepare supper.'

'We're not done here,' Cedric interrupted.

She laughed again. 'We most certainly are. Au revoir.'

Coco and Cedric watched in amazement as the diminutive woman swept from the room without looking back.

'Well, would you get a load of her?' Coco asked sounding half-impressed.

'What did you make of her?' Cedric asked.

Coco considered her response, shaking her head in disbelief. 'It's hard to tell. She's got balls of steel, I'm sure of that. Whatever she was in her past, she's not scared of us, or anything, it seems. And she's loyal to the monks, but she's also a watcher.'

'What do you mean?'

Coco stood up and began pacing across the room. 'Only that in my opinion, there's not a chance she doesn't know everything that has gone on here.'

'Then we bust her. Get her in an interview room and make her tell us what she knows,' Cedric said forcefully.

Coco shook her head. 'I get the impression she's spent enough time in interview rooms to know how to dodge questions and cover her back.'

'Then what do you suggest we do?'

'Beats the shit out of me,' Coco sighed.

Cedric stretched his arms above him and flexed the muscles in both of his arms as if he was giving himself a chance to think.

'What about that whole "look elsewhere," business?' he asked after a while, ignoring the keen look Coco was giving him as he exercised.

Coco shrugged. 'She might just be trying to distract us, to get us to look away from the Abbaye and the youth centre. All we can really do is find out who the hell she is. That might give us a chance, to find some ammunition to get her to spill her guts. Speak to Ebba, look into Estelle Grainger and shake her tree and see what falls from it. Whoever she was, I bet she had a very different sort of life before she came here.'

Cedric sighed. 'We're not really getting very far, are we? We keep going round and round in circles and no one is actually helping us. Demissy isn't going to be happy.'

Coco snorted. 'So what? That's her default setting. Even if we had a result she'd still find something to bitch about.' She stopped and looked at her watch. 'I must get home and relieve Helga. It's bingo night and she's even more hellish to live with if she misses it.' She stood. 'Tomorrow is another day, it can't get any worse, can it?'

Cedric shook his head and shuddered. 'You always bitch at me when I say something like that.'

Coco moved towards the door. 'Yeah, cos I'm a bitch. But in any event, I can't see how this mess can get any worse, can you?'

MARDI / TUESDAY

06H00

'Answer your damn phone,' Helga growled before deftly aiming the phone towards a snoring Coco. It bounced off her head, dropping onto the still-snoring form of Coco's youngest child, Esther. Coco's eyes jerked open, widening with confusion. The room was still dark, only a small slither of light slicing through a broken window blind.

'Answer your damn phone,' Helga repeated, before adding with a sneer, 'or I will break it,' she added in heavily accented broken English. 'And you know I can break it with my bare hands if I choose to.'

Coco scrabbled desperately around until she found the phone and slapped it against her ear. 'Who the hell is this? I hate you,' she mumbled incoherently.

Sonny laughed. 'Bonjour, Charlotte.'

'I hate you,' she repeated. 'Someone better be dead, or they will be when I get my hands on them.'

'Be careful what you wish for,' he replied.

Coco pushed herself up in the bed, suddenly wide-awake.

'You'd better get down to *Abbaye Le Bastien*, right away,' Sonny added. 'I'll meet you there.'

It only took Coco a moment, even with her foggy early morning brain, to pull herself together. 'Merde!' she cried. 'I had to open my big fat mouth, didn't I?'

Coco sucked irritably on a cigarette and drained the contents of the café. The drink was lukewarm and tasted disgusting, so she tossed it onto the ground, watching it bounce away. It satisfied her irritation.

She pressed her body against the bonnet of the car and prepared herself to enter the Abbaye. The gates had been pushed open and a pair of officers were standing sentry as Ebba and the forensic team moved hurriedly backwards and forwards.

The tip of the cigarette illuminated Coco's face, her eyes locked on the gates. All she had been told so far was there had been a murder reported in the Abbaye, but no identification had been made. That troubled her. Why had no identification been made? There was only one reason she could think of - the body was unrecognisable.

On the journey over she ignored many red lights and speed limits, because all she had been able to think about was a young man with jet black hair which fell in clumps across his right eye, and she had prayed to someone she did not believe in that it was not him.

'What's happening?' Cedric asked, appearing out of the darkness. The sun had barely moved across the sky, only casting shadows across the tall buildings which lined the street opposite the monastery.

'Jesus!' Coco cried dropping the cigarette down her top. 'Dammit, you scared me. Help me find the cigarette.'

Cedric sucked his teeth. 'I don't know how many more times a week I need to say this. I am not putting my hand down your top, on your ass, nowhere. Never, not again. I've been there, and I certainly don't intend on EVER going there again.'

They both stopped suddenly. Someone else had appeared behind them. He cleared his throat. Coco peered over Cedric's shoulder. Mathieu Moreau smiled at her. It took her a moment to recognise him because he was not wearing a cassock, rather a white t-shirt and boxer shorts. It bothered Coco that her first thought was, *it isn't him.* And that her second thought was, *damn he's fine.*

'That isn't how it sounds,' Cedric stuttered in the way he did a hundred times a month when Coco insisted on telling everyone the experiences they had shared together.

Coco wafted her hand. 'Pay no attention to him. Some men never get over being Coco'd.'

Mathieu's pale face pulled into a tight smile. 'As I've said before - I might be a monk, but I am still a man.' He stopped and looked over his shoulder. 'I'm glad you're here. It's awful.'

Cedric stepped around Coco. 'What happened exactly? Nobody's telling us anything yet.'

Mathieu grimaced. 'Do you have a cigarette?'

Coco smiled. 'Sure. I can almost hear my father now - *Charlotte Brunhild, corrupting innocents since the eighties.*'

'Eighties?' Mathieu questioned, his left eyebrow arching.

'Nineties… noughties…' she stuttered desperately.

Cedric tutted, glaring at Coco and whispering. *'Dead body?'*

Coco pulled herself together. 'What's awful, Mathieu? Who is dead? We're still waiting to get into the Abbaye.' She stopped and pulled two cigarettes from her pocket and lit them. She handed one to the young monk. 'Who is dead?' she repeated.

He shook his head repeatedly, almost as if he could not stop. Coco had to reach to him and touch the side of his face to stop him. He stared wide-eyed at her. She could not be sure, but he appeared to be in shock. 'I don't know,' he mumbled. 'I got up for morning prayers and… and I found him… just lying there. I… I've never seen anything like it before. He was just on the ground and there was so much blood. And his face… his face…'

'His face?' Cedric asked soothingly.

'I didn't recognise his face,' Mathieu spat the words out slowly in such a way it appeared they were too painful for him to voice.

Coco noticed he had begun to shiver, the hairs on his legs and arms standing on end. She looked around and realised all she had was her trusty woollen coat. Decisively she removed it and quickly wrapped it around him. It fitted badly, barely covering his thighs, but he pulled it tight around his chest, emitting a sigh as if he was grateful for the warmth. She looked at Cedric and he shrugged as if he did not know what to do either.

After a minute, Mathieu's eyes suddenly widened. 'How didn't I recognise his face? He was one of my brothers…'

'Mathieu,' she began. 'I have to ask you a question. Did you leave the gate unlocked again last night?'

He stared at her as if he did not understand what she was asking. 'Non, I didn't, I swear. You do believe me, don't you?'

Before Coco could respond, she noticed Sonny moving slowly away from the Abbaye. He gestured to her.

Coco looked desperately at Cedric and he shrugged. *I'm not babysitting him,* he mouthed. She leaned in and whispered into Cedric's ear. 'Then make sure someone keeps an eye on him.'

'Hey, Mathieu,' Coco said finally, taking him by the arm and gently guiding him in the direction of her car. 'Why don't you have a seat in my car? It's warm and you can listen to some music. It's Barbra Streisand, so sorry about that because you've probably never even heard of her, but you should have, so now's probably a good time to start, so sorry not sorry, really. Anyho…'

'Captain,' Cedric interrupted irritably.

'Oh, yeah,' Coco responded. She manoeuvred Mathieu into a seat, pushing pizza boxes and fast-food wrappers out of the way. He slumped forward without saying a word. Coco turned on the ignition, immediately filling the car with a burst of heat and too-loud music. *It was raining when I met you.* 'You're lucky,' she smiled, 'it's a classic. So just listen and I'll be back before you know it.'

Mathieu turned his head slowly to her. There was no doubt he was in shock, she decided. 'Don't be long,' he mumbled desperately.

Coco winked at him. 'I'll be back before you know it, sailor.'

06H15

Coco and Cedric crept slowly across the tiles Ebba Blom had placed from the entrance gates to the Abbaye, trailing in the direction of the anteroom at the entrance of the monastery where they had interviewed the monks and Estelle Grainger the previous evening. Coco stopped suddenly, causing Cedric to crash into her. He followed her gaze. A sandal was sticking out from underneath the table, attached to an uncovered leg. Coco lowered herself to her haunches, immediately recoiling at the bunched-up cassock.

'Come to the head of the table,' Sonny directed. 'Just follow the tiles. There's an awful lot of blood, so be careful where you tread.'

The two detectives gingerly made their way around the edge of the room. Coco shivered. She was still wearing her pyjama top after leaving her coat with Mathieu. The room was damp and cold. She stopped abruptly once again upon seeing the twisted body at the head of the table. The face was turned an unnatural angle away from the body but that was not the worst of it. The entire face was unrecognisable, covered in blood and cuts. One eye was open but it was dark and covered in blood. Coco could not even make out what colour it was.

'Jesus!' Cedric cried. 'Somebody really went to town on him, didn't they?'

Sonny's jaw flexed. 'They certainly did.' He stepped backwards. 'I don't think I've seen anything like this for a long time.'

Coco stepped next to him. 'Seems like overkill to me,' she said, 'if you pardon the expression.'

Sonny gave her a sad, tired smile. 'You might well be right.' He pointed to the face. 'I can't be certain yet, but I think the damage to the face came after death.'

Coco frowned. 'Really?'

He shrugged, bending down and lifting up the cassock. The torso was also bloodied and bruises were already appearing. 'He took quite a good beating. I'd put time of death at somewhere within the last six to eight hours. Rigor has started, mais it's not fully developed yet.'

Ebba appeared in the doorway. 'I had the stroppy housekeeper do a headcount,' she stated, 'and the only person unaccounted for is Frère Gerard Leroy.'

Coco took a sharp breath. She stared at what remained of the face. 'I wouldn't have recognised him.'

Cedric stepped forward. 'We talked with Frère Leroy at about 19h00 last night and then he was going off to evening prayers with the other monks, so that might help narrow down the timeline a little.'

'What the hell happened to him, Sonny?' Coco demanded.

'I need to spend some time figuring that out,' he replied after a few moments. He pointed at the torso again. 'He was beaten, I can't tell what with exactly. I've performed a preliminary examination but I don't think any of the blows were fatal.' He moved back towards the body and slowly lifted the head.

'Ouch,' Coco gasped. There was a large open wound on the back of the skull. 'That had to hurt.'

'And was most likely catastrophic.' He stepped away again and moved across the walls. In the centre of the wall was a tall, large open marble fireplace. He gestured to the lefthand corner.

Coco followed him, narrowing her eyes to stare at it. She could not quite make out what it was, other than it appeared to be a blob of lumpy gloop. 'What's that mush?'

'Ebba's taken swabs,' Sonny replied, 'but I think it's likely we're looking at blood and brain matter from the deceased.'

Coco took a step back, her eyes moving slowly back and

forth between the position of the body and the fireplace. There was a gap of only a few feet. 'It's possible someone pushed him against the fireplace, which caused the catastrophic head injury, and then he fell forward again, landing in the position we found him.'

'Or he could have just fallen backwards and hit his head,' Cedric suggested. 'It could have been an accident,' he reasoned.

'I don't see how,' Coco insisted. 'Look at his face. He took a hell of a beating.' She turned to Sonny. 'Pre or post mortem?'

Sonny stared at the bloodied face. 'Like I said, it's actually very difficult to tell. There is a lot of damage to the face, and also a lot of blood. We could be looking at a mixture of both.'

Coco pursed her lips. 'Then it seems to me he was beaten and either pushed or fell backwards onto the fireplace and that is what ultimately killed him.'

'That would be my hypothesis, also,' Sonny confirmed.

She pointed to the face. 'This is wrong in so many ways. Mais, I don't think this was an accident. The fall on its own, possibly, but the beating and mutilation tells a different kind of story.'

'What do you mean?' Cedric asked.

'Post-mortem destruction like this is different, it's… it's…'

'Personal,' Sonny concluded.

'Exactement!' Coco exclaimed.

Cedric stared at the desecrated face. 'Then you think he knew his killer?'

'I'd certainly say so,' Coco answered. She stared, shaking her head. 'And more importantly we can't rule out the similarity to what happened to Odilon Sander. His face looked pretty much the same. She studied the face carefully. 'Which makes me wonder. Just how similar are we talking?'

Sonny moved next to her, lowering himself onto his haunches. He pulled a magnifying glass from his apron and held it over the face, moving slowly across it. 'Ah-ha,' he exclaimed after a minute had passed.

'What have you found?' Coco asked keenly.

Sonny pointed to the dead monk's left cheek. 'I'll need to get him cleaned up properly to be certain, but look in the centre of the blood pool. Do you see it?'

Coco stared. It did not take her long to see the two round burns, an inch apart. 'He was burnt,' she stated.

Sonny raised himself to his feet. 'I'd say it's likely. Probably a Taser.'

Coco looked at Cedric. 'Exactly like Odilon Sander.'

Cedric stepped across the tiles, moving to the fireplace. 'So, whoever attacked him subdued him with a Taser, and then what? He stumbles backwards and cracks his skull open on the fireplace?' He frowned. 'Then why the beating afterwards?'

'To hide the Taser marks?' Coco suggested. 'Peut être they didn't want us to be too quick to link the two murders, or more importantly the way he was murdered. How easy is it to get a Taser, or a stun gun, or whatever? Are they traceable?'

Ebba shook her head. 'Not in this case. If it was a Taser there would be traceable confetti in the room, with tiny serial numbers printed on it and I don't see any so it must be an ESW, an electroshock weapon. They work on the same principle but are for close quarters defence so don't fire out the electrodes, just zap like a cattle prod. You can buy them easily enough and you don't need to register them. You just have to "justify" yourself if you discharge one on someone. There are several different models. I have five myself.'

'Damn girl,' Coco exclaimed. 'Remind me not to cross you.'

Ebba flicked her eyes over Coco. 'I wouldn't waste the volts on you,' she stated.

Coco frowned. 'Merci,' she replied, 'I think...'

'It would be a waste,' Ebba continued. 'A person your size is harder to subdue quickly. I'd probably use a twelve-inch serrated hunting knife. Quick and effective. Does the job.'

Coco raised her eyes at Sonny. He smiled. 'Wow, you've really thought this through, haven't you?' Coco asked.

Ebba shrugged. 'Why not? You have to know what you're going to do if you need to take someone out in a hurry.'

'And what about me?' Cedric interrupted with a laugh. 'You'd knee me in the nuts, I suppose?'

Ebba's eyes flicked over him. 'I would if I thought you had any, steroid boy.'

Sonny clapped his hands. 'Enfants! Enfants! Do I have to remind you why we are here…' He stopped, pointing at the body of Frère Leroy.

'Yeah, désolé,' Coco said. 'Ebba. So, you're telling me they're not unique, like bullets, par example?

'Not really,' Ebba replied. 'If you find me the stun gun in question I might be able to compare the burn mark seperation and burn depth. It may even have DNA transfer from the dead guys.'

Coco pondered. 'Well, it might just explain why someone wouldn't want us to look too closely at the Taser link in case we could somehow trace it back to them.'

Cedric flashed her a doubtful look.

'It's a lead,' Coco stated defensively. 'And if I'm right about it, then it means they really didn't want us looking too closely at it, which means they're scared they've made a mistake.'

'Peut être,' he conceded, 'mais, that's not really going to help us too much. We're not going to get mandates to search everyone's house.'

'And if they've half a brain, the stun gun's probably at the bottom of the Seine by now,' Ebba added.

Coco emitted a loud, long sigh. 'Either way, we've got a dead monk, who didn't meet a nice end.' She stared at Frère Gerard Leroy. 'I'm sorry this happened to you, mais I will find who is responsible.' She spun around and clapped her hands. 'D'accord.

Ebba - what do we have so far in this crime scene?'

Ebba's face contorted. 'I don't think the floors have been properly cleaned for decades, so there are probably thousands of footprints in this room and the same goes for fingerprints. I'll take what I can, but I wouldn't get too excited about finding anything helpful.'

'Story of my life,' Coco said glumly. She turned to Cedric. 'Round up some officers and do a door-to-door, see if anyone saw or heard anything last night.'

'According to the housekeeper, the gate was locked from the inside and it's the only way in and out,' Ebba interjected.

Cedric snorted. 'That means nothing.' He stole a look at Coco. 'We know *some* of the monks open the gates when it suits them.'

'Okay,' Coco said with determination. 'Line up the monks and we can...'

'Can't,' Ebba interrupted.

'What do you mean, you can't?' Coco demanded.

Ebba shrugged. 'Apparently they're in morning prayers now, and "praying for the soul of their brother" and therefore can't be disturbed.'

'The hell they can't...'

'I stole a look at them,' Ebba added. 'And for what it's worth, I didn't see any bruised knuckles.'

Coco tutted. 'They could have worn gloves, which means there's all the more reason to drag them out of their sodding prayers...'

Sonny touched Coco's arm. 'Charlotte. They've just lost one of their brothers. Let them process that, at least for a little while. These are holy men, men of Dieu who need to pray. It's important to them.'

'Fine,' she snapped tartly. She looked at her watch before turning to Cedric. 'I'm hungry. I spotted a café across the street, so

I'm going for breakfast. Stay here and keep an eye on them. Make sure no one leaves the monastery or makes a phone call. In fact, keep them apart so they can't concoct any more lies and get the chance to destroy any evidence.'

'Actually, they pray in silence,' Ebba stated.

Coco frowned. 'What's the point in doing anything in silence?' she demanded. 'Silent prayers or not, all I know is that someone beat Frère Leroy to death and then butchered his face.' She pointed towards the doorway. 'And someone in this monastery knows something they're not telling us, I'd bet my life on it.' She took a deep breath. 'D'accord. Sonny, you'll call me when you're ready for the autopsy?'

'Bien sûr.'

She nodded. 'Merci.' She looked around the room as she headed towards the door. 'I really hate this damn place.'

07H00

Coco stared at the pile of food on the plate and felt guilty. Money had been tight in the Brunhild household for a long time, but not more so than in recent times. The breakfast was substantial and not expensive, however like everything else in her life, each cent she spent on herself felt like a cent she was stealing from her children.

She took a mouthful of sausage and moved it slowly around her mouth, chastising herself for feeling guilty. She knew she was about to experience another full and most likely traumatic day, so she needed as much substance as she could get. She reached to her coat, feeling for the reassuring shape of a packet of cigarettes. Her hand stopped and moved around quickly in a desperate search for them. And then she remembered. Her coat was currently wrapped around the toned body of a monk she had no business in thinking about. She took another bite.

'You look like you're enjoying that.'

Coco did not need to look around to know who the voice belonged to.

'I was watching the monastery from across the street. I kept trying to go back inside, but I just couldn't. And then I saw you coming out,' Mathieu Moreau said. He smiled, looking at the plate of fried food in front of her. 'That looks… *healthy.*'

Coco pursed her lips. 'I haven't eaten for a d…' she stared at the overflowing plate, *'fortnight.'* She stabbed the fork into another sausage and nibbled the end in as demure a way as she could manage. She dropped the fork suddenly. 'I hope you don't think I was being suggestive,' she murmured.

Mathieu frowned. 'About what?' He smiled. 'Do you want your coat back now?'

Coco flicked her eyes over him. 'Are you dressed yet?'

He shook his head. 'Non. I told you, I haven't been back to the monastery since...'

'Mathieu. Is that you?'

Coco noticed the instant change in Mathieu's face and it was an expression she recognised. It was the face of a child who had just realised he was about to be chastised by a parent. She knew it because she had experienced the same thing herself on more than one occasion. It was the voice of disapproval and a clear exertion of authority. *You are my child and you will listen to me when I talk to you.*

Mathieu's eyes widened and he continued staring at Coco. *She's behind me, isn't she,* was the clear message. Coco nodded her response.

Mathieu turned around. 'Maman,' he said moving quickly towards his mother.

Coco pushed her breakfast plate away as if it did not belong to her, suddenly very conscious she was wearing a faded *Wonder Woman* pyjama top.

'What on earth are you wearing?' Mathieu's mother demanded. The voice was cold with the clear lilt of an upper-class Parisian who had most likely been educated abroad.

Coco shook her head, unruly blue hair falling in front of her eyes. It allowed her to steal a look at the other woman and immediately her heart sank. She was likely not much older than Coco herself, but they were worlds apart. She was dressed in a fur coat, platinum hair swept high above a long, narrow unlined face. If she had work done, which Coco assumed she had, it had been done well and discreetly.

Mathieu looked down at Coco's wool coat that he was still wearing. 'Ah, this belongs to my friend, Charlotte.'

His mother raised an eyebrow, a feat which did not crease her forehead. Coco clambered to her feet and extended her hand which she quickly realised was dirty. She glanced around for a napkin but could not find one, so instead she wiped them on the back of her jeans before offering a hand again. Mathieu's mother stared at it as if she had no intention of taking it.

'Captain Charlotte Brunhild,' Coco blurted, thinking how nasal and annoying her voice sounded.

'Oh, désolé,' Mathieu gushed, clearly flummoxed. 'This is my mother, Deidre.'

Deidre Moreau tipped her head slowly but said nothing to Coco, instead facing her son, her eyes flicking over him with evident despair. 'Dr. Allard called. He told me what happened to Frère Leroy. It's awful, just awful.'

Coco was taken aback, wondering how Joël Allard had discovered the news of the death of Frère Leroy, and more importantly why he had called Mathieu's mother. Coco hoped the news had not come from Sonny, though she was at a loss to think of a reason why he would.

'Come,' Deidre barked at her son. 'I must pay my respects to the other brothers.'

'I'm afraid you can't right now,' Coco interjected.

Deidre gawped at Coco, her eyes widening in surprise. 'Bien sûr, I can. In fact, I *must*. I am chairman of the trustees of *Abbaye Le Bastien*, it is my…'

'All the same,' Coco interrupted. 'Only police and forensic officers are allowed in or out of the monastery at the moment.'

'Nonsense,' Deidre sniffed, her nostrils flaring with irritation in a way which told Coco she was not used to being questioned in any way.

Coco shook her head. 'Soz, but that's the way it is.'

Deidre opened her mouth to respond, but before she could Mathieu gently touched her arm. 'Can we just go home, Maman? I really don't want to go back to the monastery right now. I found his body and I just don't think I can face it.'

Deidre's face went visibly pale as she studied him. 'How

terrible of me. I didn't think. Oh, my darling, come here.' She pulled her son into a tight embrace. 'My driver is outside, of course he'll take us home.' She glared at Coco. 'I shall expect you to inform me as soon as I am able to pay my respects,' she commanded, her tone completely changing. It had been soft and gentle with Mathieu, as if she was speaking to a much younger child, but when she had turned to Coco the coldness had instantly returned.

'You'll be the first to know,' Coco said cheerfully.

Deidre pointed at Coco's coat. 'Give that back to her, right away, Mathieu,' she scolded.

Mathieu nodded and silently removed the coat and handed it back to Coco, mouthing an apology to her. Deidre manhandled her son out of the café without acknowledging Coco. She slumped back into the seat and watched them leave, realising suddenly how young Mathieu seemed. She sighed and reached for the plate of food. 'Waste not, want not, Charlotte,' she muttered to herself.

07H45

Coco found Cedric engaged in a heated debate with Ebba at the entrance to the monastery. She exhaled, suddenly feeling very tired knowing that at such an early hour her day was about to become very, very long.

She looked at her watch, realising that yet again she was not able to walk her two youngest children to school. They would walk in silence, hand in hand with Helga, who would be the one to kiss them on the cheek and turn away, relieved that for at least another six or seven hours her day would be her own and one she could do as she pleased with.

There were days when Coco envied the elderly German nanny who had, despite her earlier life, settled into something comfortable and safe. Coco hated the fact she could only pay Helga so little, but it appeared she did not mind so much because she was living a life where she was in charge of her own destiny and not be beholden to anyone, particularly the man who had ruled her for so long.

Coco was aware Helga still carried the mental and some physical scars from her previous life - marriage to a man whose brutality was so severe he often left his wife chained to a radiator in the basement. Coco and Helga talked little of those times, but it was never far from Coco's mind that Helga's husband could turn up one day and she was prepared for it. Whatever he had done to Helga before, he would not do so again, not if Coco had anything to do with it.

'What's going on?' Coco called out to Cedric.

'The monks are still refusing to talk,' Cedric hissed.

'We'll see about that,' Coco snapped pushing past him. He grabbed her arm.

'Demissy called while you were away,' he said. 'And she was adamant we're not to speak to the monks until the Church clears it.'

Coco frowned. 'Why didn't she call me?'

Cedric smirked. 'She said she wanted to make sure one of us understood her command and that she didn't have the strength to argue with you about it. We're to return to the station and await further instructions.'

'The hell we are,' Coco snapped. 'We now have two murders to investigate. If Demissy thinks I'm going to sit around waiting for pompous frock wearers to instruct me how to do my job, then she can kiss my,' she stopped, smiling demurely, 'pert and admittedly very cute ass.'

Ebba guffawed, before offering a quiet apology.

'She did, however, agree no one is allowed in or out until further notice,' Cedric continued. 'And that Ebba and the forensic team are to have full access to the monastery and grounds.'

'Well, that's something, I suppose,' Coco grumbled irritably. She pursed her lips, a smile appearing on her face. 'Wait, she said we weren't to speak to the monks, she didn't mention the housekeeper, did she?'

Cedric's eyes flashed. 'Non, mais I think that was implied.'

'Might be to you, it isn't to me.' She turned to Ebba. 'Did you have a chance to look into Estelle Grainger yet?'

Ebba nodded. 'Yeah. And you were right. She's got a criminal record, quite a hefty one, as it goes.'

Coco raised an eyebrow. 'Well, well, well. Mademoiselle Prim and Proper butter-wouldn't-melt has a history.'

'She didn't really deny it, or seem ashamed about it,' Cedric reasoned. 'Didn't she say something about the Abbaye saving her?'

Coco turned back to Ebba. 'But what did it save her from, exactly?'

'Busts for prostitution and selling drugs,' Ebba replied.

'Though she's been clean for a long time - no arrests at least.'

Coco laughed. 'I can't imagine anyone paying for her, although I suppose everything is a fetish these days.'

'Oh, I don't know,' Cedric interjected. 'Even that sack cloth of a dress she was wearing couldn't hide the fact she's hiding a pretty impressive rack.'

Ebba tutted. 'You really are a sexist pig, aren't you?'

He shrugged. 'Truth's the truth.'

'He's got a point, though,' Coco conceded. She looked down at her own chest. 'I'm pretty proud of mine, but even I was a little jealous.'

Cedric stared at her. 'In your dreams.' He noticed the glare from Ebba and held up his hands. 'Hey! Don't shoot the messenger, I'm just keeping it real.'

Ebba stomped away. 'If I had a gun, I just might. I'm going back to finish up at the crime scene.'

Coco watched her go. 'I think she loves you really.' She stopped to consider something. 'What is interesting though is that Estelle Grainger seems to have had a lot in common with our mysterious benefactor, Gasper Peron.'

'Not so weird really,' Cedric reasoned. 'Once people come off smack, or whatever they're doing on the streets, they often look to replace one drug for a possibly less lethal one. We've seen it before, people always think the Church is going to solve all their problems.'

'It's my experience anything to do with the Church causes more problems than it solves. But, what do I know?' Coco replied with a sigh. 'C'mon. Let's go and find the housekeeper and see what she has to say for herself.'

07H50

They found the housekeeper, Estelle Grainger, in the kitchen, arms deep in a sink, scrubbing plates with a fiery determination, stabbing a brush against a worn dish. Coco cleared her throat but Grainger did not respond. Coco inched forward, the other woman seemed to be muttering but Coco could not make out any of the words. She coughed but there was no response, so she coughed again. Estelle's head jerked upwards and she slammed her hands on the surface of the water causing it to splash everywhere.

'You scared me,' Estelle cried.

'Désolé,' Coco replied evenly. 'I didn't want to interrupt you while you were busy demolishing the dishes.'

Estelle snorted, staring down at the plates in the foamy water. Her face creased. 'I'm not sure what I was supposed to be doing. I came in here and instantly forgot what I came in for.'

Coco laughed. 'It happens to me all the time,' she said in her best soothing tone. 'You've had a tremendous shock.'

'I saw him you know,' Estelle replied after a moment had passed. 'I was in bed, for some reason I'd slept badly. I'm usually a very sound sleeper, which is odd y'know?' she asked, suddenly appearing confused. 'I grew up in the projects with four brothers and three sisters and my mother and my grandmother. Can you imagine the noise? We had two bedrooms and they were tiny and there was aways something happening. Anyway, when I first came here to the monastery, it was hard because it was so quiet. I'd never known quiet before, not in anything. But here, every noise scared me because I imagined something bad was about to happen. And then one day I slept all through the night because I realised something I'd never had thought possible. Nothing bad was going to happen.'

She stopped abruptly, fixing Coco and Cedric with a puzzled look. 'What was I talking about?'

Coco inched forward. Despite her initial misgivings about the monastery housekeeper, she could see that Estelle Grainger was clearly in shock. 'You said you slept badly last night,' Coco said softly.

Estelle's eyebrows knotted. 'Ah, oui. I tossed and turned most of the night, so of course, I slept longer than I should have. I suppose it's because of everything that's happened recently. I like to get up before morning prayers and prepare breakfast. But this morning it was Mathieu's screams that finally roused me.'

Coco took in a sharp breath. The thought of Mathieu Moreau screaming was hard to bear.

'I ran downstairs in the direction of the screams,' Estelle continued. She vigorously shook her head. 'I couldn't believe my eyes. It's one of the most terrible horrible things I've ever seen,' she added as if she had witnessed quite a number of terrible events in her life.

'Did you know who it was?' Cedric questioned.

She nodded quickly. 'Bien sûr, I did. I've known Gerard for a long time. He was not just my employer. He was a friend, a dear, *dear* friend who was always there for me, not just for me even, for everyone,' she stopped, her voice cracking. 'It didn't matter what they had done to him, I knew right away it was him and it broke my heart.'

Coco touched her arm. 'I am sorry for your loss, and I want you to know that we are going to do our very best to find out who murdered your friend.'

Estelle turned her head sharply, her mouth twisting angrily. 'You don't understand yet, do you?'

Coco frowned. 'Understand what?' she demanded.

Estelle took a deep breath. She stepped away from the sink and dried her hands on a towel. She slowly turned back to Coco and Cedric. 'You've stepped into a game where you don't understand the rules, or who you are playing against.'

'A game?' Cedric questioned keenly.

She nodded.

'You're going to have to be more specific,' Coco said forcefully. 'Because, as far as I'm concerned, we're investigating a double homicide and I don't intend to let anyone prevent us from doing so.'

'Then you're foolish if you believe you wield any sort of power over these people,' Estelle retorted.

'These people?' Coco repeated. 'Are you talking about the Catholic Church? Because believe me, I've come up against them before and managed to stand my ground, and I'll do so again. The only people I have to answer to are the poor schmucks who pay their taxes to have people like me and Cedric here do our best to keep shitty assholes off the streets. I don't care about playing politics.'

Estelle snorted again. 'Then you're either stupid, or foolish, or both.'

Coco bowed her head in agreement. 'You're probably right, but the bastards haven't got me yet. So, what's say you spill your guts to a couple of hardworking and underpaid civil servants and we'll see what we can do to make sure whatever happened to your pal doesn't get swept under the carpet?'

Estelle gave her a doubtful look.

Coco smiled. 'Listen. I get you probably don't like me. Believe it or not, I get that a lot. I'm not a woman's woman. I'm barely a man's woman, but I get by, y'know?'

She ignored the loud tut coming from Cedric. 'Excuse Monsieur Rude over there. My point is this - I am many things, but mostly I am tenacious and I hate being told what to do, by men, women, anyone who tells me I shouldn't do something just "because." Ask my commander. She hates me, but I think even she knows that all I'm going to do is my job to the best of my ability, and if that means rubbing people up the wrong way, then that's their problem not mine. I've locked horns with the Church before and that's okay, they tried their best and so did I, nobody came out of it particularly smelling of roses, but the crux of it was that some very bad people ended up paying for their crimes. And that's why I do what I do and why I'll keep doing it. Do you understand what I'm saying?'

Estelle pulled back her head. 'I'm not fucking stupid, so oui.'

Coco cackled, slapping Estelle on the back. 'Hey, you're not so bad after all.' She paused, narrowing her eyes before adding quickly. 'So, you used to be a whore, eh?'

Estelle spluttered, covering her mouth with her hand.

Coco noticed Cedric's despairing look. 'What? There's no point in burying the headline, is there?' She faced Estelle. 'Yeah?'

Estelle's head dropped. 'It was a lifetime ago.'

Coco shrugged. 'That's what they all say, which gets me thinking. What kind of housekeeping do you do for the monks here, exactly?'

'Captain,' Cedric cried despairingly.

Estelle glared at Coco. 'You really have a disgusting mind.'

Coco's mouth twisted in evident agreement. 'True enough. Mais, is it true though? Do you provide "extras" for the frock wearers?'

Estelle moved away and sunk onto a chair. 'Bien sûr, non. I told you, my life before bears no resemblance to my life now. Not in any way, shape or form. I don't even know the woman I was before, and,' she laughed bitterly, 'she certainly wouldn't know me. She'd hate me.'

She moved her fingers across the chipped wooden table before fixing Coco with a stern look. 'I understand the reason for your question, I may not like it, mais I know it is a question that will be asked were any of this to come out.' She shuddered. 'I can just imagine the headlines in the newspapers.'

Coco flashed her a smile. 'Believe me, I know all about headlines that have bugger all to do with reality,' she replied through gritted teeth. In previous years her own private life had been newspaper fodder through no fault of her own and it still smarted. Coco knew her own children had been dragged into something which had nothing to do with them, and while she had little interest in protecting herself, she had taken great umbrage in her four children bearing the brunt of scandal by adults in their orbit.

She looked at Estelle and suddenly saw the woman in a new light. She had taken an initial dislike to the monastery housekeeper, and she was not sure why because she had certainly met enough bolshy women in her life and Estelle Grainger was nowhere near the top of the list of most ferocious. The fact remained, Coco was convinced Estelle Grainger knew something, and she was keeping it from them.

She took a breath because she knew at that moment she had little to go on other than her gut instinct. There was something off in *Abbaye Le Bastien* and the youth centre formerly attached to it, Coco was certain of that, but she understood there were likely very few people who would, for their own reasons, be reluctant to assist her in any meaningful way.

Coco moved over to the table and sat down, turning her head to the side. 'Listen, I need your help. What do you think happened to Frère Leroy?'

Estelle tapped blunt fingernails against the table, her mouth twisting as if she was contemplating what to say. 'You've seen the grounds. The fence, the walls, the gate, they're all too high to climb over, and even if someone could, there are spikes to stop them getting over the other side. We used to have a problem with foxes, you see. The brothers make preserves and wine for sale in our shop, and the vermin rather likes to destroy the gardens, so it was a necessary evil.'

Cedric nodded. 'I had a look around. There are also tall trees around most of the walls and it's quite a drop to the ground,' he added with a shrug. 'I'm not saying it's impossible, but I imagine it would be difficult for anyone to gain access to the monastery from the outside, unless…'

'They were allowed in, or…' Coco took over. 'The murderer was already here.'

'That's preposterous!' Estelle exclaimed. 'This is a monastery full of great men. This isn't a prison filled with criminals.'

Coco extended her hands in front of her. 'That may be the case, but as you've demonstrated, people sometimes come to places like this to escape a past they are ashamed of. You did. And so did Gasper Peron.'

'The brothers are NOTHING like Gasper Peron,' Estelle spat.

Coco stepped forward. 'Did you know him before?'

Estelle laughed. 'To say I knew him is a stretch, but oui, our paths crossed in our previous lives.'

Coco and Cedric exchanged an interested look. 'Only in your previous lives?' Coco questioned. 'Only it is my understanding Peron was involved in the youth centre.'

She laughed again. 'It's amazing what money does, how it opens doors and erases memories. And all you have to do is profess your sorrow about your past and how you want to atone for your sins.'

'Isn't that what you did?' Cedric questioned.

Estelle glared at the young lieutenant. 'I met Gasper thirty years ago, give or take. I was a teenager then and he was in charge of the banlieue I lived in. He ran it, you might say. The drugs, the girls. And in a way, it wasn't so bad. When you have nothing and somebody offers you something, you tend to take it and ask questions later.' She shrugged. 'By the time I got around to asking questions it was too late.'

'What do you mean?' he asked.

'I was in too deep,' she answered. 'In more ways than one. Hooked on drugs and desperately sleeping with anyone who would pay me so that I could buy more, or pay off my debt, but of course, it was never enough. There were never enough men to settle my bill, and never enough money to buy more drugs. It was the same with every woman and girl. If you couldn't pay with money, there were other ways to pay,' she added with bite, before adding, 'but because he "believed" in Dieu, he wouldn't allow the use of condoms.' She snorted. 'What a good Catholic!'

Coco nodded. 'And Gasper Peron was responsible for all of this?'

'Yeah,' Estelle agreed, 'or one of his men, it didn't really matter.' She pointed at Cedric. 'When anyone fell behind or wasn't doing a good enough "job" he sent around thugs who looked like him. All muscles and cold, hard faces who said little but made sure you understood.'

Coco smiled, thumping Cedric on the bicep. 'Hey my guy here's a lot of things, a bit gym'ed up for my liking, but he's a pussycat really.' She stopped, she had a myriad of questions bouncing around her brain but she was having trouble figuring out what was important and what was not. 'How did you both end up here?'

Estelle sank onto a chair. 'I don't understand why any of this is important,' she said after taking a deep breath.

Coco moved to the chair next to her, indicating for Cedric to also take a seat. 'We have two murders,' Coco began. 'And not much of a suspect pool right now, if I'm honest, which is why anything might be important. Asking questions is how we figure out what is and isn't relevant.'

Estelle took a deep breath. 'That woman is gone, and in a way it was because of him. As much as I hated Gasper Peron, he did, I suppose, save me,' she said reluctantly.

'In what way?'

She clasped her hands together in front of her before fixing Coco and Cedric with an ice-cold stare. 'I hate you for bringing this all up again,' she hissed, before adding, 'but if it helps understand what happened to Frère Leroy then I will tell you. The last time I left prison, I came out and that night I overdosed. I nearly died, in fact I suppose you might say, I DID die. I don't know how, but word got to Gasper. And when I woke up he was there. I recognised him instantly, although he had changed. He'd gained weight, he was wearing different clothes, and he just looked,' she searched for the correct word, 'normal.'

She continued. 'You have to understand, the world we lived in before was very different. Anyway, he came to me and said he'd heard about what happened and he wanted to help. I laughed at him, telling him I didn't need the help he could offer, but he took my hand and said, if I followed him he would show me a world I could only imagine. A world of peace and tranquillity, where the quiet of our mind would not make us go crazy and do stupid things.'

Estelle took a sip of water. 'Obviously, I thought he was just trying to get me back on the game, or whatever, but as it happened, I didn't really have a lot of choice. I was homeless and penniless, and I just really couldn't face life on the streets again. Prison had been tough on me and I knew the only clients I'd get would be the ones who weren't really interested in treating me like I was a human being. So, against my better instincts I went with him and he brought me here.'

She stopped and looked around the room, her face suddenly brightening. 'It was difficult at first, especially because I was in withdrawal. But Frère Leroy took me by the hand, gave me this job and said Dieu would show me the way.'

'And he did?' Coco asked, trying to hide the doubt in her

voice.

Estelle smiled at her. 'I didn't believe it either. Not at the beginning. Mais… here I am, and here I am saved.'

'And it's all thanks to Gasper Peron,' Coco concluded.

Estelle shook her head. 'He showed me the direction of the path, but that's all. His words were never truthful.'

'You don't believe Gasper Peron was sincere?' Coco asked.

'I don't believe a word that ever came out of that man's mouth,' Estelle retorted. 'No matter how he changed, the good he did, it did not change the fact he was not truthful.'

Coco shook her head. 'I don't understand, what wasn't Gasper Peron truthful about?'

'He was lying…'

Frère Henri Aries appeared in the doorway. The rotund monk clapped his hands together as if he was trying to get the attention of an errant child. 'Mademoiselle Grainger!' he shouted, his voice cold and commanding.

Estelle gasped and jumped to her feet. 'Frère Aries,' she spluttered.

Henri's tired, watery eyes flicked angrily between Estelle and the police officers. 'It is almost 08h00,' he snapped at Estelle, pointing at the empty stove. 'And it appears you haven't even begun the breakfast.'

Estelle's eyes widened. 'Breakfast? It's just… well, it's just I thought under the circumstances…'

'I was thinking much the same myself,' Coco agreed, wiping an egg splatter from her lapel.

Aries gave Coco the sort of disparaging look she was more than used to. He swished his body back to face Estelle. 'The brothers need to eat, despite… despite what happened.'

'They also need to talk the flics,' Coco bawled.

Aries turned his head, fleshy lips twisting into a sarcastic smile. 'The only people they need to talk to right now is Dieu, as I am *sure* you have already been informed.'

'And I'm *sure* you must also know a criminal investigation trumps everything else, in one way or another, sooner or later. I mean, you know what the press are like, they'd have a field day imagining what went on here.'

She noticed the undecided expression on his face and decided to attempt to win him over. 'All I want to do is make sure we run a quick and thorough investigation into the tragic murder of not only your friend, but also Odilon Sander. I'm sure you'd agree it's in all of our best interests to make sure that happens, the Catholic Church included. Which means I can either treat you and your brothers as witnesses, or suspects, but either way, I will have to speak to you all and I will have to speak to you all sooner rather than later.'

She narrowed her eyes. 'A crime is a crime, no matter on what holy ground it has been committed.'

Aries took a deep, long breath. 'We have been though a traumatic experience. I would hope you would allow us a certain amount of lenience and consideration at this time.'

Coco nodded. 'Absolutely, but I would also hope you would give all the assistance you could. If you have nothing to hide, what's the harm?'

'We have twenty monks here, Captain Brunhild,' he responded, his tone still one of an irritated older person talking to a child. 'And we lead a solitary and peaceful existence. Over half of us have taken a vow of silence, so talking to them would seem rather redundant, non?' he added with a sarcastic tone which made her want to slap him.

Coco shrugged, her irritation with the rotund monk growing by the second. 'Well, I assume they can write, can't they? They don't have to open their yaps, they can write their answers, or is that not allowed either?'

Aries slammed his fists on the table. 'I will not allow this level of insubordination in the monastery!'

Coco leaned forward, pressing the palms of her hands onto the table. 'Do you think that kind of toys thrown out of a pram shit works on someone like me? Try it Frère and we'll see who has the biggest balls…'

'You really are the most uncouth woman,' he snapped.

She shrugged again. 'Yet another thing I'm sure will be written on my tombstone. However, let's just cut to the chase. Talking or not, I need to interview all of the people who were present in this monastery at the time of the murder, because it seems to me one of them must have seen something, or was involved, and until I can establish which it was, then I can't move my investigation forward. Do you understand that?'

'I'm not a plebeian,' Aries retorted. 'Mais, you are ignoring one simple fact. You have already established that two nights ago some person or persons "unknown" trespassed on our monastery and committed a heinous crime. You also know they did not do it alone. And,' he paused as if for drastic affect, 'it appears the person most likely to have assisted in that has chosen to remove himself from the monastery when we were all clearly "told" to remain here.' He stopped, a sly smile spreading voluptuous cheeks. 'Peut être you could start there with your "investigation?"'

Coco formed her fingers into quotation marks. 'Saying as you're so fond of these, perhaps you might "elaborate" as to exactly what YOU believe has transpired here.'

His mouth twisted. 'It's not for me to say. It is not my place to speculate. In any event, my brothers need breakfast and we need to return to some degree of normality. As has already been explained to me, no one is allowed to enter or leave the monastery other than police personnel, so what is the problem if you have to wait to speak to us until we have finished our prayers?'

Coco pulled back her shoulders. 'Because I hate the thought of giving people a chance to get their stories straight before they talk to me. It smacks of conspiracy and it mightily ticks me off.' Her eyes flicked over him. 'But I get your point. Eat, pray, do whatever you want to do, but know one thing - you might think me uncouth, and I probably am, but I can also be the biggest pain in the ass when I feel as if I'm getting the run-around. We'll be back later, Frère Aries and if you cared a jot about your friend Frère Leroy, you'll do whatever you can to make sure whoever brutalised him doesn't get away with it. Was that as succinct and uncouth as you like, Frère?'

Aries waved his hand dismissively. 'We'll talk later.' He turned away, calling over his shoulder. 'Peut être.'

08H15

Coco slapped her hands onto the steering wheel, before removing a cigarette from the pack on the dashboard and lighting it. She sucked irritably and stared out of the dirty windscreen. Cedric watched her but said nothing. He yanked the seatbelt but it did not move, so he pulled it again. It snapped backwards and he yanked it again.

'Jeez! Give the poor thing a break, you're not jerking it off,' Coco cried.

'Oh, she's back in the room,' Cedric responded, finally pulling the seatbelt over his chest and clicking it into place.

They had left the monastery in silence, trudging through the gates and making sure they were locked behind them. Once satisfied, they had continued their journey, walking slowly around the walls. Coco had insisted on a full circuit, stating she wanted to satisfy herself there was no secret door, or other entrance where someone could have gained access to the monastery. They had remained in silence, Cedric watching his Captain constantly as if confused. Finally he turned to her. 'What the hell's going on? The only thing that annoys me more about you being annoyingly loud and obnoxious is when you are quiet.'

'Pourquoi?' Coco demanded.

'Because usually something bad is about to happen.'

They had continued their lap of the monastery in silence, finally returning to the car. Coco inhaled the cigarette, blowing the smoke out of the gap in the open window. 'I hate being lied to,' she said finally.

Cedric moved muscular shoulders. 'Yeah, and? We spend every day being lied to. People aren't generally straight with flics. Why is this any different?'

'Because it is,' Coco pouted. She was not sure why she was irritated particularly. Cedric was correct. Not a single investigation was easy, and she was used to being lied to, and more importantly she was used to being told what she could and could not do in order to further her investigations.

Cedric pointed to the steering wheel. 'You actually have to move that thing if you want to move forward. We should get back to the commissariat.'

'I don't want to go back to the station,' Coco stated huffily. 'I don't know if you know this about me, but I'm not destined for cooling my heels and having Demissy breathing down my neck, telling me who I can and can't speak to.' She tipped her head towards the monastery. 'Doesn't it bother you that we're being frozen out?'

Cedric shrugged again. 'Not when we don't have much of a choice. What would you have us do? Drag twenty monks into the commissariat and demand they relinquish their vows of silence to tell us everything they know? Even if they know anything, which is doubtful, are they actually going to be honest with us?'

'My point exactly!' Coco cried. 'And it busts my chops that they're hiding behind their damn cassocks. Frère Leroy was murdered in a brutal, horrific way. So, why aren't they all stumbling over themselves to help us? There's only one reason I can think of.'

'They're protecting someone,' Cedric concluded.

'You heard Estelle Grainger,' Coco said, her eyes locked in front of her. 'She was about to break ranks and actually spill the tea on Gasper Peron, former bad guy who found Dieu. She knows the truth about him, and probably more besides, I'm sure of it. But you saw Frère Aries. I mean had he just arrived, or was he listening to make sure she didn't say too much?' Coco pondered. 'Either way, he shut her down pretty damn quickly, which probably means he's going to do whatever he can to keep her quiet and stop her from talking to us. And she's so wrapped up in the whole damn monastery, she'll probably go along with it.'

'We can get her out of the monastery and into the commissariat,' Cedric reasoned. 'The amount of time she spent in a cell in the past might actually loosen her tongue.'

'It's not a bad idea,' Coco agreed. 'What did you make of the whole Gasper Peron story?'

Cedric considered his answer. 'I'm struggling to see the connection. You heard what Dr. Allard said. Peron was terminally ill anyway. Whether you believe him or not, you have to believe Sonny and he confirmed the prognosis. At best, someone may have helped him along earlier, peut être to make sure they got his money, or just to put the dude out of his misery. Either way, I'm struggling to understand what significance it might have with what happened this week.'

'I hate the fact they're keeping us at arm's length,' Coco grumbled again. 'I should still have the chance to crack some skulls if they give me the runaround.'

Cedric laughed. 'They're monks, Captain, not hardened criminals. Let them have their prayers and their porridge, if they're still hiding after that, THEN you can go crack some skulls.'

Coco grinned at him. 'You mean it?'

He nodded. 'Now, c'mon, let's go and do something productive.'

Coco turned the key in the ignition, the police issue car roaring into life. 'You're right. Let's go and see Deidre Moreau. She seems to know a lot about the comings and goings in the monastery.'

'Who?'

'When I was having breakfast earlier, Mathieu Moreau's mother came in the café,' Coco replied. 'A real piece of work, as it happens. It appears she has a lot to do with the monastery, not just by giving them shitloads of money, but I got the impression she's pretty hands on. We should go and see her, Mathieu went home with her too, so we might just be able to get something tangible from him away from the monastery. Something that might give us some leeway to bringing those brats back in. Demissy can hardly complain about that, can she?'

Cedric gave her a doubtful look. 'You just want to see your boy toy, don't you?'

Coco tapped her fingers on the steering wheel, considering whether to lie to her lieutenant. 'Maybe,' she said finally. 'I'm not saying I dig the dude…'

'The *young* dude,' Cedric corrected. 'The *very* young dude.'

Coco shrugged. She stared at him. 'Tell me this. Do you choose your partners because of their age, or how they look?'

He considered. 'Non, of course, not.'

'Then why the hell should I?' she demanded. 'Hypocrisy is boring, but it's real only because people don't fight against it.'

Cedric laughed. 'So, you screwing a twenty-year-old monk redresses the sexist balance?'

She shrugged. 'Why the hell not?' she demanded. 'Not that I've screwed him, you understand, or intend on screwing him, for that matter.'

'But you want to?' Cedric asked with obvious reluctance.

She did not answer. 'I can't talk about this with you,' she said finally.

Cedric clapped his hands. 'Thank fuck for that. Find a woman to talk to, or better yet, a damn shrink.'

'I can't afford a shrink,' Coco retorted.

'I'd gladly chip in, if it meant you becoming normal,' Cedric stated seriously.

She stuck her tongue out at him. 'You'd hate it if I was normal. I'd bore the tits off you.'

He laughed. 'It's a risk I'm prepared to take. You must have a girlfriend you can talk to.'

Coco stared straight ahead. The truth was she did not have

many friends, male or female. It had used to bother her, but she had reasoned it was simply because she did not time to have friendships. Her time and energy were divided between her children and her job. There had rarely ever been time for anything else. 'Where do I have time for friends? I practically work seven days a week and it's never nine to five,' she said glumly, before pulling herself together. She was not a woman prone to self-pity. 'Besides, most chicks are worried I'm going to steal their husband or fella.'

'Fair point,' Cedric mumbled. 'What about Dr. Bertram? She's a woman and she seems to like you,' he added.

Coco's eyes widened. 'My point exactly! I think I exude some kind of sexual intoxication. Stella has the hots for me, poor thing. Therefore, it would be cruel to tell her my innermost fantasies, especially if they don't include her.'

Cedric shuddered. 'All the same, it would give the rest of us a break.' He tapped the dashboard. 'Anyway, let's get out of here. What do you want to do?'

She touched the steering wheel. 'I still think Deidre Moreau's worth a punt. At the very least, she seems to have some kind of control over the monastery, so either she wants to help, or she's going to make sure she hampers us. Either way, that's important to figure out, non?'

Cedric nodded, before flashing her a tight smile. 'D'accord. Then we have to think about this logically. Either one of the monks did it, or someone from the outside did. And if that's the case, then we have to figure out how they might have got into the monastery. And,' he paused, 'I think we know there's only one possible way that might have happened.'

'We know no such thing!' Coco shouted. She dropped her head, mouthing *désolé* under her breath. She lifted her head slowly. 'I don't care what you say. He's not my boy toy.' She stopped, turning to him, her mouth forming a smile, before adding, 'not yet, at least!' She shook her head dismissively. 'Mais, you might have a point if Frère, *admittedly*, sexy pants is up to the waistband of his Calvin's in all of this, then we also need his help if we're going to stand a chance of getting those rich brats who think they're above the law. And if Mathieu is, then I'll personally slap the handcuffs on him myself,' she added with a wry smile. 'And not in the way I might like to.'

Cedric clenched his fists. 'We know those kids stole the coffins,' he stated angrily.

'Know and prove are two different things,' Coco reasoned. 'And we have nothing to tie them directly to it. No prints, nada. Mathieu left the gate open for them, but he doesn't know, or won't say, whether he knew who exactly was coming in.'

'Which is why we need to get them all into an interview room and force the truth out of them,' Cedric snapped.

Coco laughed. 'By what? Attaching electrodes to their nipples? Listen, I agree. I think they stole the coffins. But was it just another prank? Do we really see them as murderers?'

Cedric shrugged. 'As I said, pulling them in again is the only way we're really going to find out.'

Coco shook her head. 'Maître Duchamp, or some other fancy asshole of a lawyer isn't going to let us near them unless we have more to go on, we know that already.'

Cedric took a long breath. 'And how are we going to get that if no one is willing to talk to us?'

'We speak to Mathieu.'

'Boy toy,' Cedric mocked.

Coco stuck her tongue out at him. 'Don't be a bitch, lieutenant. As it stands, boy toy is the only one we've met so far who is actually willing to talk to us.'

'And why is that?' Cedric retorted. 'It could be because he's up to his neck in it and is trying to lead us down the wrong path. Remember, we only have his word for it that he found Frère Leroy already dead. Mathieu Moreau could be as much of a suspect as a witness.'

Coco's face twisted. 'You could be right. And therefore all the more reason we talk to him when he's still willing to talk. The monks are shutting down, and I don't want his mother to shut him down before we're sure either way what his deal is. Whatever you think of my motives, or desires,' she added with a wink. 'You gotta know by now that no matter what I think, if someone needs to go down, I'll kick them down myself, no matter who they are or what they might mean to me.'

Cedric lowered his head. 'I know that,' he whispered.

Coco turned away from him, gulping. 'After Deidre, we should go and see Chantel Sander again,' she said, changing the subject.

'Why?' Cedric asked.

'Don't you remember what she said yesterday?' Coco demanded.

Cedric considered. 'Not really. She said a lot of things.'

'When we were leaving she said we should give Frère Leroy a message for her,' Coco recalled. 'Something about telling him if he was involved in her husband's death, she'd make sure he paid.' She shrugged. 'Sounds a bit like a threat, non?'

'It could,' Cedric conceded. 'Or it could just be a wife pissed off because her husband had just been murdered. You said it yourself, everyone is being tight-lipped for whatever reason, self-preservation, protecting someone, we can't be sure, mais, Chantel Sander has just lost her husband. She made it clear she hated the monastery and the youth centre, it stands to reason she'd be angry and lashing out.'

'All the same, I'd at least like to know what she has to say about his death, wouldn't you? And more importantly, what she was up to at the time of his murder.'

'Oui,' he agreed.

She nodded with determination. 'Okay, let's do that. Look up

Deidre Moreau's address and we'll go and pay her a visit. Then we'll see Sonny and get some details of the murder so we can confront Chantel Sander. Demissy might expect me to sit on my hands and wait for permission to do my job, but she's going to have to realise sooner or later, that's not how I work, and that's not how we get results.' She looked at Cedric. 'Are you with me?'

He looked at her, the muscles in his cheek flexing. 'I have been this far, haven't I? Why would I stop now?'

08H30

Coco and Cedric were led in silence by a tall, thin man along a wide, expansive hallway, lined with antique furniture and paintings Coco imagined all belonged in a museum.

It was not a home which felt lived in, something which could not be said about her own home, the ramshackle tiny apartment on the tenth floor of a building badly in need of repair. But it was a home, and it was filled with love in all its forms. For the life of her, Coco could not imagine Mathieu Moreau living in this home, because it was not a home in which a child would be allowed to roam freely. The floors were lacquered, and the rugs appeared old and valuable. Coco could not see a child playing on the ground with toy cars in such a space. She looked at the walls and remembered her own. Pencil marks of growing children and doodles of naughty children. She loved it all and had no desire to remove it.

The tall man stopped finally, knocking discreetly on a door.

'Enter.'

Coco instantly recognised the cold, distant voice of Deidre Moreau. Coco and Cedric moved forward, stepping into a living room which would comfortably fit Coco's entire apartment several times over. Like the hallway, the salon was lined with antiques.

'I don't recall inviting you to my home,' Deidre snapped.

Coco opened her mouth to speak, but before she did, she noticed a man standing by the window, staring out into the street. It took her a moment to recognise him. Aaron Cellier turned away from the window, his face instantly clouding in a way Coco read as him being afraid, or as if they had caught him doing something wrong. Coco could not imagine how a high society dame like Deidre Moreau would know the man in charge of the demolition of the old youth centre, but she supposed it was not so unreasonable after all and they were likely to have crossed paths and lived in the same neighbourhood.

Still, she could not imagine them being friends. Cellier was a serious man and she could not imagine him fitting into the sort of life Deidre demanded. Coco stopped herself, realising she was summing up Mathieu's mother a lot despite having only met her once and for a short period of time, and she could not understand what it was about Deidre that bothered her so. Coco knew she could never be like the grand dame, but she had met several women like her in the past and it had never bothered her then. This time, Coco could only think of one thing that was different. *Mathieu.*

Deidre extended her hand towards Cellier. 'Have you met Aaron Cellier? He is an old friend.'

Cellier nodded and stepped forward. 'Oui, we've met.' He dropped into a chair next to Deidre. 'I came to offer my condolences to Deidre.'

Or to get your stories straight? Coco wondered. Deidre pulled back her head, suddenly fixing Coco with a curious look. It was the first time she had looked at Coco with anything other than mild contempt. She was now staring at Coco with interest. 'Has there been an arrest made?' she demanded.

Coco threw back her head and laughed louder than she had intended. Her mouth twisted. 'Désolé,' she apologised. 'It's just I'm not sure how we're meant to make an arrest when everyone appears either unable or unwilling to speak to us.'

Deidre's lips pulled tight. 'As I said earlier. We are devastated by what has happened. We have suffered immeasurable losses, we have…'

'To help the police,' Coco concluded for her. 'Or else, whoever is responsible is going to walk away free as a bird.' She pointed to a chair. 'May I?'

Deidre's eyes flicked over Coco's coat, barely able to hide her distaste. She nodded with obvious reluctance.

Coco flopped onto a rigid sofa, wincing uncomfortably at its firmness. She gestured for Cedric to sit next to her. She continued. 'Let's all cut to the chase, shall we?' She stopped and looked around. 'Say, is your son around? I'd like him to be here, too.'

Deidre pulled her arms around her chest. 'He's resting. As I'm sure you can understand, what happened... what he discovered, has affected him very much. We're waiting for our doctor to arrive to check on Mathieu. You can't talk to him. I won't allow it.'

Coco raised an eyebrow. 'It's not really a question of what you will or won't allow...'

Deidre cut her off. 'Then let the doctor decide if you won't allow a mother the courtesy of attempting to protect her only child.'

Cedric leaned forward. 'And what are you protecting him from, exactly?'

Deidre closed her eyes. 'Well, isn't that obvious? Further trauma. My Mathieu is a very sensitive boy and I fear, well, I fear this entire business will be too much for him. When we decided he should join the brothers of *Abbaye le Bastien*, it was because we knew it was where his destiny lay.' She suppressed a smile. 'I realise you may think that sounds a little fanciful, but it is true.'

'I'm sure you believe that,' Coco responded. 'Mais, tell me - you said "we" knew, was that your decision, or Mathieu's?'

Deidre stared at Coco quizzically. 'I don't know what you mean. The decision was not mine, nor Mathieu's. It was Dieu's, and it was a decision made long before any of us could comprehend. It was, you might say, pre-determined. My father was a devout man who was always troubled by the money our family held. He was determined it be used for the benefit of the community.'

A sadness passed over her face. 'He tried to love me, but he could never disguise his disappointment he only produced a daughter. That disappointment was only really eased when Mathieu was born. He wanted more than anything for one of his kin to devote their life to Dieu. Mathieu was raised to fulfil that desire. There was never any doubt amongst any of us that it was his destiny.' She paused, fingers tracing slowly across her skirt. 'I swear my father only hung to life so long so he could see Mathieu join the Abbaye.'

'Your father is dead?' Cedric asked.

Deidre shook his head. 'Non, he isn't. Not really.'

'I don't understand,' Coco interrupted.

'My father is unwell. He has advanced Alzheimer's disease,' Deidre answered, covering her mouth with a delicate lace handkerchief. 'He is in a clinic in Switzerland. It is very sad. It was always his wish for Mathieu to join the monastery, and I think he held on for as long as he could for it to happen. He knew he was ill, but he waited until Mathieu fulfilled his destiny. The man I knew as my father may no longer be here, but he lasted long enough to see his dream come true.'

Coco moved her head slowly, suddenly aware of how sorry she felt for the young man who most likely was never allowed to decide his own destiny. Her own life could have been very different if she had followed the pre-determined path her own parents had designed for her. She had stepped away, not just from the destiny but from the parents who had sought to speak for her. As much as she still had problems with them, they had allowed her to move away from them, and it occurred to her in that moment it might not be so easy for everyone to abandon everything and everyone they knew, as she had.

There were occasions when she missed her family, but the older she got, the fewer and farther it became. It did not make her sad, and was not something which she found troubled her. Some pasts are best left where they are, just shadows which appeared in the night. She knew she could close her eyes and that eventually the shadows would dissipate into the morning light.

Cedric nudged Coco, causing her to snap back from her thoughts. 'I need to speak to your son,' Coco stated, 'doctor or not. He is a vital witness to what happened.'

Deidre shook her head. 'Witness to what? He told me what happened. He came downstairs and saw the door to Frère Leroy's office was ajar, so he went to close it, and that's when he discovered… when he…' She paused, shrugging her shoulders slowly. 'He went to raise the alarm and waited with the brothers for the police to arrive. That is all he can tell, so I see no sense in disturbing him more.'

'Je comprends,' Coco said in the most soothing tone she could muster. 'However, the fact remains, Frère Leroy was murdered and that the murderer either came from the inside, or was let in, because as far as we can tell, that is the only way they could have access to the monastery. They locked the gate when the police arrived this morning, but we know it has been opened in the past. And we also know it was Mathieu who opened it so that his friends could sneak into the crypt.'

'That's an outrageous thing to say!' Deidre shouted.

Coco turned to Aaron Cellier. 'You know it's true though, don't you, Monsieur Cellier? Because your son was one of the people involved.'

'I don't know that,' Cellier responded in a not entirely convincing manner.

Deidre clenched her fists. 'If that was the case, why are you troubling us? If you had any evidence, you wouldn't be here.'

Coco ignored her and faced Cellier again. 'When we first met, you intimated you weren't exactly sorry to see the back of the youth centre and that it had affected your son, Idris.'

Cellier's eyes darted towards Deidre, her mouth pinching tightly. She said nothing, fixing Coco with a look she clearly understood. *We don't talk about matters such as this with people like you.* It reminded Coco of her own mother and the way she would lower her voice, indicating with her eyes whether she deemed a conversation to be too delicate or important to discuss in front of others she deemed to be beneath her.

Undaunted, Coco pressed on. 'And yet, Monsieur Cellier, we discovered your son partying with the others we suspect of being involved in the stealing of coffins and the murder of Odilon Sander.'

'My son had nothing to do with any of that!' Cellier cried.

'How am I supposed to know that if no one will talk to us?' Coco demanded. She turned away from Cellier, back to facing Deidre. 'This will not go away until we understand what happened and who is responsible. And listen, whatever you think of me, I can either be your best friend, or the biggest pain in your ass.' She nudged Cedric. 'Ask him, he knows.'

'I know,' Cedric agreed wearily.

Deidre grimaced at the word *ass*. 'What do you want?'

'The same thing I always want,' Coco answered. 'Minimum bullshit. Which means I want you to go get your son, and,' she turned back to Cellier, 'for you to get your son to come to the Commissariat de Police du 7e arrondissement and stop hiding behind the coattails of kids you say were bad for him and to him.'

'This isn't about our children,' Deidre snapped. 'This is about the children who think they are better than us. They are not. They are unholy. Raised from stock not fit to walk in our society. Mathieu turned to the light, but some demons are difficult to escape.'

'Demons?' Cedric interrupted.

She nodded. 'Those children have always been a blight, spewing poison, attempting to infect innocent children into following them like some ridiculous cult.'

'You're talking about Jericho Martin and Sofia Charton?'

Coco asked, recalling the three suspects she had removed from the party boat along with Aaron Cellier's son, Idris. They had seemed to be spoilt brats to her, particularly Jericho Martin, but she had trouble imagining them to be anything other than what they appeared. And yet she knew, she *felt* instinctively, that whatever they had done, whether youthful hijinks, or something altogether more sinister, until she got them in an interview room, she was never going to really know for sure. She needed Mathieu Moreau and Idris Cellier to break ranks and give her something she could use as leverage.

'They weren't bad kids,' Aaron Cellier said finally. 'Not really, not in the beginning, at least. It just seemed that as time went on, they became more and more cruel.'

'Like I said,' Deidre added, 'the devil fed them poison, and they ran with it, trying to infect anyone decent they came into contact with.'

Coco nodded. 'Then that's why you both need to speak to your sons and get them to talk to us. At worst, they'll clear up a mess and then we can move on and stop wasting our time.'

Deidre Moreau and Aaron Cellier stared at each other. Without saying a word, Deidre stood and slinked out of the room. Coco watched her leave, her eyebrows knotting in confusion. 'Something I said?' she quipped. Nobody responded. Coco tapped her foot on the ground, silences always made her feel uncomfortable, and she was left with the underlying need to punctuate any silence with inappropriateness. 'So, you schlepping the monk's mother?' she asked Cellier.

He spluttered. 'Quoi?'

Cedric dropped his head, muttering something incompressible.

Coco shrugged. 'Well, I was just wondering why you were here? I mean, you don't seem natural bedfellows, but I saw the way she looked at you.'

Cellier appeared surprised. 'You did?'

Coco nodded. She had not been sure, but she had detected there was something between the two of them. 'She's pretty good at hiding it, mais,' she tapped the side of her nose, 'a woman knows.'

Cellier exhaled. His breaths were long and sad, as if he had been holding them in for a long time. 'You might find it difficult to believe, but Deidre and I were actually childhood sweethearts back in the day. Her father hated it,' he added bitterly, 'he thought I wasn't from "good enough breeding." He absolutely refused to allow us to date. Deidre, being Deidre, agreed with whatever her Papa said. His approval was everything to her. I hated the man, but he did a lot of good with the money that came with his privilege, there's no doubt about that. I just wish he'd cared more about the people around him than impressing the people who weren't.' He extended his hands in front of him. 'He was a cold man, and he railroaded Deidre into marrying a man she didn't love and who didn't love her, just so they could produce a child that they could serve up like an offering to the Catholic Church.'

'Phew. You didn't like him much, eh?'

Cellier shrugged. He scratched his head. 'I hated him, but so did most people. In the end, it didn't really matter because, as I'm sure you know, at the end of the day, money talks.'

Behind them, Deidre Moreau cleared her throat. Coco turned her head, wondering how long she had been there.

'Mathieu has gone,' Deidre stated.

'Gone? Gone where?' Coco asked.

'Well, he didn't leave a note, if that's what you're asking,' Deidre snapped. 'And he doesn't have a cell phone, so I can't even call him. He has taken a bag, however,' she added, as if she did not want to be sharing the information.

Coco looked at Cedric. She stood. 'A bag?'

Deidre nodded. 'Just a backpack. I can't be certain, but he

appears to have taken a few items of clothing he kept here.'

He's running. The thought stabbed against Coco's skull. She still could not believe it of him, but she had realised she had nothing to go on other than a rotten instinct when it came to men. Still, she was not prepared to write him off just yet. 'Where would Mathieu go?'

Deidre shrugged. 'The only place he could go is back to the monastery.'

Cedric stepped next to Coco. 'The monastery is locked down. No one is allowed in or out, so it would be pretty pointless him going there.'

'Then I don't know where he would go,' Deidre whispered, her voice cracking. She turned away, staring out of the window. 'He was so upset about what happened to Frère Leroy. I've never seen him like that before.'

Coco gestured to Cedric. 'We should go.'

Cedric nodded. 'Monsieur Cellier, talk to your son and get him to talk to us. We need his help.'

Deidre stepped into the room. 'There can be no more secrets, Aaron,' she said simply.

'Is your son in danger?' Coco demanded.

Deidre sank into a chair. 'I don't know, however, if anyone hurts my son, they have no idea what I am capable of,' she gave by way of an answer. 'Mais, they will regret crossing me.' She glared at Aaron. 'Call Idris. Now! And tell him from me that if his instinct is to protect his friends, or anyone else for that matter, he had better think twice about it.'

Aaron Cellier nodded and pulled his cell phone from his pocket.

09H30

Coco sucked angrily on a cigarette, blowing the smoke into the extractor fan in the corner of the morgue. She stuck her tongue out at the *No Smoking* sign above her.

'Why are you so pissed off?' Cedric demanded. 'Are you worried about boy toy?'

Coco took another drag. 'Do you think he killed the other monk?'

Cedric considered his answer. 'Peut être. Why else would he run?'

'We don't know he's running,' Coco snapped. 'For all we know, he could be in some kind of trouble.'

Cedric shrugged. 'We've put out an alert for him. Half the cops in Paris are looking for him.'

Coco snorted. 'For all the good that's going to do. He's not even wearing his monk dress, he has no cell phone, what are the cops gonna look for? Random hot guy who used to be a monk? May or may not be a murderer?' She looked at her watch, she was waiting for Aaron Cellier to do good on his promise and present his son for interrogation. She wanted him to give her something she could use.

'You really think Idris Cellier is going to give up his friends?' Cedric asked. 'Even if he's been bullied by them, he's not likely to grass them up to the flics because that would only make it worse for him. When this is done and we walk away, he's still got to be here, living with these people. Kids don't spill their guts unless they have to.'

Coco sighed. 'What else can we do?'

Cedric regarded her warily. 'We should really run this all by Demissy.'

'Demissy can eat my ass,' Coco snapped. 'I'm sick of her always hiding behind regulations and at the same time riding us to get results. Where was her support today? Who was she protecting? Herself? You bet! Instead of worrying about either of the dudes in this morgue, all she cares about is not upsetting anyone above her. She's shit scared of upsetting the apple cart. And me? I fucking hate apples.'

Sonny appeared in the doorway. He smiled. 'Before you talk yourself out of a job *again*, Coco, how's about we look at Frère Leroy and figure out what happened to him?'

Coco stubbed out the cigarette. 'Lead on, doc, lead on.'

Sonny moved slowly across the morgue, staring into the open chest cavity of Frère Gerard Leroy. He jotted something on a pad, before tapping the pen against his chin as he contemplated something. Coco and Cedric watched in silence, knowing that he needed the time to understand what was in front of him.

'As I thought, Frère Leroy was murdered somewhere between 22h00 and midnight,' Sonny began. 'Death was as a result of catastrophic head injury. The beating, as I surmised, came after death.' He pointed at the face. 'The blows are superficial and I imagine meant only to cause confusion as to the cause of death.'

Coco nodded. 'Yeah, it's not like it was meant to disguise who he was. This was about hiding the fact he was Tasered. But, why? There's not a lot of chance we can trace the weapon used, they have to know that. Therefore the beating seems extreme.'

'Or personal,' Cedric suggested.

'It's possible,' she replied. 'Anything else, Sonny?'

He moved around the body. 'For a man of his age, late fifties, he was in pretty good condition. Nice clean lungs, liver, heart. None of the trappings of normal life.'

Coco snorted. 'Good for him. I intend to give my organs the

maximum workout I can. Hell, we're only here once, what's the point in dying with shiny bits and pieces?'

Sonny gave her a disapproving look. 'As a doctor, I can't say I approve of that statement, Charlotte.'

She blew a raspberry. 'There was nothing on the body that might help?'

Sonny shook his head. 'The clothes were clean and there was nothing under his fingernails. Ebba's still going over the monastery, but I think it's fair to say it's going to be difficult to obtain anything conclusive.'

'What about the beating?' Coco pondered. 'I mean, wouldn't the attacker have marks on their hands?'

'Not really,' Sonny responded. 'The beating didn't actually cause a lot of damage to the face, I'm not sure what affects it would have left on the perpetrator. They could have bruised knuckles, par example. All I can tell you is there was no obvious transference of skin or any other fibres. We couldn't find any evidence of who attacked him. They could have worn gloves, so if you find them, then...' he trailed off, a mischievous smile on his face.

'You might as well say, fat chance,' Coco conceded. 'So, what exactly do we have?'

'I compared the burn marks on the faces of Odilon Sander and Frère Leroy, and I can tell you they are the same size,' Sonny added, 'but that doesn't necessarily mean it was from the same device, it could just be from the same *sort* of device.'

'I'm happy to believe it's the same device,' Coco stated, 'because it's too much of a coincidence to be otherwise.'

Cedric shook his head. 'We can't rule out the fact it could be a copycat.'

Coco shook her tongue out. 'It's possible, but I feel it's unlikely.' She rose to her feet. 'Let's go and see Chantel Sander and see what kind of alibi she has.' She moved to the door, and stopped, biting her lip. 'Sonny, I have to ask you a question,' she stated reluctantly.

The doctor met her gaze, his eyebrows creasing as if he was confused by her serious tone. 'Bien sûr. What is it?'

'Did you speak to Dr. Allard this morning?' she asked, her tone gentle.

Sonny continued looking confused. 'Joël? This morning?' He shook his head. 'Non, pourquoi?'

'Because he knew about Frère Leroy's murder,' she stated.

His eyes widened. 'Not from me. What makes you think he knew?'

'Deidre Moreau told me. Apparently he informed her,' Coco replied.

'Well, he didn't hear it from me,' Sonny repeated, his tone harder.

'I didn't say you did.'

'Mais, you thought it,' he snapped. 'And I didn't, because that would have been extremely unprofessional.'

Coco shook her head. She touched his arm. 'I didn't think it, but I had to ask because I have to wonder how he did know. I mean, who would have informed him, and why?'

'One of the monks? How the hell am I supposed to know?' Sonny snapped again. He bit his lip. 'Désolé. I know you didn't mean anything by it. And yeah, you're right. How did he know?'

'The how is just as important, but I also have to wonder why,' Coco added. 'I know he was your friend back in the day, but can you honestly say you know him well enough to believe him to be on the level?'

Sonny carefully considered his answer. 'He was a good pal. We spent a lot of time together at college and he helped me a lot. If you're asking do I believe he could be involved, my gut is going to have to say no. He's as straight as a die, I'd bet money on that. Although…' he trailed off.

'Although?' Cedric asked keenly.

Sonny shrugged. 'I don't know what to tell you, or even how to explain it. Listen, Joël's a good guy and a good friend. For a man who is very religious, he could be a lot of fun, and not as straight and boring as you might imagine. In his job he works hard to differentiate between his beliefs and what he needs to do. I'll give you an example. One of his first cases was for a man who committed suicide. It troubled Joël immensely, because his beliefs told him it was a sin, but he worked through it and he was as careful and considerate to the deceased as he could be, and more importantly he fought for the dead man to be buried in the cemetery he wanted.'

'But Joël is devoted,' Sonny continued, 'there's no doubt about it and I can imagine he would be torn if he was asked by someone in the Church to do something, or to act in a certain way. I can't really tell you what I base that on, other than I have seen him interact with religious people and I would probably describe him as being subservient in those instances. I realise that's not much of an answer, but it's all I have. He is a good man in my opinion, however, I don't know how that translates into his interactions with people in authority in the Catholic Church.'

Coco listened to him keenly. 'Your opinion matters, Sonny. And I actually agree, from what I saw of Dr. Allard, he seemed like a swell guy.' She stopped and moved across the room. 'But we have to know who called him this morning and why.'

'I don't know, truly I don't,' Sonny said quietly.

'There could be a reason,' Coco continued. 'Someone could have asked him to get involved, to keep an eye on what we were doing…'

'It would be completely unprofessional and probably illegal!' Sonny shouted. 'That isn't his case, I'm sure of it. Do you want me to call him and ask?'

Coco considered before shaking her head. 'Not until I have a better idea of his involvement. I think we'll drop in on him ourselves.'

Sonny shook his head. 'I just can't see it, I truly can't.'

'But he has been involved,' Cedric commented, 'and if he wanted to, he could be again, and that could be because like the Captain says, someone wants him to see how the case is progressing and keep them informed.'

'You're talking like he's a spy! He's just a doctor who happens to be religious, that doesn't make him a bad guy,' Sonny cried, his voice rising.

Coco cleared her throat, suddenly feeling edgy. She had never really seen Sonny angry and it bothered her. She had not meant to upset him. 'Hey, chill Sonny. If I didn't know better, I'd think you had the hots for him!' she said, immediately regretting it.

Sonny turned to her and said nothing.

Coco pulled her cell phone and looked at the screen. It was blank. 'Oh, would you look at that, we gotta go!' she said, gesturing to Cedric.

Sonny watched them as they headed towards the door. 'If Joël calls, I won't tell him anything, I promise,' he called out, before softly adding, 'désolé.'

10H15

Coco stared straight ahead, her eyes locked on the road in front of her. She was thinking about so many things at once she was not sure what to make of it all. Images flashed before her and she realised that, not for the first time, she was running on empty, trying to juggle too many things at once without ever really taking a moment to stop and think about the life that was passing by her. There was always too much to do and too little time to do it.

In the rear view mirror she saw a young couple passing by, their hands entwined and their eyes locked in a powerful embrace. Coco realised she had never really experienced love like that. There had been lovers, some she cared to remember more than others, but she was not sure she had ever really experienced anything approaching the level of intimacy she saw in others.

Cedric broke the silence. 'You're going to have to do something about the Sonny situation sooner or later, you know,' he said.

Coco turned her head briefly towards him and then turned back to face the road. 'I have no idea what on earth you're talking about,' she said forcefully.

Cedric sighed. 'Believe me, I don't want to get involved in this, but I like Dr. Bernstein. He's a great guy, and you…' he trailed off as if he was searching for the right words, 'you're not so bad,' he added in a low voice. 'Listen. I'll say this only once and I'm only doing it because you don't seem to have anybody else to talk to. Choose right. Don't choose the one with the tightest ass and six-pack just because you know it's not going to work out.'

Coco pulled back her head sharply. 'Still, I have absolutely <u>no</u> idea what you're talking about,' she stated huffily.

'Yeah, you do,' he shot back. 'You're looking around and

ignoring what's right in front of you because you're worried it won't work out.' He held his hands up. 'All I'm saying is that you've got choices.'

She shook her head. 'Non, I don't. I can't choose someone just because I… because I have urges, or they have urges. I can't lose someone who means something to me, because I don't have a lot of those types of people in my life.'

'Do you like him, or not?'

'Who are we talking about?' Coco demanded.

'Whoever? What does it matter?' Cedric responded. 'If you have the need to be with someone, do it, but do it because you want to, not because you're afraid of losing them. Or else, what's the point? This is the last I'm going to say on the subject, because believe me, I have zero minus many many zeros interest in assisting you in getting laid.' He smiled at her. 'You know what you'd say to me if I ever talked to you about this sort of shit? And by "ever" I obviously mean, never in this fucking life, you'd say something along the lines of: *Stop being a drama queen and drop your drawers and stop overthinking things.*'

Coco looked briefly at him once more. 'Drop your drawers?' she cried with incredulity.

Cedric shook his head. He pointed in front of them. 'Anyway, enough with this monstrosity of a conversation, we're here. Merci Dieu!'

Chantel Sander yanked back the door with such ferocity it bounced against the wall. She narrowed her eyes angrily towards Coco and Cedric. 'What are you doing here?' She glanced over her shoulder. 'We have people here paying their respects to Odilon. Now, is NOT the best time.'

Coco looked to the crowd gathered behind Chantel. She did not recognise any of them and it reminded her of every such scene she had experienced. Rich people paying respects to other rich people. Bathed in wealth and sharing anecdotes about someone they likely barely knew, or in her experience, barely liked. 'We need to talk,' Coco stated in hushed tones.

Chantel shook her head angrily. 'Not now, not here.'

Coco stepped forward, placing her boot in the doorway to prevent Chantel from closing the door. 'This is serious,' she mouthed. 'And either we talk here and now, or else you'll have to come to the commissariat with us, and I'm sure you really don't what to do that in front of all your friends, do you?'

Chantel's mouth fell ajar, a horrified expression shadowing her face. She began to speak, but stopped mid-sentence. 'Very well, follow me into the kitchen, but for Dieu's sake, be quiet.' She glanced down at Coco's boot. 'And wipe your feet.'

Coco looked down at her boot, other than the tape holding the soul together it appeared fine to her. She made a big deal about wiping them on the mat, slapping the boots loudly against the mat. Chantel tutted and grabbed Coco's arm and dragged her away, a smiling Cedric falling into step behind them.

They proceeded quickly down a long hallway, turning into a wide, open-plan kitchen which appeared to have more appliances than Coco knew existed. Chantel stopped in front of a large island, her mouth twisting as if she was contemplating slipping into her usual good-host mode, or not. She seemed to decide against it, slapping the palms of her hands on the island and glaring at Coco and Cedric. 'What is this about?' she demanded with a ferocious hiss.

'Maman?' Vichy Sander appeared in the doorway. 'What's going on?'

Chantel waved her hand dismissively. 'Go back to our guests, darling.'

He shook his head. 'Non, I won't. Sycophants who looked down their noses at Papa and what he did and are now suddenly pretending they were his best friend?' His nose crinkled. 'The hypocrisy stinks and I won't be a part of it.'

'Vichy...' she wailed.

He ignored his mother, moving towards Coco and Cedric. Coco noticed his acne appeared even angrier than the last time, with large red welts all over his cheeks as if he had been scratching at his skin. 'Why are you here? Has something happened? Do you know what happened to my father?' he demanded, his voice cracking making him sound much younger than he was.

'We're still investigating,' Coco replied. 'Mais, oui, something else has happened. I'm afraid there's been another murder.'

'Another murder?' Chantel cried.

Coco nodded. 'Oui. I'm sorry to inform you that Frère Gerard Leroy was murdered earlier today in the *Abbaye Le Bastien*,' she said quickly.

'Maman, what...' Vichy began but stopped abruptly.

Coco watched the young man, sure he had been about to say - *Maman, what have you done?* She moved across the room. 'I'm afraid it's too early to say what happened exactly, other than we are treating it as another murder.'

'The same person?' Chantel asked. The tone of her voice indicated she had lost the earlier irritation. Now, she just sounded panicked.

'We can't be sure,' Cedric responded. 'But nor can we rule it out. There were similarities,' he added cautiously.

Vichy gasped. 'Similarities?'

Coco nodded again. 'Oui. Although, again, we can't really go into specifics at the moment.'

Chantel stared wide-eyed before blinking rapidly several times. 'Why are you here? What does this have to do with us?'

Coco moved closer to the other woman. 'Do you remember the last thing you said to me before we left yesterday?'

Chantel turned her head. 'You can't possibly imagine I meant that.'

Cedric stepped next to Coco. 'You did make what sounded remarkably like a threat.'

She waved her hand dismissively. 'Rubbish. I did no such thing.' She moved across the kitchen, stopping in front of the window and staring into the expansive garden behind it. 'Did he suffer?' she asked without looking back.

Coco watched her, trying to decide whether she sounded hopeful. She was sure she did. 'No murder is without pain,' she answered. 'And the fact remains, I haven't heard from a single person who has a bad word to say against the monk, other than you, of course.'

Chantel turned abruptly. 'And you think what, exactly? That on the day I discovered my husband was murdered I went and extracted my revenge?'

Coco shrugged. 'It wouldn't be the first time something like that has happened. People often react out of character when they are faced with tragedy. Often the first instinct is to get revenge for the loss of a loved one. As a police officer, I can't condone it, but as a woman and a mother, I most certainly understand the instinct for revenge.'

Chantel laughed. 'For you, maybe, but as I'm sure you recall, my feelings and my relationship with my husband were not the sort which would inspire me to murder someone for ridding me of him.'

'Maman!' Vichy gasped.

'Désolé, cher,' Chantel said softly. 'You have to know that while I wished your father no harm, I was not entirely fond of him these days, and it appears by the double-life he was leading, nor was he fond of me.' She moved to her son and pulled him into an embrace. He was reluctant, his body stiff. She kissed the top of his head. 'You're old enough to understand that.'

Vichy pulled himself away. 'Bien sûr, I'm old enough. I'm not stupid, either. I knew exactly what was going on between the two of you, and everyone else for that matter.'

Coco and Cedric looked sharply at one another, realising the young man had just said something that was potentially important. Chantel pushed her son away. 'You know nothing about any of this,' she snapped.

He laughed. 'You'd like to think that, wouldn't you? The spotty geek always in the background because he's frightened of stepping out of the shadows in case anyone takes too hard a look at him? Well, you know what, Maman? Standing on the sidelines is a pretty good place to be, as far as I'm concerned, because it means you see what everyone doesn't want you to see.'

'And what did you see, exactly?' Coco interrupted.

'He saw nothing,' Chantel snapped. 'And it is none of your business.'

Coco shook her head. 'I have two corpses in the morgue who tell me different,' she retorted. 'And until I know what happened, I'm not going away. So, let's start with this. Where were you last night?'

Chantel smirked. 'Here, obviously. We were both here. Where else would we be? I realise I'm hardly a grieving widow, but nor am I in the mood yet to the hit the town to celebrate my sudden single status.' She clasped her hands. 'We had friends with us until 20h00 or so, and then we went to bed.'

Vichy looked oddly at his mother. 'Non, we didn't,' he stated matter-of-factly. 'Why are you lying?'

Chantel gave her son a puzzled look. 'I'm not lying.'

'The hell you are,' he snapped. 'I don't know what you were up to last night, because I wasn't here.'

'Where were you?' Cedric asked quickly.

Vichy looked at the lieutenant, but said nothing.

'Where were you?' Cedric repeated.

Chantel took a step closer to her son. 'Say nothing, Vichy,' she warned.

Vichy pulled back, yanking his arm away from his mother. 'I have to get out of here. I need to think.' He glared at Chantel. 'Whatever happened, don't use me as your alibi.' He moved quickly towards the door. 'I have to get out of here,' he repeated.

Chantel called after her disappearing son. 'If you're not my alibi, then I'm not yours, remember that, Vichy!'

Coco nudged Cedric. 'Get after him,' she ushered.

Cedric nodded and took off after the young man. Coco turned back to Chantel. 'Well, that was interesting.'

'I don't see how,' Chantel retorted. 'We were in all last night. That was not a lie. I went to bed and I assumed my son had too. I can't say any different to that.' She paused, giving Coco a sad smile. 'I'd had rather too much wine, I'm afraid, so I don't really recall too much.'

Coco stared at her, her eyes widening. 'Being wasted isn't a defence, you know? Claiming you don't remember isn't either.'

Chantel shrugged. 'I don't know what to tell you. That is what happened.'

'If you left, we will find out,' Coco stated. 'I don't know if you've noticed, but there are cameras everywhere. If you left here and went to the monastery, we will find out.'

She shrugged again. 'Then do it. Mais, I didn't leave this house last night, or this morning, so unless you can prove otherwise, then I don't think we have anything left to discuss, do you?'

Cedric appeared in the doorway panting. 'He got away,' he said angrily.

Coco turned back to Chantel. 'So, your son, also without an alibi, is apparently on the run. What a predicament we're in, aren't we?'

'My son did nothing wrong,' Chantel said, slamming her fists on the island. 'He's just lost his father, for Dieu's sake! This has nothing to do with him!' she shouted, before quickly covering her mouth and glancing over Cedric's shoulder to make sure none of her visitors had heard her raised voice.

'How are we supposed to know that?' Coco suggested. 'All we know is there was apparently no love lost between your family and Frère Leroy, and now, less than twenty-four hours after the death of your husband, he winds up dead too, in a very similar way. And then there's the fact that you tried to give us a false alibi which your son contested, the same son who is now on the run.' She turned to Cedric. 'Did I miss anything out, Lieutenant Degarmo?'

Cedric considered. 'Nope, I think you pretty much covered it all, Captain Brunhild.'

Coco nodded. 'Bon.' She faced Chantel again. 'D'accord. Here's what we're going to do. We're going to put out a warrant for your son's arrest. We're also going to have his cell phone tracked. So, either you come clean, or he will, but either way I'm pretty much on my last nerve with this case. There will be no more lies.'

'We just lost Odilon,' Chantel said desperately. 'Why are you doing this to us?'

'I'm doing nothing,' Coco retorted. 'If you were being honest with us, then I would be the first person to make sure you were allowed to grieve in peace, but I don't think you are. I don't think any of you are, and until that changes it is my damn job to be all up in your faces.' She edged forward. 'Alors, what's it gonna be? You gonna level with us, or not?'

Chantel held Coco's gaze in a way which told Coco she was considering her options. Chantel lowered her head. 'My husband is dead, what does this matter?'

Coco faced the other woman. 'Because I have a sneaking suspicion you have an idea why he was murdered and also why Frère Leroy was, too. So, I have to work on the assumption that either you are involved, or there is another reason you're unwilling to talk to us.'

'Another reason?' Chantel demanded.

'Yeah,' Coco replied. 'And it's bugging the shit out of me. So, spill.'

Chantel shook her head. 'I have nothing else to say, and I want you to leave.'

'With pleasure,' Coco snapped. She moved to join Cedric in the doorway. She turned back. 'Your son will be arrested, is that what you want?'

Chantel turned away. 'He's done nothing wrong, and you can't prove otherwise.'

'I don't need to,' Coco reasoned. 'However, until he's in police custody then we can't help him either way.'

'What do you mean?'

'Two people are dead and it seems to me that someone is pretty determined to finish what they started,' Coco suggested. 'If your son isn't involved, then he also isn't safe. If you want him to be safe, then if I were you, I'd think long and hard about what you are not saying. We're running out of time, and I'd hate Vichy to get caught up in this, if he doesn't need to be.'

'I asked you to leave,' Chantel repeated.

Coco nodded. 'Sure. But hey, if you leave this house, I'll have you arrested. How's about that?'

'You wouldn't dare.'

Coco laughed. 'The hell I would.' She paused. 'Oh, and one last thing - do you have a Taser?'

Chantel's eyebrows knotted with confusion. 'A Taser? What on earth are you talking about? Of course I don't have a Taser.'

Coco nodded, studying Chantel's face and realising if she was lying, she was very good at it.

Coco continued. 'Call your son and get him to come to us before he gets himself in more trouble, and you stay here until I know whether you're in danger, or the one posing the danger. Is that clear?'

Chantel nodded and dropped her head.

11H25

Dr. Joël Allard opened the door to his office, his eyes widening in surprise when he saw Coco and Cedric standing in the hallway. 'Captain Brunhild, Lieutenant Degarmo, this is a surprise,' he said in a way which told Coco it was not entirely a pleasant one. 'Was I expecting you?' he asked with a frown.

'Non,' Coco replied. 'You might say we're just filling in some blanks. Can we come in?'

'Oh, oui, bien sûr. Désolé,' he appeared flustered, gesturing for them to follow him into his small, cramped office. He pointed to a pair of chairs and he quickly removed piles of folders from one of them and placed them on his desk haphazardly, causing a pile of them to crash onto the floor. He uttered a curse and bent over, scrabbling to put the papers back into their folder. Coco stooped to help him. 'Désolé,' he mumbled again.

Coco finished picking up the papers and led Allard by the arm around his desk and guided him into his chair. He flopped heavily. 'Merci,' he whispered. 'I don't know what's wrong with me this morning.'

Coco sat opposite him. 'The death of Frère Leroy must have come as a tremendous shock to you,' she said.

He nodded. 'Oui. Gerard was a dear friend. Not just to me, but to everyone he met.'

'Not quite everyone,' Cedric stated.

Allard gave the lieutenant a quizzical look. 'Oh, I see what you mean,' he said finally.

Coco leaned forward. 'You really can't think of anyone who might have to wanted to do Frère Leroy harm?'

Allard did not need to consider his answer. He shook his head emphatically. 'Non, absolutely not.'

'And yet, someone did,' Coco reasoned.

'A madman, surely? Nothing more,' Allard countered.

Coco shrugged. 'It's possible, I suppose,' she answered with little conviction. 'And with the stealing of the coffins, and the similarities in the murders, I suppose we could be looking at pointless crimes committed by a lunatic…'

Allard pulled his head back sharply, slamming his hands onto the desk. 'What do you mean by similarities?' he demanded.

'We can't really go into that too much as this stage,' Coco replied.

'You must,' he interrupted. 'It could be important. It could be relevant.'

Coco and Cedric looked at each other. Coco shrugged at the young lieutenant. 'There's evidence both victims were subdued the same way before their death,' Cedric stated.

'Subdued?'

'Oui,' Cedric confirmed but did not elaborate.

'Subdued,' Allard repeated, staring off into the distance. He turned back to Coco. 'And you really can't tell me in what way?'

'The truth is,' Coco replied cautiously, 'we can't be certain of anything right now, particularly because it might be the murderer chose to hide the way they subdued the victims. I'm sorry, we're not trying to be obtuse.' She cleared her throat. 'Tell me. How did you find out about Frère Leroy's death this morning?'

'Frère Aries called,' Allard responded. 'He wanted me to come to the monastery and take charge of Gerard. Of course, I explained to him that was not possible,' a wry smile crossed his face. 'I'm sure you're aware by now, that Henri Aries is not a man who takes kindly to being told no.'

Coco laughed. 'Yeah, he's a peach that monk. What did Frère Aries tell you exactly?'

Dr. Allard considered. 'Not a lot, really,' he answered. 'He just called and said he had some terrible news to share with me and that Gerard was dead. He didn't really go into much more detail, other than he repeated again he wanted me to take charge of Frère Leroy to ensure he was cared for properly. I explained again why I could not, but I continued to reassure him that Dr. Bernstein is a close friend and a doctor I trust very much.'

He smiled again. 'Henri said something derogatory about Sonny's ungodliness and that was about it. I've been sat here all morning trying to make sense of it all and getting on with my work, but I'm afraid I haven't managed to do much of either. I don't understand what happened to Odilon, and I certainly don't understand what happened to Gerard Leroy. They were both, in my opinion and experience, exemplary and very decent, honourable men.'

'When was the last time you saw or heard from Frère Leroy?' Coco asked.

'He actually called me yesterday evening, around 20h00' he replied.

Coco was surprised. 'Really? And what did you speak about?'

Allard bit his lip. He stroked his chin slowly and deliberately, clearly taking his time to decide what he was going to say, before removing his glasses and rubbing his eyes. It bothered Coco because she imagined he was about to lie to her. He locked eyes with her briefly before lowering his head as if it was too difficult to hold her gaze. She smiled. 'That's right. I have a finally honed bullshit detector.'

Allard frowned. 'I don't know what you're suggesting…'

Coco sighed. 'What did he have to say?'

'He was worried,' Allard said after a moment. 'And heartbroken, but he was certainly worried.'

'Worried about what?' Cedric asked. 'His own safety?'

Allard shook his head. 'I don't think so. He certainly never mentioned it, and in hindsight I don't recall getting the impression he was worried about himself, rather about what had happened.'

Coco nodded. 'What did he say, exactly?'

Allard tapped the side of his head as if he was trying to force himself to remember. 'He was worried.'

Coco shook her head irritably. 'You said that already. How's about you stop pretending you don't want to talk to us, and actually start talking to us?'

Allard's eyes widened. 'There's no need to be so abrupt.'

'There's every damn need,' Coco countered. 'I have two murders on my desk to solve and all I'm getting is the run-around and to be frank, it's getting on my tits.'

Allard gasped, his cheeks flushing with embarrassment.

Coco mouthed an apology. 'You get my point though, don't ya?'

He nodded, lowering his head. 'This is a complicated issue,' he began, 'and something I am not at liberty to discuss.'

'Not even with the police investigating a double homicide?' Cedric asked irritably.

'And don't give us any of this, "I answer to a higher authority," shit,' Coco added.

Allard smiled sadly. 'Even though I do?' He swallowed, his throat croaking as he did. 'Listen, I should make clear that I have always struggled with the juxtaposition of my two lives. I work between two masters, it's true. However, as difficult as it might be for you to understand, or to even believe, I have managed to serve them both.'

Cedric shook his head. 'I don't see how that's possible. At this very moment, the Catholic Church are stopping us from speaking to the brothers in the monastery. For what reason, we don't know, but what I do know is this wouldn't be allowed in any other situation.'

'What he said,' Coco added with a smile. 'There are so many questions we need answering if we are ever to begin to understand what happened to Odilon Sander and Frère Leroy, and to be honest, I don't even know where to begin. We really need your help, Dr. Allard. We REALLY need your help, and if you're half the man Sonny says you are, you have to tell us what you know. I can't say I understand your other master, mais I do understand the master, or rather the mistress, that I serve,' she added with a wink. 'And all she cares about is sending bad guys to prison, so that decent people can manage to walk the streets without fear of the afore mentioned bad person caving their skulls in, capeesh?'

'I need to pray,' Allard said finally.

'The hell you do,' Coco snapped. 'You need to open your damn mouth and talk to us.'

Cedric reached over and touched her arm, his eyes widening. Coco knew he was trying to tell her to go easy, but she could not because her level of tolerance for bullshit had reached its maximum. Still, she was aware that antagonising Dr. Allard was probably not the smartest of moves. 'Désolé,' she said softly. 'Everyone says my mouth is going to get me in trouble one of these days.'

Allard smiled at her. 'Sonny told me you could be…' he laughed, before adding, 'colourful. Mais, he also said you were one of the finest police officers he knows,' he looked at Cedric, 'both of you.' He sighed, taking a long, deep breath. 'I don't know what you want from me, but believe this, if I thought I could tell you something that would help, I really would. This isn't about protecting the Church, because honestly, my loyalty ends when it comes to the murder of people I cared about.'

'I hope so,' Coco responded. 'Listen, I realise we're clutching at straws, but until we figure out exactly what we're dealing with anything might be important, no matter how inconsequential you might think it is. Do you understand what I am saying?'

'Two people are dead,' Cedric continued. 'Two men who you claimed were your friends. And whoever did this, well, you've seen yourself what they are capable of. Until we know more, they could do this again, and that is why everything could be important.'

Allard nodded quickly. 'Tell me what you need,' he said softly.

'Merci,' Coco said with a warm smile. 'Firstly, I need you to get us into the monastery.'

The doctor gave her a surprised look. 'What do you mean?'

'Because they're not talking,' Coco replied, 'or the ones who normally talk, aren't talking, and we really need to speak to them.'

'You can't possibly think one of the brothers did this?' Allard demanded.

Coco shrugged. 'Until we talk to them and rule them out, all twenty of them are our prime suspects.'

'Nineteen, now,' Allard corrected.

Coco covered her mouth, mumbling an apology. 'You get my point, though,' she added. 'As it stands, your powers that be have called my powers that be and told us to lay off.' She shrugged again. 'And see, that's not something I do very well, especially when I'm on the hunt of a scumbag.' She took a breath. 'I can understand how you don't want to believe someone in the monastery could be responsible for what happened. If that's the truth, then we have to assume someone else was allowed into the monastery last night. And as far as we can tell, that's pretty difficult without someone opening the gate and letting them in.'

Allard nodded. 'That is true. Access to the monastery is limited, deliberately so, for a myriad of reasons. Have you spoken to Frère Moreau?'

'Oui,' Coco replied, immediately remembering at that precise moment she had no idea where Mathieu was, and although she could not rule out the fact he may have gone on the run, her most pressing concern was that he could be in danger. A thought which terrified her. She coughed. 'Frère Moreau claimed he did not leave the gate unlocked, not this time at least.'

'And you believe him?'

Coco ignored the look on Cedric's face. 'I have no reason to suppose otherwise. I can't call him a liar unless I have the opportunity to interview everyone else before I draw conclusions, now can I? That wouldn't be fair, and I'm nothing if not fair, you ask anyone.'

Allard sighed. 'Then I'll take you to the monastery.'

Coco smiled gratefully. 'And you're not worried about getting into trouble?'

'Non, I'm not. As I said, even though I *technically* serve two masters, I do so with a conscience to both of them, and I cannot do so by ignoring one to placate the other.'

'No matter where it leads?' Coco asked.

He nodded. 'Bien sûr.'

'Bon,' Coco replied gratefully. 'Tell me, what do you imagine happened?'

Allard considered his answer. 'I don't know,' he answered. 'I keep going over and over it in my head, but I have to tell you, I'm not making any sense of it. The crimes are despicable, even taking out the personal connection I have. When I relate it to my job, I have to admit I see terrible things all the time, and all that experience tells me one thing about these crimes.'

'It's personal,' Coco concluded.

He nodded his agreement. 'I don't understand how, or why. But, oui, I do believe there is some kind of personal motivation attached to these crimes. And that is what troubles me the most. I can't imagine for a moment why someone would want to hurt these people in such a way.'

'How long did you know them?' Cedric asked.

Dr. Allard whistled. 'A long time. A very, very long time. Frère Leroy is… *was*, one of the best men I have ever known. He was truly devoted, not just to Dieu but to the community as a whole. I don't think I've ever met anyone who had a bad word, or thought, against him.'

'Then why this?' Coco pondered. 'We go back to the personal nature of the crime, or could it be he saw or heard something, or knew something?'

Allard considered, his mouth twisting back and forth. The desperate sadness was clear on his face. 'Each scenario is as permissible as it is incomprehensible.' He turned to Coco and Cedric. 'Could this not just be an unavoidable tragedy? In our occupations we see the terrible effects of insanity all the time. This may not be about anything other than the mental deficiency of someone. A person whose illness makes them react to things created by the imbalance of their mind. Surely, the most logical reason would be there is no logical reason, at least, not one which has anything to do directly with Frère Leroy and Odilon?'

Coco spread her hands in front of her. 'Hey, listen I'm not against any scenario. I just want the perp in jail so we can all go about our business without worrying they're going to do it again. The only way we're going to manage that is if everyone starts to tell the truth and quit hiding. So, how about for a starter, you spill the beans about the conversation you had with Leroy last night?'

Allard stood and moved across the cramped office before quickly returning to his chair. He crossed his legs, uncrossing them again as quickly. He was still wrestling with something, Coco was sure of it. He pressed his fingers against his temples. 'There is so much I cannot imagine having anything to do with what happened. However, like you said - how do we differentiate between what may or may not be significant?'

Coco cleared her throat. 'Let's start with the coffins. Three coffins lined up in that way - either it's relevant, or it's a red herring, and if we're ever to stand a chance of understanding this, we need to know. What can you tell us about it?'

Allard closed his eyes.

11H40

Dr. Joël Allard tapped long fingers on the desk in front of him. It was almost as if he was playing a musical instrument. Coco imagined he was silently singing some kind of hymn. Normally it would bother her, but she realised she needed his help if she was to ever make sense of the investigation in front of her, because she knew if she did not, another would land on her desk before too long.

'You know about the hazing,' Allard began.

Coco nodded. 'Oui. And I don't really understand it. What's that all about?'

He shrugged. 'It isn't really what you might think. Obviously, children can be cruel, we all know that. Some can be more cruel than others. And once you factor in wealth and privilege, things can change. Often it amplifies cruelty. There are many reasons for that, and it is my experience it often comes from a place of abuse.'

Coco took this in. 'Are we talking about Jericho Martin?' she asked, recalling the dark-skinned youth she had first met at the boat party on the Seine. His arrogance was one thing, his choice of avocat in Pierre Duchamp another, both indications of how unlikeable he was, but it had been more than that, she was sure. He was trouble.

'Oui. Mais, not just him,' Allard responded.

'You mean Sofia Charton and Idris Cellier?' Cedric suggested.

Allard's eyes flashed with worry as if he was afraid of saying too much. Coco locked eyes with him, sending the clearest message she could. Be more afraid of me than anyone else, if you know what's good for you. He nodded. 'It wasn't just them, there was a gang of them you might say.'

Coco took a breath. 'Mathieu Moreau?'

'Oui, and Vichy Sander.'

Coco raised an eyebrow. 'Odilon's son?' She pursed her lips. 'I sort of got the impression he was never really part of the gang.'

'He wasn't,' Allard confirmed. 'Not really. It was sad to see. He was always desperate for approval, and he would pretty much do anything to be part of the gang, which of course only made it worse. The harder he tried, the harder they made him try. You know how kids can be.'

'Cruel, evil little bastards,' Coco added.

Allard smiled sadly. 'Well, I'm not sure I'd go quite that far. Mais, oui, they can be, I suppose. It seemed to only get worse after what happened to Paul.'

Coco scratched her head. 'Paul Lecourt? The kid who died ten years ago.'

He nodded. 'Oui. He was such a sweet child, despite what he'd experienced in his short life, he seemed to bear no malice or lasting damage. His smile brightened a room.'

'But he was bullied?' Cedric interrupted.

'I'm afraid so,' Allard confirmed. 'It wasn't just because he was a gentle child, although I suspect that had something to do with it.'

'It was because he came from the wrong side of the tracks, huh?' Coco suggested. She had seen the cruelty of children first hand. Her youngest son, Cedric, had returned home from school on more than one occasion with a blackened eye, a bloodied nose and a bruised knee, sometimes all three. At first, and with little comment from him, she had assumed it to be youthful hijinks, but as it had continued she had realised something altogether different was going on.

Back then, as she walked slowly towards his school, her thoughts preoccupying her, Coco realised she knew with utmost certainty what was happening to her child. Cedric was being targeted by bullies because of who his father was and what he had done. Each day he came home from school without any evidence of an attack, Coco felt herself breathe properly for the first time that day. It was all she could do to stop herself from tearing over to the home of the tiny punk who was terrorising her son and ripping his parents a new one. Coco loved her children more than she loved anything, but she was sure that if one of them was doing something wrong, she would be the first to make sure they never did it again and that they would apologise with their tail between their legs.

'I never understood that sort of mentality,' Allard contended. 'I mean - are you better just because you were born in a certain place, to rich or famous parents? I mean - what does that matter? Rich, poor, eh? What about just being a decent person?'

Coco gesticulated between her and Cedric. 'We were both brought up on the wrong side of the tracks, or not, I'm still not sure what any of that means. What I do know for certain is that whatever your past, the only responsibility any of us has is to be the best person we can.' She noticed Allard appraising her. She smiled. 'Obviously, it's subjective. I most certainly AM the best person I can be, as far as I'm concerned. And do you know why that's important? Well, I'll tell ya, sailor. Cos I don't give a shit what people think about me. I know people say that sort of thing all the time, but in my case it's really true.'

Cedric nodded slowly. 'I can sadly confirm that Captain Brunhild has no shits to give.'

Coco stuck her tongue out at him. 'Don't get me wrong, sailor,' she addressed Allard. 'I'm not arrogant, all I know is that I do my best. I do my job and I treat everyone fairly, so long as they deserve it. No matter what life throws at you, you've got to take it on the chin. That's my mantra.'

Dr. Allard smiled at her. 'It is a mantra that Dieu would approve of.'

Coco mock bowed. 'I aim to please.' The smile disappeared

from her face as she recalled what they had been discussing. 'Paul Lecourt. We've been told his death was accidental. Is that your recollection also?'

Allard hesitated. It was only a second or two, but it was enough for Coco and Cedric to notice. 'I was there. It was an accident,' he gave by way of an answer. 'A terrible, terrible accident.'

'There was never any suspicion of foul play?' Cedric asked.

Allard turned his head away from them. 'It was a tragedy, that's all.' He faced them sharply. 'What on earth does this have to do with what happened now?' he snapped.

Coco spread her hands in front of her. 'I didn't say it had anything to do with it, however we really can't ignore the fact we're on the tenth anniversary of young Paul's passing.'

Allard took a deep breath. He locked eyes with Coco. 'Frère Leroy thought so,' he said in a whisper.

Coco looked surprised. 'So, that's why he called?'

He nodded. 'He remembered something, but he wasn't sure if he misremembered it and wanted to check with me because he knew I was also there the day Paul died.'

'Odd that we saw him last night and he didn't bother to mention it to us,' Coco snapped.

'I don't think there was anything untoward about it,' Allard said reassuringly. 'Gerard certainly wasn't trying to keep anything from you.' He noticed the doubtful look on Coco's face and he gave her a sad smile. 'I get it's part of your job to assume everything you hear is a lie until you know otherwise. All I can tell you is I am sure Gerard Leroy was a good man with the heart of a lion. He wouldn't lie to you, he wouldn't lie to anyone.'

'No offence, doctor,' Cedric interrupted, 'but you would say that, wouldn't you? He was your friend and it seems to us you all cover each other's backs when it comes down to it.'

Coco leaned forward, she understood the direction of

Cedric's questions, but she was tired and she was worried, and at that point she did not want to risk alienating Joël Allard, not least until she had convinced him to talk. 'You said Frère Leroy remembered something?' she pushed. 'What was that exactly?'

Allard bit his lip. 'As I said, he'd almost convinced himself it was some sort of false memory, triggered by what happened to Odilon Sander.'

Coco took a sharp breath. 'He thought there was a connection?'

Allard slouched. 'He wanted my advice. He didn't want to report something that might have no bearing on what happened to Odilon.' He stopped, before continuing cautiously. 'The arrangements of the coffins reminded Gerard of something. He called because he was concerned and wanted my counsel. It wasn't so much about how the coffins were arranged, but the way in which Paul's body was discovered that was odd.'

'Odd?' Coco asked, her voice rising sharply.

'Oui,' Allard replied. 'He wasn't wearing shoes.'

'He wasn't?' Cedric asked. 'That's odd. I thought he was discovered outside the youth centre.'

Allard took a moment. 'That is correct, however his shoes weren't. They were found *inside* the youth centre.'

'That's weird, non?' Coco suggested.

'Peut être,' the doctor conceded. 'Mais, as you know, there was no suggestion of anything untoward. I examined the poor child myself. He fell and hit his head.'

'Or was pushed?' Coco interrupted. 'By a taunting bully, maybe?'

Allard shrugged. 'Possibly, however, I don't think it's that simple. There was no one around. No one came forward to say they had witnessed anything. What would you have had us do differently? I mean, the police came and they too saw it for what it was. A tragedy.'

'What about the shoes? You said they were discovered inside the youth centre?' Coco asked. 'Surely someone must have thought that odd?'

'I suppose,' Allard conceded with obvious reluctance. 'Remember though, it was summer and it was hot. Kids often kick off their shoes and run around. I don't really recall any of us thinking there was anything unusual about it. They were just little plimsolls, the ones that flop on and off feet all of the time.'

'Where were the shoes found?' Cedric asked.

The reluctant look appeared again on Allard's face. Coco shook her head irritably. 'If you're thinking of lying, Dr. Allard, think twice. Now answer the lieutenant's question and let us determine whether it's relevant, or not.'

'The third floor, and the ground floor,' Allard blurted.

Coco looked at Cedric. His eyes widened and he shrugged his shoulders. Coco closed her eyes briefly, a scenario running through her mind, a scenario she did not care to consider possible. Her eyes snapped open. 'That's where we found the coffins.'

Allard nodded. 'Je sais, mais…'

'There's no connection, yeah, I get it,' Coco grumbled. 'But, what if there is?'

Cedric turned to her. 'What are you thinking?'

'Oh, I don't know,' she reasoned. 'I mean, we could imagine a scenario of a kid running carefree through the youth centre, happy and gay, his shoes falling off as he skips happily along, and that could be possible, I guess, but there's something not quite right about it, as far as I can tell.'

Cedric snorted. 'We're not living in a fucking Pippi Longstocking movie?' he laughed.

Coco stuck her tongue out at him again. 'You're so rude,' she grumbled. She winked at Allard. 'He's so rude.' She narrowed her eyes. 'Despite the reference, there is one other reason I can think of that a ten-year-old kid may lose his shoes in two different places and not stop to pick them up.'

'He was being chased,' Cedric concluded.

Coco nodded. She kept staring at Allard. 'And you're telling me none of this concerned any of you? I mean, you're a smart guy, but I don't believe for a second you didn't think it was odd. And I also can't believe that the police called to the scene wouldn't have also thought it was odd. Unless, of course…'

'Unless?' Allard questioned without looking up.

The thought occurred to her suddenly. 'Frère Leroy didn't call you last night because he remembered something. He wanted to confess something, didn't he?'

Dr. Allard said nothing. Coco repeated the question.

'For what it's worth,' Allard said after a time, 'Gerard said they never believed there was anything wrong. And also for what it's worth, I believe that too.' He took a long breath. 'They found his shoes and put them back on his feet,' he spoke as if saying the words was a relief. 'When he called, he said he hadn't thought about it in ten years. I don't mean the death of the poor child. I think we've all thought about that over and over, but he said he had never thought about the shoes. Not until yesterday and with what happened to Odilon Sander. Not until the anniversary. I don't really understand it myself.'

'And you told Frère Leroy that?' Coco asked.

He nodded. 'I said, as I wasn't privy to the problem with the shoes, I couldn't really think of a reason why there might be a connection. I told him I thought it was odd, but that ultimately, it was likely inconsequential. I thought I had reassured him, but he didn't seem convinced. He said he had to go because he needed to speak to someone.'

'Who?' Coco demanded.

Allard shook his head quickly. 'I don't know.'

'I don't believe you,' Coco snapped.

'It's true!' Allard cried desperately. 'I swear I don't know who he was going to speak with. Don't you think I would tell you if I knew? Gerard is dead, and I was probably one of the last people who spoke to him before he was murdered. If I knew who murdered him, I promise you I would tell you.'

'To be frank, doc, your word means bupkis to me right now,' Coco responded. 'Because you could have told me this earlier. We're only hearing it now because we came to you and that was just because I wondered how you knew about his death. Tell me this - were you going to call me?'

He turned his head. 'Oui. I was.'

Coco shook her head. 'I guess I'll have to take your word for that.'

Allard sighed. 'It was a difficult situation, not just for me, for Frère Leroy also. When he refused to tell me who he was going to speak to, I understood why.'

'And what was the reason?'

Allard clasped his hands together. 'I know this isn't likely to sit well with you, but men of belief are bound by rules you might not understand or agree with.'

Coco frowned, wondering what he meant. It dawned on her. 'Ah, you're talking about the seal of the confessional, aren't you?'

He nodded. 'I suspect so. Somebody may have spoken with Frère Leroy in confession, and that obviously meant Gerard felt unable to talk about it.'

'Pile of crap,' Cedric grumbled. 'Especially when we're talking about a crime.'

Allard smiled sadly at him. 'I told you, you wouldn't understand.'

'And you do?' Cedric retorted.

Allard considered his answer for a few moments. 'I understand the complexity of such situations, and the need for utmost secrecy. Without it, it renders the whole purpose of confession redundant.' He stood up and immediately sat back down again. 'With hindsight, however, I do wish I had pressed Gerard as to who he might need to speak with. I assumed it was someone in the monastery.'

'Not necessarily,' Coco reasoned. She looked at Cedric. 'Get Ebba to check the phone logs in and out of the monastery, not just for last night, but for the last few days.'

Cedric nodded and pulled out his cell phone. Coco faced Allard again. 'Say I believe you didn't know about the missing shoes - what did you think when Frère Leroy told you about them?'

'I'm not sure,' Allard replied with a deep sigh. 'I suppose like you, I thought it was odd, but I didn't really think it meant he was murdered. I didn't back then, and I'm not sure I think differently now. Whatever happened to Paul Lecourt was a tragedy, but I still believe it was an accident.'

'An accident that was covered up?' Coco suggested.

'I can't answer that, because I don't know,' Allard replied. 'Gerard was definitely confused about it, but I don't think he was entirely convinced. He wanted my advice and I gave it to him, that's it. The ten-year anniversary and the death of Odilon all brought it to the surface again, that's all.'

'Who else knew about the shoes?'

'I don't know, and he didn't tell me.' He smiled sadly at Coco. 'I know I can't convince you otherwise, but that is the truth. You do believe me, don't you?'

Coco shrugged. 'I don't know what to believe, other than the fact it seems to me Frère Leroy wasn't the only person to have withheld this fact, for whatever reason, whether it was important or not.' She jumped to her feet. 'Let's go. You're going to take me to the monastery and we're going to talk to the remaining monks, and you're going to make sure they don't lie, because if they refuse to talk to us a second longer, I'm going to make all of your lives a misery. And believe me, I can do that.' She smiled at Cedric. 'Tell him, lieutenant.'

Cedric covered the mouthpiece of his cell phone. 'She can do that, and she can do that very easily and without breaking a sweat,' he informed Allard.

'He's right,' Coco agreed. 'So, let's stop all this pussyfooting around.' She stood. 'I can't profess to know exactly what happened ten years ago and whether it has anything to do with what happened this week, but all I know is that I'm ready to find out. And that begs the question, are you?'

Allard rose slowly to his feet. 'Let's go to the monastery.'

12H15

For what felt like the hundredth time, Coco wrapped her fingers around the gate railings which provided the only entrance to *Abbaye Le Bastien*. She turned her head slowly, taking her time to examine the building. Like the former youth centre, it appeared to be badly in need of repair, but despite the cracked walls, and the ivy traipsing slowly around the brickwork, she could not dispute the fact it appeared to be a place of peace and serenity. But she was also acutely aware of how appearances could be deceptive.

Dr. Allard pulled the bell again, the shrill sound echoing from the monastery. The journey from the hospital to the monastery had been in all but silence, the only sound Cedric typing rapidly into his cell phone. Coco had decided to allow Allard the time to reflect on what he needed to do. She imagined him to be a good man, but a man torn between his religious beliefs and his medical ones. She hoped Sonny was right about him and that he could be trusted. She was not entirely convinced.

Finally, the door to the monastery swung slowly open and Estelle Grainger exited. She stopped, her eyes widening when she saw who was waiting on the other side of the gate. She did not move, hesitation clearly spreading across her face. She looked back to the monastery and Coco realised she was considering going back into the building and closing the door behind her.

Coco stood on her tip toes, grabbing her ID and waving it in the air. 'Woo-hoo!' she shouted waving and pointing to the ID. 'Police!'

Estelle's lips twisted angrily and after a few further moments began walking slowly along the pebbled walkway in the direction of the gate. She walked so slowly it caused Coco to tut. 'No hurry, love,' she grumbled irritably.

'What do you want?' Estelle demanded when she finally made it to the gate.

Coco pointed to the lock. 'I want you to open the damn gate, that's what I want,' she snapped.

Estelle sneered. 'I thought you had already been told your presence here was not allowed.'

Coco shrugged. 'I get that a lot, believe it or not,' she answered cheerfully, 'and when I do, I know it's the only place I need to be, if I don't want to get shafted, that is.'

Estelle's nostrils flared and she fixed Coco with a disgusted look.

'Estelle, please let us in,' Allard said in a calm, even tone.

Estelle turned her head abruptly to him. 'I didn't realise I was taking orders from you now, Dr. Allard.' She pronounced the word *doctor* as if was a dirty word. 'Unless you've suddenly found Dieu again and turned away from your heathen beliefs?'

'Open the gate,' Allard said, his tone sill passive. 'Or else I'll call the bishop and have him come down here.' He smiled. 'I know the bishop well, but I also know he's not here for a reason. He does not want his presence to bring even more attention to what has happened in the last few days.'

Estelle turned back to Coco. 'The brothers are resting and cannot be disturbed.'

'Resting, praying, eating. They certainly spend a lot of time doing shit that means they can't be disturbed,' Coco replied. 'So either open the gate or I'll have a locksmith here within the hour to force our way in.'

'Estelle,' Allard pleaded. 'The gate, s'il vous plaît.'

She tutted loudly and pulled back the lock. 'There'll be hell to pay,' she muttered as she began heading back to the monastery.

Coco nodded. 'There always is,' she laughed.

12H20

Estelle Grainger led Coco, Cedric and Dr. Allard down a long, narrow hallway. It was dark, with wood panelled walls and dark floorboards. The only light came from candles lining the walls in ancient holders. Estelle stopped abruptly causing Coco to crash into her. They were in front of a closed door, bearing a carved sign. *The Grand Hall.* Grainger pushed open the door and stepped backwards, gesturing for Coco and the others to move forward.

Coco stepped into the room and was startled. She gasped, covering her mouth. There was a row of monks, all dressed in cassocks and staring po faced straight at her. It was all she could do to stop herself from screaming an expletive. Instead she curtsied in front of them. It did not change the stoic expressions on their faces. She took a moment to recover her composure, her eyes scanning the faces. She guessed there to be seventeen or eighteen men, but there was no Mathieu Moreau, she realised with disappointment. At the head of the line was Frère Henri Aries, the small, rotund monk with the cold impassive face. He fixed cold eyes on her which showed clear contempt.

'You bother us at such a time?' Aries broke the silence. He pointed at Dr. Allard. 'And you brought them in?'

Coco suppressed a smile, by his tone she half expected Aries to call the doctor, Judas.

Allard stepped into the room, moving past Coco and Cedric. He stood in front of the monks and bowed his head, quickly uttering a prayer. The monks, all except Aries who did not stop looking at Coco, joined in. He slowly turned his head to the other monks in the line and raised his fingers to his lips, pushing them across as if he was gesturing for them to be silent.

'The hell you will,' Coco snapped striding forward. 'Unless

you want me to think you're all up to your starched cassocks in the murder of Frère Leroy. The time for silence has passed.'

One of the other monks turned to Aries. 'She has a point, Henri.'

Frère Henri Aries snorted. 'I doubt that very much,' he murmured.

Cedric stepped in front of Coco. 'Hey, show some respect. We are police officers and we're investigating a double homicide. You want us to respect your job, then you'd better respect ours.' He smiled at Coco, before adding, 'capeesh?'

'What do you want to know?' Aries demanded.

Coco stepped in front of him, her eyes flicking over him as she tried to decide what it was about the elderly priest. She had encountered her fair share of grumpy old men, stuck in their ways and reluctant to change their opinions, but Aries appeared different. And it occurred to her there may be another reason for it. Protection. He was protecting someone, or likely protecting himself and the monastery. Either way, it mattered little to her. She wanted him to stop fighting her and if there was one thing she was sure of, she would not rest until he told her everything he knew.

'I want to know everything that happened yesterday,' Coco began. 'And I want you to all stop fighting me. I'm here for one reason and one reason only and that is to figure out who murdered Odilon Sander and Frère Leroy, and for the life of me, I can't figure out why you don't want to help me.'

'There are considerations to be made,' Aries interjected.

'Bullshit,' Coco snapped.

The monk grimaced. 'I don't know why you insist on being uncouth, Captain Brunhild, it is hardly…' he trailed off.

'Ladylike? Decent?' Coco suggested.

'Professional,' Aries added.

Coco laughed. 'Professional? You want to talk to me about being professional?' She pointed at Cedric. 'Because as far as I can tell, Lieutenant Degarmo and I are the only ones who seem to give a flying f…' she bit her lip, before adding, 'who seem to care about what happened to your brother and Odilon Sander.' She raised her hands, waving off his impending objections. 'Don't get all huffy with me when you know I'm speaking the truth.' She clapped her hands together and turned her head, moving it slowly across the line of monks. An image she was sure would come back to her late at night when she could not sleep and one which would manifest itself quite differently than how it looked at that moment.

Coco pulled out a cigarette and lit it. She noticed the disparaging look from Aries. 'Oh, what you gonna do? Grass on me to Dieu? That ship has sailed. He knows me and I know him and we're okay with each other.'

Aries laughed. 'Are you sure?'

Coco narrowed her eyes at him. 'You're damn right I'm sure. If there is a God, I know for a fact <u>she's</u> more interested in me stopping bad men and women from walking the streets than she is me smoking a fag and having sex with random men.' She stopped suddenly. 'Ignore that last bit, it's not relevant. Mais, what is, is that me and the man above are okay with each other, and I don't need to bow and curtsy to him for him to know that.' She noticed one of the older monks in the line was attempting to hide a smile. She pointed at him and winked. 'Hey, sailor, I knew you were the trouble one in the line.' She faced Aries again, serious. 'So, we go back to the point. Two men are dead, and it appears two more people are missing. Maybe they're on the run, they could be guilty, or they could be scared, at this point, who the fuck knows? But, moi? I'm ready to start dragging you all down to the commissariat.'

A trio of monks cried out loud, others reassuring them. Aries spoke something to them in a language Coco did not understand. She did, however, understand the intonation of his speech. Be silent. She folded her arms across her chest. 'And that brings us to the burning question. Who murdered Paul Lecourt?'

She had spoken the words quickly because she wanted to see their reactions. Most of the monks dropped their heads and began praying again. Only Frère Henri Aries continued staring at her, his face as impassive and as cold as always. His mouth twisted. It took a long time for him to speak. 'I expect you already think you know that, don't you?' he asked finally.

Coco nodded. She was not sure she understood at all what had happened to the young man ten years previously, or how the anniversary of his death had triggered a whole new series of events, but she could almost see the clouds in front of her disappearing.

Aries swept past her, heading brusquely in the direction of the door. 'We'll talk in private,' he hissed.

Coco nodded, gesturing for Cedric and Dr. Allard to follow her. She noticed Estelle Grainger lingering in the recesses of the hallway, skulking as if she wished to disappear into the walls. Coco wiggled her finger at her. 'You come too,' she commanded.

12H45

Frère Henri Aries lead Coco, Cedric, Dr. Allard and Estelle Grainger along the narrow dim-lit hallway, only stopping to pause momentarily outside Frère Leroy's office. Aries moved his fingers slowly across the police tape which blocked the doorway. Coco noticed the cloud passing across his face and the way his eyes widened and darkened showed her he clearly cared about what had happened to his brother and friend behind the door. He swept away again, cassock flapping around his short legs.

They continued in silence for a few minutes, turning left and right as they moved down further into the bowels of the monastery, passing one unmarked closed door after another before Aries stopped in front of a final door at the end of the hallway. He reached into this cassock and retrieved a long ornate key. He placed it in the lock and pushed the door open, immediately filling the dim hallway with coloured light. Coco and the others followed him inside, Coco's eyes widening as she took a moment to take in her surroundings. The room was clearly some kind of chapel, with rows of uncomfortable looking wooden benches lined up in front of a large altar, filled with a giant bejewelled cross.

'It's been a long time since I've been in the chapel,' Dr. Allard stated breaking the silence. He turned his head slowly as if he was taking in the majesty of it all.

'It's lovely, I'm sure,' Coco agreed, 'but why are we here?'

Aries moved across the chapel and stopped in front of the altar, genuflecting. Allard and Estelle Grainger joined him and did the same. Coco and Cedric looked sheepishly at each other. Coco looked at her feet and noticed she had a crisp wrapper stuck in the broken sole of her boot. She bent down and discreetly removed it, stuffing it into the pocket of her coat.

Aries returned to face the detectives. 'We are here because it was Gerard's favourite place. He came here not just for prayers with the rest of us. It was here that he shared his private, most intimate moments with Dieu. It was…'

'Why did you want to see us privately?' Cedric interrupted irritably.

'I wanted to spare my brothers any more grief,' Aries answered. 'They are burdened with the sadness of what has happened. They need to reflect and pray, they don't need to carry any more.'

'I think that's our call,' Coco stated. 'And I have to tell you, I'm getting more and more pissed off at being told who I can and can't speak to…'

Aries raised his hands as if he was pacifying a child. 'With Frère Leroy gone, I am now in charge of the monastery. I will allow the brothers to make statements, but I will not require those who have taken a vow of silence to break that vow, however, that does not mean you can't "talk" with them. However, I am hoping that will not be necessary, because I can assure you they will have nothing to tell you which would be useful. I, on the other hand, do.'

Coco raised an eyebrow. 'Well, we'll see about that. Spill your guts, Frère.'

Aries moved his head slowly around the chapel. 'Gerard came to me last night. He asked me to come with him to this room and when we were here he asked me to hear his confession.' He stopped, wide lips pulling in a sad smile. 'I said - *what have we to confess about? Two old monks who barely leave the monastery.* I laughed and added - *if I had an impure thought these days, I wouldn't know what to do with it.*'

Coco covered her mouth to stop herself from snorting.

'Gerard didn't laugh,' Aries continued without looking at her. 'That's when I knew it was serious.'

Coco stepped forward and lowered herself onto one of the wooden benches. It creaked under her. 'Jeez, everyone's a critic,' she complained. 'This is SO uncomfortable. How don't you all have haemorrhoids from sitting on these damn things?'

Cedric shook his head despairingly and stepped in front of her. 'What was he serious about?' he asked Frère Aries.

Aries cleared his throat. 'He told me he believed the death of Odilon Sander was somehow connected to something that happened a long time ago.'

'The death of Paul Lecourt,' Coco said.

Aries nodded. 'I said he was crazy. The death of the child was a tragedy, but that's all it was. He shook his head and told me he had been carrying a burden for a very long time. A burden he had borne because he believed it was the right thing to do.' He paused. 'I took his confession,' he whispered.

Coco slammed her fists on the bench. 'Not this damn nonsense again,' she cried. 'I'm on my last nerve of you guys in frocks all hiding behind that dogma, because as far as I can tell, the only people it protects are the guilty, because it certainly doesn't give a flying… doesn't care about the victims.'

Aries shook his head quickly. 'Gerard told me he took a confession and after much deliberation and prayer, he knew no good would come from him telling anyone what he knew.'

'So he let a child murderer walk free?' Coco snapped with incredulity.

'Non, bien sûr, non,' Aries replied with force. 'It was an accident. It really was. It just didn't happen exactly as everyone believed.'

Coco snorted. 'Yeah, right. Listen, monk. We know about the shoes.'

Aries looked sharply at Dr. Allard. The doctor nodded. 'Gerard called me last night and told me.'

'Had quite the confession party, the three of you, didn't you?'

Coco whistled.

Aries moved his head to the side. He tapped his chin as he continued staring at Allard. 'I suppose that makes sense.'

Coco scratched her head. 'Well, I'm glad it makes sense to you, Frère, because it's as clear as mud to me.'

Aries smiled. 'He wanted to stop me from having to break his confession.'

'But why?' Cedric demanded. 'Unless he knew he was going to die, why confess to you and hope that you and Dr. Allard would pass on the story to us?'

'Because he wasn't done with his little chats,' Coco reasoned. 'His next call was to his murderer.'

They all lapsed into silence as if all processing the possibility. 'So, confession or not,' Coco said finally, 'we need to know everything he said to you, Frère Aries.'

Aries locked eyes with Coco, but did not speak immediately. 'I suppose it would do no harm now.'

'Henri,' Allard interrupted. 'You can't break the seal of the confessional.'

The rotund monk shrugged nonchalantly. 'I'm an old man. What are they going to do? Throw me out onto the streets?' He shook his head. 'Non, my oldest friend is dead, I won't be party to helping his murderer go free.' He continued staring at Coco. 'Not that I imagine it will help you much. The person responsible for Paul Lecourt's death ten years ago is also dead.'

'Odilon Sander?' Coco suggested.

He shook his head again. 'Non.'

Coco frowned, suddenly confused. 'Dead, you said?' she mused, before noticing the expression on Estelle Grainger's face. 'Are you talking about Gasper Peron? The old ex-con who dropped his fortune on the monastery and youth centre?'

Aries nodded. 'Oui, I am.' He moved back to the altar, his back to them all. 'Gerard told me Gasper came to him and told him there had been a terrible accident. He took him to where the young boy had fallen and Gasper explained what had happened. He had been on the third floor and the boy was there and something happened to spook him. He got frightened and ran away. Gasper went after him, following him out of the youth centre and into the gardens. He was calling out, trying to reassure him, but the child did not stop, and then he tripped, banging his head on the rockery. By the time Gasper reached him, the poor boy was already gone.'

Coco did not respond. She shared a look with Cedric that was clear. After a few moments, she clapped her hands. 'And Frère Leroy bought that shit?'

Aries looked at her quizzically. 'Bien sûr he did. Why wouldn't he? He arrived soon afterwards and examined the boy himself. It was exactly as Gerard had explained.'

'And the shoes?' Cedric asked.

'The shoes fell as the boy ran,' Aries replied.

Cedric laughed with incredulity. 'And they just thought it would be cleaner to put them back on the kid's feet?'

'Gasper was in a state of shock when he made his confession,' Aries continued. 'And in that confession he told Gerard about his past and how he believed it would make people look at the accident differently and it was in nobody's interest for that to happen.'

'So, a deal was struck,' Coco said through gritted teeth. 'Keep my secret or the gravy train ends.'

'It wasn't that simple,' Aries sighed. 'There was no crime. What good would it have done to dredge up ancient history?' He looked imploringly at Dr. Allard. 'Joël, tell her.'

Allard nodded. 'I examined the boy, I told you this already. It was just an accident. And if Frère Leroy saw no reason to suspect anything untoward, then why should we?'

'Well someone apparently did,' Coco interrupted.

'I'm still not convinced there is a connection,' Aries said, before conceding reluctantly, 'other than the timing of the two events.'

'We can't ignore it,' Coco replied. 'Especially when we have so little to go on. It's not only a clue, it's a great big, humungous fucking clue!'

Aries tutted. Coco apologised. He tutted again. 'You apologise a lot, Captain Brunhild, but I notice it doesn't actually ever temper your behaviour.'

Coco spread her hands in front of her. 'Them's the damn breaks, brother.' She turned to Estelle Grainger. 'What did you know about any of this? I get the impression you weren't exactly the biggest fan of Monsieur Gasper Peron.'

Estelle spluttered, clenching her fists. 'I hated the bastard.'

Coco clapped her hands. 'Finally, we have some honesty coming through! Tell me, did you know what happened to Paul?'

She shook her head. 'Non, but if I did, I would have known Gasper was lying.'

'And why's that?' Cedric asked.

Estelle snorted. 'Because I knew Gasper Peron and the only thing I can tell you, the ONLY thing I can tell you with utmost certainty is the only time you knew he was lying was when his lips were moving.'

'Sounds like most of the men I've dated,' Coco quipped. She narrowed her eyes. 'Then you think he was lying about what happened to Paul Lecourt?'

Estelle looked anxiously between Frère Aries and Dr. Allard. 'If you're asking do I believe he killed the kid? Then, I have to say, I don't know. What I do know is that I believed in Frère Leroy and I trust his judgement.'

Coco watched the other woman keenly. 'There was a great big BUT in the tone of your voice,' she stated.

Estelle shrugged. 'I don't know what you mean.'

Coco considered her response. 'Because you thought the

same thing I did. What was Gasper Peron doing that scared a ten-year-old boy enough to make him run away, and for Peron to run after him?'

Estelle shrugged again. Coco turned to Aries. 'Do you think the same thing occurred to Frère Leroy?' Aries said nothing. 'There was more to the confession, wasn't there?' He still did not speak. 'Dammit, talk to me!' Coco yelled.

Aries took a deep breath. 'There was more that Gerard wanted to tell me, mais, he didn't.'

Coco gave him a doubtful look. He noticed it. 'It's the truth,' he retorted. 'And all I can tell you is he left me stating there was something he had to do.'

'Something he had to do?' Coco repeated, recalling Frère Leroy had also said something similar to Dr. Allard. 'Were those his exact words? Or did he say he had to see someone?'

Aries considered his answer. He shook his head irritably, before finally saying. 'I can't be sure. He left me and I swear I did not think anything was wrong, or untoward. By that I mean, he did not appear overly worried, or scared, or anything else which might have caused concern.' He stared at Coco and Cedric. 'I sensed no fear in my old friend. All he said was he was going to speak to someone and he believed that would be the end of it.'

'The end of it?' The words puzzled Coco because she could not understand who Frère Leroy would contact. Then a thought occurred to her. She squared up between Frère Aries and Dr. Allard. 'How am I supposed to believe either of you? You've spent years telling lies, it's like a second nature to you all. And now, you expect me to accept your platitudes? Well, forget that. All I can see is that it appears two people are dead because of what happened to a young boy ten years ago and no one is bothering to tell us the truth. And that's not Dieu's way, as far as I'm concerned. It is the way of man. Selfish and self-preserving.' She pressed her hands on the altar. 'And I'm only going to say this once. Either tell me everything you know, or be prepared for the consequences.'

Frère Aries chortled. 'That sounds remarkably like a threat, Captain Brunhild,' he bristled.

Coco nodded several times. 'Then my grasp of the French language isn't as bad as some would have me believe,' she quipped, before narrowing her eyes at him. 'But be clear, the threat is real, it is not implied. I don't care what altar you pray in front of, the only master I'm interested in serving is the one who pays me and allows me to feed my kids.'

'Captain Brunhild…' Dr. Allard wailed.

Coco waved her hand to fend him off. 'I don't want to hear it,' she snapped. 'I'm not sitting on the fence. My only duty is to serve the dead and do what I can to honour them. I only met Frère Leroy a day ago and it seems I care more about what happened to him than either of you do.'

Aries clenched his fists. 'That's a despicable thing to say.'

'And yet you're still lying to me,' Coco countered.

He turned his head away. 'You know nothing about us, or our circumstances.'

'That may be true,' Coco replied. 'And I'm not actually sure I care. Not until I know what is going on here, and until you all level with me, that's not going to happen, is it?'

The chapel descended into an ominous silence. Coco watched the light streaming through the stained-glass windows, throwing colour and sparkling light into the dark chamber. She looked at the various men and women depicted in the glass and she realised she did not know who they were, or what they represented. They were people from a story she had never understood or ever completely believed in, but looking at the light shining through their images in the glass, all she saw was peace and serenity and for a moment she understood why people were comforted by such images.

Dr. Joël Allard finally broke the silence. He crossed the

chapel and placed his hand on Aries' shoulder. 'Henri. This isn't the time to remain silent. Captain Brunhild is correct, this isn't just about the confessional, it can't be. I left the Church to enable me to do a job I believe Dieu wanted me to do, but I had to leave because it was the only way I can truly do my job. It took me a long time to realise I can honour our Lord and serve him, but for it to only inform my work, not to control it.'

He paused. 'I know it is different for you and your brothers. I understand the sacrifice you make to live your life in His honour. But I have to tell you, there are times we must all step back and face the light.' He pointed to Jesus on the altar. 'We face Jesus every day and we pray to him, we talk to him, however I don't know about you, but the Jesus I pray to wouldn't want us to protect murderers.'

Aries' mouth twisted angrily. 'It must be nice to be so sure of such things. I, however, am not.'

'Try,' Allard whispered.

Coco stepped forward, lowering herself onto another wooden bench next to the altar. 'Tell me about Odilon Sander,' she said.

Frère Aries spoke. 'I don't know what I can tell you,' he replied with clear reluctance. 'Other than to confirm, I have never taken confession from Odilon. We were friends, you might say, but not confidants.'

'And Frère Leroy?' Cedric asked.

'They were friends,' Aries conceded. 'Very close friends - if you're asking do I believe if they shared confessions? Then I truly can't say.'

Coco nodded 'What about the other monks?'

Aries shook his head. 'Only Gerard and I are allowed to take confession, because we have made priestly vows.'

She frowned. 'There's a difference?'

He smiled. 'Oui. Not all monks take vows, they're not

required to offer a life of subservience and service to Dieu. Gerard and I met at college and were the only two in our class who knew that the life of a "normal" priest was not for us. It was our intention to come together in the community in a different way.'

He extended his hands. 'A monastery and a youth centre and a haven for the homeless in the heart of a thriving community was both of our dreams, but really it was instigated and led by Gerard. He was an expert in tending to those who needed his guidance, but that was only a small part of the job. There was the rest of it. The finance, the paperwork, the bowing and curtailing to those who could provide the funds for us to continue our work. He was very good at it.' He flashed a wry smile. 'I don't know if you've noticed this about me, but I don't share many of the same traits.'

'You're a peach, just like me,' Coco laughed.

Aries gave her a horrified look. 'Don't make me feel worse than I already do, Captain, I beg you!' He offered a smile that she understood. It was as close to a white flag as she could imagine he would go.

'I'll level with you,' Coco said in as cheerful a tone as she could muster, 'it's like shooting fish in a barrel right now.'

'Am I the fish?' he asked with a wry smile.

She winked at him. 'Keep it up and you just might be, sailor. Let's be honest. Something horrible has happened here. We can't ignore the connection to what happened to Paul Lecourt ten years ago. We now know that Frère Leroy was somehow caught up in it all, either by what he saw, or what he heard, or what he was told. If you're telling us you don't know what that is, I don't imagine I can beat the truth out of you, but there is something we're missing. Something that involves Odilon Sander.'

'I wish I could help,' Aries responded. 'Whatever happened to Odilon, whatever he knew, whatever he saw, I was not privy to it. And that is the truth.'

Coco nodded. 'Will you allow us to take statements from

your brothers?' she asked.

'It won't help, mais oui, I won't stand in your way.' The monk stepped away, moving again to the altar. 'I think I need to be alone. Dieu may just give me the answers you need.'

Coco sighed. 'This is not the first time we've been brushed off, and TBH it's getting pretty fucking boring.'

Aries moved his shoulders slowly, wincing as if it caused him discomfort. 'Pour moi aussi. Give me a little more time, Captain, and I will try my best to reassure you that Dieu does not have to work against you.'

Coco gave him a doubtful look. 'We'll see. I'll send some officers to interview the brothers and to make sure no one enters or leaves the monastery, but you have to understand, this can't go on any longer. One of your brothers is missing and we don't know whether he is in danger or a perp and it's all because nobody is helping us.'

Aries nodded, he moved across the altar and wrapped his arm around Dr. Allard's shoulders. 'We will pray together.'

In the corner, Estelle Grainger cleared her throat as if she was asking for permission to speak, or to leave. Coco turned to her, and her first instinct was to say something cutting, but she saw the older woman's face and there was something about it which stabbed at her heart. It was almost as if she was standing stock still on the spot, unsure what to do, where to move, or what to say. Like she was waiting for permission, or instruction. Coco moved to her and touched her arm. 'If I'm going to be sending over four or five cops, they're going to want refreshments. Can you fix that?'

Estelle's eyes widened, suddenly alert with the prospect of something tangible to occupy her time. 'I'm not running a damn café here, you know,' she responded with what appeared to be forced irritation.

Coco turned away from her abruptly and gestured to Cedric. 'C'mon, let's get back to the commissariat and talk.' She addressed

Frère Aries and Dr. Allard again. 'I'll be back in an hour, so be quick with your call with Him,' she said pointing above her head, 'or else I suspect we're all in for a very, very long day.'

13H30

Coco threw herself into the swivel chair opposite her desk and yanked a cigarette from a packet. She lit it, immediately puffing smoke into the air. The forensic technician, Ebba Blom wafted her hand, coughing in an exaggerated fashion. 'Drama queen,' Coco sniffed.

'If I die, I'll sue,' Ebba stated grumpily. 'And you know, if anyone can come back from beyond the grave, it would be me and I'd be back for my pound of flesh.'

Coco snorted. 'Good luck with that.' She pointed at her boot. 'You can try selling these, though I suspect you'd have to pay someone to take them off your hands.'

Ebba moved to the opposite side of the office, muttering something in her native Swedish.

Cedric poured himself a coffee from the percolator on top of a filing cabinet, grimacing as he tasted it. He turned around. 'What did you make of the monks?'

Coco shrugged. 'I still don't think they're telling us all they know, but I'm not sure what we can do to make them, short of dragging them by the scruff of the frocks and throwing them in a cell. You can imagine how Demissy would take to that, and I'm not sure I'm feeling brave enough to take the risk putting my job on the line just because of some lying monks.' She sighed deeply as if she had just had enough of it all.

They had travelled back to the commissariat in silence. Coco had been preoccupied with it all, trying to make sense of a situation that made little sense. She had come to one conclusion - everything she needed to solve the crime was in front of her, she just needed to clear the fog in her brain and she was sure it would become clear.

She reached into a drawer and searched amongst the papers and files. 'Ah-ha!' she cried triumphantly, extracting a small whisky bottle and adding a healthy slug to her café. She noticed the horrified look on Cedric's face. He pointed to the wall clock. She shrugged again, rubbing her throat. 'It's medicinal, I have a tickle.'

'You are ridiculous,' Ebba muttered, picking at her fingernails, before adding, 'in more ways than one.'

Cedric laughed loudly. 'You're just realising that?'

Coco tutted. 'Don't be bitchy, the pair of you!' She slurped her drink. 'I need this because it helps me negate the bullshit we have to deal with every day.'

'And it helps?' Ebba countered.

Coco poured another. 'Nah, but it makes me less likely to slap the silly out of suspects. And, I don't know if you are aware, but we've pretty much reached our quota of silly this time around. So, what you got to make it better for us?'

'I have a few things,' Ebba replied, 'but I'm not sure what help it might be.'

'Any help is some help, as far as I'm concerned,' Coco interjected. 'We're in the dark here, Ebba.'

Ebba gave a contented smile. 'I don't get paid enough,' she stated.

Coco gave her a surprised look. 'And you think I do? You sound as if you have something, do you?' she asked keenly.

Ebba pulled out her laptop and notepad and slapped them on the desk. 'Okay, we have a couple of interesting things. Firstly, I've finally found out where Odilon Sander has been when he was pretending to be in China.'

Coco clapped her hands excitedly. 'Finally!' she exclaimed.

Ebba shot her a filthy look. 'Don't judge me, judge the damn legal system in this stupid country and the hoops we have to jump through to get a warrant just to make sure rich and powerful people never really have to be accountable for what they do…'

Coco's mouth contorted. 'Anyho… let's move on from that *particular* raw nerve. Where has Odilon Sander been dipping his wick when he was supposed to have been eating sushi in the Orient?'

'Sushi is from Japan not China. Anyway, he was in Northern France volunteering at a shelter for women and children, victims of domestic abuse,' Ebba replied.

Coco was surprised. She was not sure what she had been expecting, but it was not that. She scratched her head. 'And why was he doing that?'

'For fun? A hobby? Repentance?' Cedric suggested slowly.

Coco stood up, sucking on the cigarette. 'Repentance sounds about right. Mais, wasn't it a weird way to go about it?'

Cedric shrugged. 'We have no idea what he did, or what he was involved in, maybe this was his way of making sense of something from his past.'

Coco sighed. 'And yet again, we have no idea what that might be.' She faced Ebba. 'Any indication of what he was up to there?'

Ebba shook her head. 'Not really. It seems as if he was an exemplary volunteer. I found no evidence of any crimes committed in the region, or reports of abuse in any way. By all accounts, he was just a man who spent his down time volunteering to help what I gather were some pretty poorly disadvantaged kids.'

'Then why hide it?' Coco asked with a frown. 'If you're doing good deeds, why the hell hide it? Nobody I know would do such a thing, it's probably even a tax write-off.' She locked eyes with Cedric. 'Why did Odilon Sander disappear two or three times a year and not brag about it? Not even brag about it, but blatantly lie about it?'

Cedric extended his hands. 'He was atoning for his sins, without having to admit something he knew would likely throw a hand grenade into his nice rich life in Paris.'

Coco nodded her agreement. The thought had occurred to

her as well, but it did not make a lot of sense. They were still missing so much. 'It's weird all the same,' she concluded. 'Why not tell his wife and his child or his friends? Was there anything else you found out about his time away from Paris?'

'Not really,' Ebba concluded. 'Once I got the mandate I went through all of his bank account records and I have to admit it was all pretty boring. He took cash out, probably to pay for his hotel and food when he was away, but there wasn't a lot of it. It seems he lived like,' she stopped giving a wry smile, before adding with a grin, 'a monk.'

'And there was nothing odd about his time away?' Cedric demanded.

'I don't think so,' Ebba replied. 'Like I said, it all seemed to be above board, nothing but good words about him.'

'Then what was he up to?' Coco mused. She turned to Cedric. 'It might be worth putting out a call to the local police there and asking them to sniff around and see if there was any indication of Odilon Sander being up to something untoward.' She noticed his hesitant look. 'Je sais, it's a long shot, but long shots are about all we have right now. Did you find anything else?' she asked Ebba. 'What about the phone records in and out of the monastery.'

'There were no calls out of the monastery last night,' Ebba replied.

Coco frowned. That was not what she had been expecting. She had been sure Frère Leroy had called someone, and whoever that had been, was someone who had either been directly involved in his death or had information which would most definitely assist with the investigation. 'Well, that's odd,' she mused. 'Both Frère Aries and Dr. Allard said Leroy was going to speak to someone. So, either they lied, and they do have cell phones, or it was someone in the monastery.'

'Or someone could have come to the monastery,' Cedric added.

Coco shook her head. 'That doesn't make sense either. How would they know Leroy had remembered something unless he told them? Non, there must be a cell phone.'

'I searched the monastery myself,' Ebba interrupted. 'And didn't find anything.'

'Did you search everywhere?'

The forensic expert shrugged. 'I'm not stupid, but if you're asking did I search all the coffins in the crypt, then no, I didn't.'

'Well, perhaps you should have,' Coco quipped. 'Mind you, old buildings like that often have hidden rooms, cupboards, a hidey-hole where all manner of things can be locked away from prying eyes, like the monk's porn stash, par example.'

Ebba sighed. 'You want me to go over it again?'

'It might be worth a go,' Coco agreed.

'Like I've got nothing else to do,' Ebba grumbled under her breath. She looked at her pad. 'I finished all the background checks and there's nothing that stands out, I'm afraid.'

'And I heard from the Swiss police,' Cedric added, 'and there's no evidence Paul Lecourt's adopted parents left Switzerland any time recently, in fact the officer who interviewed them said unless they were damn good liars, he didn't get the impression they were too cut up about the anniversary of the death of the kid. If anything, he wasn't sure they even remembered. They're getting on and have four other children they're looking after, so their hands are pretty full. He also asked them if they thought there had been anything suspicious about Paul's death and they claimed they didn't think so.'

'Another dead end,' Coco grumbled. 'In a case filled with dead ends, I suppose I shouldn't be surprised.' She stubbed out the cigarette and took a swig of the laced café, emitting a contented sigh. Her telephone rang and she grumpily snatched it. 'Allô, Brunhild. Ah, he is? Bon, show him up to interview room one.' She replaced the receiver and jumped to her feet, draining the remains of the drink. 'C'mon, Lieutenant. Aaron Cellier is here with his son Idris. Ebba, you'll go over the monastery once more? Find me a phone, or something, anything I can use, okay?'

Ebba whistled. 'You mean you want a miracle?'

Coco grinned. 'Well, you're going to the right place for one, aren't you?'

14H00

Coco moved swiftly along the hallway outside her office, pounding the floor of the commissariat, her coat billowing behind her, Cedric a few steps behind was struggling to keep up with her. She stopped abruptly, causing Cedric to crash into her. Aaron Cellier was in front of the interview room, his head bowed as he spoke hurriedly into his son's ear. Idris Cellier jerked his head back, glaring at his father and mouthing something Coco was sure was not pleasant.

'Bonjour messieurs,' she announced cheerfully. 'Et merci for coming…' she glanced at her watch and shook her head before adding sarcastically, 'so promptly.'

Aaron Cellier pushed against his son's arm. 'Junior here decided hiding from me was a good idea.'

'Toujours,' Idris Cellier snapped.

Coco stepped in-between the two of them. 'Hey, kid. I'm the expert in dealing with kids who think they know better than us old folks and I'm here to tell you, you don't! Do you know why I know that? Because twenty-some years ago, I was exactly like you, only I had a kid growing in my stomach.'

Idris looked down at her. 'Looks like you still do,' he commented.

Coco touched her stomach. 'Bitch,' she mouthed. 'Any-ho, let's go and talk,' she said kicking open the door to the interview room. She pushed Idris into the room and went after him. Aaron Cellier followed her, she stopped and shook her head. 'You stay out here,' she said, pointing to a seat opposite.

'Non, he's my son, I have to be with him, he's only a child,' Aaron snapped.

Coco shook her head. 'Non, you don't. He's old enough to

be interviewed without you, and that's exactly what should happen.' She touched his arm. 'Listen, it's my experience kids are more willing to talk openly when their parents aren't breathing down their necks judging them. Give us a few minutes and I guarantee we'll know pretty quickly whether your son has anything to tell us.'

Aaron turned his head quickly between his son and Coco, his eyes narrowing in confusion. After a few moments he nodded. Coco ushered Cedric into the interview room and slammed the door behind them.

'Take a seat, kid,' she commanded.

'Non, I won't,' Idris replied in a cold and antagonistic way.

Coco cackled. 'Hey, you think surly adolescent works on me, kid? Well, I'm here to tell you, it doesn't. Been there, done that, wrung the necks of those who tried, that sort of thing. So, take a seat and we'll talk, d'accord?'

Idris Cellier moved slowly across the interview room, eventually throwing his body into one of the seats. He glared at Coco and Cedric, his mouth twisting into a petulant pout. Coco understood it completely. It was antagonistic and at the same time it was a child issuing an ultimatum. *I don't understand what is happening and I hate you.* It was not unlike every experience she had with her own children.

'What is this about?' he demanded.

'You know exactly what this is about,' Coco responded. 'Three missing coffins and two murdered men.'

'And I had fuck all to do with it,' Idris stated cockily.

Coco studied the young man's face. He was not as his father had described him. Aaron Cellier had said that Idris was once a cheeky young boy but had been changed by his time at the youth centre, presumably from being bullied, but at that moment, in the interview room, Idris Cellier did not seem frightened of anything, least of all his own shadow.

'We have proof you and your two friends, Sofia Charton and

Jericho Martin removed the coffins from *Abbaye Le Bastien*,' Coco stated. It was a lie, but a lie she was prepared to make to get him to talk.

His eyes flashed anxiously. 'Non, you don't,' he said with forced bravado. 'Mathieu Moreau can say what he likes, but it doesn't make it true. He's a hanger-on that's all. Desperate to be part of something he can't belong to anymore.'

Coco felt the familiar stab upon hearing his name, but this time she was filled with an overwhelming sadness for a young man living a life not of his choosing. She cleared her throat and shook her head. 'We don't need his word, we have other proof.'

Idris looked anxiously between Coco and Cedric, and they remained stoic faced. 'You're lying,' he said. The fear he had been hiding had returned.

'Nope, we aint,' Coco said cheerfully. 'We found evidence on the coffins. We know it was you and your pals.' She paused, studying his face. His eyes were wide and darting from side to side as if he was having a dozen thoughts at the same time. Coco did not want to push him too far for fear he would clam up and demand an avocat.

'Listen, kid,' she began reassuringly. 'I know you were cajoled into this, and that it was just meant to be a prank, but if you want Lieutenant Degarmo here to believe that, then you're going to have to level with us. He doesn't believe you just removed the coffins, he believes you murdered Odilon Sander too, and now we have proof tying you to the coffins, well...' she trailed off, letting out a loud, long whistle before adding, 'it just doesn't look good for you, does it?'

'I should talk to an avocat,' Idris whispered.

'You could,' Coco reasoned, 'but once you do, there's not a lot else we can do for you. We'd have to charge you with double murder.'

Idris slammed his fists on the desk. 'I didn't murder anyone!'

he wailed. 'It was just supposed to be a joke, I swear.'

Coco smiled reassuringly. 'You see, I knew it was,' she said playfully punching Cedric's bicep.

Cedric narrowed his eyes to Idris. 'Tell us everything that happened, and tell us right now or I'll throw you in a cell and to hell with helping you.'

Idris nodded incessantly. 'Okay, okay, I'll tell you everything,' he blurted. 'We went into the crypt, because we go there to party. It's weird, but it's also kinda fun.'

'How often do you go?' Coco asked.

'Sometimes every weekend,' Idris replied. 'But usually once a month because we didn't want to risk getting caught. Jericho would call Mathieu, and he would leave the gate unlocked for us.'

Coco scratched her head. 'What was different this time, because I'm fairly sure you never hijacked coffins before? Was it because it was the anniversary of Paul Lecourt?'

Idris did not answer immediately. 'I don't really know, he didn't make sense.'

'He?' Coco interrupted. 'You're talking about Jericho Martin?'

Idris shook his head. 'Non, Vichy.'

'Vichy Sander? Odilon Sander's son?' Coco demanded with a confused frown. She had not imagined the dead man's son was part of the gang.

'Yeah. He came with us. He didn't always come, but this time he did,' Idris replied. 'Vichy called Sofia. She always felt guilty about the way we treated him when we were kids, so she talked Jericho into letting Vichy come this time.'

'How did this all come about?' Cedric asked. 'I mean hanging out and getting wasted in a crypt is one thing, but stealing three coffins and dragging them to the youth centre is a whole other level of craziness.'

'I told you, Vichy wasn't making a lot of sense. He just said it was our last chance to do something.'

Coco leaned forward. 'And what did he mean?'

Idris shrugged. 'I don't know. He just kept saying over and over that once the youth centre came down then it would be the end of it all and there would never be justice.'

'Justice? Justice for Paul Lecourt?' Coco suggested.

'Yeah,' Idris continued.

Coco considered for a few moments. 'And it was his idea to steal the coffins?'

He nodded again. 'He chose them and then...'

'He chose them?' Coco repeated, her voice rising sharply.

'Yeah. Kicked up a big fuss because he couldn't find Frère Bardot.'

Coco and Cedric turned to face one another. A look swept across Coco's face as she recalled a conversation with Frère Leroy. 'Frère Bardot's first name was Paul wasn't it?'

'I think so, yeah,' Cedric replied. 'Why?'

'Leroy said he died about nine years ago,' Coco recalled. 'And he also told us that Paul Lecourt was found abandoned outside the monastery and that he was named after the person who found him.'

'Frère Bardot?'

'It would be logical,' Coco conceded. She pursed her lips. 'But what isn't logical is - why would Vichy Sander deliberately choose Frère Bardot's coffin?'

'I have no answer for that,' Cedric conceded.

'Don't look at me either,' Idris added.

'It has to be connected,' Coco mused. 'It just can't see how. What about the other two coffins?' she asked Idris. 'Did he deliberately choose them too?'

'Yeah, weird bastard,' Idris quipped.

Coco mulled it over, a myriad of thoughts competing for attention in her muddled brain. She pulled open her notepad and looked at her indecipherable handwriting. *Anna Nols - Gasper Peron.*

'Did you know Anna Nols and Gasper Peron?' she asked Idris.

'The dyke and the creep?' Idris responded with a sarcastic, cruel laugh.

Coco tried to recall what she could about Anna Nols. She was sure Frère Leroy had described her as single woman with no family and a patron of the monastery. Gasper Peron, on the other hand was a man of dubious character and a lengthy criminal record. 'How did you know them?' she enquired.

'They were always hanging around the centre. She was always watching us kids, standing looking. It was weird. And Peron was the same, always watching, like some goddamn pervert.'

'Calling someone a pervert just because they were watching you at a youth centre is a bit of a stretch,' Cedric suggested.

'It's the way they watched us that was weird,' Idris replied. 'I can't really explain it, but it wasn't like the other adults. It was like… like…'

'Like?' Coco pushed, sensing it could be important.

He shrugged. 'Like they knew us, I guess. My grandfather used to look at me like that when I was a kid playing in the park. Like he cared, or some shit like that.'

Coco leaned in and whispered in Cedric's ear. 'Find out when Anna Nols died and what she died of and get someone to pick up Vichy Sander.' He nodded and quickly moved out of the interview room. She turned back to Idris. 'Your father seems pleased the youth centre has gone. Why do you think that is?'

'Cos he's an idiot,' Idris snorted. 'He thinks I got mixed up with the wrong crowd and that it "changed me." Maybe it did, who cares? I don't care what anyone says about them, they're my friends and that's all that matters.'

Coco watched him and recognised the loneliness on his face, because she had seen it a hundred or so times on her own son Julien's face. He had grown up a sensitive child, most likely gay, and that, combined with his natural awkwardness, had seemingly put a target on his back for bullies. She was not sure if Idris was gay, but he was most certainly awkward and self-conscious and as she recalled, Jericho Martin was the sort of kid who was likely popular with both girls and boys. She could understand why someone like Idris Cellier might look up to him.

'So, Idris, tell me what happened that night,' Coco continued. 'Didn't any of you try to stop Vichy Sander?'

'Not really,' he replied. 'I guess we thought it was funny. I didn't really think we'd go through with it, but before I knew what was happening we were dragging the damn coffins from the crypt.' He laughed. 'I suppose you think that's weird, don't you?'

Coco snorted. 'Yeah, a little. So, the four of you dragged three coffins from the monastery to the building site and then what? Whose idea was it to arrange them that way?'

'His. It was scary dragging them up the stairs, I kept thinking the floorboards were going to give way,' Idris replied.

'And then what?' Coco pushed.

'And then we left.'

'All of you?'

He shook his head. 'Vichy stayed.'

Coco leaned forward to get a good look at his face. When she asked her next question, she wanted to be sure he was telling the truth. 'And what about his father? What about Odilon Sander? How did he end up in Gasper Peron's coffin?'

Idris's eyes widened. 'I don't know, I swear!' he cried. 'I never even saw Monsieur Sander. I don't know how he ended up in the coffin.'

Coco nodded. 'Did Vichy talk about his father?'

He thought about it for a while. 'I don't think so. I don't remember him mentioning him at all.'

Coco studied the young man. She did not think he was lying. 'Why did Vichy say he was staying with the coffins?'

'He just said he was going to hang around,' Idris shrugged.

'And you didn't think that was odd?' Coco countered.

'Not really. Jericho was bored and wanted to go and score some weed.'

'And you all left apart from Vichy?'

'Yeah. I didn't pay a lot of attention to what was going on, to be honest. The whole thing was giving me bad vibes and I just wanted out of it.'

Coco understood what he was saying and despite it all she was grateful to the young man because she was sure he had been one of the few people who had finally been honest with her. She was also positive the information he had shared was likely to be instrumental in making sense of what had actually happened two days earlier. She stood, pushing the chair back, the metal feet squealing against the tiled floor. 'I'm going to send an officer in to take your statement.'

'Am I under arrest?' he asked, panicked.

Coco studied his face. The truth was she was not sure yet. He had told her a version of the truth, she was sure, but quite what was truth and lies, she had little idea, but her gut instinct was, he had still not been entirely truthful. 'Make your statement and tell us EVERYTHING,' she stated forcefully. 'And then we'll see. But in the meantime, until we figure out what the hell happened, as far as I'm concerned, everyone is a suspect.' She moved to the door and stopped. 'Is there anything you want me to tell your father?'

His face clouded. 'Tell him I'm sorry.'

14H35

Coco walked quickly into her office, lighting a cigarette as she did. She looked at the clock on the wall and realised she had missed lunch again, but she was also sure she was supposed to have been somewhere else. It was not lost on her that her life appeared to be a lesson in moving from one disaster to another and never actually managing to achieve anything.

Cedric appeared in the doorway. 'How was it with the kid?'

'Beats the shit out of me,' she answered honestly. She filled him in on the rest of the conversation after he had left the interview room.

'You buy it?'

Coco took a long, deep breath. 'I buy nothing, especially when someone opens their mouth.' She frowned and pointed at the clock. 'Was I supposed to be doing something today?'

'How the hell am I supposed to know? I keep telling you to go and see a shrink, but you always think you know better,' Cedric quipped.

She stuck her tongue out at him. 'Tell me what you found.'

'I've sent officers to pick up Vichy Sander, Jericho Martin and Sofia Charton,' he replied. 'Although if they're anything like your missing boy toy monk, they're probably hiding out somewhere.'

'I hate you,' Coco stated matter-of-factly. 'I don't know why I keep you around.'

'Because no one else would work with you,' he retorted. He bit his lip.

'Bitch.'

He smiled at her. 'So, Frère Bardot and Anna Nols. Anna Nols died in 2013, Bardot as well. Her death certificate states she died of an accidental overdose.'

Coco raised an eyebrow. 'Accidental?'

Cedric nodded. 'She was on medication for diabetes and apparently she took too much of it.' He met her gaze. 'There was no indication of anything untoward. She had no criminal record, and I couldn't find anything to suggest she had any sort of problems or enemies. She never married and had no family. I've requested her medical records but I'm not sure we'll get them anytime soon.'

'Who signed the death certificate?'

Cedric met her expectant gaze. 'Dr. Allard,' he answered reluctantly. 'Mais, I don't think we can read too much into that. He probably was doctor to most of the people involved with the monastery. For the record, he also sighed Frère Paul Bardot's death certificate.'

'He did?' Coco questioned with interest.

Cedric sighed. 'Like I said, all probably perfectly normal. Bardot died of a heart attack. I called Sonny and had him access the autopsies for both of them. He sounded grumpy by the way, so you should still talk to him...'

Coco stuck her tongue out at him again, indicating for him to continue.

'He said he couldn't be certain unless he spent more time on it, but his initial assessment is that both autopsies were above board and there was no suggestion of anything untoward. Nothing in the blood or toxicology screens. Maybe Sofia Charton killed herself, maybe she didn't, but I don't think there was anything suspicious about it. Same with Frère Bardot.'

Coco sucked on the cigarette. 'They both died nine years ago,' she mused, 'the year after Paul Lecourt also "accidentally" died.' She shook her head. 'There's a whole lot going on here we're not seeing, but we're close to understanding what happened, I'm sure of it.' She irritably stubbed out the cigarette. 'We need those kids here, all of them. Or else we've got nothing.' She stopped as her cell phone beeped. She picked it up and stared at the screen. It was from a number she did not recognise. 'I don't know this number.' She narrowed her eyes to read the message.

'Hey, this is Mathieu, I bought a new phone. Sorry I took off, I just need some time to think about what happened. I'll be in touch soon, I promise. I don't understand, but I think I was responsible somehow for Frère Leroy's murder. He came to me last night and asked me for my cell phone. I had one hidden in the monastery, I didn't even know he knew about my hiding place - there's a false wall in the communal bathroom and it's behind there. Anyway, find the phone and you might just figure out who murdered him. We'll talk soon I promise. Don't give up on me?? MX.'

Coco quickly rang the number, cursing as it went straight to voicemail. 'Dammit, he's turned it off,' she cursed. 'We need to get to the monastery and find that phone.' She jumped to her feet and grabbed her coat. 'We're close to figuring out what the hell happened to these people, Cedric, we're close.'

He gave her a doubtful look, adding. 'I hope so.'

15H00

Coco watched as Ebba deftly moved across the bathroom, her hands tapping against the wall, her ear cocked to the side as she listened for a change in sound.

Cedric nudged Coco. 'Are you so sure boy toy isn't playing you for a fool?'

'What the hell do you mean?' she snapped.

He shrugged. 'Only he sends you a weird message, suggesting you may, or may not find a clue? And all the time he's on the run? If he's so bothered about what happened, why didn't he come to the commissariat and tell us in person?'

Coco glared at him, but found herself unable to answer, because she had no answers, and she did not understand it herself. But still she held out hope that whatever Mathieu Moreau had done or was involved in, he had sent them a very clear message and a clue. She had to believe it because she had trusted his face. She had believed his words and she could not face losing trust again in another man. 'How the hell am I supposed to know?' she grumbled.

Ebba continued her search, moving into one of the cubicles. 'Ah-ha!' she exclaimed, pointing behind a toilet bowl. 'One of the bricks is loose, see?'

Coco peered over her shoulder. The brickwork looked the same as the others to her, old and badly in need of repair. She watched as Ebba used her long fingers to scrap away some loose concrete and then began wriggling the brick back and forth. It only took a few moments for it to give and the brick to fall away, crashing to the ground. Ebba pulled a torch from her pocket and shone it into the now open space. She reached in and pulled out a cell phone and handed it Coco.

'Is there anything else?' Coco asked hopefully.

'Yeah, there's a Taser,' Ebba replied.

'Wow!' Coco cried excitedly.

Ebba chuckled wickedly. 'Only kidding, it's empty.'

Coco balled her fists. 'I oughta slug you!'

Ebba raised an eyebrow. 'You could try but I'd take you down before you landed the first blow.'

Cedric nodded. 'She has a point.'

'You're just lucky I'm in a good mood,' Coco said. She lifted up the cell phone. Luckily it was an old model and she was able to turn it on and wait for it to boot. 'Odd that a rich kid like Mathieu Moreau would have a phone like this,' she mused. 'It's the same kind Helga has.'

'And a lot of drug dealers,' Ebba added. 'Because they're impossible to trace.'

Coco handed it back to the forensic technician. 'Here, access the call history and see when it was last used.'

Ebba snatched the cell phone and began searching. 'If this belonged to a twenty-year-old, he had a pretty fucking boring life,' she laughed. 'Looks like pretty much the only calls he made was to "Maman." I mean, how sad is that?'

Coco looked to Cedric. 'The only calls from that phone were to Mathieu's mother?'

Ebba turned around. 'Sorry. Wasn't what I just said clear to you?' She shrugged. 'There's also a couple to Idris and Jericho.'

Coco shook her head despairingly. 'And when was the last call placed?'

Ebba looked at the screen. 'Last night. 20h00. No name.'

Coco pursed her lips. 'Call it from your own phone and just say it was a wrong number, but see if you can find out who you're talking to, okay?'

Ebba tutted loudly and quickly input the numbers on her own cell phone. They all waited expectantly. Coco cocked her ear to listen. Her eyes widening as she heard the voice on the other end of the line. She gestured wildly for Ebba to disconnect, causing her to drop the phone.

'What the hell's wrong with you?' Coco demanded.

Coco faced Cedric. She was not sure what to make of the voice she had just heard on the telephone. 'Frère Aries said he took confession from Frère Leroy and that he had to speak to someone. Mathieu Moreau told us Leroy used his cell phone. Now, what are we supposed to make of that?'

'He's pointing us in the wrong direction?' Cedric suggested.

'Or the right direction,' Coco countered before shaking her head irritably. 'Either way, I think we have something here and the only way we're going to make sense of it is to…'

'Have a denouement,' Cedric interrupted.

Coco threw back her head and laughed, throwing frizzy blue hair over her shoulders. 'Who are you, Agatha fucking Christie? Hell yeah, time to drag in all the suspects and beat the crap out of them until they confess.'

He raised an eyebrow. 'Beat the crap out of them? Really? Shall I call Commander Demissy to join in as well? I'm sure she wouldn't want to miss it.'

Coco sucked her teeth. 'Don't bother,' she said petulantly.

'Do you know what you're doing?' Cedric asked cautiously. 'I mean, I don't, so….'

Coco took a moment. 'All I know is that we can't wait around any longer because it might just result in someone else getting the chop.' She smiled sweetly at him. 'All the same, let's not mention it to Demissy until we have a better idea of what we're dealing with, or I have something to repel her with. If the murderer got to use a Taser I don't see why the hell I shouldn't.'

Ebba reached into her backpack and extracted something. She handed it to Coco. 'It's unmarked,' she said.

Coco looked at it before grabbing it and thrusting it into her bag, ignoring Cedric's disproving look. 'Well, you never know when it might come in handy,' she stated walking quickly towards the door. 'I need to think, meet me back at the commissariat and we'll make a plan.'

15H25

Coco moved slowly around the gravelled pavements which wrapped around *Abbaye Le Bastien*.

She was silent as she tried to bring everything together in her mind. She knew she was missing something vital, or rather, she was sure she was missing something obvious that was right in front of her. It was always the same in a murder investigation she reasoned, every conversation she had was replayed over and over in her head, often at the same time, and none of it made any sense because she was bombarded with too many voices and too much information. Her friend Hugo Duchamp had once told her the only way to listen, to *really* understand, was to be silent, to sit and listen to her thoughts without interruption and only then was there a chance everything would become clear.

She spotted a bench between two hedges and moved towards it, dropping heavily onto the wooden seat and pulled a cigarette from her pocket and lit it, taking a moment to enjoy it and hope it helped clear the fog in her brain. She noticed a plaque on the wall. *Grâce à la famille Moreau.* It caused her to take a sharp breath. She did not believe Mathieu Moreau was a murderer, but she was also acutely aware her barometer was not entirely reliable all of the time. And that was why she was sure whatever his involvement, there was something he was lying about, and she only hoped it was not as serious as she imagined it could be.

Her cell phone began ringing, jolting her. 'Allô, Brunhild,' she snapped.

'Coco, c'est Mathieu.'

Coco took in a sharp breath. 'Where the hell are you?' she hissed.

Mathieu sounded concerned. 'You're mad at me?' he asked.

'You bet your ass I am,' she replied. 'I asked, where the hell are you? Because as far as we know, you're on the run.'

He laughed. 'On the run? That sounds rather romantic, non?'

Coco sucked her teeth. 'Stop… stop…' she searched for the word before adding, 'just stop and answer my fucking question.'

'I like it when you swear,' he said. 'I guess you do it because it disarms people, but actually, I find it rather cute.'

Coco laughed. 'I couldn't give a fuck about disarming people, I swear because I have a fucking potty mouth. Now, quit stalling and tell me where the sodding fuck hell you are.'

The line went silent. 'I wasn't running,' he responded finally. 'I was looking for someone to put an end to all of this.'

'Vichy Sander?'

'You know?' he asked, clearly surprised.

'I know…' Coco trailed off, 'not as much as I should.'

'I found Vichy. I have him,' Mathieu stated.

'You have him?' Coco interrupted, suddenly alarmed. 'What do you mean by that?'

'He was hiding,' Mathieu responded. 'I just figured out where he was hiding. I wanted to make sure he was okay, and he is, sort of.'

'Did he murder his father?' Coco demanded.

Mathieu took a deep breath. 'I've given you all you need to solve this,' he said mystically.

Coco frowned. 'You've said nothing.'

'Not directly, peut être, mais I've said and done as much as I could.'

'Mathieu, stop it!' Coco shouted. 'Stop playing games. Just because you're young, you're also not a kid. I get that your life may not have been the one you hoped it would be. Believe me, I'm the Queen of understanding that particular scenario, but it also means I'm not blinded by it. Tell the truth, that's all you have to do. As some song I can't remember right now says only the truth will set you free, or some bullshit like that.'

He was silent again. She could hear him breathing. Finally he laughed. 'I hate the fact you make me laugh so much.'

'That's not a bad thing,' she countered.

'It is for me,' he replied. 'Because it means something.'

Coco shook her head quickly as if she was trying to eliminate thoughts from her head. 'What does it mean?' she breathed.

'It means something,' he repeated, 'and that freaks me out.'

Coco cleared her throat, narrowing her eyes angrily. She could not afford to get distracted, because she was almost sure that was exactly what he was doing, distracting her. 'You said you'd given me all you needed to solve the crimes - what did you mean?'

He remained silent. 'Listen, I have to go,' he said distractedly. 'Can we meet at the monastery later, say 18h00?'

'What's going on, Mathieu?' she demanded.

'I just have to find someone else, and we'll all come and meet you at the monastery. Okay?'

Coco exhaled irritably. 'I'm sick of all this cloak and dagger nonsense. I'm a goddamn cop, Mathieu.'

'Je sais, je sais,' he cried. 'But I must do this my way, it's the only way I know how to do it. Meet me later?'

'Are you in danger?'

Mathieu took several long, deep breaths before finally answering. 'Non, not really. This will all make sense soon, and then we'll see.'

'We'll see?'

'We'll see,' he repeated. 'I really have to go, but listen, I meant what I said, I tried to tell you all, because I wanted to stop it, but I did something stupid, and I think that got two people murdered.'

Coco clenched her fists. She was growing angrier and impatient, replacing the concern she had felt for the young monk. 'You're really pissing me off, Mathieu.'

He gave a long, soft laugh that was tinged with sadness. 'I'm sure it won't be the last time,. At least I hope it won't. Ciao, Coco.'

'Wait, Mathieu,' she cried desperately. 'Give me something,' she pleaded.

'This all began with Gasper Peron,' he replied.

Coco tutted. 'I'd gathered that, but how? Everybody has done a pretty good job of only telling half the story. I need the rest if I'm going to make any sense of what happened to Odilon Sander and Frère Leroy. You HAVE to give me something.' She stopped, hearing loud, muffled voices in the background of the call. 'Mathieu, are you okay?'

'I have to go they're here…'

'They?' Coco interrupted. 'Who are they? Who's there, kid?' She could tell he had covered the mouthpiece and was talking in hurried tones to someone with him, but she could not make out any of the conversation.

'I have to go. Listen. Look at Gasper Peron again. This isn't about who he said he was, it was always the opposite. It was who he *didn't* say he was.'

Coco scratched her head. 'I don't understand,' she wailed, but it was too late and the line went dead.

16H15

Coco stared at the clock on the wall, nibbling on the corner of a semi-stale cheese baguette. She tossed it disgruntledly onto the desk and instead lit a cigarette, quickly inhaling and exhaling, blowing plumes of smoke into the air. She was having trouble focusing, something which was *almost* unusual for her. The fact was, there was too much going on. A double homicide investigation with few leads, and then there were the other aspects of her life which refused to dissipate.

Cedric and Ebba appeared in the doorway. Coco jumped, alarmed by their sudden appearance and also by the concerned expressions on both of their faces. She was not used to it and she suddenly felt as if she was an old woman being looked upon with pity by a younger generation. 'I'm only forty-one, you know,' she snapped.

Ebba chuckled. 'What in, dog years?'

Coco clapped her hands. 'And she's back in the room! Welcome back, you shaved-haired strop bag.' She turned to Cedric. 'What's with your face? Gym ran out of steroids?'

Cedric flexed his pectoral muscles, flashing a confident smile. 'Nothing. It's just you were staring at the wall.'

Coco shrugged, looking around her cramped, overflowing office. 'What the hell else is there to look at in here?'

Ebba tutted. 'Anyho, boy toy's cell phone has been turned off since his last call, which was to you.'

Coco glared at her. 'Don't you start with the boy toy schtick.' She turned to Cedric. 'And you quit gossiping about me.'

Ebba flashed her a sweet smile. 'Understood. So, your *friend* the monk is AWOL and his cell phone is off. Same for Vichy Sander.'

'His mother doesn't know where he is either,' Cedric added. 'Or at least that's what she claims.'

Coco pouted. 'Well, we have a deadline. 18h00 at the monastery.'

'What's that all about?' Cedric replied.

Coco shrugged. 'I don't know. What Mathieu said has been bugging me.'

Cedric stared at her. 'He's playing you because he's up to his neck in this complete shit.' He noticed her irritated expression and held up his hands. 'Don't shoot the messenger!'

'Anyway,' Coco continued. She had relayed the conversation to the both of them, hoping that it would help, but so far, it had not. 'He had to be making a point about Gasper Peron and what he was lying about.'

Ebba shook her head. 'I've gone over and over Gasper Peron. He was who he was. A criminal who led a pretty horrible life and then found God. I don't know what else to tell you. His criminal record was lengthy, and his business dealings were too. He had money hidden everywhere. I think even forensic accountants would have trouble working out what he was into and whether or not it was legitimate.'

'And yet, what did Mathieu mean?' Coco demanded. She pointed at Cedric. 'Don't say a word. Put all your misconceptions to one side and help me work out what we're missing.'

He nodded. 'I'll try, mais…'

Coco turned back to Ebba. 'What about Mathieu? Did you finish your check on him and his family?'

'Yeah. Nothing new turned up. Rich as a Russian oligarch. Deirdre Moreau is widowed, she never remarried and has no siblings and no other family. Her father, Bastien Moreau, set up the monastery with her help and left her as the executrix. He's gaga now though, living out his days in a Swiss clinic specialising in different forms of dementia. She seems pretty hands on at the monastery and also the former youth centre.' She paused, giving a bored yawn. 'Same goes for everyone else. They all seem pretty boring.' She reached into her backpack. 'When I finally got the warrant, I was going through the autopsy reports for Anna Nols and Paul Bardot, the two stiffs in the stolen coffins. There was nothing odd as such, certainly nothing to contradict the findings of the pathologist, but there was this…' She handed Coco a folder.

Coco flipped it open and scanned the contents of the paper. She stubbed out the cigarette and frowned. 'I don't get what I'm supposed to see.'

Ebba moved around and pointed at the bottom of the paper. 'The pathologist reported that Anna Nols had given birth at some point.'

Coco shrugged. 'Et?'

'And according to everyone we've spoken to, Anna Nols was a confirmed spinster who had never married,' Ebba said. 'And once I saw that, I checked her medical record and there was no record of her having ever given birth.'

Coco frowned and smiled at Ebba. 'I think I love you, but I don't know exactly why yet.' There was something about this revelation which made perfect sense to her, but she could not be sure what it was or what it meant.

'You're not my type,' Ebba snipped, 'or anyone else with good taste, I would imagine.'

Coco opened her mouth to respond, but stopped suddenly. 'Wait, a damn minute,' she exhaled. Something else had popped into her head. A memory of a conversation, a difference in words. The question was - did it mean anything or was it just a throwaway comment? She could not be sure, and yet… and yet. A scenario was appearing in her mind's eye, an implausible scenario, but one which just might explain everything, or perhaps nothing, but the only thing she knew for certain was that it was a lead, and a lead which someone had perhaps being pushing her towards.

'What's up, Captain?' Cedric asked.

'I need you to find out everything you can about Mathieu Moreau's grandfather,' she said.

'Like what?'

'Like how long he's been gaga in Switzerland for a start,' Coco replied. She picked up the baguette and took a bite, smiling widely. 'I think we're on to something.'

Cedric and Ebba exchanged a doubtful look.

Coco stood up. 'I'm going home to see my kids and have a shower. Meet me at the monastery in an hour and keep me updated.' She hurried towards the exit.

17H55

Coco moved her eyes between the cell phone and the plaque on the monastery wall, *Grâce à la famille Moreau*. Thanks to the Moreau family suddenly seemed to make much more sense to her. There was still so much of the picture missing, but she was sure there was enough to finally begin putting the pieces together. Cedric stood in silence beside her, peeking at her from time to time, but saying nothing.

'None of this makes sense,' Coco said finally.

Cedric snorted. 'You're only just figuring that out?'

She lit a cigarette and traced her fingers around the sign. It was clearly old, but it was obvious it was well taken care of because of the highly polished sheen.

'Does the information Ebba gave not help?' he asked.

Coco took a long drag on the cigarette. The information had been what she had expected, even though she was not sure why and what it meant. 'It did, but it's not proof, and I don't want to drag anyone into the commissariat without proof or Demissy will just turn them right back around.' She stared at him. 'We only have one chance at this, Cedric,' she stated. 'Unless we walk out of this monastery with a confession, then I don't think we'll ever be able to prove anything, because all we have are vague rumours and speculation.'

Cedric grabbed the cigarette from her and took a drag before handing it back to her. 'We've done it before. This time isn't any different. Let's go figure this out.'

She smiled gratefully at him, then punched his arm. 'Hey, don't steal my cigarette again. I don't know where your lips have been!'

He flashed her an incredulous look. '*My* lips!' he cried.

18H00

Deidre Moreau stopped mid-sentence as the door to the chapel was pushed open, and Coco and Cedric walked in. 'What are you doing here?' Deidre hissed.

Mathieu Moreau stood up from one of the benches, flashing Coco with a warm smile, his dark eyes sparkling. 'I told them to be here, Maman,' he said.

Her eyes widened in clear horror. 'What are you doing, Mathieu?'

Mathieu moved across the room. 'What I should have done a long time ago. If I had, then Frère Leroy and Monsieur Sander might still be alive.'

Coco took a moment to survey the chapel. As well as Mathieu and his mother, she noticed Vichy Sander and his mother, Chantel Sander. Next to them were Idris and Aaron Cellier. In the corner of the chapel, Frère Henri Aries and the monastery housekeeper, Estelle Grainger were sitting, their faces pale and stoic betraying their anxiety.

'Quite a little gathering we've got here,' Coco stated breezily. 'Tell me, if you weren't expecting the police to show up, what was this all about?'

'That is none of your concern,' Deidre snapped. She was dressed all in black, platinum blonde hair swept upwards, blood-red lips twisted into an angry stance.

'The hell it is,' Coco retorted. 'Because I don't think this was an ordinary get together. It was a council of war, you might say, or rather more accurately, a chance for everyone to get their stories straight.'

Frère Aries cleared his throat, causing his chins to wobble. 'I don't know what you're suggesting, Captain Brunhild, but I advise you to be careful with your words…'

'Or you'll do what?' she demanded, standing in front of him, hands on hips. 'You'll call in the big Catholic guns? You see, I don't think you want to do that because you don't want this whole sorry business to be made public.'

Before Aries could respond, the door to the chapel opened again, and Dr. Joël Allard entered. 'Désolé, I'm late,' he announced. 'The traffic was bad.' He stopped dead in his tracks upon seeing Coco and Cedric, his face creasing in confusion as he looked at Deidre.

'This has nothing to do with me,' Deidre stated through gritted teeth.

Coco moved across the chapel. 'Ah, I was wondering if you'd show up,' she said. 'The altar boy with his toe in two worlds, never really loyal to either of his masters.'

Allard sighed. 'We've been through this before, Captain. I have done nothing wrong.'

Coco swept away from him. 'I'll be the judge of that.' She stepped in front of the altar, moving her head slowly between the people who had gathered. The only ones missing were the two punk kids, Sofia Charton and Jericho Martin, and she wondered why. She filed the thought away. She would deal with them later. Right now, she had to concentrate on the task at hand. Unmasking a cold-blooded murderer. 'Let's begin, shall we?'

18H10

Coco extended her arms. 'So, here we are,' she began. 'In the place where it all started. From the beginning, I had thought it actually began with the death of little Paul Lecourt ten years ago, but in reality, I actually believed it started much earlier than that. However, the ten-year anniversary of his death was certainly a catalyst to what has happened this week.'

'I don't know how many times this has to be said, but Paul Lecourt's death was an accident, a horrible, tragic accident, but an accident none the less,' Frère Aries interrupted angrily.

'I can't say I necessarily disagree,' Coco conceded. 'About the accident, at least. I believe it was an accident, but not in the way it has been portrayed. The missing shoes that were put back on the young boy prove it.'

'It proves nothing,' Aries snapped.

'I disagree,' Coco replied. 'And as my opinion is the only one that counts right now, tough titty!' She ignored the furious look on the monk's face and pressed on. 'They found the first shoe on the third floor of the youth centre. Tell me, what was on the third floor ten years ago?'

Aries shrugged. 'The staff rooms and offices,' he answered. 'And we strictly forbid the children to be on that floor, so there was no reason for Paul Lecourt to be there.'

'Except he was a kid, and kids go where the hell they please,' Coco suggested. 'I believe Paul was on the third floor and while he was there, he overheard a conversation. A conversation he was not meant to here. The chances are he probably didn't even understand what he had heard, but the people having the conversation weren't willing to take that chance. I suspect they ran after him, probably just to talk, but it spooked Paul enough for him to run away, first losing one shoe on the way and then the other downstairs. He ran out of the youth centre and it was then that he fell and tragically died.'

'*Suspect… believed… probably.* You have an awful lot of nothing but supposition as far as I can tell,' Deidre interrupted with a bitchy bite. 'And even if what you described was an accurate reflection of the events, it was still nothing but an accident.'

'But an accident that was buried and covered-up,' Coco countered. 'There can only be one reason for that. Whatever had happened couldn't come out. The people involved couldn't take the risk of questions being asked. Why was Paul Lecourt's shoe on the third floor? What was he running from?'

Dr. Allard shook his head. 'I hate to be the one to state the obvious, but what did it matter? He was dead. There was no way of anyone knowing why he had run, even if he had, and for what reason, or what he had overhead. As Deidre says, there is nothing but supposition here.'

Coco avoided making eye-contact with Cedric. 'You're right, of course,' she responded to Allard. 'However, I don't think it was about that so much as the people involved in the conversation. We'll come back to that shortly, because I think there are two different issues here. And first we have to understand why what happened ten years ago suddenly came to light. And I admit I was confused about that, but I think if we look at it logically, and oui, use a little supposition we can begin to work it out.'

She continued. 'Par example, when I discovered that as an infant baby Paul Lecourt was left outside of the monastery, I didn't think too much about it. I mean, you hear about that sort of thing all the time. Even the fact I was told he was named after the monk who discovered him, in this case Frère Paul Bardot, didn't strike me as too odd, not until you start to see a pattern forming. Two nights ago, three coffins were stolen from the crypt and placed in the soon-to-be demolished youth centre. The coffins of Frère Paul

Bardot, a woman by the name of Anna Nols, and a mysterious unnamed benefactor, who we soon came to know as Gasper Peron.'

She took a deep breath before continuing. 'It didn't strike me as odd Anna Nols was described to us in such a way that I imagined she was an elderly spinster, but of course it wasn't really true, and I suspect it was designed to lead us away from another line of enquiry. However, as we looked further, I was surprised to see both Anna Nols and Frère Bardot died soon after the death of Paul Lecourt, and that's when the picture started to become clearer. Anna Nols' autopsy report showed she had given birth, but yet there was no evidence of a birth in her medical records. I've come across this before and there are generally few reasons why a woman might choose to hide her pregnancy, and one of them is that she does not want the father to be known.'

Coco stepped to the side and turned her head towards the altar. 'If it was true that Anna Nols was a religious woman, then you could say it makes sense for her to abandon her child here. But what if there was another reason? What if it was because this was where the father lived? And that brings us to Frère Paul Bardot.'

Frère Aries slammed his fists on the wooden bench. 'That's an outrageous assumption!' he roared.

'Peut être,' Coco conceded. 'Mais, it is one I am prepared to make, especially considering something we discovered later. The way they arranged the three coffins puzzled me from the beginning, primarily because if the purpose was to hide a dead body, why not do it on the higher level where it was less likely to be discovered? Non, it could only have been deliberate. Then the question is - why? And why choose three seemingly random coffins?' She faced Vichy Sander and Mathieu. 'Only it wasn't random at all, was it, Vichy?'

Vichy Sander lowered his head and said nothing. His mother, Chantel, pushed his arm. 'What is she talking about, Vichy?' she demanded. Again, the young man did not respond.

Coco turned away. 'This piece of information changed things for me. If the coffins were chosen deliberately, then there had to be a reason. And there was only one I could think of. Whoever did this was sending us a clear message. Anna Nols and Frère Bardot were the parents of Paul Lecourt. Anna likely abandoned the child because she wanted Frère Bardot to acknowledge the child, peut être? Or peut être because she was overwhelmed and just wanted his assistance. Unfortunately, we can't be sure of that because they're both gone.'

'You don't seem to be sure of a lot,' Deirdre Moreau muttered under her breath.

'Maman,' Mathieu cried in a way which caused his mother to give him a surprised look.

Coco ignored them both. 'We can't be sure of it because they both died in 2003. Anna Nols from a drug overdose and Frère Bardot from a heart attack.'

'There was nothing suspicious about either of their deaths, I'm sure of it,' Dr. Allard interjected.

Coco nodded. 'Oui, I noticed your handprints were all over that, too,' she stated.

Allard glared at her. 'I don't know what you're suggesting, mais…'

Coco raised her hands. 'I'm not suggesting anything. I'm merely proposing a pattern. Anna Nols killed herself not long after the death of Paul Bardot, and then Frère Bardot drops dead not long after. Sounds like heartbreak to me.'

'You know nothing about these people,' Frère Aries spat.

Coco shrugged. 'You have a point, and I can't say I disagree. But we have to look at it logically. It also reminded me of something you said, Idris.'

Idris Cellier lifted his head slowly. 'Moi?' he breathed.

She nodded. 'Oui. You told me Anna Nols was always watching the kids, and that it was creepy, didn't you?'

Idris shrugged and dropped his head again.

Cedric moved next to Coco. 'What if she wasn't being creepy? What if she was just watching the son she could never admit was hers? That wouldn't be creepy, it would be perfectly normal. But then he died, and I can only imagine she decided life wasn't worth living, so she took an overdose.'

'And it's not too much of a stretch to imagine the death of both of them was too much for Frère Bardot,' Coco added.

A silence descended on the chapel.

Coco clapped her hands together. She stared straight at Mathieu and Deidre Moreau. 'And that brings us to the final piece of the puzzle. Gasper Peron.'

18H20

'Gasper Peron was always the biggest part of this puzzle,' Coco continued. 'Was he just a former drug dealer who found his way to Dieu following stints in prison and the death of someone using his drugs?'

She paused. 'I wondered whether it was something to do with that, but I think the main part of the problem was something I didn't even consider until two very different thoughts came to me.'

She stopped and looked at Mathieu. His face was tight, staring straight at her. 'And I think the truth is, were it not for you, Mathieu, we may never have understood what happened here, not just this week, but also in the past.'

Deidre Moreau reached over and touched his arm. Mathieu jerked it away. 'Say nothing,' she hissed.

He turned his head to her. 'It's too late. Don't you get that, Maman? We have to stop lying.'

Chantel Sander suddenly spoke. 'I don't understand what any of you are talking about. What does any of this have to do with the death of my husband?'

Coco stared at her. 'I think I'm beginning to understand, finally,' she replied sadly. She moved back in front of the altar. 'Gasper Peron's involvement in all of this is confusing. A drug baron who found Dieu?' She shrugged. 'I suppose it happens, but in this instance there was more to it.' She faced Estelle Grainger. 'I recall a conversation we had about Gasper. You said he took his pick of the women on the estate. If they couldn't pay for their drugs, then they had to pay in some other way. *With their bodies.* But you also said something else. Something which only occurred to me later as being important. You said he didn't care about what he was doing to the women, but he cared about Dieu and refused to wear a condom.'

Estelle Grainger looked ahead. 'C'est vrai,' she mumbled before spitting. Frère Aries shot her a disparaging look.

Coco exhaled. 'One of those refusals resulted in a baby. Maybe the realisation changed Gasper. Either that, or the death of someone using his drugs, or the prison sentences, or watching too much Judge Judy. Who the hell knows?

'He found Dieu,' she continued, 'and he came here to this monastery, and I have to wonder why. I think Gasper Peron wanted to start a new life, or rather, he wanted to give a new life, a *legitimate* life, to his child. To do so, he created the mysterious persona we've all come to know. And that's why he came here. He knew he had to make a new start, and to do so, he created a life for his child. A life he probably didn't want to be a major part of because he didn't want his chequered past to interfere with this child's upbringing, but I would imagine he wanted to be near enough to watch. Just like Anna Nols, and probably Frère Bardot. They all wanted to be near their children in one way or another.'

'What does this have to do with anything?' Frère Aries interrupted.

Coco narrowed her eyes. 'Because I believe Gasper Peron was talking to his child on the day Paul Lecourt died. And it was because of that he chased after the poor boy. Gasper Peron had created an elaborate lie, and he wasn't prepared for it to come crashing down around him.' She stopped and turned. 'Isn't that right, Madam?'

18H35

Deidre Moreau's eyes widened in abject horror. 'What are you talking about, you stupid woman?' she demanded.

Coco stepped around, being careful to ignore the expectant gaze of Mathieu Moreau. 'Again, I think this has all been about subterfuge. And it was subtle, so I didn't really pick up on it. However, there were two separate conversations which later told me something was off. Firstly, your son Mathieu told me about how he had joined the monastery at the bequest of you and his grandfather, Bastien Moreau.'

'That is correct,' Deidre responded, without looking at her.

Coco nodded. 'Except the pair of you don't seem to be able to agree on what exactly happened to old Monsieur Bastien.'

'What do you mean?' Deidre asked with a puzzled frown.

Coco faced her. 'Your son told me your father was dead, and yet when we spoke with you, you said your father was in a clinic suffering with dementia. I had to wonder - which was true? So, today we checked. Bastien Moreau is indeed alive in a Swiss hospital, but he isn't your real father. Not really. Bastien Moreau was a business acquaintance of your real father. We found his business records. Bastien Anders was an investment banker who worked with Gasper Peron, presumably to create a legitimate life for him. Bastien Anders was also pretty broke, with no family and, as it turns out, early onset Alzheimer's. Again, I'm guessing, but I imagine that at some point a deal was struck between Gasper and his banker, something along the lines of - *give me your legitimacy and I'll make sure you live out your days in peace and comfort*, that sort of thing. We can't ask the patron of this monastery because apparently he doesn't talk much these days.'

'Real father?' Dr. Allard asked. 'What do you mean by that?'

Coco stared at him. She was still not sure how involved he was. 'Gasper Peron came to this monastery and the youth centre because he wanted to escape his past, but crucially, he wanted to make sure his only child escaped the stigma which would surely follow if anyone discovered who had actually fathered her.'

Dr. Allard looked confused. 'I don't understand what this has to do with anything.'

'Nor did I,' Coco countered. 'Mais, if you look at another way, we may just have a way to make sense of it all. We now know Gasper Peron had something to hide, and it's not too difficult a proposition to extrapolate it might just have something to do with what happened to Paul Lecourt. It wasn't just Frère Bardot and Anna Nols who were watching the children. Gasper Peron was too.' She turned to Mathieu. 'He was watching his petit fils.'

Mathieu lifted his head slowly and met her gaze. 'My earliest memory was him telling me I couldn't tell anyone who he really was. I didn't understand it, but I did as I was told.' He sighed. 'I always did as I was told, but not anymore,' he added with a sad smile. 'Not anymore,' he repeated.

Coco continued. 'I believe ten years ago, Paul Lecourt overheard a conversation between Gasper and his daughter, you, Deidre. Had you always known he was your father?'

Deidre lifted her head, glaring at Coco. She said nothing, but nodded.

'I suppose he wanted you to have a life away from the constraints of his past,' Coco said. 'He had the money, but he didn't have the name or the social position, but by striking a deal with Bastien Anders, he found a way to legitimise his past life and create a new life for his daughter. And by contributing to the monastery in his own name, he found a way to be around and see his daughter and eventually his grandson, on more or less a daily basis. In the end, it was much like the scenario of Frère Bardot and Anna Nols. People wrapped in lies,' she added sadly.

'And you're saying this has something to do with the death of Paul Lecourt?' Chantel Sander asked.

Coco nodded. 'I imagine Paul stumbled upon a conversation between Gasper Peron and his daughter. It was enough to scare Peron. He'd spent so much time erasing his past, or creating a new one, I guess he panicked when he saw Paul watching him. As I said earlier, I'm not even sure he meant to hurt the poor kid, but I think he chased him, probably just to stop him to make sure Paul hadn't heard something he shouldn't have.' She stopped, staring directly at Deidre Moreau.

Mathieu reached across and touched his mother's hand. 'Maman, je t'aime,' he whispered.

'My father panicked,' Deidre said finally. 'I told him he didn't need to, but he didn't listen. He just said he couldn't take the risk. I remember following him as he chased the boy. I was shouting for him to stop, but it all happened so quickly, and then... and then...' She stopped. 'It was over.'

'What happened next?' Cedric asked.

Deidre took a moment. She stared at Mathieu before finally answering Coco. 'We went to Frère Leroy,' she said. 'He was close with my father, his confident you might say. My father confessed to Gerard. We talked it over, and we all understood the situation and that there was no point in making more out of it than we needed to.'

Coco frowned. 'What do you mean?'

'It was an accident, that's all,' Deidre stated matter-of-factly. 'What was the point in ruining our lives over it?'

'Your lives?' Cedric cried as if he could not believe what he was hearing. 'What about Frère Bardot and Anna Nols? Their lives were destroyed.'

Deidre shook her head with determination. 'We couldn't have known about that. We did what we had to do to protect our family, and I don't regret it. My father was a good man, and I didn't want to lose him.'

Estelle Grainger threw back her head and laughed. 'A good man? You're delusional if you believe that. I knew him back in the days when he strutted around Paris as if he owned it, trampling on anyone who got in his way. Reformed? He just didn't want to go back to jail, that's all. I was here when poor Paul Lecourt died and I remember what happened. There were no witnesses to the so-called accident, therefore we only have your word Gasper Peron didn't throw the child to his death just to protect himself.'

Deidre bowed her head. 'My father was a good man,' she whispered.

Coco stared at Deidre and could not imagine how she had produced someone like Mathieu. But then again, did she really know him at all? She had thought she had known Mordecai Stanic, but in the end, his whole life was a lie.

Chantel Sander stood and approached Coco. 'What does any of this have to do with my husband's murder?'

Coco turned to Mathieu Moreau. 'I think Frère Moreau here can better answer that question. Isn't that correct, Mathieu?'

18H45

Mathieu clasped his hands together, pressing his fingers hard again the skin.

'Keep your mouth shut, Mathieu,' Deidre hissed.

Chantel Sander's eyes flicked over the young man. 'I've known you all your life, Mathieu. Why would you do something like this? Odilon was like a father to you at that centre.' She shot Deidre a filthy look. 'Especially when you had no father of your own to speak of.'

Mathieu opened his mouth to speak, but no words came out.

Coco moved towards Chantel. 'Mathieu didn't murder your husband, Madame Sander. In fact, I think he did his best to ensure those responsible would not get away with it.'

Frère Aries shouted from the corner of the chapel. 'You're not making any sense, Captain Brunhild. And to be frank, I don't think you have the first clue what actually happened.'

Coco gave a sad laugh. 'I admit this investigation has been challenging, but lies and deception have also complicated it.' She pressed her body against the altar, ignoring the loud disapproving tut coming from Frère Aries. 'The fact Monsieur Sander was murdered exactly ten years to the day of Paul Lecourt's death was obviously something we could not ignore, and that became even more evident when we discovered that Vichy Sander had personally insisted on choosing which three coffins were used. The question is, jeune homme, why?'

She stopped and moved directly in front of him to prevent him from looking at someone in the room. 'She won't help you now,' Coco stated.

Chantel moved next to her son and wrapped her arm around his shoulders. 'Vichy, what is she talking about?'

Vichy looked blankly at her. 'I... I don't know what to say,' he replied, his voice cracking.

She turned her head, staring at his face. 'What have you done?'

'When we discovered Odilon Sander was leading a double-life,' Coco carried on, 'we automatically assumed, wrongly, as it happens, he was having an affair. But instead he was donating his time to charity, working particularly with young, disadvantaged children. Not so surprising, you might say, especially considering his time at the youth centre, however the question had to be - why keep it a secret?' She looked at Chantel Sander. 'I understand things may have been difficult between you and your husband, but I have to ask - would it have bothered you if Odilon had told you what he was really up to?'

Chantel considered her answer before finally shrugging her shoulders nonchalantly. 'I stopped caring what my husband did years ago. Whatever he was doing, whether or not it was another woman, I wouldn't have minded. Our marriage was a marriage of convenience, for appearances only, nothing else.'

'Maman,' Vichy choked.

She shrugged again. 'It seems I wasn't the only one keeping secrets. What were yours, Vichy?'

Vichy dropped his head. 'I don't want to talk about this.'

Cedric sat next to him. 'You don't have a choice, kid. This has gone too far.'

'Vichy,' Coco called his name softly, 'this doesn't have to be difficult. We're here to help you.'

His head jerked back upwards. 'None of this makes sense. It wasn't meant to be this way. That wasn't the plan.'

Coco looked at Mathieu. His eyes had widened and in that moment something made sense to her. Mathieu had informed her in a roundabout way that he had been trying to help and for the first time she actually believed he was telling the truth. She continued blocking Vichy from seeing anyone else in the room. 'What did you mean? What was the plan?' she pushed.

Vichy took a deep breath. 'I came home early from college one day and Papa was in the living room. I was about to go in when I heard voices. I realised it wasn't Maman, and I was going to go upstairs when I heard something that made me stop.' He gulped several times. 'They were talking about Paul Lecourt. Papa was saying something like he'd had enough of carrying the guilt and that the youth centre being demolished had stirred it all up for him. He said he was going to make it right. And then the person he was talking to said something. *If you dredge this up again, your own son will be implicated, and who's to say he won't get the blame? You talk and we'll all go down.*'

Coco frowned. 'And what did you take that to mean?' she asked.

He shrugged. 'I don't really remember, Paul. I remember the accident and seeing him lying there, but that's about it. But she said she would tell a different story. She said she would say she saw me pushing Paul and that he fell and died. She said it was in all of our best interests just to keep quiet.'

'Did you speak to your father about it?' Cedric asked.

Vichy nodded. 'I told him what I heard, and he said I wasn't to worry and that he would deal with it. I told him I didn't remember, and he just kept saying not to worry.'

Coco pursed her lips. 'Who was your father talking to, Vichy? I need you to say her name.'

Vichy moved his head to the side. 'To the woman who murdered him. Deidre Moreau.'

19H00

Deidre Moreau threw back her head and laughed. 'Ridiculous! I did no such thing.'

Coco moved closer to her. 'Oh, you did. We've already heard how far you were prepared to go to protect your family secret. You are your father's daughter, after all. I imagine you thought this was all behind you. Your father was dead, the secret gone with him. And then out of the blue, along comes Odilon Sander with his conscience and you saw it all slipping away again and you couldn't have that. So you murdered him. I have to wonder. Did you plan to?'

Deidre patted her platinum blonde hair and pulled her thin lips into a malevolent smile. 'You have nothing.'

Coco shook her head. 'That's not true.' She turned back to Vichy. She decided to take a chance and lie to him. 'What happened, Vichy? We know she called you the night your father died. We have the phone records. What did she say?'

'She was at the youth centre demolition site,' he answered after a few moments. 'She said there had been a terrible accident and that my father was dead. I couldn't believe it and I said I would call the police. It was then she told me I couldn't, unless I wanted the truth to come out. She told me that ten years ago she had seen me pushing Paul Lecourt and him falling and dying. She said they had all been keeping the secret to protect me and that she needed protection now.'

Chantel Sander shook her head. 'Even if what she said was true, you were ten years old. You were a child.'

'I wasn't thinking like that,' Vichy cried. 'She just convinced me it was what I had to do, or I'd go to jail. I didn't know whether or not it was true. I told you I didn't even remember what happened to Paul. And if I had something to do with it, then maybe Madame Moreau was right. I needed to help her because I couldn't leave Maman without both me and my father.'

Chantel cried, making the sign of the cross on her chest.

'Whose idea was it to send the fake email?'

Vichy pointed at Deidre. 'She said that if left the body in the demolition site, we could make it look as if my father had just run off with someone. She said everyone knew what a miserable marriage my parents had, so it wouldn't be too difficult for people to believe he'd chosen just to leave. Madame Moreau said we needed to make it look real, so as not to raise suspicion. I told her I knew my father's email password and she said to send some emails and after a while, send one confessing he had fallen in love with someone else and was sorry, but he wouldn't be coming back.' He stopped abruptly, his voice cracking even more than usual. 'She said it was the perfect plan and it meant no one else had to get hurt. I didn't like the way she said it, because it sounded like a threat.'

'It probably was,' Coco agreed.

Chantel touched her son's arm. 'Oh, Vichy,' she cried before glaring at Deidre Moreau. 'I ought to scratch your eyes out, you pathetic bitch, but you know what? You're not worth it. Everyone is going to know you were nothing but the bastard child of a murderer and a drug dealer. And that will be enough to see your shame.'

'I'm sorry, Maman,' Vichy cried. 'She really made me believe I had killed my friend.'

'That's not what happened, child,' Frère Aries interrupted. 'The Captain is right. It was a tragedy, but an accident nonetheless. You had nothing to do with the death of Paul Lecourt.'

'It was,' Coco confirmed. 'Mais, what happened this week was not a tragedy. It was cold-blooded murder, nothing more, nothing less.' She pointed at Deidre. 'You manipulated a young, vulnerable man to satisfy your need to protect your family name.

And you murdered Odilon Sander and Frère Gerard Leroy to facilitate that.'

Deidre mouthed slowly. 'P R O V E I T,' she stated before laughing.

19H15

'I don't need to,' Coco said with confidence. 'You've gone too far this time and you've run out of lives. The truth will come out and it will come out now.'

She stepped across the room, stopping briefly in front of the altar. 'You called Vichy Sander and told him his father was dead and that he needed to help you, or else face the consequences. What I don't understand is why the elaborate staged crime scene. Unless... unless....' She looked in-between Vichy and Mathieu and then back to Deidre. 'The plan was elaborate, over the top even. Why take those three coffins in particular? Because all it would do was draw attention to the crime. You would have had to know we would look into it and that there was a very real chance we would understand what had happened.'

Vichy looked at Mathieu. Mathieu smiled back at him and nodded.

Coco felt her heart pounding against her chest. 'Oh, Dieu,' she exhaled. She reached into her pocket and lit a cigarette, and noticed Frère Aries giving her a scolding look. 'Really?' she laughed. 'After everything that went on in this damn place...' she stopped abruptly and attempted to make the sign of the cross in front of the altar. 'Désolé, Dieu. Anyway,' she continued, 'I think I finally understand what happened.' She looked at Vichy. 'You didn't choose the coffins, did you?' She faced Mathieu. 'It was you, wasn't it?'

Mathieu stood and took the cigarette from Coco and took a long drag. He stared at her and smiled. 'Clues,' he whispered.

'What the hell's going on?' Cedric demanded. 'If you knew something, why the hell didn't you call the police?'

Coco answered for Mathieu. 'Because he didn't want to

denounce his mother, but he also didn't want to let her get away with her crimes.' She paused. 'It would be quite sweet if it wasn't so fucking annoying,' she said, snatching the cigarette back from Mathieu. She moved away. 'We know for certain Odilon Sander came to see Frère Leroy on the morning of his death. He was supposed to be in China but didn't want to go. He also didn't want to be here for the demolition. He felt guilty and he wanted to end that guilt. I imagine he saw what happened to Paul Lecourt in one way or another and had just turned away from it. It had worn him down and with the youth centre about to be demolished, he wanted to confess.'

She took a deep breath. 'I don't know what he said to Leroy, nor what advice Leroy gave to him, but the only scenario I can go with is that he called you, Deidre and you arranged to meet with him. Perhaps you suggested the demolition site, or he did? It doesn't really matter. I think he wanted to talk about it again, but you didn't. He wanted closure and I imagine you just wanted him gone.' She stared at Deidre. 'Did you go there with the plan to rid yourself of someone who might bring your past back to haunt you?'

Deidre lifted her head slowly. 'I couldn't allow it to happen. Not after all of this time. Not after everything my father had done to create a life for my son and I. And for what? Guilt? Guilt for a stupid child who had died a decade ago? Odilon claimed he saw my father chasing after the child but that he didn't see what happened just before his death. He implied my father was responsible. I couldn't allow such an implication to become public.' She shook her head forcefully. 'Non, it wasn't going to happen. Not then, not now. Not ever.' Her lips pulled into a tight smile.

Coco continued. 'And what happened? Did you really mean for him to die?'

Deidre shook her head. 'Non, not really. He was going on and on and on and I just couldn't take any more. Before I knew it, I had reached into my purse and pulled out the Taser I use for protection. It was a gift from my father, you know. He worried about me so,' she added with pride.

'And then what happened?' Coco pushed. 'Because the Taser attack didn't kill him. You beat him to death.' Her eyes flicked over the woman and she could scarcely imagine her to have the strength, but she realised she had seen before the power of adrenaline. She imagined Deidre Moreau thought she was fighting for her own life.

Deidre clasped her hands together. 'I had no choice. Don't you see that? Odilon Sander and his damn conscience were going to bring down my entire family, everything we've built and sacrificed…'

'Sacrificed?' Mathieu interrupted angrily. 'The only thing you've sacrificed in your life was me, your son, pushing me into a life I didn't choose or want.'

Deidre laughed. 'And what would you rather your life be? Running with the wolves? Getting into trouble with your friends…'

Mathieu nodded, interrupting again. 'Yeah, being a normal twenty-year-old would be nice.'

'Well, you're certainly as ungrateful as one,' Deidre sniffed. 'My father would be ashamed.'

'I hope so,' Mathieu whispered, dropping his head, dark hair falling over his face.

19H30

Coco cleared her throat, eager to move the discussion forward. 'After he was dead, I suppose you reverted to the original plan,' she stated.

'You'd already tried to stop Odilon by threatening to expose his son. But with him out of the way, you went directly to the source. You called Vichy following your murder of Odilon because you needed help to dispose of the body. Was it your idea to hide the body in the building that was about to be demolished?'

Deidre smiled. 'It was a good idea, you have to admit,' she stated simply. 'Nobody would even notice his body amongst the debris and rubble.'

'That's not what happened, though,' Dr. Allard interrupted.

'Non, it isn't,' Coco agreed. 'And that misdirection cost us valuable time.' She tapped Mathieu's shoulder and he lifted his head slowly, fixing dark eyes on her. He appeared to be on the verge of tears and it was all she could do to stop herself from hugging him. 'I think I understand the reason for the misdirection.'

Frère Aries shook his head irritably. 'I really don't understand what is happening here,' he grumbled.

Coco fought the urge to say, you're not the only one. 'Idris Cellier told me it was Vichy's idea to remove the coffins, but I don't believe it was.' She moved in front of Idris. 'Vichy wasn't even there was he, Idris? You lied about that, didn't you?'

Idris said nothing. Mathieu spoke instead. 'I asked him to tell you that.'

Cedric scratched his head. 'What on earth for?'

'I think I know,' Coco responded. 'Clues,' she repeated Mathieu's earlier word. 'How did this all start?'

'I saw Odilon at the monastery that morning talking with

Frère Leroy and I could tell he was worried,' Mathieu replied. 'I was praying in the chapel and they were outside. I only heard snippets but when Odilon mentioned having seen something Gasper Peron had done, it got my attention. The last thing he said was that he was going to speak to "her." I knew instantly who he meant. I didn't know what to make of it. I should have gone right then, but it was prayers and I couldn't get away… if I had… if I had…'

Coco reached over and touched his arm. It was warm and soft. 'None of this is your fault,' she whispered.

'I should have gone,' he replied shaking his head.

Coco considered her response. 'How did you find out Odilon was dead?'

'Later that afternoon, I left the monastery and went to my mother's house. When I got there, I heard mother on the phone.' Mathieu continued. He looked at Deidre. 'She was cold and commanding. At first, I thought she was speaking to me, that's why I stopped and listened,' he added with a sad smile. 'It soon became clear she was talking to someone else. I only heard one side of the conversation, but it was enough to get the gist of what had happened. Odilon Sander was dead and my mother was trying to drag Vichy into her mess, and at that moment, I knew I couldn't let it happen.'

'Then why the hell didn't you just call us?' Cedric demanded.

'Because I just couldn't,' Mathieu replied weakly.

Coco smiled at him. 'But you left us enough clues and hoped we'd figure it out.

'It was quite an elaborate plan,' Cedric suggested.

Mathieu shrugged. 'Not really. I was walking back to the monastery, a thousand thoughts running around my head. I can't tell you how many times I stopped by a payphone, just staring at it. I knew I should call the police, I knew it, but… I just couldn't. And then I ran into Jericho and Sofia. They were wasted as usual, and when they saw me I guess they figured they could carry the party on at the crypt like they used to. I agreed, and then it came to me. We used to play pranks with the coffins, we could again, but this time it could have a purpose. Revenge for Odilon Sander and Paul Lecourt and his parents who never even got the chance to enjoy him because of some pointless religious dogma.'

He took a deep breath before continuing. 'I told them to wait an hour and come to the monastery and I'd leave the gate open for them. I sat in my room, just going over and over it in my head. I couldn't stand the thought Odilon would just be blown up with the old youth centre. I needed to get someone's attention and moving the coffins might just do that. You're right, it wasn't Vichy who chose the coffins. It was me. Vichy wasn't even there. Sofia, Jericho, Idris, me even, never really allowed him to be part of the "clique."'

He gave Vichy a sad smile. 'I am sorry about that, Vichy. I always liked you and I should have done more to bring you in, but I guess I was always aware of what my mother said, that I had to "fit in" and not make a fuss or draw attention to myself. I guess I was like you. I just wanted to be popular, and that kinda disappeared when I joined the monastery. Anyway, that night I was crazy. I didn't know what to do. I came here, to the chapel and I prayed and I prayed and I prayed and the only answer I got was from me. *This can't happen.*'

'Shut your damn mouth,' Deidre hissed to her son. 'Stop talking, maintenant!'

Mathieu smiled at her. 'Too late, Maman. I won't be the next generation of liars.'

'Don't you understand what could happen?' Deidre demanded. 'Our name, our money, they could all be lost if you keep talking.'

He laughed. 'You made me a monk with no money and a fake name. What do you imagine I have to lose? I have no money and my only family is a woman who murdered two men just to keep a secret that really REALLY wasn't worth keeping. That's not a lot to lose, or to move on from.' He stole a look at Coco. 'Mais, I will move on.'

Deidre snorted. 'Even if it lands you in jail?'

Mathieu shrugged. 'That's up to Captain Brunhild. If she thinks my crimes deserve it, then I will accept whatever she offers me.' He smiled at Coco. 'I convinced Sofia, Jericho and Idris that we could pull one last prank before the youth centre went. They agreed, why wouldn't they? It was just a laugh to them. So, we took the coffins to the youth centre, and that was it.'

'They saw the body of Odilon Sander?' Cedric asked.

He shook his head. 'Non, we left the coffins on the ground floor. I knew Vichy had moved the body onto the third floor, so I didn't want Sofia, Jericho, and Idris to see him. I have enough dirt on them, so I wasn't worried about them talking, but I just didn't want anyone else involved. So, I sent them home and told them I would clean up. All I had to do was drag the third coffin to the third floor and swap the... swap the bodies.' He stole a look at his mother, but she did not turn her head, her gaze was fixed firmly on the alter.

Coco watched Mathieu closely. His face was pale, but his eyes were bright and alert. He was not lying; she was sure of it. In fact, she was sure he appeared relieved to be talking about what had happened. 'And you removed the skeleton of Gasper Peron?'

Mathieu nodded. 'I knew I shouldn't, but I had to. It was the only way I could think of to make the police look into the whole thing. I found somewhere to put him that I knew was out of the way, but not so out of the way that they would never find him. To me, he was just an old man who was kind to me, whatever else he was before. That's what he was to me, and that's all that mattered. I just wanted this to be over, mais I didn't want to...'

'Grass up your mother,' Cedric concluded. He looked to Idris. 'How did you get involved in all of this?'

'Mat told me what had happened,' Idris replied. 'And he said he needed my help. If the police were to ask, I was to tell them it was Vichy's idea to choose and move the coffins. He figured even if it wasn't true, if he was questioned, the chance was he would come clean and confess.'

Coco took a long, deep breath. 'What about Frère Leroy? How did he die?'

'That was my fault,' Mathieu spoke quickly. 'I shouldn't have done what I did…'

'You asked him to take your confession, didn't you?' Coco asked.

He nodded again. 'I couldn't stand keeping it in. Gerard had always been a mentor to me. He understood the Catholic Church was not really my calling, but he allowed me to be here until I figured out what I was going to do. I told him what had happened, and he was so calm. So, SO calm. He told me Dieu would forgive me and that I should go to my room and rest and that "it would be better tomorrow."' Mathieu snorted. 'Mais, that wasn't true. Tomorrow was worse, because Gerard was dead, and it was because of me. You have to believe, I never imagined for a second she would… she would do what she did, not to Frère Leroy of all people.'

Coco stepped across the chapel again and positioned herself in front of Deidre. 'He called you. We know he did. We have the proof. So, you came here, and you silenced him, again to protect your family name. It was cruel, and it was nasty. I can't even imagine he was going to turn you in.'

Deidre glared at Coco. 'He wanted to save me. He always wanted to save me.' She stomped across the floor of the chapel, throwing her hands into the air. 'I reminded him that all of this, the monastery, the youth centre, the homeless kitchen, were all down to one person. My father. And that we owed him the respect he had earned by his deeds. Don't you see? This all began with a foolish young child who stumbled into something he shouldn't of. It should have ended ten years ago, and what has happened now is because Odilon Sander grew a conscience and dragged us all down with him. That's it, that's all there is to it.' She smiled, moving slowly back towards Coco. 'You weren't right about a lot, but you were right about one thing. I am my father's daughter and I believe what he taught me. The family name is something you cannot lose.' She shook her head. 'And I won't allow you to drag us down.'

Coco laughed. 'And what do you propose to do? Murder me like you murdered Odilon and Frère Leroy? And how do you propose to do that in front of a room full of witnesses?'

Deidre shrugged. 'My time is up, I accept that, but it doesn't mean I have to be a good loser.' She stopped and reached into her bag.

Coco watched her slowly, and it took her a moment to realise what she was doing. Coco exhaled and reached into her pocket and yanked something out. She pressed it against Deidre's chest. Deidre's eyes widened in horror as her chest began vibrating rapidly. Coco smiled. 'You're not the only one with a Taser, bitch. Oh, and by the way, you are under the fuck arrest, d'accord?'

20H25

Coco's head was on her desk, snoring loudly. Commander Demissy walked into the office, shaking her head in irritation. 'Quite a mess we have here,' she announced.

Coco jerked upwards, a trail of spittle falling from her mouth. She wiped it with the back of her hand. 'Quoi?' she asked in confusion.

'I've read the reports, et… et…' Demissy threw her hands in the air. 'I don't know what to make of any of it.'

Coco shrugged. 'It'll all come out in the wash. Even the Catholic Church is going to have trouble making sense of this whole shi.. debacle,' she added demurely.

Demissy gave her a disapproving look. 'You did a good job.'

Coco's eyes flashed with surprise. 'As always, it was all down to teamwork, but the truth is, we had a lot of help.'

'Mathieu Moreau,' Demissy concluded.

Coco nodded. 'I can't quite believe what he did. He didn't want to turn his mother in, but nor did he want her to get away with her crimes. I think he's going to carry a lot of guilt about what happened to Frère Leroy, even though I don't really think he had anything to do with it.'

Demissy emitted a loud sigh. 'What are you even still doing here?' she asked.

Coco reached across the desk and lit a cigarette. 'You know exactly why I'm still here, because you asked me to talk to you.'

Demissy's face softened. 'This probably isn't the best time. Go home, be with your family and we'll try again tomorrow to sort our mess.'

'You want me to talk to *former* Commander Mordecai Stanic,' Coco snapped. 'And I'm here to tell you, it will not happen.' She raised her hands. 'And before you start, I'm not interested in the party line he's selling. Morty wants out of jail and he wants me and his kids to be back in his life. Neither is going to happen, not so long as I'm around. Is that clear enough for you, Commander Demissy?'

'He has information, <u>important</u> information.'

Coco snorted. 'He has fuck all. He's always had fuck all. He's just bored, or lonely, or desperate, whatever. I don't care, and nor should you.'

Demissy cleared her throat. 'He claims he has information about several high-ranking police officers and politicians who are taking bribes and working with criminals.'

Coco snorted again. 'Well, obviously he's claiming that. He wants attention. What the hell else is he going to claim - someone is falsifying their expenses? He knows he has to aim high to get our attention. It's classic, and it's stupid, and if we fall for it, then we're ridiculous. And I won't let that man make a fool out of me again.'

Demissy stared at her. Her face softened. 'I understand why you're angry and reluctant to believe what he is saying. I don't blame you because I would most certainly feel the same, but this is different. He says he has proof, but will only share it with you. Is he lying?' She shrugged. 'It's a possibility, but it's not something I think we, as police officers, should ignore. Corruption? I know you hate that as much as I do.'

She sat on the chair opposite Coco's desk. 'Besides all that, I didn't want to bring this to you.' She noticed Coco's doubtful look. 'Truly, I didn't. I know you think I am averse to what you've been through, but that's simply not true. I understand you and I agree with you. Mordecai Stanic is a despicable man. There's no doubt about that, but I also know one thing more important.' She stood, pressing her hands on the desk and leaning towards Coco. 'You're a good cop and he's just a stupid, arrogant man. So, go to him and look him in the eyes and you see if he's lying. If he is, kick him in the balls and come back to me and I'll call the prison governor and make sure that the rest of Mordecai's time in jail isn't what he hoped it would be. What do you think of that scenario? Shall I call the prison and tell them to expect you?'

Coco smiled at her. 'Don't make me start to like you, Commander.'

'I wouldn't dare,' she countered.

Coco rose to her feet. 'Call the jail. I'll go, but give me an hour or so. I want to see my kids before I face the bastard who sired them.'

21H00

Coco trudged slowly out of the Métro station and immediately lit yet another cigarette she knew she could not afford to smoke. The day was wearing heavily on her and all she really wanted to do was to go home, kiss the children who would allow her to and drop into a warm bubble bath and drink her body weight in cheap wine. But she knew it was not how her night was going to end, not yet at least. There were doors to close before she was allowed that.

'Bonjour.'

She heard the voice and knew instantly who it was. She spun around. Mathieu Moreau was standing outside her apartment block. He was dressed in jeans and a leather jacket and it seemed strange to her. 'How do you know where I live?' she demanded.

'I know more about you than you think,' he said, sucking on his lips.

Coco gave him a disgusted look. She could not allow herself to be distracted by him again, especially with what she was about to have to face. She shook her head. 'I don't care about that. Whatever you're doing, don't stalk me. It's not a good look,' she added. 'Why are you here?'

He stared at her in a way she had not been looked at in a long time. It made her want to lick this throat like it was a lollipop. 'After everything that happened earlier, it's given me the courage to do something I've wanted to do for a very long time.' He stamped his feet on the ground as if he was making an announcement. 'I've left the monastery for you,' he said.

Coco shook her head irritably. 'I don't know what that means to you, but your decision is nothing to do with me. It can be NOTHING to do with me. Don't use me as an excuse for what happened to you.' She reached out and touched his arm. 'Make your own decisions. It seems to me you've spent too much time thinking of other people and what they want. If you want to leave the monastery, then you can only do it for yourself, not for me, or your mother, and the legacy she created. Do you understand that, Mathieu?'

He bit his lip again. 'I love the way you say my name,' he breathed.

'What do you mean? It's just my voice.'

He shook his head. 'Non, it's more than that. When you say my name, it sounds like the beginning of something.'

She chortled. 'That sounds like a cheesy greetings card message.'

Mathieu stared at her wide-eyed. 'I want to marry you,' he announced.

Coco spluttered. 'And the hits keep on coming!' She stopped, noticing his expression. It was one of sincerity. 'Oh, Dieu, you're serious. You're twenty years old,' she stated. 'And I'm... *not*.' she added with a wink.

He shrugged. 'Age is just a number. Frère Leroy once told me he imagined I had lived before because I had an old soul. So, basically I'm a really old man. Listen, I've declared my intentions, so I'll leave it there for now. You have my cell number. I have yours. I'm not what you think I might be, and I've read your google entries so I know you're not too. We have our skeletons and that's okay. I'll be waiting for your call, Charlotte.'

'Why are you calling me Charlotte?' she asked.

Mathieu laughed. 'Because you don't let anyone call you Charlotte. So, I will. Au revoir, Charlotte,' he said as he walked toward the Métro station. Coco watched him, trying her best not to look at his ass.

'He likes you.'

Coco jumped, immediately recognising the voice of her son

Julien. He stepped out of the shadows.

'How long have you been there?' she demanded.

He smiled at her. 'Enough to know that the cute guy really likes you.'

Coco linked arms with him. 'Oh, shut up, he does not.'

Julien shrugged. 'He certainly does, which is weird because he's REALLY hot.'

'You think?' She playfully slugged his chin. 'Hey, what am I, the Hunchback of Notre Dame?' She shook her head. 'I can't have this conversation with my son.'

'Who else you going to talk to?' he asked. 'What's his name and how old is he?'

Coco lowered her head. 'He's Mathieu, and he's twenty.'

Julien pushed open the door to the apartment block. He laughed. 'So, what you're telling me is that YOUR boyfriend has the same name as mine and is exactly the same age?'

Coco narrowed her eyes at her son. 'I'm not sure that's what I'm saying at all…'

Julien pressed the call button on the elevator. 'If this family didn't need therapy before, we certainly do now.'

Coco pushed back the elevator gate and stepped inside. 'Oh, you have no idea. In an hour, I have to go and see Morty and beg him to spill his guts about corrupt cops. Sounds like fun, non?'

Julien smiled. 'Fuck Morty. Call the handsome kid afterwards, might cheer you up? Or if not, maybe give him my number?'

Coco watched him walk away, her mouth twisting. 'Well, he's certainly my kid,' she breathed, impressed.

23H05

Coco strode with fiery determination down the hallway, the sound of her boots echoing around the concrete walls. The prison was relatively quiet, though she could hear what sounded like someone having night terrors in the distance. Demissy had arranged with the governor to sneak Coco in after hours. Coco was not sure if it was for her safety or Mordecai's.

She kept walking, suddenly feeling more alone and afraid than she could remember feeling in a long while. The guard had irritably pointed and grumbled. *End of the hallway, last door on the right. He's already in there, handcuffed to the desk*, before returning to his crossword puzzle.

Coco ignored the no-smoking sign and lit a cigarette. The buzz from her third gin and tonic was giving her the extra courage she needed to face what was ahead of her. She stopped abruptly, annoyed she had run out of hallway. She turned her head slowly to face the doorway and took a deep breath before kicking the door open with her foot.

Mordecai Stanic's head jerked upwards, his eyes widening first with shock and then surprise. He tried to stand, but the handcuff would not allow him to. He scratched the scar on his cheek, a scar she herself had touched a thousand times. His mouth widened into a smile, as if he had read her thoughts. Coco noticed he had lost a tooth and a great deal of weight. His face was gaunt and there were heavy bags under his eyes. His normally round, olive face appeared like a balloon that had been deflated.

Coco stepped into the room and moved as far away from the desk and Mordecai as she could. It was not far enough. She could hear his breath and the way it had quickened reminded her… reminded her of a time before.

'Well, this is awkward,' Mordecai said. His voice had not changed, and it stung her, because her son Cedric was beginning to sound similar. Mordecai pulled his teeth together and wiggled his tongue. 'I ate his liver with some fava beans and a nice Chianti' he said in a Hannibal Lecter impression.

'Nice, how's your ass? The top dog in this shithole keeping it busy?' Coco interrupted.

Mordecai threw back his head and guffawed. 'Dieu, that felt good,' he said, pressing his hand against his chest. 'Only you can make me laugh that way.' He narrowed his eyes. 'How are the kids?'

'The kids are none of your damn business,' she hissed. 'And don't mention them again or I'll jump over the table and gouge your eyes out, okay?'

'They're my kids too,' he replied desperately. 'Don't they even ask about me?'

'Not a damn bit,' Coco spat. 'And that's the way it's going to be.'

'You can't keep them from me.'

'The hell I can't!' she screamed. Her face creased. 'Listen, I told you a long time ago I would tell Cedric and Esther about you, and where you are, but not yet, when I think they're ready. But I will not bring them here to see you. I won't put them through that. If they want, when they're eighteen and able to make their own minds up about you, then they can decide for themselves. I won't put ideas into their heads about you, because frankly, your name never comes up. I think nothing of you. Is that clear enough?'

'Wow,' he said solemnly. 'I forgot, you really don't have a filter, do you? You may think nothing of me, but I think the world of you, I always did.'

Coco held up her hands. 'Enough!' She stepped forward. 'Now, look me in the eye. Do you have information to trade, or not?'

He locked eyes with her. 'I have enough to blow the lid off at least five commissariats around Paris.'

Coco nodded. He was probably telling the truth, but the fact was, she did not really care. 'Bon. Then quit playing games and start talking, but not to me. I've played your little game now, but this show and tell is over. Tell what you know, or not, I don't much care, but I won't be back and I won't let you near our children. Capeesh? Have I said it loudly and clearly enough to get through your thick skull?'

'I'm getting out of here and then we'll all be back together…'

Coco laughed. 'You're never getting out of here, Morty. Not if I've got anything to do with it. And like I said, if the kids want to see you, that's their business. But don't drag me into this. Spill your guts, or don't, I could not care less. And if you decide to let crimes be committed all because you want to continue to play games, then that says all we need to know about you. You've only ever been interested in yourself, and that's not changed. So, I've done as I was asked and put in an appearance, but it's a one-time deal. Au revoir, Morty,' she hurried to the door.

'This isn't over. We're not over,' he called after her. 'And I will get out and get back everything that was mine, everything I lost.'

She pulled open the door and turned back to him. Seeing him wriggling against the handcuff was hard, but it did not affect her in the way she thought it would. She felt nothing. She shook her head. 'Bien sûr, we're over, Morty. The fact is, we never even began, not really, not in any way that matters.'

He raised an eyebrow. 'You've met someone, haven't you?'

Coco did not answer, but she also knew she did not need to.

'It won't work,' he said with obvious anxiety. 'You'll hate every man who touches you, because they won't be me.'

She laughed. 'You think too highly of yourself, Morty.'

He shook his head. 'Non, I don't. I know how you sound when you make love. I know every grunt, moan…'

'You make me sound like a goddamn rhinoceros,' Coco snapped. 'And your memory is certainly better than mine. You were distinctly average at best. In fact, I'd go so far as to say I have more fun sitting on top of my washing machine when it's on the spin cycle.' She stepped away, calling back over her shoulder. 'Talk to Commander Demissy, or not, I don't care, but that's it between us, as far as I'm concerned.'

'You can lie as much as you like, Coco, but I'm the only man for you, you know that deep down, don't you?'

Coco did not answer, instead moving quickly along the hallway, desperate to be free.

23H55

Coco slumped in the driver's seat of her car and lit a cigarette, a thousand thoughts crashing against her skull. She needed to escape. She needed a very large, very alcoholic drink and she also needed… She shook her head, desperate to rid herself of the thoughts now invading her. Mordecai Stanic could not get in her head, not again, and certainly not now. She needed to be alone, but she needed someone to wash away the shadow of Mordecai's hands on her body. She pulled out her cell phone and searched for the call history. Three names appeared at the top of the list.

Sonny.
Cedric.
Boy Toy Monk.

Coco took a deep breath and pressed one name.
'Allô?' came the surprised reply.
'It's me. Can we meet? I don't want to be alone tonight.'

COCO BRUNHILD WILL RETURN IN A NEW MYSTERY:

Séance de Spiritisme

Printed in Poland
by Amazon Fulfillment
Poland Sp. z o.o., Wrocław
17 August 2022

0b55c1ab-29dc-4904-9dec-5fd42c13efdeR02